S0-ABC-968

WHILE MANY OF Charlie's male friends might be jealous that he had had the guts to do what they wished they could, they could never be seen to admit it, so they tended to ignore Meg, while their wives clearly saw her as a "Betrayer of Women." Although they'd be perfectly friendly when she and Charlie visited them, they'd manage to communicate their feelings by various methods. Often, Meg was treated to a seemingly inexhaustible supply of stories concerning self-sacrificing women who had been shunted aside in favor of the dreaded Trophy Wife. This was a blisteringly direct form of attack.

For the most part, though, they'd be a touch more subtle. They'd place pictures of Helen and Josh and David in strategic spots, so that Meg, while she was sipping her coffee, would be face-to-face with her predecessor. Or, if they didn't have a recent photo of sad-eyed Helen, they might leave a postcard from her lying around casually, so that Meg would find her gaze drawn to the familiar writing, and read a plaintive message such as: "I'm in Florida. I'm not sure what to do with myself. Love, Helen." Well, Meg wasn't sure what to do with *herself* on these occasions. She'd become tongue-tied or find herself spouting inanities, thus behaving in a way that made her appear to be the Trophy Wife they so despised.

There was no way to win.

Unless she had a baby.

"An energetic and spirited comic novel . . . what sets it apart from its sibling blockbusters is Blake's intelligent and razor-sharp wit . . . great fun." —*The London Times*

"This novel makes for amusing, compulsive reading that anyone looking for a fast-paced, involving, and often funny story about relationships between men and women will enjoy." —*Library Journal*

SECOND WIVES

CINDY BLAKE

St. Martin's Paperbacks

First published in Great Britain by Simon & Schuster Ltd.

SECOND WIVES

ISBN: 0-312-97121-4

Printed in the United States of America

St. Martin's Presss hardcover edition / May 1999
St. Martin's Paperbacks edition / December 2000

St. Martin's Paperbacks are published by St. Martin's Press, 175 Fifth Avenue, New York, N.Y. 10010.

10 9 8 7 6 5 4 3 2 1

for my sister, Diana Blake,
with all my love, always
March 11, 1946–June 2, 1994

"There is none like her, none.
Nor will be when our summers have deceased."

—TENNYSON

I promise I'll meet John Prine one of these days.

If someone breaks into your house and steals your most precious possessions, you have rights, don't you?

If you hear the burglar creeping around downstairs, fooling with the silver, what do you do?

If you have a gun, do you use it?

I think so.

I would.

I will.

Chapter One

"THIS IS A disaster, Leo," Meg said, trying to sound calm. "You can't do it. You just can't. It's a huge mistake."

"I wish you wouldn't say that," Leo replied simply, looking at her sister with that forlorn little frown Meg knew so well, the one that brought out all her protective instincts.

"What do you expect me to say? You're my sister. I love you. This guy is almost twice your age—he's married already, he has a daughter—it's a recipe for disaster."

"You keep saying the word 'disaster.' We're not talking about an earthquake or a plague of locusts. I've fallen in love. I wish Nick weren't married—I *hate* the fact that I'm in love with someone else's husband—but I can't help it. I can't change the way I feel. It's not the end of the world." Leo twisted in her chair. "Is it?"

"How much alimony does his wife want?"

"Meg—" Leo's eyes widened in disbelief. "Money's not the issue."

"Not yet. It will be, believe me. How often will he see his daughter?"

"I don't know," Leo sighed. "As often as possible, I hope."

"And how do you think she'll feel about you?"

"What is this, the Inquisition? I don't know how she'll feel about me. I hope she'll like me, but I'm sure it will take time. I'm not expecting miracles, Meg. I know things will be tough, but there's no choice anymore. We're together. We *have* to be together."

"I think I'd better call Beth," Meg mumbled and immediately saw the anger surface on Leo's face.

"Sister Shrink will sort me out, is that what you think? How could Beth help me? She doesn't know a thing about love." These were the harshest words Leo had ever spoken and Meg was relieved that they were directed at Beth, not at herself.

"But we have to tell her, Leo. You know that. And we have to tell Amy too. Among the four of us, we'll work it out. We've always managed to work things out. You know that."

At a certain point, Meg reflected, the number of siblings in a family becomes a critical mass—at the number four. She and her three sisters were individuals, of course, but they were also a recognized group, a power. Acquaintances referred to them as the "Four Preston Sisters" and were fascinated by their physical similarities and differences, while friends enjoyed discussing their psychological similarities and differences. When they were all out together, Beth sometimes introduced herself and her sisters as John, Paul, George and Ringo. Meg never dared ask which one Beth thought was Ringo.

"There is nothing *to* work out," Leo shook her head. "And besides, I've already told Amy. She's behind me— one hundred percent. She understands. As usual, it's you and Beth who still think I'm a baby."

Struggling to hide her disappointment, Meg forced the corners of her mouth into a lame smile. Leo had talked to Amy first—that shouldn't be a surprise. In the shifting nature of the relationships among the four of them as the years went by, one constant prevailed—the completely attuned psyches of Amy and Leo. They had never argued, never even disagreed. Amy held the place in Leo's heart both Beth and Meg wanted for themselves and could never have.

If only Amy had objected to this romance, Meg thought. Then *I* could have been the one to support Leo one hundred percent. But Amy, practical Amy, who *should* have seen the potential complications, had come down firmly on Leo's side, leaving Meg with the messy business of pointing out all the pitfalls. It wasn't fair.

"You can't marry that man until he gets divorced, so at least you'll have some time to consider all this," Meg said, clearing away the cups of coffee from the table, moving toward the kitchen.

"That man's name is Nick."

"Right," Meg said, over her shoulder. "Nick."

"You'll love him too, Meg. Really you will."

Nick, whoever he was, whatever he was like, was clearly a father substitute for Leo. An older man had finally paid some attention to her and she had rushed straight into his arms. The classic scenario.

Beth was going to have a field day with this news, Meg decided, sighing as she loaded the dishwasher. Beth's stand on psychiatry was oddball, focusing as it did on the therapeutic value of rage, but at the heart of it all was her view that every relationship between any two people was actually a parent-child one. She felt that the Oedipus Complex was right on target when it concerned children wishing to murder their parents, but went completely haywire when it came to the bit about wanting to have sex with one's father or mother. Basically, Beth believed that all people involved in a relationship want to kill each other. Period. Her practice was flourishing.

Leo followed Meg into the kitchen and hoisted herself onto the counter, looking at most sixteen years old in her jeans and Red Sox T-shirt. Her short, dark hair was combed back like a boy's, and she had two gold studs in one ear, one in the other. Achingly thin and waiflike, with deep brown eyes and a pale complexion, she was one of life's fragile beauties, a woman who should have had "Handle With Care" stamped on her high forehead. Meg couldn't imagine Leo sleeping with a man, tumbling around on a bed. She'd break. Or she'd suffocate.

She's a little girl, for Christ's sake! What does this Nick person think he's doing?

Every time Meg looked at Leo, she saw her as an eight-year-old; she replayed the same scene over and over again until the tape was almost worn in her memory bank. Leo, standing in a little black dress in the hallway of the family house on Chestnut Street, leaning against a wall, pulling on her earlobe, ready for their mother's funeral. Grabbing Leo's hand, Meg had tried to lead her outside to the big black limo.

"I feel sick," Leo had said, pulling away. "I don't want to go."

Beth breezed in then, acting as if she were hurrying them all along to a cocktail party.

"We're all waiting in the car, Leo. None of us *wants* to go, okay? It's just one of those shitty things we have to do because we're supposed to. Like brushing our teeth at night."

Whoa, Meg thought. Going to your mother's funeral was like brushing your teeth? Beth was really stretching it this time. But maybe it would work—Leo had stopped tugging at her ear, anyway. She looked up at Beth with a quizzical expression.

"But I skip some nights," she said softly. "Mom said it was okay if I skipped brushing some nights. So I can skip this too, can't I? She wouldn't mind. I know."

Beth shrugged and threw her hands up in the air.

"Little sis has a good point," she said, turning to Meg. "Frankly, I wouldn't be surprised if Mom had missed *our* funerals. So why don't we all skip hers? We could go to a movie instead."

"Beth—" Meg couldn't finish her sentence. Beth managed to render her speechless most of the time. With her seraphic face, her long, blond hair and her pale blue eyes, Beth looked like someone who should be playing the harp. Actually, Meg knew, Beth would have been more comfortable playing with Semtex.

"What's everyone doing? We're supposed to be leaving for the church *now*," Amy said as she ran into the hallway. The scene was beginning to resemble a farce, with sister after sister tumbling out of the lead car in their mother's funeral cortege.

"We're discussing which movie we'd like to see this afternoon," Beth replied. "What do you think, Amy? *Or-*

dinary People or *The Elephant Man*? Or would you prefer to go ten-pin bowling?"

Amy stared at Beth and Meg recognized the look: it was full of fear. How could this happen? she asked herself. Meg was the oldest sibling of the family. How could Beth, a year younger, have so much power? Why was everyone so scared of her?

"Leo feels sick. She says she doesn't want to go," Meg explained to Amy, who immediately went over to Leo, and knelt down in front of her.

"Leo. We're going to say good-bye to Mom. All of us. I feel sick too—I think we all feel a little sick—but I think we'll feel better once we've said good-bye. And I'll be beside you the whole time, all right?"

"What if she comes back here while we're away saying good-bye? Then she might miss us and leave again when we're not looking." Leo stared at her fifteen-year-old sister with a desperate intensity.

Beth rolled her eyes; Meg hung her head.

"You know she's not coming back, Leo. You know she's dead. We talked about it all, remember? And you know how you like me to say good night to you every night before you go to sleep? Well, when you're dead, you want people to say good-bye, I think." Amy hugged Leo to her, then stood up and took her by the hand. "Come on. Dad's waiting."

She and Leo went out first. Meg and Beth followed them.

"What are the odds Dad's been getting the telephone number of the lady who's driving the limo while we've been dealing with Leo?" Beth whispered to Meg.

"Pretty high," Meg whispered back, thinking: just please, God, let this day be over without any major disasters.

There hadn't been any to speak of, Meg later reflected. Well, the minister had backed his car into one of her father's friends' Mercedes on his way out of the church, which caused some genuine angst, but all in all the funeral

had gone according to plan. Other mourners had glanced
covertly at the four daughters and made whispered comments about how hard life would be for the motherless
Preston girls; how tragic Victoria's sudden death had been
and what a burden life now would be for the widower,
Mark.

Meg was aware even as she listened to the sermon that
her family made an affecting portrait, sitting in order of
age—first their father, then herself, nineteen; Beth, eighteen; Amy, fifteen and the eight-year-old Leonora—in the
front pew of Trinity Church, all five heads bowed in grief.
She contemplated trying to force tears from her eyes to
make the picture more pitiful, but knew that Beth would
catch the fraud and tease her mercilessly for it afterward.
So she sat still, watching the only face in the family that
showed any pure emotion—Leo's.

It was a dignified and restrained ceremony; a truly Bostonian response to death—no wailing or gnashing of teeth,
rather a few simple hymns and equally simple words of
eulogy from Victoria's brother, the girls' uncle Hugh. There
was an air of politesse throughout, Meg noticed. As if
WASP society felt that it had to be gracious in defeat, especially when one of their number was defeated by such a
worthy opponent as death.

After the service, when they buried the ashes in the family plot at Mount Auburn Cemetery, Leo burst into hysterical tears, but Amy was right there to comfort her.

"You can always come here and talk to Mom," Amy
said. "I'll be getting my driver's license soon and I can
drive you here and we can talk to her."

"We can talk to Steven then, too," Leo said, calming down.

"Yes," Amy replied quietly, shooting a quick look at her
two older sisters. "We can talk to Steven then, too."

Meg felt the familiar surge of despair and jealousy she
experienced whenever she heard Steven's name spoken.
During the graveside rites, she had avoided looking at
Steven's headstone, and she could see that Beth and Amy

were also refusing to turn their heads the minimal amount it would take to see their brother's grave. Their father, however, kept shifting his glance back and forth between his wife's and his son's resting places as if they were two equally beautiful women who were talking to him at the same time.

Dad must have loved Mom once, Meg found herself thinking. He'd sometimes looked at Victoria with a frightening passion in his eyes, but Meg had believed that passion was anger, not love. Until now. She stepped back a pace, stunned by a sudden breathlessness. And then she felt Leo's hand steal up and grab her own.

There were disadvantages to being born into a wealthy East Coast family, Meg reflected as they drove back from the cemetery to their house. It meant that you were sent to private school, for one. And that meant that you didn't go to a normal high school so you didn't get to go to a prom. No prom, no prom queens, no cheerleaders, no all-American activities. At the core of the Boston WASP ethos was one overriding tenet—real WASPs don't lower themselves to the rowdy American lifestyle. They are British at heart. Well-bred, well-mannered, gracious and graceful. Tasteful people who shun attention and any public display of feeling.

Meg would have liked to go to a prom. She would have liked to try out for a cheerleading team. And if she had to go to her mother's funeral, she would have preferred an Irish wake. She had seen them on television shows and envied the black humor, the raw emotion. However, if she were to be totally honest with herself, she wasn't sure that she had any raw emotion to vent; rather a confused mix of sorrow, self-pity and bewilderment. It was just as well, then, that she take her part in what seemed a carefully orchestrated event, designed to keep everything on an even keel. Back at their house, maids passed around hors d'oeuvres, while a bartender served drinks from behind a table covered in white linen. People stood in corners, speaking in hushed tones.

It was a hot Friday in July, and her father's law partners looked as though they couldn't wait to get out, don their sailing clothes and head for the North Shore or the Cape. Still, they stood politely making small talk; not crass enough actually to discuss business, but discreetly working the room socially nonetheless.

"Meg—" Mrs. Pembury, a friend of her mother's, approached her. "How are you? I'm so sorry about your mother." She paused as Meg tried unsuccessfully to respond. "But she never was the same after Steven's death, was she?"

"I guess not," Meg answered.

"Your sister Beth"—Mrs. Pembury waved in the direction of Beth, who was stuck in a corner with Mr. Pembury—"looks just like Victoria did at her age. She was so striking then. That blond hair. Your father and she were like Gregory Peck and Grace Kelly—a real film star couple. Beth inherited those genes, didn't she? Of course *you're* the one who knows how to dress properly," she added hurriedly. "You have a real sense of style. And I hear Amy has your father's brains. It's too early to tell what Leonora will be like, isn't it? She's so young."

Nodding dutifully, Meg silently willed Beth to escape from Mr. Pembury and help her out. Beth would know what to say—she'd know how to shut Mrs. Pembury up. ·

"None of us knew how Victoria managed to look so young all those years. We used to joke with her about her secret fountain of youth. But then of course, she aged so much after Steven's death—she was unrecognizable, really—so terribly old." Mrs. Pembury's voice trailed away, her right hand moving up to touch her own cheek, and Meg was left wondering what would happen next. Beth was heading in her direction now, she could see, and Amy as well, bringing Leo along with her. Welcome relief.

"Well, look—here you all are!" Mrs. Pembury exclaimed. "The Little Women. I always meant to ask Vicky why she never called one of you Jo. Meg, Beth, Amy, but no Jo. And one Leonora. Why was that, do you think?"

"Maybe Mom thought Jo was a touch too much of a tomboy," Beth said, smiling angelically. "It's so nice to see you Mrs. Pembury. You know, I've often wondered myself, were those girls all a little dubious? Little lesbians, perhaps?"

"Beth—" Mrs. Pembury laughed, then looked around quickly to see if she'd been heard.

"A lesbian is a girl who likes other girls too much," Leo said, obviously proud of herself. "I saw one on television. Is there a name for a boy who likes girls too much?"

"Yeah—Dad," Beth whispered, but Meg was sure the aside had been heard.

"It was wonderful to see you all again. I'm only sorry it was in such sad circumstances," Mrs. Pembury said, edging away from the sisters. "Come and visit any time. I have such fond memories of your mother."

"Thank you," Meg said, feeling that the afternoon was beginning to slip out of control. She wished Beth would stop whispering to her. She wished she could grab Leo and take her away from the house, from Boston; move to Colorado or Montana and live a quiet, normal life.

As Meg looked down at her younger sister, she knew she'd never lose the image of her standing there in the warm afternoon light. Unconsciously, Beth and Amy and Meg had formed a ring around Leo, as if to protect her from any onslaughts of a capricious life. Leo, her little black dress still clean and creaseless, clung to Amy with one hand, tugged at her earlobe with the other. She was innocence incarnate. Just looking at her made Meg want to weep for being unable to fix everything that went wrong in the world.

And now, Meg thought, fast-forwarding her mental tape to the present and to her twenty-two-year-old sister sitting on the kitchen counter, Leo was involved in her first big love affair. She was involved with a married man.

"I have to say it, Leo. This relationship is a huge mistake," Meg repeated.

"Charlie was married when you met him, remember?"
Leo was tugging at her earlobe, another childhood gesture
that tore at Meg's heart.

She's so young, so young and so naive. She doesn't have
a clue.

"That's the point. I know Charlie was married when I
met him and I wish he hadn't been. It was a mess." *And it
still is a mess.* "But I was older than you are now, and
Charlie's only a couple of years older than I am. This
man—"

"Nick."

"Right, Nick. Nick is forty and you're twenty-two."

"I love him, Meg." The Leo frown returned and Meg
sighed. It was such a desolate frown, so sad, that it added
to Leo's fragile beauty. At the same time it made you want
to do anything to remove it from her face.

Meg poured powder into the dishwasher and was silent
for a moment, considering the word "love." After he had
married her, Charlie had stopped saying "I love you." "It's
a given, I don't need to say it, do I?" he'd stated quite
reasonably, Meg made herself believe, although there had
been a distressing number of moments lately when she
could have used reassurance on the subject.

"I love Nick," Leo repeated the words in a stronger
voice. "And I'm going to marry him—when he gets divorced." The last line was less forceful, but Meg recognized
the will behind it. Leo was so rarely assertive, it was impossible not to take her seriously when she made an un-
qualified statement.

"It's not easy being a second wife," Meg stated, hoping
she didn't sound too much like a schoolteacher. "People
resent you. They think you've stolen something that belongs to someone else. Like a car thief."

"A car thief?" Leo laughed. "Do you think all married
men should have alarms fitted? As soon as a strange woman
talks to them, sirens go off?"

"It's not funny, Leo. I mean it. I saw an Oprah Winfrey

program about second marriages the other day. It was really scary. The—"

"Please—" Leo interrupted, still smiling. "Let's lose Oprah. I'm sure she was talking about second wives who have had sex change operations and now lust after their manicurists. No one who goes on that show is normal. Anyway, you know Beth's going to go berserk about this, so why don't you let *her* do all the ranting and raving? She'll probably tell me Nick and I will end up murdering each other."

"Beth *can* get things right sometimes."

"I know you're trying to be helpful, Meg, and I appreciate it, really. I know you feel responsible for me. You keep looking at me as if I were about to self-destruct, but I'm fine—Nick and I can make things work. Look—you've managed to become friends with Charlie's ex. Divorce doesn't *have* to be bloody. Maybe Nick's wife wants out of the marriage as much as he does. Maybe she won't resent me. I don't know—I don't really know anything about her."

"You will," Meg said grimly. If this all goes through as planned, you'll know more than you need to, more than you want to. You'll be inextricably bound up with her and it will be hell.

Leo twiddled with the tap on the kitchen sink, turning it off and on.

"So, anyway, I mean . . ."

Meg knew what was coming then; Leo always began to mumble awkwardly when she wanted to talk about their mother.

"What do you think Mom would feel about me and Nick?"

"I don't know, Leo. I have no idea."

"Why won't you ever talk about her?"

"I'll talk about her. But I can't second-guess a dead person. I just don't know how she'd respond, okay?"

Leo shut the tap off with a vicious tug, hopped off the counter, and kissed Meg on the cheek. "Okay. I think I'll

get going now. Tonight's the first night Nick and I get to
spend on our own together without any subterfuge. He's
told his wife about us now and he's moving out tonight.
You wouldn't believe how wonderful it feels to be out in
the open, not to have to hide. I can't wait." She looked at
her watch. "Three more hours—that's all. Not even your
doom-and-gloom, disaster talk can get to me. You'll see
how right this is. I promise."

Shit, Meg thought, as she hugged her sister's body and
felt the sharp ribs jutting out. How much of this is my fault?
Mine and Beth's and Amy's? We were so busy trying to
protect her, to give her at least a semblance of a happy
childhood, we went overboard and she's ended up this innocent, trusting girl who would happily take candy from a
stranger. Then invite him home. Then marry him.

"Hey, you're killing me," Leo laughed, breaking away
from Meg's hug. "I'm out of here. Give my love to Charlie,
will you? And the kids. Is it their weekend here?"

"Yes," Meg nodded.

"Thea—Nick's daughter—she's around Josh's age.
Maybe we could get them together some day."

"Sure." Meg heard how dismissive her voice sounded
and tried to change the tone. "That would be nice." She
found she couldn't sustain the momentary optimism. "Being a stepmother isn't easy, either."

Seeing Leo's face fall yet again, Meg decided to relent.

"But Josh and David love you, and they don't give their
affection easily. So I'm sure you'll find the stepmother
business easier than I have."

The fact that Josh and David were so fond of Leo both
pleased and distressed Meg. Why can't they be as open and
affectionate with me? she often asked herself, before reminding herself yet again that she would have to put in a
lot of time and work to clear the hurdle intrinsic to the
image of the wicked stepmother.

"*I* think you're a great stepmother. You're a great
mother. Look how well I've turned out!" Leo grinned and
headed for the door. "You and Beth and Amy have brought

me up so well I'm incapable of making mistakes. You'll see that as soon as you meet Nick. In the meantime, stop worrying, okay?"

"Okay, I'll try. I promise."

"Thanks. I know deep down, underneath it all, you're a true romantic."

I don't think so, Meg thought. *Not anymore.*

As Leo made her way out, Helen and the kids arrived. Meg watched Josh and David throw their arms around Leo and give her good-bye kisses. Helen, their mother, Charlie's first wife, was standing behind them, holding a huge dish with aluminum foil over the top.

"Come in everyone," Meg tried to sound cheerful.

"I've brought you a casserole for tonight, Meg," Helen announced. "I know how much you hate to cook, and I've got plenty of time on my hands, so I thought I'd help you out. Besides, I know Charlie and the kids love this particular dish."

Which means: I know you can't cook. I know the kids hate your food. I'm pointing out to you exactly how inadequate you are.

"Bye guys," Leo waved. But before she walked off down the street, she gave Meg a little nod of the head. This was a signal, saying: look, *you've* done it. You've become friendly with your husband's ex. She's even bringing you cooked suppers. I was right. Divorce *can* be civilized.

Oh, Leo, if you only knew.

"Helen, how sweet of you. Thanks so much. Listen, make yourself comfortable in the kitchen, make yourself some coffee or tea. I'll be right with you. I just have to make a telephone call, okay?"

"No problem," Helen replied. As always, she was dressed in her thrift-shop clothes. A long, dark brown plaid skirt, a print blouse, a stained yellow sweater, all of which hung badly and made her appear both helpless and hard done by. Her hair was unwashed, her skin blotched—picture of a rejected, dejected first wife, Meg thought.

For Christ's sake, pull yourself together. You're only thirty-four years old. Stop being the fucking victim, she wanted to scream at Helen.

Instead she said: "Right, I'll be back in a few minutes." Heading upstairs to her bedroom, she could hear the sounds of Helen and Josh and David trooping into the kitchen together. She sat on her bed, picked up the phone and lit the second of the two cigarettes she allowed herself each day. She'd smoked her first one when Leo had told her about Nick.

Why, exactly, was she so upset by Leo's love affair? Jesus, she'd been so excited when she'd first started out with Charlie. Just like Leo was. Just as sure of her love, just as determined that the marriage would work.

And now?

She didn't want to answer that question.

Beth's answering machine responded to her call, and Meg took a deep drag, exhaled, then proceeded to deliver a somewhat hysterical monologue to her absent sister.

Chapter Two

BETH KICKED HER shoes off, headed for the CD player, slotted in the Mary Chapin Carpenter disc, poured herself a glass of wine and settled down on the sofa. What a lousy day it had been. A few times that morning she had felt herself falling asleep as clients droned on about their lives. Her head would nod forward, and she'd quickly jerk it back, hoping she hadn't been noticed. Although it didn't much matter if she had been caught. She could always say: "Look, I was bored. I fell asleep. You should be angry with me, right? Why can't you express that anger? What's wrong with you? You should walk out on me. Boy, do you need help." It was amazing what shit people would take from their therapists. But then most people took shit from authority figures ninety-nine percent of their lives.

Which is why she was all set to be spiky and confrontational with the policeman who stopped her for speeding on Storrow Drive on the way home. She wasn't going to flutter her eyelashes and say "Oh, I'm sorry officer, I had *no idea* I was over the limit. Please take pity on a poor pathetic female." Just because the guy wore a uniform didn't mean he deserved to be kowtowed to.

He sauntered up with a real police swagger; cool, calm, his gun resting easily on his hip. Straight out of a cop movie, Beth thought. Life does an imitation of bad art. Before he could speak, she started in:

"Listen, I know what I've done wrong. Five miles or so over the designated limit. But what I don't know is why you bother with little things like this when people are getting robbed and knifed and shot. It's a waste of taxpayer's money. So give me the ticket and spare me the lecture, whatever your name is, okay?"

He clapped his palm against his forehead, widened his eyes.

"Gee whiz," he said, shaking his head. "You mean to tell me that people are getting *robbed? Shot?* Hey, I better go do something about that now."

He turned and walked away. Beth sat in the car, stunned, waiting for him to return. He hesitated as he opened his patrol car door, looked over at her and said loudly enough for her to hear, but without actually shouting, in a perfect mimic of her voice: "It's Steven. Okay?" Then he smiled, slid in behind the wheel, put his siren on and sped off.

What the hell was *that* all about? she wondered, feeling utterly upstaged. Despite the fact that she hadn't been given a ticket, she knew she'd lost the game. The experience still rankled. Some wise-ass policeman named Steven had made her feel stupid. Jung would have approved of the synchronicity of names on that one. Steven.

Saint Steven: the brother from hell.

She couldn't remember exactly when she knew who Steven was, what had happened to him, why he meant so much in her life. Children study sounds and letters, gradually putting them together until they can read, but the precise moment, the Eureka, I can read! was often hard to pinpoint. Steven's presence she now knew had hovered in the house from the moment Beth was born; but although she had always received messages about him, she couldn't be sure of the age she was when she actually deciphered the code.

The key was simple: Steven was perfect. Beth, in her teens, referred to him as "Do No Wrong." "It's Do No Wrong's birthday next week," she'd say to Meg. "Mom won't be coming out of her room for a couple of days at least."

In her early childhood, though, Beth hadn't been able to be so flip. All that she understood was that Steven was perfect, she wasn't, and she wanted to be. It took her a while to put together two simple facts: Steven was perfect. Steven was dead. Therefore death equaled perfection.

One afternoon, when she was twelve, and Victoria had failed to pick her up at school yet again, Beth sat silently and considered the different ways she could kill herself. She was serious about it, as she was about everything, because she wanted to be the best at everything. Her teachers often discussed "how to handle Beth Preston's overly competitive nature" but Beth never responded to any of their initiatives. When she contemplated suicide, she took a long time weighing up the different methods.

She wanted her mother to find her body—that was crucial. But she didn't want any blood around. She had a distinct memory of her mother coming upstairs to her room one night a few weeks before. Beth had thought Victoria might be coming to tell her a bedtime story, a rare and startling event; instead she sat on the edge of Beth's bed and told her how perfect Steven had been in death.

"When Steven was hit by the car, he didn't bleed," she said, staring at Beth as if daring her to contradict this statement. "He lay there, so peaceful and quiet. As if he were playing dead. Tricking me. He liked to do that sometimes. Tease me. He'd hide and pop out at me and I'd pretend to be scared. That's what he was doing then, too. Hiding behind the car, trying to surprise me. He didn't scream or cry out. I think sometimes—" her voice trailed off and Beth lay back, waiting, but the story was over. Her mother got up and left the room, without saying good night.

Bleeding was out if she wanted to be perfect, Beth knew. That ruled out guns and knives. Eventually, she decided that hanging herself was the answer. She scoured the house for some rope, checked the attic for a suitable beam. Finding a chair or stool the right height was a problem, but one she solved within days. The next big question was whether she should write a note or not. She would have liked to leave a specimen of her brilliant vocabulary for Victoria to treasure.

But Steven didn't write a note. Not that he was old enough to write when he died, not that he knew he *was* going to die; still—if she wanted to be as perfect as Steven, she'd better not write a note.

Beth could imagine the future. Beside every picture of Steven in the house, there'd be a picture of herself. They'd have to find some photographs the school had taken of her because Victoria didn't take any pictures of her daughters; Beth was sure, however, that once she was dead, her mother would make an effort.

Even better than having her picture placed beside all of Steven's was the fact that Meg, Amy, and the baby Leonora would have to hear stories about *her*. They'd have to sit and listen to how perfect she'd been as a baby, how perfect she'd been as a toddler; they'd be forced to hear even more about her than about Steven because she would have lived longer. Steven had died aged two and a half and his life seemed to stretch on forever in stories; just think how long it would take to tell about Beth's twelve years. She couldn't lose.

She considered killing herself on her birthday, which was on February 4, three months away, but she reasoned that Steven had two days that sent Victoria into total seclusion—his birthday and the anniversary of his death. If Beth combined her birth and death day, she'd be one short of Steven. And it would be better to do it soon, before Thanksgiving, before the Christmas rush. Beth set a mental date for herself—November 12.

Two days before, on the tenth, Victoria remembered to pick Beth and Meg up at school; she even managed to arrive on time, bringing Leo and Amy along with her. They drove off, Meg in the front seat beside her mother, the others scrunched into the back, toward Chestnut Hill. They were going to visit their Uncle Hugh and his family.

Victoria didn't speak in the car after informing them of their destination, but Beth was used to her mother's silences. The four girls, even two-year-old Leo, were preternaturally quiet in the car.

Beth looked forward to their visit to Uncle Hugh and Aunt Sarah. They had identical twin eight-year-old boys who were fun to play with, and, most important of all, they had food. There were always cookies, ice cream, a refrigerator full of goodies; all in brilliant contrast to the empty Amana fridge and freezer sitting at home on Chestnut Street. Beth knew every time she opened its door, the only thing she'd see for certain was the light.

She had heard that prisoners condemned to die were served one last great meal. Perhaps this was going to be it for her.

After the visit was over and Beth had stuffed herself and hidden cookies in her coat pockets for later, Victoria did something completely out of character. She stopped at the Star Market on Route 9.

"Your aunt says how thin you all look," she commented in a flat, distracted tone. "I suppose we should get something here."

The four girls trailed after her, as she grabbed a shopping cart and headed off into the aisles. Her choice of food was eccentric. Sardine tins, olives, artichokes. Victoria tossed them into the basket, then turned to Meg and said: "Take your sisters and get whatever you want." Hoisting Leo in her arms, Meg took off for the aisle marked "Candy," with Beth and Amy close behind. They grabbed handfuls of M&Ms, Reese's peanut butter cups, Milky Way bars, loading them all into Amy's arms, until she looked as if she were carrying a baby as well.

They were all giggling happily, Beth remembered clearly, as they went to find Victoria. They continued giggling when they couldn't find her, heading straight back to the candy aisle and loading up Beth this time. When they searched for their mother again and couldn't find her, they stopped laughing.

"Look—" Meg said, pointing at the meat counter. "There's her cart, so she must be around here."

Other shoppers swore as they negotiated their way around the abandoned cart. Meg stood with Leo's head resting on her shoulder, turning around in circles.

"Let's put Leo and the candy in Mom's cart—then we

can take it around the aisles looking for her," Amy suggested.

They went up and down aisles for what seemed like hours, thinking all the time that Victoria must be doing the same and just missing them. So they tried staying in one place, figuring that she'd have to pass them.

"Why don't we go to the car?" Amy finally said as Leo began to cry. "She may be waiting for us there."

"But we can't pay for the food." Meg was on the verge of tears herself.

"If she's in the car," Amy responded, "we can get her to come back and pay for it. If she's not, we'll know that she's here still. See? It's like a math problem."

Beth had always been envious of Amy's mathematical talent. Amy had skipped a grade in school and, at nine, was capable of working out problems Beth still had difficulty with at twelve.

The dark green BMW wasn't there. They searched the parking lot methodically, led by Amy. There were twenty rows of parking spaces, each able to take ten cars. As they took turns holding Leo, they began to march up and down each row. Various adults, both male and female, asked them if they were lost, but each time Meg would say "No, we're just playing a game."

"Dad said never to talk to strangers," she explained after the first offer of help. "They might kidnap us if they think we're on our own."

After they'd covered the lot for the sixth time, however, the November night was beginning to set in and with the dark came panic.

"What are we supposed to do now?" Meg asked, her voice shaking.

"We should find a phone booth and call home," Amy answered, but she began to cry quietly as she spoke the words.

"Phones cost money. We don't have any," Beth said. She could be as logical as Amy if she chose. "Oh, forget it," she said as Leo let out a wail. "This is stupid." She walked straight up to a man who was getting into his car three spaces away. "Excuse me, sir, but my sisters and I have lost our mother. She was in the market with us and now she's gone and so is her car. We want to go home and we're not sure how to get there."

"I think I should call the police," he replied immediately, looking over at Meg and Amy who were holding Leo between them. They were huddled together, terrified, Beth could tell. But she wasn't. The man was nice. He had sandy hair and a kind face and a lovely voice. He wasn't about to kidnap them. He wasn't some old creep. He looked pretty young, actually. She knew she'd done the right thing, she'd saved them all. "Where do you live?" he asked.

"Sixty Chestnut Street. How long will it take to get the police? We're starting to freeze to death. I mean the others are. My sisters aren't as strong as I am."

"Evidently not," he smiled. "Listen. Why don't you tell me your telephone number and I'll call your house and see if your mother is there? If she isn't, I'll call the police. If she is, I'll drive you all home myself. All right?"

"Great," she said. "Thank you very much."

"The phone is there—" He pointed to a booth a few hundred yards away. "I'll go call now—wait here. And watch out for cars backing out, will you?"

She nodded happily, told him their home number and then went over to Meg and Amy to fill them in. As he walked back to them after a few minutes in the booth, she knew she was in love. If only her mother was at home, she'd get to ride in his car. He was frowning as he approached them, but stopped when he saw Beth staring at him.

"It seems your mother *is* at home," he said and Beth felt herself light up. "I don't quite understand how this happened, how you were left here."

"She forgot us," Amy said. "She forgot the food too."

"My name is Stuart," he said, extending his right hand and shaking first with Meg, then Amy. He put his left hand on Beth's shoulder. "Who are you guys?"

"I'm Beth," she said quickly, wanting him to know she was in control, even if she was a little younger and shorter than Meg. "This is Meg." She pointed. "That's Amy. Like in *Little Women*. Only there's no Jo. Our baby sister is called Leonora."

"Leonora? That's unusual. Right. Well, let's get you home. You'll have to squash into the back with my shopping bag, okay?"

"No problem." Beth couldn't stop herself from smiling. As he got in the driver's seat, she opened the back door of his car, pushed Meg, Amy and Leo in, shut it and went in the front herself. As soon as she'd settled in, she reached into her coat pocket.

"Would you like a cookie?" she asked him.

"No thanks," he smiled again, glancing over at her. "You're really something." He shook his head. "Has your mother ever forgotten you kids before?"

"Not exactly. I mean, she forgets to pick us up at school pretty often. Meg and me. We go to the same school— Winsor—do you know it?"

"No." He was frowning again.

"But you live around here, don't you?"

"No. I live in California. I went to Boston College. I graduated last year and I'm back visiting a few friends."

"Oh."

"What about your father? Will he be at your house when we get there?"

"No. He'll be at work. He's a lawyer. He works late all the time. Do you think you'll move back here, maybe?"

"I doubt it." He passed his hand through his sandy hair.

"We have a great summer house you could come visit. Dad has a boat."

"Right. Are you okay back there?" he asked, looking in his rearview mirror.

"We're fine, thank you," Meg replied. "Did Mom say—"

"Our house is right on the beach. You'd love it. But if you don't like swimming, we have a tennis court."

Stuart smiled but didn't respond. Beth couldn't believe

all the traffic lights were green. They were passing Coolidge Corner now. Which meant they'd be home in a few minutes.

"Is there anyone else who looks after you? Besides your mother?"

"No. Do you live in Hollywood?"

"San Francisco. You don't have any older brothers or sisters?"

"We had an older brother Steven," Amy said before Beth could reply. She was leaning forward, sticking her head between the front seats. "He was the oldest. We never met him. Mom backed up her car and ran over him by accident when he was two and a half. He didn't bleed or anything."

"Jesus," Stuart muttered, and Beth pushed Amy back.

"I might come to San Francisco soon."

"This is none of my business," he said softly. He was silent as Beth told him how much she liked the idea of San Francisco. And he remained silent as Beth told him she was going to save up her allowance to take a trip there. "Is it number sixty?" he asked as he slowed the car.

"Yes," Meg replied.

"Right. Your chauffeur has delivered you to your door." The car pulled to the side of the street and Stuart got out. Beth sat watching as he opened the door for Amy and Meg and Leo. She continued watching as he walked with them to the front door and rang the bell. He turned around and beckoned for her to join them, but she didn't move. She saw her mother arrive, she saw her sisters troop into the house. She could tell that Stuart was saying something to her mother, then she saw him nod his head in her direction. Her mother stood waiting with a vacant expression, her head tilted, her hand on the edge of the door.

Stuart came back, opened her door, crouched down so that his head was level with hers.

"Time to go home, Beth," he said. He reached out, took her hand and pulled gently, straightening as he did so, until they were both standing on the sidewalk. "I'd love to see you when you're twenty-one. You're going to break a lot of hearts, kiddo," he said, bending down and kissing the top of her head. "Remember, you broke mine first." Then he closed the door, walked around to the driver's side, got in, started the engine and drove off.

Beth didn't look at her mother as she walked straight past her, into the house, and up the stairs to her room. In the space of one afternoon, she had changed her mind about everything. She no longer cared whether her mother thought she was perfect or not. No way was she going to kill herself—they could have all been murdered in the parking lot and her mother wouldn't have blinked. There was no point in trying to compete with Steven in the perfection stakes because there was absolutely no chance to tie, much less win. Victoria didn't care about any of her daughters. She never had.

But Beth cared now. She cared desperately because she was in love with Stuart. And when she turned twenty-one she was going to go to San Francisco, find Stuart and marry him.

Meg came into her room and collapsed on the end of her bed.

"I've changed Leo and put her in her crib," she said. "She fell asleep right away."

"Good."

"Mom told me that she thought she saw Steven in the store, Beth. That's why she took off. She followed him. I mean, she even followed him when he got in a car with a lady. She followed them to their house. And then she saw him and she realized it wasn't Steven and she said she was so sad she had to come home."

"Right."

"But doesn't that mean she's crazy? Steven's dead."

"Yeah."

"Should we tell Dad? I mean what are we supposed to do? I think she's really crazy."

"Listen. Dad doesn't care. Haven't you noticed how he stares off into space whenever she talks to him? What good is telling him going to do?"

"Maybe she should go to a loony bin or something."

"Then we'd have to go visit her there. I saw a movie where some lady had a nervous breakdown and her family had to visit her in a loony bin every weekend. Do you want to go visiting a loony bin every weekend?"

"No."

"Okay. So we don't tell Dad what happened. We took care of ourselves this afternoon. We can take care of ourselves fine. And we can take care of Amy and Leo too. We don't need Mom."

"I don't know—"

"You know how she never does anything anyway. She just sits around looking goofy and telling us stories about Steven. Okay, so she sometimes goes to those Garden Club meetings but she doesn't bother to wash our clothes or cook us food. You know how different she is from other mothers, Meg. You know what it's like when you go to a friend's house to stay, how different it is."

Meg nodded.

"Right. Well, I kept thinking she might change. You probably did too. But she's not going to. So we have to do everything ourselves. I'm going to be twenty-one soon."

"What?"

"Okay. In ten years. But that's not so far away. I can learn how to do everything so I'll be ready then."

"Ready for what?"

"Never mind. But let's just forget about Mom and forget about Steven. There are more important things in life."

"I don't know—"

"Well, *I* do. I figured out what to do this afternoon, didn't I?"

"Yeah, I guess so—"

"Right. Now leave me alone. I've got things to think about." As Meg left her room, Beth leaned over to the table beside her bed and switched on the radio. Gladys Knight and the Pips were singing "Midnight Train to Georgia." She lay back and closed her eyes, seeing Stuart's dark blue eyes and sandy hair. Midnight Train to San Francisco, she thought.

Any train, any plane to San Francisco. In ten years life will be perfect.

Opening her eyes, Beth looked around her apartment. Eighteen years had passed and nothing was perfect. Asshole cops were making fun of her, most of her clients were stupid idiots and her love life was little more than a form of diversion. She hadn't been able to find Stuart, even though she'd tracked him down to San Francisco after getting his last name from a Boston College yearbook. He'd moved. No one knew where he was. He'd vanished while Beth was growing up for him. Five years previously she'd hired some dipstick private investigator to find him. He came back with nothing but a bill.

If anyone knew about this obsession, they'd think she was crazy.

What the hell, she thought. All shrinks are crazy. That's why their patients identify with them.

Getting up from the sofa, she wandered over to her answering machine, hit the replay button and stood listening to her messages. Two from clients wanting to reschedule sessions, one from her friend Robin asking if she'd like to see a movie the next night, and then the last—Meg. She replayed Meg's message twice, stunned by this story of Leo and the married forty-year-old. What did Leo think she was doing? More to the point, why hadn't Leo told her herself, why did she have to hear this from Meg, who sounded as if she'd been mainlining speed?

The Parents. The fucking Parents. Beth felt the familiar rage engulf her once again and did exactly what she counseled her clients to do—she gave in to it. She stomped her feet like a demented female Rumpelstiltskin, she threw her wineglass at the wall, she shouted every expletive she could think of. The redeeming sensation of expressed rage kicked in, as she knew it would, after she'd hurled her tennis racquet at the sofa, barely missing the antique vase on her side table.

Then, and only then, could she settle down and think clearly about this problem. This disaster, as Meg had called it. Yes, disaster. A man-made disaster: Leo throwing her life away on an ancient, married idiot; some Woody Allen thinkalike, who, doubtless, had taken one look at Leo's childlike beauty and decided he wanted to hijack it for himself. It was unforgivable. So much in life was unforgivable, and so many people wasted so much time trying to forgive.

How could Leo think of marrying anyone at her age? Beth shuddered, remembering the complete losers she had dated in her early twenties. What if she'd married one of them? As it was, she felt herself fortunate not to recall their names. Had she and Meg and Amy wasted all this time trying to look after Leo only to see her stuck in a kitchen with a baby on her hip? No—Leo was supposed to blossom when she left college. She was supposed to do everything all the others hadn't. Christ—she was supposed to have *fun*.

Beth poured herself another glass of wine. She'd clean up the shards of the old one later. What she had to do now, she knew, was to figure out a way to save Leo. Poor, misbegotten Leo who had no clue how to save herself. One of life's few innocents.

What had happened to that innocence? Beth wondered as she worked out all the ramifications of Meg's news. Leo must have been having an affair with this man for a while, at least, to decide that she was going to marry him. Therefore, Leo must have been lying for a while. How many times in the past month had she spoken with Leo? At least twenty. During those conversations, Leo had never mentioned a man in her life. She'd been as she always was—sweet, eager to please, full of questions about Beth's job. Not once did she allude to a boyfriend, much less a married man.

Leo had been lying, if only by omitting the truth. That fact was more shocking than the truth itself. The thought of a jaded Leo sneaking off for trysts with a deceitful married man made Beth feel physically sick.

This man, whoever he was, had done something criminal. He'd corrupted a pure soul.

At the bottom of it all, though, she knew that he wasn't the real one to blame. Their mother and father were the true villains of the piece. Victoria and Mark, the beautiful, perfect couple who managed beautifully to create a perfectly dysfunctional family.

Meg had said in the message that Nick was obviously a father substitute for Leo. "Well, wake up and smell the coffee, sis," Beth wanted to say. "Your hubby Charlie is a botched carbon copy of Dad—a man with all of Dad's flaws and none of his saving graces. At least Dad is charmingly impossible. Charlie is just impossible."

Beth shook her head and sighed. Meg, Amy and now Leo—each one linking up with men who had been married before. What did that say about their pysches? A whole hell of a lot. They accepted their role in life as the perpetual runners-up, the second choices. Even Leo, who she hoped might have escaped the parental trap, had fallen for the Preston line: you don't come first. Steven does. Or, in their father's case, work.

What a load of shit, Beth thought. But her three sisters bought it. They were too frightened or too nice to fight back.

Beth had been the only one to stand up to her parents. She waged guerrilla warfare against them both, disregarding any attempts by her father to discipline her, while ignoring her mother completely. In her teens, she would occasionally decide to be outrageous. She might gather together all the pictures of Steven in the house and hide them, or show up at her father's office wearing the punkest clothes she could find. Most of the time, however, she lived her life as if her parents didn't exist.

Meg and Amy kept trying to improve the parent-child relationships. A total waste of time and energy. They made allowances for Victoria and Mark. Poor Mom, they'd say: she accidentally killed her son. We should forgive her any-

thing. We should take care of her. Poor Dad. Living with
Mom can't be easy. He has his reasons for working so
much, for being away so much. And, okay, he flirts with
women, but he's not obnoxious about it—most of the time,
they flirt with *him*.

"Yeah, right," Beth often said. "But what about *us?* Why
did Mom keep having children after Steven died when she
knew she could love only Steven? Was she trying to have
a boy to replace him? Is that it? And we all turned out
second-class citizens, unworthy people just because we're
female? Fine. Terrific. And Dad couldn't deal with Mom's
increasingly loony behavior. So he stayed away as much
as he could. Great. But what about *us?* He left us to deal
with Mom. Plus he seemed to have plenty of time to flirt
with plenty of other women. I don't care whether they
winked at him first or not. The point is, neither of them
cared about us. How can you forgive them?"

Meg and Amy would stand speechless then, incapable
of responding to what Beth knew was the obvious truth.

She never lectured Leo like that, though. She couldn't
stand to see Leo upset. She and Meg and Amy had covered
for Victoria; they'd done Leo's washing, done her cooking,
read her good-night stories, taken her back and forth to
school every day, acted like the mother they'd never had
themselves, thus allowing Victoria to waft in and out of
Leo's little life whenever she chose. As if she were the
female President of IBM and they were the nannies. The
fact that Victoria didn't go out to work, aside from attending the occasional Garden Club meeting, but stayed at
home doing absolutely fuck all, made the Mothergate
cover-up more difficult still.

Beth remembered absurd times when Leo would be doing her homework, and Victoria would wander into her
room to give her ten millionth speech on the virtues of
Steven. Meg and Amy and she would then have to distract
Victoria and deflect her attention in such a way that she
would end up droning on to one of them instead. As far as

Beth was concerned, Victoria's death had been a blessing. It almost made her believe in God.

Leo loved Victoria's memory and she worshiped Mark from afar. She had no idea how fatally flawed her parents were.

Big mistake to go along with that, Beth told herself. Huge mistake not to tell Leo the facts of life early on. We were trying to spare her. A modus operandi that goes against all my instincts. Cruel to be kind is more like it.

And now Leo is in deep shit.

Beth became suddenly aware of the silence in her apartment. She stood up, restarted Mary Chapin Carpenter, and listened to "Something of a Dreamer, Something of a Fool." Then she picked up the telephone and dialed Amy's number.

Chapter Three

"AMY, PICK UP the phone if you're there, will you?"

"No, I won't," Amy said to the answering machine.

"Right, you're out. Here's my message. Meg told me about Leo and obviously I'm very upset. She mentioned that you approve of Leo's plans, but I find that hard to believe. You can't really think she knows what she's doing. I'm sure you agree that we have to find a way to stop this idiocy. So call me and I'll arrange a time when you and Meg and I can get together and plan our strategy. Okay?

"Oh, and by the way, I saw you in the Square a couple of days ago. I was in a rush, so I couldn't stop, but I think that new haircut is a major mistake. You look like someone's secretary. Bye for now."

Smash. Beth had a distinctive way of hanging up. She crashed the receiver down as if she'd just realized her apartment was on fire. It was another form, Amy supposed, of venting her anger. So was her unfailing instinct to wound.

Given that she knew full well Beth would throw in a stinging remark at some point during every conversation, Amy was amazed by how unprepared she was each time for the actuality. This time it was her haircut. Last time it had been the curtains in her living room. Beth knew exactly where the weak point was and went for it. The curtains were, indeed, "better suited to a funeral parlor in Las Vegas." Amy had quite liked them before Beth's remark, but once Beth had spoken, she saw the truth in what her sister said. Every time she looked at them now, she imagined a seedy, tacky, Las Vegas mortician's idea of style.

As for her haircut, well, once again Beth had it dead-on. What had at first struck Amy as a grown-up, efficient, working woman's cut—subtly layered, shoulder-length—

was instantly transformed into a bourgeois secretary's misjudged notion of chic.

Tears snuck into her eyes, and she shook her head to clear them. If only Beth would leave her alone. But there was no hope of that. The three oldest Preston sisters had an agreement: they would all stay in the Boston area, at least until Leo graduated from Harvard.

It was impossible to escape Beth when she lived only ten minutes away. Actually, Amy reckoned, it would be impossible to escape Beth even if they lived continents apart. There were telephones everywhere. Beth would make it her business to keep tabs, to try to run her life. She wasn't someone who could give up.

Poor Leo, Amy thought. Beth will be on her case with a vengeance, seeing herself as the guardian angel. And poor Nick. To deal with an impending divorce and Beth at the same time was not an enviable position. He probably assumed that Leo's sisters were similar to her in temperament. Well, he was in for a shock.

Amy had given Leo total support when told of the Nick situation, but then she would have given Leo total support if she had come to her and confessed to being a serial killer.

Carefully erasing Beth's message from her machine, Amy went into her kitchen and began to prepare supper for Jimmy. *I'll deal with Beth later*, she told herself. *When I feel stronger*.

How could she argue on behalf of Leo when she wasn't sure herself whether this marriage was the right thing? Of course she had gushed and enthused when Leo had told her, but secretly she was nervous as hell about it. The age factor was one problem, but not, to Amy's mind, the real issue. The major obstacle was Nick's wife, whoever she might be.

How was this unknown woman going to react to being shunted aside for a twenty-two-year-old? What problems would she cause for Leo, what kind of spiteful behavior might she indulge in? Leo had no concept of what it was like to be a second wife or a stepmother. Amy knew all too well the landmines scattered through a second marriage. She stepped on them herself continually.

Meg might have pulled off the miracle and become friends with Charlie's ex, Helen, but Amy knew that she would never come to terms with her own husband's ex. Rachel haunted her like an evil spirit; thoughts of Rachel dominated her psyche. She was obsessed by a woman she'd never met. Was that what Leo was going to let herself in for?

Beth maintained that there was some deep psychological meaning lurking in the fact that Amy and Meg were second wives. "You're just confirming the belief you both have that you're second best," she had stated. "You both picked men who have already sworn undying love for someone else. Think about it."

Amy *had* thought about it and decided that she and Meg were natural statistics in a world dominated by divorce. If one out of every two marriages is terminated, and the total number of marriages was not decreasing, it was reasonable enough, mathematically speaking, for two out of four daughters to marry a divorced man. Leo entering the equation changed the odds. Three out of four *did* seem a little excessive.

Still, Amy had been married once before and she knew that it was possible to make a vow of eternal love twice and mean it on both occasions, in different ways. Her first husband, Patrick, had been a feckless, irresponsible, charming kid. He liked to drink, gamble and quote poetry. He also liked to walk out of jobs or take unscheduled vacations. He believed in "living life to the fullest." It took Amy far too long to realize that this actually translated into "living life for myself."

"I let people down," he'd confessed on their second or third date, and she'd thought, *How sweet of him to be so honest about himself. He doesn't really mean it, though. He'd never let me down.* She had laughed when he'd described all the dull, meaningless jobs and courses he'd abandoned. "Absolutely," she'd agreed. "Life's too short to spend behind boring desks."

A year later, he'd walked out on his twenty-year-old-wife and their baby daughter as if they were some tedious job he'd wasted too much time on.

Her sisters had rallied around her then in their different ways, but each time she saw Meg or Beth the same thoughts would assail her. *Patrick would have stayed with Meg because she's more sophisticated than I am. Meg knows how to dress, she knows how to put on makeup, she knows how to present herself. And Patrick would have stayed with Beth because Beth is as beautiful-looking and as crazy as he is.* It didn't hurt her as much to think that Patrick would have stayed with Leo because Amy believed that any man with a tenth of a brain cell would stay with Leo.

Still—what it came down to was that the only one Patrick would leave was her. Amy. The loser in the family. The others were prettier. The others were funnier. The others were more interesting.

When she married Jimmy, five years after her divorce, she wasn't worried about his possible preference for her sisters. She had studied him closely in their presence. She'd even set little tests: would he compliment Meg on her clothes once too often? Would he laugh too much at Beth's jokes? Would he look longingly at the young Leo? He'd passed all the tests and he'd done better. He'd excelled because he hadn't criticized them either. He'd admired them all, but just the right amount. Only Amy knew how tough a line he'd had to walk, how easily she could have dismissed him if he'd said or done one wrong thing.

What *did* make Amy nervous at the altar was her sense of déjà vu. She could feel her mouth twitch as the minister said "till death do you part." *We've both said this before,* she thought. *Jimmy said it to Rachel and I said it to Patrick. Does that make this ceremony a sham? Does God understand that I didn't know what I was doing before? I meant what I was saying then, too. But I was nineteen and I didn't know what marriage was all about. Neither did Patrick. It was one of his crazy whims. Does God realize that this marriage to Jimmy is the one that counts?*

The telephone rang again and Amy swore. It would be Beth, calling back to make another point. Beth liked to use the telephone as a pulpit when she knew the answering machine was on. It was a perfect opportunity to lecture to a captive, speechless audience. Amy waited for the click, dreading Beth's insistent voice.

"Jimmy. Fishbone. You won't believe this. I just heard that Sal and Pete are getting a divorce. I mean, after us, they were the perfect couple. Remember how cute they were together that night in Denver? What a trip that was. Anyway, they're splitsville, history, toast. I gotta run now. Talk to you soon."

A double whammy, Amy sighed. Beth followed by Rachel.

What was she supposed to do when she heard a message like that? Why did Rachel have to use her creepy nickname for Jimmy all the time? "Fishbone." It made her feel ill. She wished she could shove a fishbone down Rachel's throat.

Within the space of twenty seconds, Rachel had managed to convey a shared intimacy with Jimmy—one that didn't recognize Amy's existence, of course. Every sentence was full of their past—their old friends, old trips they'd taken, the fact that they'd been thought of as the perfect couple.

If you were such a perfect couple, Amy wanted to scream at Rachel, why did you leave him and run off with another man?

More importantly, why can't you leave him alone now? He has a new life and a new wife. Why do you think you have the right to call him anytime you feel like it, any hour day or night? Your marriage is over. You're history. Toast.

How ironic that Rachel wouldn't leave Jimmy alone while Patrick never once contacted Amy. Their daughter, Charlotte, hadn't seen her father since the day he left. He sent her birthday and Christmas cards from wherever he happened to be, but that was it.

Amy knew that Beth would advise some acting out at this point. Throw a chair, she'd say. Smash a vase. Sure. Then try to explain it all when Jimmy walked through the door. It might be perfectly acceptable to trash your apartment when you were living alone in it, but not when you had a husband to deal with. Jimmy couldn't comprehend her attitude toward Rachel; he thought Amy was over-reacting and jealous when she had no need to be. "Rachel's an old friend now, that's all," he would say patiently. "She's no threat, so don't treat her as one."

"If Patrick kept calling me, you wouldn't be pleased, either," she had argued.

"I wouldn't have a problem with that," he'd countered. "Besides, Rachel has valid reasons for calling me. We have Zoey to discuss."

"Of course," Amy replied. "You have Zoey." The fourteen-year-old product of his union with Rachel, Zoey was a sprite who darted in and out of their lives at odd moments. Never one to keep to any schedules, Rachel would send Zoey over to Jimmy when it was convenient for her; sometimes six weeks at a time would go by without a sighting of the girl. Whenever she did turn up, Zoey would dazzle Jimmy with her intelligence, wit and beauty. She'd entertain them with humorous stories of nights out with her mother.

Amy was amazed at the places Rachel would take Zoey to: gay bars, wild parties—completely inappropriate hangouts for a young teenager. But Zoey seemed to take it all in her stride, a complacent chaperon to her mother's more bizarre forays. Why Jimmy allowed Rachel to treat their daughter in this blasé fashion astounded Amy. It didn't jibe with his conservative nature. Yet Zoey displayed such remarkable equanimity and maturity, it was clear that this strange parenting was beneficial to her nature. With her dazzling red hair and green eyes, Zoey was irresistible. Jimmy adored her and Amy, despite her implacable hostility to Rachel, found it hard not to love Zoey as well. What she hadn't figured out yet was whether she felt sorry for the girl.

Nevertheless, Rachel's calls rarely seemed to concern Zoey. As far as Amy could gather, Rachel had a real problem talking about anyone but Rachel. Jimmy's defense for her constant telephoning was flawed. And he could say he wouldn't mind if Patrick began to communicate, but how could he know what it felt like to be plagued by an ex?

How easy it was to be a rational, balanced person in hypothetical situations, Amy thought. There were times when she longed for Patrick to appear out of the blue and start hanging around, just so she could see Jimmy's real-life response.

Rachel might be an "old friend," but she didn't fit Amy's notion of one. How many old friends take an exorbitant amount of money from you every month? Child support was only a fraction of what Jimmy handed over to her. And how many have no compunction about calling you up at three A.M. to tell you something "crucial" like they've been out dancing at a hot new club? What kind of old friend takes no notice whatsoever of your new wife? If Amy answered the phone when Rachel called, Rachel would say "I'd like to speak to James" in a repulsively superior voice, as if Amy were Jimmy's secretary.

Perhaps that's what she *should* be, Amy thought. After all, she looked like a secretary now. She was and always had been extremely efficient and practical. Not like Rachel, who was, by all accounts, "zany" and "different."

Amy began to peel potatoes at her kitchen sink, hacking away at them with a growing sense of despair. She was so tired of being the nice, sensible person; a woman who knew everything there was to know about neuroscience without any idea of how the brain actually interacted with the heart. Neural networks were one thing, emotions another. The one person she felt totally at ease with was Leo; everyone else confused her.

Had Jimmy married her because he loved her, or because

he was on the rebound, licking his wounds after Rachel had deserted him? Was Beth actually conscious of the hurt she caused when she made her negative comments, or was she completely unaware of the effect she had? Did Patrick have any desire whatsoever to see his now seven-year-old daughter?

Questions like this tormented her. She tried to live her life rationally; she wanted more than anything to be on an even keel, unaffected by other people's whims or caprices, but she knew the effort was doomed. One wrong word from Beth and she felt as if she'd been stabbed. If she overheard Jimmy on the phone to Rachel, listened to the softened tone of his voice, she thought she'd implode. When Charlotte showed even the slightest signs of unhappiness, Amy would blame herself for being a bad mother.

When she felt most insecure, Amy took refuge in science. Everyone's character was founded on how synapses fired, how chemicals interacted in the brain. Soon a computer would be able to simulate a human personality, complete with all emotions, including those ineffable ones like love and pathos. Classic psychiatry was on the wane. Freud was being discredited more with each passing day.

She needed to reprogram herself, that was all. Rewire her brain and remove all channels that caused her self-confidence to falter.

There were times, though, when she wished that *she* could be zany and different and say whatever she felt like to anyone. Those were the interesting people, the ones who made an impact, who got what they wanted out of life. Beth had a limitless string of male admirers who considered her to be "the most fascinating" woman in the world. They never seemed to mind being treated like pathetic, loyal dogs. If anything, they lapped it up. Beth never failed to get attention; people always noticed her because she had an aura of compelling power.

And Jimmy's friends never stopped talking about Rachel. "What's the crazy lady up to now?" they'd ask him, smiling in anticipation of Rachel's latest adventure while

Amy served out some dinner she'd cooked, playing the loyal wife-cum-chef.

Outrageous behavior scored points. Amy didn't see, though, how she could suddenly become outrageous. What would she do? How would she do it? If she tried to copy some of Beth's more bizarre antics, people would laugh at her, not admire her. You had to be born different to be different; you couldn't give yourself a personality transplant in five easy lessons. Besides, she had Charlotte to think of. Children didn't like having wacky, off-beat, different mothers. Well, maybe Zoey did, but not most children. That was one thing she knew for a fact.

When she'd been living with Patrick, life was such a roller-coaster ride, she hadn't had time to analyze herself. Those were the days, Amy thought. Romance and sex and excitement had occupied all her thoughts. She hadn't felt like an old married woman with thousands of responsibilities then. She hadn't felt like a secretary, either.

What would I be doing right now if Patrick hadn't walked out? she wondered.

Amy heard Jimmy's key in the lock and decided to stay in the kitchen, listening. He would hang up his jacket, sort through his mail on the hall desk and check for phone messages. She crept toward the kitchen door, waiting for the sound of Rachel's voice being replayed. If she flattened herself against the wall, she'd be able to spy on his facial expressions as he listened to his ex-wife.

He stood there, opening a bill, hearing the message with a smile on his face. Was it a wistful smile? Was he remembering that "night in Denver," wishing he could be there still? Amy felt sick as she watched.

"Amy? Are you home?"

She crouched down, out of view, edged back to the sink, straightening up just as he walked in.

"Oh, hi," she said, trying to sound nonchalant. "I didn't hear you come in."

He came and hugged her, gave her a kiss on the cheek. "How's it going?" he asked, rolling up his shirtsleeves and moving toward the kettle to fix himself some coffee.

Why doesn't he ever lose himself in passion? Why can't he ravish me right now, right here on the kitchen floor? Amy looked at her husband, then turned back to the potatoes. And what if he did just that? I'd think it was because he'd been turned on by Rachel's message.

"Fine," she replied. "Although Beth's gone ballistic about Leo and Nick. She wants to meet with me and Meg and find a way to stop her." She paused for a second. Go ahead, she decided, fish for a compliment. "And she thinks my haircut makes me look like a secretary."

"I know. I heard the message. But what's wrong with looking like a secretary?"

Well, I walked right into that one, Amy thought. And I'll make another appointment tomorrow, have the whole lot chopped off. Or shave it. Do a Sinead O'Connor.

"Where's the brat?" he asked and she felt her bones tighten. Relax, she cautioned herself. It's a term of endearment.

"She's been invited to Georgia's house for the weekend."

"Ah," he said, relief and pleasure sneaking into his face. He couldn't know how easily he betrayed himself, Amy thought. He'd be embarrassed if he knew. Her jaw locked; her entire body went on the defensive. *He's thrilled that my daughter's gone away*, her racing heart said. *He doesn't want her here*.

"But *I* was happy when Charlotte told me about the invitation," her brain shot back. "I wanted some time. Time for myself. And time alone with Jimmy. Why should I blame him for being pleased? What's the difference between his reaction and mine?"

The difference is that I love Charlotte and he doesn't.

That's about as big a difference as you can get.

Jimmy was leaning against the kitchen counter, coffee cup in hand. She wanted to go over and wrestle him to the ground, pin him down, put a gun to his head and force him to love Charlotte. She loved Zoey, or at least she was extremely fond of her. Why couldn't Jimmy feel the same for Charlotte?

"Let the line out." She could hear her father's voice. "Take your time, make him tire himself out. You don't have to be so forceful, do it gently." Why was a fish always assumed to be male? she wondered, remembering the first bluefish she'd hooked. Her arms ached from the strain of the rod, she was exhausted and wildly excited simultaneously. Her first fish, and a big one.

Her father was as excited as she was, giving her instructions, refusing to take over himself. "You've got him," he said. "He's tired now. Bring him up close to the boat." Amy was thrilled when she saw the fish rise to the surface, clearly done in, giving up the struggle. She'd won and her father was there to see her triumph. Meg and Beth had taken Leo for a walk on the beach, Victoria had stayed in Boston, so Amy was alone with Mark. It was too much to hope for, this fish, but there it was, its gills panting wildly, ready to be netted.

"He's a beauty," her father announced, leaning over the side of the boat, net in hand. "Foul-hooked, though." With one effortless motion, he swooped down, caught the fish, pulled him up to the boat. "Look where he's hooked, poor bastard. Right through the eye." Amy watched as the proverbial fish out of water flopped around desperately, trying to struggle free. Her father clubbed it on the head, and the fish lay quiet, in submission. Mark twisted the hook around, trying to wrest it out of the eye. The fish bucked one last time, sending the hook straight through her father's thumb.

"*Damnation*," he shouted, and Amy burst into tears.

"So—" she said to Jimmy, aware that her voice sounded a false note of calm. "Did anything interesting happen to you today?"

"No," he replied. "You should know by now, nothing interesting happens in an insurance office."

Jimmy had a job Patrick would have done a comedy routine on.

"What about that movie—*Double Indemnity*—that was

all about an insurance scam? I'm sure people murder for insurance money all the time."

"I'm sure they do. But not on my watch." He smiled and brushed the hair back from his forehead in a gesture that always reminded Amy of films she'd seen of Robert Kennedy. Are you going to tell me about Rachel's message? she wondered. Or has it gotten to the point where you're afraid to mention Rachel's name, because you're afraid I'll react badly? Just as I'm afraid to push you too hard when it comes to Charlotte. Should I bring it up? But if I do, will you ask me why I didn't answer the phone myself? Why I hid behind the answering machine?

"What do you want to do this weekend?" She took the chicken breasts out of the fridge.

"I don't know. What do you want to do?"

This was like a conversation between eight-year-olds, she thought. What do you want to do? I don't know, what do *you* want to do? I don't know, I asked you first. Is this the inevitable effect of years of marriage? Playground talk? Or does it happen only when two people are busy avoiding dangerous subjects?

"Well, according to Leo, Nick has told his wife that he's leaving her, and he's moving out tonight. So maybe we should invite them over for dinner tomorrow."

"Sounds fine to me. I think it's time we met this guy, Nick."

"Absolutely," Amy nodded. "Meanwhile, though, what should I do about Beth? She's on the rampage."

"So what's new?" Jimmy shrugged. "You know, I love to watch Beth in action. It's a trip. Someday someone is going to stand up and yell at her. Maybe it will be me. It's not as if I don't know what she thinks of me."

Beth had no time for Jimmy. He wasn't on her wavelength, didn't understand her humor, so she dismissed him as a lowly family appendage. She had approved of Patrick, probably because she had been responsible for Amy and Patrick's first meeting. They'd been on their way to visit Uncle Hugh when Beth had pulled over to the side of the road to pick up a hitchhiker—Patrick. "Do you want to come with us to visit our aunt and uncle?" Beth asked when he'd climbed in. "Or would you rather rob and rape us?"

He'd gone along with the game, and Beth had introduced him to Aunt Sarah as Amy's French fiancé. Patrick didn't miss a beat. "Enchanté," he'd said, bowing to kiss Aunt Sarah's hand. As he lifted his head, he winked at Amy. That was the beginning. She should have known the end would have been just as unpredictable.

"You know *I'd* like to stand up and yell at Beth sometimes. But I can't," Amy sighed. "I can't ignore her either. Not unless I take the phone off the hook for the rest of my life and skulk around Cambridge with my head down."

"Hey, I like Beth, despite the fact that she thinks I'm an amoeba. And I know you love her—she's your sister. But I don't like the way she treats you sometimes. I don't like the way you let her get to you. I think you should stand up for yourself. Or I should stand up for you."

"It's better just to leave it alone. Standing up to Beth isn't worth the hassle. Really."

He shrugged and frowned.

"Okeydokey. Whatever you say. It's your life."

Beth's voice was in the back of her head now: *Okeydokey? Does he think that's cute, or is he verbally challenged?*

"Do you want peas or broccoli with your chicken?"

"Broccoli's fine."

Beth came back again as Amy chopped the broccoli: "You know that Congreve play—*The Way of the World*? There's a line that goes something like: 'As soon as a woman marries a man, she starts to dwindle.' Look at you, Amy. Standing there cutting up vegetables. You should be cutting up brains, kiddo. We're in the nineties, remember? But, hey, if that's what you want, dwindle on."

"I'll be right back," Amy told Jimmy. She fled to their bedroom, sat down on the floor, her back up against the bed, pulled the telephone to her, and dialed.

"Leo. It's me. I'm making supper for Jimmy and Beth's

in my head again. You know that speech she gave me about
women dwindling? Is she right? I mean, is that what I'm
doing? Dwindling?"

"Of course not. Listen, when is the last time Beth had a
real relationship? Can you remember? Because I can't. So
she tries to trash other people's relationships. That way she
can feel better about herself."

"But what *am* I doing chopping vegetables?"

"You're cooking supper, aren't you? What's wrong with
that? People have to eat. And you're a good cook. Who
says you can't be a good cook *and* a great neuroscientist?
Is there some law against that?"

"Rachel called. I listened to her message on the machine.
She referred to herself and Jimmy as the 'perfect couple.' "

"Sure. So that's why they're divorced. Come on, Ames.
You can't let Rachel get to you, either. It's exactly what
she wants. I bet if you weren't in the picture, she wouldn't
be calling Jimmy. She can't stand the fact he's happy with
someone else, that's all. Don't let her win, okay? She's a
control freak."

Amy took a deep breath and smiled.

"Thanks. I needed some sanity in my life. Listen, will
you and Nick come to dinner tomorrow night? I don't think
I can wait any longer to meet him."

"Definitely. Now that we're out of the closet, we can do
whatever we want. I'm so happy, you wouldn't believe it."

Oh, Leo, Amy wanted to say. Be careful.

"See you tomorrow evening, then. Meanwhile, watch out
for Beth. Meg told her about you and Nick and she's not
exactly thrilled."

"I didn't think she would be. Don't worry, I'll be on
Beth Alert. I'll put on the heavy armor, gird my loins, as
it were. I bet she's already called a family meeting with
you and Meg, right?"

"Right."

"Well, it's bound to be a strange meeting. I know Meg
has a jumpy nature and I know I dropped a bombshell on
her today, but she looked so unhappy. She had on the per-

fect clothes as always, but her eyes looked defeated. Maybe that was all because of my news, but I don't think so. I've got a gut feeling about it, Ames. I think she's miserable."

"You know Meg wouldn't confide in me about anything," Amy said.

"Do you think I should try to talk to her? I hate seeing her like that."

Leo's voice had such concern and sadness in it that Amy found herself desperately wanting to cheer her up.

"I think you should concentrate on yourself and Nick for the moment. Maybe Meg woke up this morning and realized who she was sleeping with."

"Watch out, Ames—that's dangerously close to a Beth comment."

"No, no—anything but that—I promise I didn't mean to be so bitchy about Charlie. I just couldn't resist," Amy laughed, then said good-bye to Leo and returned to the kitchen. She kissed Jimmy fiercely.

"What's that for?" he asked, looking surprised and boyish.

"The kiss of life," she said and went back to the broccoli.

Chapter Four

THE PHONE WOKE her. She had to reach across Nick to grab it, thinking as she did so, My God, he's *here*, he's been with me *all night*. She saw the time displayed on the clock as she said hello: 3:14 A.M. The fear suddenly hit when there was no immediate response. *Something's happened to Meg or Beth or Amy*, she thought. *There's been an accident.*

"Hello," she said again. "Is anyone there?"

"I want to speak to Nicholas," the voice said. "Now."

A terrible voice, Leo thought. Full of pain and anger. The voice of a woman who had been up all night crying and drinking.

Leo put her hand over the receiver, not sure if she was trying to shield the woman or herself. With her other hand, she gently shook Nick awake.

"I think your wife's on the phone, Nick. She wants to speak to you."

He sprang upright immediately.

"Shit," said, as she handed the phone to him. He kept his hand firmly over the receiver as well, she noticed. "Can you turn on a light?"

Leo nodded, feeling herself begin to tremble. When she turned on the bedside lamp, she saw Nick motioning to her to get him a cigarette. He pointed to his trousers, lying in a heap on the floor, and she got up from bed, delved into the pockets and came up with a pack of Marlboros and a lighter. She lit one for him, passed it to him, took her robe from the hook hanging on the bedroom door, pulled it close to her and left the room—just as he was saying: "Jackie. What do you want?"

She was tempted to stand outside of the door, listening

to his end of the conversation, but she walked instead to the kitchen, fixed a cup of coffee.

She couldn't stop herself from imagining the scene. A forty-year-old woman sitting in a house by herself, drenched in pain and anger and frustration knowing that her husband had left her for another woman. How many bottles of wine had she consumed, how many old scrapbooks had she looked at? How desperate must she have been to make that phone call?

Leo couldn't bear to think of the pain for which she was responsible. Yet when she'd first been assailed by this overwhelming sense of guilt, she'd been unable to do the right thing and tell Nick to go back to his wife. The only way she could conceivably give Nick up would be to lock herself in her room and chain herself to a radiator. So she'd entered into the lies and the deceit and the betrayal, trying to keep the thought of Jackie from her mind.

Was it possible to build your happiness on the back of someone else's suffering? Meg had managed, she reminded herself. Meg and Helen were friends now; they had somehow constructed a working relationship. Anything was possible, given time and effort and understanding. Leo wished she could fast-forward the tape of her life a few years and get to the point where Jackie had accepted the situation, maybe even found a new man.

"Leonora—" Nick was standing in the doorway of the kitchen, fully dressed, smoking a cigarette. "I'm sorry, but I have to go home and see her. She's hysterical."

Home, Leo thought.

"Do you think she'll be all right?"

"I don't know." He rubbed his forehead. "I thought we'd said all we had to say when I told her I was leaving. But that was too much to expect. You can't make a clean break of a messy marriage in one fell swoop."

"No. Of course not."

Yet another night when he left her alone. She was almost used to it by now. The first time he'd taken a shower, washed all traces of her from his body before going back to his wife, had been the most difficult. She'd kissed him good-bye and then sat in her bed, sleepless, holding the towel he'd used to dry himself off. I'm dirty, she'd thought. A dirty little tramp. This is not how I wanted love to be. Why couldn't I have had a choice?

"How did you meet him?" was the first question Amy had asked when she'd told her about Nick.

"I stalked him," Leo replied, laughing. But it wasn't particularly funny. In fact, it was pretty insane. She'd noticed him one morning, sitting at a corner table in her local Dunkin' Donuts. He was reading the newspaper, smoking a cigarette, occasionally sipping at his coffee. She was three tables away, but she couldn't stop staring at him and she couldn't understand why. He looked old and tired and sad, nothing like the image she had of an attractive man. He never smiled, not even when she caught his eye as he was leaving. *She* had smiled then, but he had continued as if he hadn't seen her, just carried on and walked out the door.

What's the matter with him? she wondered, and then dismissed him from her mind. Except she went back at the same time the next morning. He was at the same table, reading the *Globe* again. She bought her coffee and moved one table closer. He didn't acknowledge her existence, didn't even take one sideways glance. When he left this time, he strode past her table, and kept his eyes straight ahead. She got up and followed him, lagging behind a few paces. Fishing a pen and a piece of paper from her bag, she copied down the license plate number of the tiny blue Honda Civic he scrunched into.

Beth, the queen of random contact with strangers, had once seen a Jeep with the license plate "BORED." So enamored was she by this statement on the back of a car, she called the Massachusetts Registry of Motor Vehicles and asked who the owner was. They informed her that if she sent a check for twenty-five dollars, they would provide the name. As soon as she had received it, she called the male owner and asked him out for coffee. "It won't be boring," she'd said, and he fell for it. Subsequently, he fell for her.

He became one of a band of male admirers who were continually rebuffed. He failed to see the twenty-four-hour neon BORED sign that lit up in Beth's heart whenever she was the object of devotion.

With this precedent, Leo knew exactly what to do. She wrote off to the Registry, enclosing the license number and a check. While she waited for the reply, she went to Dunkin' Donuts every morning and watched the man in the corner. She knew now how he sat, how he walked, the way a vein in his forehead stood out slightly when he concentrated on his paper. She knew he spent most of his time reading the sports section, that he smoked two cigarettes in the twenty minutes that he spent there. If there wasn't an ashtray on the table, he'd use the floor. Once in awhile, he'd have a honey-dipped doughnut, but usually he stuck to coffee. He was, she realized, too thin for his height—like her—and she worried about his health. His hair seemed to grow thinner by the day. He was definitely sad—she was certain of that, too. What she didn't know, however, was why she cared so much.

His name was Nicholas Booth.

Be Beth, she told herself as she walked to Dunkin' Donuts on the day after the Registry office's reply to her request. Be bold and crazy and don't worry about what he may think of you. She remembered a dinner party Beth once hosted, when a guest rang early in the evening, saying he was stuck in New York and couldn't come. "Damn Fred," Beth muttered. "We'll have to find a replacement."

Leo was helping Beth prepare the food. "Nobody will mind if you're one person short, Beth. They don't even know Fred. Don't worry about it," she said, trying to be a comfort as she mixed dips for the nachos.

"Well, *I* mind," Beth had replied. "We'll find another Fred."

"Who? Nathan? Larry?" Larry was Mr. BORED.

"No. It's time for some new blood. Let's get someone we don't know."

"What? Someone off the street?"

"Why not?" Beth smiled her wicked angel's smile.

"A homeless person?"

"Come on, Leo. I'd never do anything that nice. Look, you finish the dips and I'll go out and invite a stranger to dinner. I'll tell him his name is Fred and that he's from New York and he's an art dealer. There must be plenty of guys wandering around who wouldn't mind a good meal and a little playacting."

"I don't believe you," Leo said, but of course she did. This kind of behavior was par for Beth's course. Half an hour later Beth came back with a man in tow. He was somewhere in his late twenties, overweight, red-faced and clearly baffled.

"Is this for some kind of TV show?" he asked, looking around Beth's apartment for hidden cameras. "Were they filming when you picked me up in McDonald's?"

"Fred. How did you guess?" Beth nodded gaily. She was in her element. "But don't worry. All you have to do is eat and mention the occasional painting. Or not, if you don't know any paintings. There's no set script. Just eat and smile a lot. The bathroom is down the hall on your left, if you want to comb your hair."

"Fred" had had a whale of a time. He guzzled the wine, beamed at the other guests, told lousy jokes, all the while scanning the room for hidden cameras and not so discreetly combing his lank hair.

"So when does the show air?" he asked Beth at the end of the evening, when everyone else had gone home.

"I'd say in about two years," she answered.

"Two years?"

"We're trying to get Alec Baldwin and Kim Basinger. It takes a while, you know. To pin the stars down."

"Right. Of course." "Fred" grinned. "You'll let me know, though, won't you? Can I call you?"

"Nope. I'm off to Hollywood now. But give me your number and I'll be in touch. Okay?"

"I wish I understood the plot, the concept—whatever."

"You will," Beth said, gently steering him toward the

door. "All good things come to those who wait."

"Hannibal Lecter," "Fred" said proudly. *"The Silence of the Lambs."*

"Exactly," Beth sighed. "The true meaning of life lies in the art of waiting. Even psychopaths understand that concept." She opened the front door, gave "Fred" a shove and closed it quickly behind him.

"Wasn't that a little cruel?" Leo asked. "Getting his hopes up like that?"

"We've made his day, Leo. *And* we've fed him something a lot better than a Big Mac. Two years from now, he'll see some Alec Baldwin movie and think his bit has been left on the cutting room floor. No problem."

Nothing was a problem for Beth. And Leo had to admit, the evening had been fun with a fake Fred. After years of tagging along with Beth's crazy schemes, Leo knew she could combat her natural shyness and approach a stranger. All she had to do was pretend she was Beth.

So she walked straight up to him.

"Mr. Booth?"

He raised his eyes from his paper.

"Can I join you for a coffee?"

"Who are you?" he asked and his voice was so severe she immediately wished she'd never approached him. It was a stupid idea and a silly obsession.

"I'm sorry." She shook her head and started to back away. "I'm really sorry." All traces of Beth had deserted her. Leo felt awkward and humiliated. What had she been thinking? Who did she think she was?

"How do you know my name?" he asked. He sounded offended, angry.

"I don't," she mumbled, spilling her coffee at the same time. Her hand burned from it, but she didn't move. He had her fixed in his glare, and she stood paralyzed, a little girl ashamed.

"So you just guessed Booth? Because I'm sitting at a table?"

She shook her head again, unable to speak.

"You come in here every morning for the past week and a half and you stare at me and now you know my name. What is this, some kind of sorority challenge? A college prank?"

She turned then and fled, her head down.

"Leonora—" she heard her name called as she was half-way across the parking lot. "Wait a minute," he said, approaching her, then stopping as a car drove between them and into an empty space.

"How do you know *my* name?" she asked, completely puzzled.

He started toward her again, then halted as another car drove in. She saw him smile. In that one instant, that short smile, she recognized a lifetime of hope and possibility.

"This is a dangerous place to hold a conversation," he said. "Why don't you come back inside and we'll have that coffee?"

They returned, not speaking, to his table in the corner, where his cigarette pack, his newspaper and his coffee lay waiting.

"Let me get you a fresh cup," he said. "Black, right?"

"Right."

"Would you like a doughnut, a muffin, a bagel?"

"No thanks," she smiled.

"You should eat something sometime, you know. You're much too thin."

"I know," she nodded. "So are you."

She watched him as he waited at the counter for his turn in line. The girl behind the counter smiled when she took the order and glanced at Leo. He brought the coffee over, walking that slightly loping walk she knew so well, and placed it in front of her, then sat down himself.

"Do you mind if I smoke?"

"No. One of my sisters smokes. I'm used to it."

"How many sisters do you have?"

"Three. Meg, Beth and Amy. Meg's the one who smokes."

He laughed. "What happened to Jo? Or shouldn't I ask?"

"It's a family mystery. We all have different theories."

"I see," he nodded.

They were silent for what seemed to Leo a very long time. She automatically reached for her earlobe.

"I'm going to make a little speech, Leonora. Is that all right?"

"Yes." She was surprised by the gentle tone of his voice.

"Okay. Here goes. I noticed you that first morning you came in here. You smiled at me when I left and there was something about that smile that stayed with me all day. Now, that's unusual in and of itself. You tilt your head when you smile, you know. The light was behind you. I felt as if I'd seen the most beautiful painting in the world. I felt privileged.

"The next morning, you came in and you sat at that table over there, one table closer to mine, and I wondered if that was pure chance or design. I decided it was chance and I walked right by you because I couldn't stand it if you didn't smile at me again.

"On the third morning, when I saw you walk in, I thought I was going crazy. I realized that I'd been waiting for you all night. I realized how disappointed I would have been if you hadn't been here. I was angry with myself and angry with you for creating this absurd longing. It didn't seem fair. You were some kind of sprite who was playing with me, having a game at my expense. Have you ever read *Lolita*?"

"No," Loe replied.

"Well, what no one seems to understand about that book is that Humbert *loved* Lolita, that she was willfully torturing him, but that's another discussion. On the fourth morning, when I left here, I parked my car down the street. And I followed you when you came out. At a discreet distance, of course. It's not as easy as it looks in the movies to follow someone, especially if she's walking. It's hard to keep the car at a crawl, but I managed. You went up the porch stairs of what must be your apartment building. By this time, I was close enough to see and to hear the woman who was waiting for you at the top of those stairs. She had long blond hair and a lovely face that looked a little like yours. And she said, 'Leonora, you fucker, where have you been?' "

"That was Beth," Leo laughed. "I forgot I was supposed to meet her that morning."

"I sat in my car—I don't know how long I sat there— but I decided that I had gone temporarily insane. I'm forty years old and I'm following a child around in my car. I'm waking up at four A.M. every morning, thinking about going to Dunkin' Donuts. This is not healthy or desirable. This is—" he paused, pulling on his cigarette—"reprehensible. And—" he paused again, narrowed his eyes. "This is *war*. I could have stopped coming here every morning. But that would be an admission of defeat. Why should I avoid a young girl, whatever game she may be playing? I like having my coffee here in the mornings. Why should I give that up?

"So I continued to come here and I determined to wait you out, figuring you'd get bored watching some old guy in the corner read his newspaper. What I wasn't prepared for was your initiative. It was a surprise attack and I didn't like it. I snapped. But when you walked away you looked so hurt and distraught I couldn't let you go like that. I guess I wanted to see you smile one more time.

"End of speech. I've been honest with you. God knows why. What do you want from me, Leonora? And how do you know who I am?"

"I took down your license plate number and sent away to the Registry of Motor Vehicles for your name." Leo took a sip of coffee, wrapped her hands around the coffee cup. "I don't know what I want from you. I guess I just wanted to talk to you. It wasn't some prank. I just wanted to talk to you."

"Is this a habit of yours?" he asked. "Do you normally pick people up in Dunkin' Donuts?"

"No. My sister Beth picks up strangers all the time. I've never done it before." She frowned. "I didn't mean for this to be a pickup." The frown turned into a grimace. "I don't know what I expected. I just sort of did it. I wasn't thinking. Oh God. I can't explain it. I'm sorry."

"Don't be," he said, leaning back in his chair, looking relaxed for the first time. "Tell me something. Why does Beth pick up strangers?"

"She gets bored with the people she knows. I think she's always looking for someone who will fascinate her. She's volatile—what she needs is someone to calm her down, but what she wants is someone who'll excite her."

"That's a pretty shrewd comment, Leonora."

"No. It's a very obvious one—if you know Beth."

"So. Meg smokes. Beth is volatile. That leaves Amy. Will you have coffee with me tomorrow morning and tell me about Amy? I have to get to work now, I'm afraid."

Leo nodded, feeling absurdly happy. He rose from his chair, stuffed his cigarette pack in the pocket of his corduroy trousers and gathered the paper together.

"Did the Registry inform you of my first name, by the way?"

"Yes. Nicholas."

"Nick," he said.

"Most people call me Leo."

"Not me," he shook his head. She smiled up at him. "I'll see you tomorrow morning." He tapped her on the shoulder with the *Globe*. "Good-bye, Leonora. And eat something, okay?"

They continued to meet every weekday morning. Within the space of a few weeks, she had told him all about her childhood, her family, all the stories she'd never shared with anyone except Amy. He grilled her with question after question, very rarely talking about himself. Early on, in the first week, he'd informed her that he was married and had a daughter, but when she asked him about them, he said he didn't think it was "appropriate" to talk about them.

"I don't discuss you with them, so I don't believe I should discuss them with you. Fair enough?"

She had nodded, relieved. If he'd told her how happily

married he was, she knew she'd be irrationally upset. Conversely, if he'd gone into any detail about how unhappy he was, if he'd told her his wife didn't understand him, she'd be disappointed in him. She wanted him to be loyal to his wife. At the same time, she hoped he didn't love her.

He was the theater and movie critic for *The Boston Globe*. Occasionally, he'd bring a play along with him and hand it to her. "Read this," he'd say. "You don't have to discuss it with me later, but I'd like you to read it. I'm very impressed with your linguistic ability"—she'd told him that she was majoring in Russian at Harvard—"but you should take a break from Chekhov and Co. and check out some of the contemporary playwrights."

Leo began to dread the weekends. She'd go to Dunkin' Donuts on Saturdays and Sundays anyway, feeling perversely deprived and alone. Sometimes she'd manage not to think about him for an hour or two, but usually he invaded her psyche every few minutes and she'd try to shake him off, physically shake him off, tossing her head and shoulders like a dog after it has been in the water. "He's just a friend," she'd tell herself then. "My new best friend. Nothing else."

On one Sunday afternoon in October, as she was struggling with the Russian verb tenses in Chekhov's short story "The Black Monk," her buzzer rang. "Leonora, it's Nick," the voice said over the intercom. She buzzed him on in, quickly ran to her bathroom, picked up her comb, threw it down without using it and headed for the door.

"Am I interrupting something?" he asked, standing on the threshold.

"No. I was sitting here reading Chekhov. Just what you told me to take a break from, but I couldn't face Mamet either. Beth took me to *Oleanna* last year and—you're not going to believe this—but in the middle of it, she said so loudly everyone could hear: 'Shouldn't these people consider Prozac?' Everyone stared at us. I've never been so embarrassed. Come on in."

He smiled and walked over to her window, which

looked onto Huron Avenue. His back was to her as he said: "I've just been to the MGH to see my father. I never told you, but he's been sick for a long time and now he's sicker. I don't know why I came here. Except it's the only place where I thought I might be able to breathe normally."

"Nick," she said softly, going up to him and putting her hand on his shoulder. "I'm so sorry. Are you all right?"

"No," he answered. "I'm not."

She wanted to put her arms around him, but took her hand off his shoulder instead.

"Do you have a roommate?" he asked.

"No. My father's been very generous to me. He pays the rent for this place. When I graduate, he expects me to support myself, but for now, he's funding me. After all those years living with my sisters, I have to admit, I like having my own place."

Nick turned away from the window and went to sit on Leo's armchair.

"That chair is from the Chestnut Street house, the one we all grew up in," she said, going over to the sofa opposite and sitting on the floor, with her back propped against it. "So is this sofa. All of the furniture, actually. Dad sold the house and moved to a smaller one when I was accepted by Harvard. He told us we could take any of the furniture we wanted because he was going to start fresh. Meg and Beth and Amy refused to take anything. Bad memories, I guess."

"But not for you?"

"No. It's funny—do you want a coffee, by the way?"

"I'd love one," he smiled. "But keep talking, please. I need to hear you talk."

"Right. That's easy." She went and fixed them both cups of coffee, brought them in with the one ashtray she possessed and returned to her original position.

"Anyway, you know I told you about Steven? Well, my sisters spent so much time shielding me from Mom's stories about Steven and how wonderful he was—they didn't know that I *liked* hearing about Steven. It's hard to explain, but I think I loved Steven almost as much as Mom did. He was like a character in a fairy tale. To Meg and Beth and Amy, he was a bad ghost who took over the house and made Mom crazy. But to me, he was a little prince.

"I didn't mind that Mom was so obsessed because I had my sisters to take care of me. I had three mothers. The others felt neglected, but I had more attention than I knew what to do with. I was smothered in love. I think that's why I like living on my own now."

"But your father didn't smother you in love, did he?"

"No. That's true. Beth goes on and on about how distant he was, but she never puts anything in context. My mother never recovered from the accident. It wasn't her fault, she didn't see Steven behind the car. But she blamed herself. She was riddled with guilt. She must have been a difficult wife to live with. Beth says that Dad worked all the time because he was so ambitious and single-minded, but I think he just couldn't cope with Mom's pain. Besides, he *did* do things with us. She conveniently forgets the good parts.

"I've overheard Beth ranting to Meg and Amy about our parents. She thinks she's managed to hide the nasty bits from me; they all do. They don't want to talk to me—especially about Mom—because they think I should be spared. But I know a lot more about what's gone on in the family than they think. I loved Mom, and I love my father. I felt sorry for them both. I still do." She paused, looking at Nick's sad eyes. Their expression reminded her of her own when she was a child, putting on her dress for her mother's funeral.

"Do you want to talk about your father?" she asked.

"Yes. Sometime. Not now. Listen—" He stubbed out his cigarette, stood up and rubbed his forehead. "I know I don't have a right to ask you this, but I'm sitting in that hospital and I can't think straight and I can't concentrate. It's driving me crazy. I promise you it won't make a difference to anything, but I need to know. Do you have a boyfriend, Leonora? Can you tell me, please?"

"No. I don't. I did. We broke up a few months before I met you."

He nodded. "Thank you. I'm sorry I asked. It's none of my business."

"Why not?" She stood up as well, facing him.

"Because it's not." He rubbed his hand all over his face, slowly, then shrugged. "I've got to go."

"You can come here anytime, Nick. Really. Here—" She went over to her desk in the corner, wrote down her telephone number. "Please call me. Anytime."

"Thank you," he said gravely, taking the piece of paper. "I have to go."

The telephone woke her at six on Monday morning.

"My father just died," he said. "I don't know what to do."

"Do you want to come over here?" she asked.

"I can't. Maybe later. Maybe tonight. Are you in tonight?"

"I'll be here, Nick."

He didn't arrive that night, he didn't call, he didn't show up at Dunkin' Donuts. She waited, at first patiently, but as the months passed, with a growing sense of despair. She thought of all sorts of plans—standing in front of *The Boston Globe*, calling him at home with some foolproof excuse in case his wife answered the phone. But each time she discarded the notion, forcing herself to accept the fact that he didn't want to see her anymore. Whatever it was, whatever had happened between them, was over. He had disappeared from her life. She didn't tell anyone, and was surprised by her own secrecy on the subject.

She had bought a pack of Marlboros to keep in her kitchen for his arrival, but after Christmas passed she threw it out. Every morning she woke up with a pain in her stomach that receded only at noon when she forced herself to eat a half a piece of toast. Her size six clothes began to fall off her, but she refused to get on a scale and weigh herself. Food disgusted her, but so did any comments about anorexia from friends. "I can't help it if I'm not hungry," she'd say. "I'm not anorexic, I just don't feel like eating."

Ineluctably, she was drawn to Beth. Whereas she used

to visit her once or twice a month, she now dropped by a couple of times a week. Although she never said anything, she listened closely to Beth's lectures on the importance of not forgiving people.

"What is this tolerance bullshit?" Beth would say. "Why are we supposed to make excuses for the people who shaft us? We have to live with the reality. There are shitty people out there. If we get screwed by one of them, we should admit it. Then we can get pissed off and figure out how not to get screwed again. It's as simple as that."

Or as complicated, Leo thought.

Had she been hallucinating, imagining things? There were times, during those morning coffees, when Nick had said something that made her laugh so much she thought she'd collapse. And others when she felt an electric wave of total sympathy and understanding between them. Had he been playing with her for his own purposes, taking her on a ride from hell? She was used to feeling sorry for other people. Now she was feeling sorry for herself and she hated it.

After one particularly depressing evening at Beth's, when she sat there listening to a long-winded explanation of all the murderous impulses in human nature, she went home, strode straight to her desk, took a pen and paper and wrote: "This isn't fair. You are willfully torturing me." She put it in an envelope addressed to Nick Booth, looked up the address of the *Globe*, wrote it beneath his name, licked a stamp, fixed it on and then went out to find the nearest mailbox.

Three nights later, when her apartment buzzer rang, she knew it was Nick; she didn't even bother to ask who was at the door, but pushed the button immediately.

"It's going to be different now. You know that," he said when he came inside.

"I know."

"It's not right. I was *trying* to be fair, don't you understand that?"

"Yes, I do," she said. "But it *is* right. Don't you understand that?"

He reached out and pulled her to him. For someone so thin, he was surprisingly strong and his kiss, which started tentatively, suddenly entered a realm of passion Leo hadn't known was possible. The kiss took off, like a car switching into fifth gear. It accelerated, and reminded Leo, when she thought about it later, of Marcella Detroit's voice: the way she would be singing along normally and then unexpectedly skip octaves, until she'd hit a note so high it hurt.

She'd had sex before, and enjoyed it. The two men she'd slept with in her life had been more than competent in bed. They'd had orgasms, she'd had orgasms. Each time had been pleasurable in its different way. Leo liked sports; she was good at tennis, basketball, baseball. Sex struck her as a variation on a team sport. Except in this case, both teams won.

Nick wasn't playing any games. There weren't any rules. Nor was there any logical progression. They didn't even remove their clothes. He took her hand, led her to the sofa, his overcoat still cold from the February frost. They lay down and kissed, his hands covering every part of her body. Even through her wool jumper and the denim of her jeans, she could feel his touch as if it were directly on her skin.

His hands seemed to read her desire, touching every point she ached for them to touch at exactly the time she hoped they would. At the base of her spine, he stopped and began to rub in a circular motion, a gesture that produced an animal response in Leo. She reached for his belt, unbuckled it, wriggled his trousers down over his hips and slid down to take him inside her mouth. She'd never minded going down on a man before, but it had never particularly turned her on, either. It was just part of a larger agenda. This time, she was desperate to do it. It was the most intimate, personal act she could imagine and she loved every second of it. When he came, she came as well, wondering how that could be possible.

She sat up, smiling.

"Are you okay?" she asked.

"Jesus, Leonora," he laughed. "That's an incredibly stupid question." He was lying back, his overcoat still on, staring at her as if she had appeared from another galaxy.

"Would you like some coffee?"

"Anything you say." He shook his head in disbelief.

When she returned with the two mugs, he had put his trousers back on and was sitting upright on the sofa.

"Can we take these into the bedroom?" he asked. "I'd like to do that again. Properly."

"*I'd* like to do that again. And improperly is fine by me."

She handed him his coffee, turned her back and walked into her bedroom. It was the first time, she reflected, as she pulled her sweater over her head and threw it on the floor, that she had seen him look truly carefree.

A few hours later, as she lay in his arms, he kissed her softly on the side of her face.

"You know I have to go now."

"I know."

"Can I take a shower here?"

"Sure."

She stayed in bed, already feeling lonely and bereft. When he emerged from the bathroom, gathered his clothes and dressed, she remained silent, watching him. He came over and sat on the edge of her bed.

"What happens next?" he asked. He looked as miserable as she felt.

"I don't know. Can you come over tomorrow morning?"

"I can come over every chance I get, Leonora. That's what I want to do. But you're not going to like it. It's never going to be enough. For either of us."

"It's better than nothing," she said fiercely. "You can't disappear again. Not now."

"No. I can't. I'll see you tomorrow."

I'm dirty, she said to herself after he'd kissed her goodbye. *A dirty little tramp having an affair with a married man. What is his wife doing right now? What does she look like? Where will he tell her he's been? I don't care. I can't let myself care. Because I don't have a choice. I have no choice at all.*

Now, nine months later, she was saying good-bye to him again, watching his back as he loped off down the stairs. He was going to comfort Jackie, calm her down. But Leo knew the only words that could possibly help Jackie were the words he wouldn't say.

Jackie might be older than she, a mother and a wife, she might have entirely different interests in life, perhaps she was physically dissimilar as well, but they had one thing in common—their love for Nick Booth.

God, I feel sorry for her, she thought, sitting back at the kitchen table staring at her cold cup of coffee, her head in her hands. How would *I* survive if he left me?

Chapter Five

MEG PAUSED AT the threshold of Josh's room. Was she supposed to tidy her fourteen-year-old stepson's mess or not? If she did, would he be offended? She knew she didn't want to risk ordering him to do it himself, at the same time realizing that was exactly what she should do.

Josh and David had gone out with Charlie for a Saturday morning breakfast at the International House of Pancakes. Meg knew how much Charlie enjoyed having time on his own with his children, so she'd stayed behind. And now she was faced with this mayhem. How could Josh manage to find clothes to wear in the rubbish heap he'd created? She took a few steps into the room, picked up a half-empty can of Coke, put it down again.

Maybe Josh *liked* warm, stale Cokes and would be furious if she threw it away. She stared at a pile of filthy clothes splayed in the corner. Was she supposed to wash those? Had he brought all his dirty laundry over to their house to save his own mother the bother? Or were mud-stained T-shirts as hip as ripped jeans these days? *Leave it*, she told herself, backing out. *If in doubt, leave it alone.* Her eye was caught by the framed picture on his desk. This was a new addition to his room and she walked over to inspect it.

There they were, in their full glory, the Thurlow family as was. Father, mother, and two sons sitting on the beach. Charlie looking tanned and remarkably thin, Helen gazing at him, with David on her lap. Josh was sitting in front of Charlie with a bucket and spade—a tow-headed, smiling little kid. Meg zeroed in on Helen's face and winced. This was a different woman. She appeared to be at least twenty years younger than she was now, but the picture couldn't have been taken more than ten years ago. Where was this beach? What family holiday had it been? And why did they all have to look so perfect?

Even more disturbing, why did she notice a slight resemblance between herself and Helen? Meg had never seen this before, but it was unavoidable in the picture. She and Helen had the same auburn hair, the same high cheekbones, the same physical build.

The Helen who had brought the children and the casserole over yesterday afternoon had put on pounds, her hair had changed from auburn to a sickly shade of brown, her face was devoid of any trace of girlishness. She'd lost her looks completely, to the point where it was impossible to believe she'd ever had them.

Shuddering, Meg turned and left Josh's room. She went to the kitchen, made a cup of coffee, took it into her living room and opened up *The Boston Herald*. Within a few minutes, she'd tossed it away and lit a cigarette.

Beth, the first time she'd seen Helen, had pulled Meg aside and said "Goes to show how people can be misnamed. Helen's face wouldn't launch a thousand ships. More like a thousand dredgers, if you ask me." Meg had registered appropriate outrage at this bitchy comment, but she'd been secretly pleased. This was hardly a becoming sense of competitive edge, she knew, but she felt it nonetheless. The concept of a once pretty, youthful, vibrant Helen made her ill. What had happened? Could one man's desertion wreck a woman so comprehensively? Apparently so.

The first major argument Meg and Charlie had was over Helen. They were out at dinner together, a few months after their wedding, and Meg mentioned casually that she hoped Helen would find a nice new man soon. Lurking behind this comment was a host of hopes—if Helen found a new man, she might marry him. If she married him, she wouldn't need all the alimony she received. She might not find it necessary to call Charlie so often. Charlie's friends' wives might then deign to speak to Meg, instead of regarding her, as they did now, with suspicion, as if she were chairman of the board of Marriagebusters Inc.

"It's unlikely that Helen will find someone," Charlie had said dismissively.

"Why?"

"Because I'm the only man for her."

"What kind of egotistical bullshit is that?" Meg shot back immediately. "How can you think you're irreplaceable? Do you really believe you're that wonderful?"

"Calm down." Charlie put his palms up in the air. "I'm being honest, that's all. To begin with, you have to understand that Helen is a one-man woman. That's the way she's made. Also, although you might find this difficult to fathom, she always found me fascinating—my job, the people I meet—she loved all that. She loved our life, she loved me. Obviously we had our differences, the marriage was far from perfect, but the chances of her finding someone who would live up to me *in her mind* are slim."

"I don't believe you're saying this." Meg took a huge slug of her red wine. "There are other men out there, you know. Okay, maybe they're not all president of Harvard Law School, maybe they're not wildly successful or infinitely fascinating, but they might just have other attributes."

"Are you saying there are men in the world who are better in bed than I am?" he grinned.

"Of course not." She found herself essaying a feeble grin in return. How had she backed herself into this corner? There she was, trying to bring him down a peg, drive a hole into his self-confidence, while his ex-wife clearly idolized him. If there was one thing she wholly agreed upon with Beth, it was the fact that the male ego could never be sufficiently fed. To come out well in this conversation, she'd have to back down and say: "Obviously Helen sees you as the perfect man, Charlie. So do I. *I'd* never be able to replace you either."

"All I'm saying is that there's a possibility that Helen will fall for someone else, someone who measures up to you. You can't really expect to be the love of her life forever. That's putting yourself in a no-lose position. Maybe if you realize she could fall in love again, *she'll* realize she can. Through osmosis or something."

"Osmosis?" he laughed. "You're not making much sense, Meg. I can't change the way Helen feels about me. She can't change it, and neither can you. This has nothing to do with my ego, it's simply the truth. It has no bearing on our relationship, though."

Oh, no? she thought, reaching for the wine again. When I know there's a woman on the sidelines who thinks you're some kind of god? What does that make me feel like when I criticize you, or when I don't happen to find you fascinating? Christ knows, *I'd* prefer to be with someone who found me irresistible and irreplaceable. How do I know you won't go running back to the comfort of her all-welcoming, besotted arms, even if we are married now? Did you get bored with her worship, were you temporarily seduced by someone like me who challenged you occasionally? If so, when will that wear thin?

The specter of a Miss Havisham figure sitting out the rest of her days waiting for her man to come back unnerved Meg. She felt as she imagined Audrey Hepburn must have when taking the role of Eliza Doolittle in the film of *My Fair Lady*. Everyone knew that Julie Andrews deserved the starring part; she'd been slaving away at it for years on Broadway, belting out "Just You Wait Henry Higgins" every night, but when the time came to put the play on celluloid, Hollywood demanded a younger, more glamorous flower girl. One who couldn't even sing. People were outraged. Audrey Hepburn was so winsome and charming, though, that she managed to get away with this bit of poaching, and win an Oscar to boot.

Meg wasn't so lucky. No Audrey Hepburn, she. The general public was in complete sympathy with Helen. They certainly weren't about to hand out any awards to wife number two. Social outings with Charlie's friends were a trial for her, filled with awkward moments and stilted conversations.

It was easy to understand why this set of people who

had known Charlie and Helen as a couple now viewed Meg as a carpetbagger. Although Helen hadn't put Charlie through law school, she'd been there with him during the hard times, starting out in a tiny apartment in South Boston and progressing, through three moves, to a house in bucolic Dedham; the house that Helen and the kids still occupied. By the time Meg entered the scene, Charlie had established himself as the Boy Wonder. At which point he proceeded to ditch the wife who had cooked his meals, ironed his shirts, had his children and facilitated his climb to the top. A classic story, which of course produced outrage and moral judgments.

While many of Charlie's male friends might be jealous that he had had the guts to do what they wished they could, they could never be seen to admit to it, so they tended to ignore Meg, while their wives clearly saw her as a "Betrayer of Women." Although they'd be perfectly friendly when she and Charlie visited them, they'd manage to communicate their feelings by various methods. Often, Meg was treated to a seemingly inexhaustible supply of stories concerning self-sacrificing women who had been shunted aside in favor of the dreaded Trophy Wife. This was a blisteringly direct form of attack.

For the most part, though, they'd be a touch more subtle. They'd place pictures of Helen and Josh and David in strategic spots, so that Meg, while she was sipping her coffee, would be face-to-face with her predecessor. Or, if they didn't have a recent photo of sad-eyed Helen, they might leave a postcard from her lying around casually, so that Meg would find her gaze drawn to the familiar writing, and read a plaintive message such as: "I'm in Florida. I'm not sure what to do with myself. Love, Helen." Well, Meg wasn't sure what to do with *herself* on these occasions. She'd become tongue-tied or find herself spouting inanities, thus behaving in a way that made her appear to be the Trophy Wife they so despised.

There was no way to win.

Unless she had a baby.

It was remarkable how quickly a woman could turn from a scheming bimbo into an accepted member of the female community when she became a Mother. As soon as she could participate in discussions about nappies, teething, schools and the problems of being a working mother, she knew she would begin to fit in.

A baby would be the solution to the feeling Meg had of being a spurious wife. More importantly, a baby was exactly what Meg wanted. She loved working with young children, found immense satisfaction in being a mother figure for a group of six-year-olds. Although she felt ill at ease with Josh and David, she knew this was due to her position as stepmother, and also to the fact that she hadn't known them from an early age, but come into their lives when they were already eleven and nine. If they were kids at her school, she was convinced they'd be close friends by now.

The only stumbling block to becoming a mother was her husband. Charlie didn't want any more children. He'd made that clear early on in their relationship and she hadn't pushed, thinking that he'd change his mind as time went by. He hadn't. Nor, it appeared, was he going to.

"Been there, done that, got the proud papa T-shirt," he'd said recently, when she had dared to raise the subject. "I thought you understood my position on this. This isn't a conversation we should be having. And please," he continued, as he saw her tears start up, "Don't go hysterical on me. Helen pushed me into having Josh and David. I'm not saying I regret it. Of course I don't. But I didn't get remarried to go through it all again. Don't pull a Helen on me, Meg."

He had her again. He knew precisely how to stop her dead in her tracks. All he had to do was suggest that she was behaving like his ex and Meg would back off immediately. If she behaved like Helen, he might treat her the way he treated Helen. He might leave her too. Still, the horrible prospect of being abandoned, that blow he had dealt to Helen, must have been softened for her by the existence of Josh and David. What if Charlie left Meg after twelve years and she was forty-four and childless? Where would she be then? Even if she managed to break through the barriers and become close to her stepchildren, they'd most likely disappear from her life with their father and she'd be left alone. With no one but her sisters to fall back on.

She needed a baby and she needed Charlie.

Or did she? Lately frightening thoughts ambushed her at odd times. She'd begun to wonder if she might actually be a lot happier alone. This was heretical thinking. From childhood onward, Meg had accepted the idea of a family of her own as a kind of religious faith. The creeping doubt now assailing her was not unlike a Catholic's questioning of faith. Whereas a Catholic might ask himself: "What if Charles Darwin was right?" or "Is the Virgin Birth meant to be taken literally?," Meg found herself facing similarly difficult questions: "What if I could take charge of my life *myself?* What if I didn't need Charlie after all? What if a baby is *not* the answer?"

Meg sighed, stubbed out her cigarette and went into the kitchen to fix herself another cup of coffee. As she opened the cupboard to find a new pack of sugar, she saw again the jar of homemade marmalade Helen had delivered to her when she'd picked up Josh and David the previous Sunday. The handwritten label read "Magic Marmalade for the Boys." Meg laughed. Beth had been visiting when Helen came by and had been unnaturally quiet as Helen explained exactly how she'd made the marmalade. Once Helen had gone, however, Beth turned to Meg with a sly smile.

"You know what you should do with that, don't you?"

"Throw it away?"

"No. Of course not. Put slivers of glass in it. And when you're spooning it out at breakfast tomorrow, pick out a piece of the glass and say: 'Oh my God, this could have killed one of us. She couldn't have done it on purpose, but how clumsy of Helen. What *could* she have been thinking of?'"

"Beth!"

"Why not? Put a little kink in the works of Mother Earth. Murderous Marmalade for the Boys. Come on, it would be hysterical."

They both dissolved in laughter then, and Meg was grateful to her sister for putting humor into a bleak situation. Her own domestic capabilities were less than zero. The closest she'd ever come to homemade marmalade was once when she'd had a hangover and watched a cooking show on TV—and that was only because she hadn't had the energy to change the channel. Now, whenever she saw the marmalade, she giggled. For all the times that Beth had said something hurtful, Meg had to admit, there existed an equal number of times when she came up with the perfect response.

The doorbell rang and Meg went to answer, half expecting it to be Helen again, bringing more homebaked goodies to tide "her boys" through the weekend.

"Any chance of a cup of coffee?" her father asked as he strode through the door, wearing khaki trousers, a blue shirt and blue and red polka-dot tie. Meg couldn't remember ever seeing her father without a tie, except, of course, on fishing expeditions.

"Sure. I'm just making some for myself."

"Where's Charles?"

"He's gone out to breakfast with Josh and David. Come on into the kitchen."

Mark sauntered into the kitchen and sat down at the pine table, looking, as always, distracted. And handsome.

"I gather your sister Leonora is planning to get married," he said, without any inflection to his voice. Did he approve or disapprove? It was impossible to tell.

"Who told you about that?"

"She did," he replied, taking the cup of coffee from Meg's outstretched hand. "Thank you."

"You're welcome."

"Have you met her intended?"

"No." Meg hesitated for a moment before saying, "He's married, you know."

"I'm aware of that, yes." Her father suddenly smiled and Meg felt drawn in by the warmth of that smile. "When he chooses to be, he's so fucking charming he should move to India and buy a snake," Beth had once remarked.

"Do you think I should call him into my study and have a man-to-man chat? Apparently he's not exactly a boy."

"No." Meg sat down across from Mark. "He's not." It was disconcerting to have her father to herself like this. She couldn't recollect the last time they'd had a discussion without one of her sisters, or, lately, Charlie, being present.

"I suppose the general consensus is that I'm to blame for this inappropriate alliance. Leonora is looking for a father figure. Am I correct?"

Meg felt herself blush, disarmed by this wholly uncharacteristic dip into the icy waters of family history.

"I don't know, Dad. You'd have to ask Leo about that."

"Aha. Deflect the question. A nice legal tactic." He smiled again and Meg looked away. "Beth would give me a straight answer, though, wouldn't she?"

"Beth would give you an answer, yes."

"Another canny reply. Meg, I believe you should have gone to law school yourself." Mark put his coffee cup down, crossed his arms and leaned back in the chair. "You know how to tell where the bluefish are, don't you? The seagulls. They circle overhead, then dive for the bait. So when you see a group of gulls circling and diving, you know that there are fish underneath. Because the bluefish are driving the bait up from underneath. The bait is being attacked from both sides, by the gulls *and* the fish. Then we fishermen join in the feeding frenzy and throw out fake bait to hook the fish. The birds tell us what is happening beneath the surface. But to reap the benefits of this information, we humans need artifice."

"I don't think I understand what you're saying," Meg said quietly, trying to remember every word of that little speech to tell her sisters later. It would be good for a few laughs.

"I'm not sure I do either," Mark shrugged.

Charming, distracted, elusive, but not wholly indifferent? Wasn't that her father in a nutshell?

"I think you should talk to Leo, Dad. She's the one in trouble."

"And you're not?"

"What's that supposed to mean? Are you saying something about my marriage?"

"Meg, I never mentioned your marriage."

"Good, because it's fine. My marriage is fine."

"Beth and Amy—are they fine too?"

"Absolutely. We're all fine. Leo's fine, actually. She's in love with Nick. She's happy. I overreacted when I first heard about it, probably because—" Meg stopped. "We can take care of ourselves. You don't have to worry."

"Yes, of course." Mark stood up. His gray eyes scanned the room before resting on Meg with a bemused expression. "You're self-sufficient, aren't you? The Four Preston sisters. A law unto themselves. Thank you for the coffee. And give my best to Charles. He's in line to be the youngest ever president of Harvard, you know."

"I know."

"Good luck to him. Being president of the law school is demanding enough. To take on the entire university is one hell of a difficult job."

"Thanks." Meg smiled. At last they were back on familiar territory—work. Mark was in charge of Harvard's legal business. When Charlie became president, he'd be seeing a great deal of her father. Of course that wasn't why Charlie had married her. Mark might be a useful contact for him, but not an indispensable one. Charlie had told her that, early on. "Your father's a bonus in the perfect package of you," he'd said. Meg hadn't objected to herself being called a package or her father being labeled a bonus. Not then. Back in those days she hadn't objected to anything Charlie said. If he repeated that line now, she realized, an-

ger quickly taking control of her body, she'd want to smash
his face in.

Meg forced herself to smile as she walked Mark to the
door and gave him a quick kiss on the cheek. She then
peered out the window, watching him as he walked to his
car. There was a red-haired woman sitting in the passenger
seat. She turned to him as he got in and Meg could see the
flash of her gold-hooped earrings, like fishhooks in the sun.

Chapter Six

"SURPRISE! I'VE COME to check out my prospective brother-in-law." Beth swept in, bringing a waft of her trademark scent of Sunflowers, her long blond hair piled on top of her head in a messy but appealing mound.

"Nick's not here, Beth."

"So where is he? Having male hormone replacement therapy?"

"He's with his wife. He left early this morning."

"Uh-oh. Cheating on you already?"

"Would you like some coffee?"

"Absolutely. Are you on an antivanity campaign, kiddo? The clothes. Meg would have a heart attack. They have those awful colors of an old fifties movie. You know, Hayley Mills in *Please Don't Eat the Daisies*."

"That was Doris Day. Hayley Mills was in *The Parent Trap*, I think."

"Same diff. Same colors. You look best in black, you know. Mourning becomes you."

Beth took off her black overcoat, revealing a John Prine "Great Days" T-shirt hanging loose over Armani stretch jeans, and followed Leo into the kitchen. Sitting down, she tossed the coat onto the table, threw her legs up on the neighboring chair and stared at her sister as she spooned out Nescafé into two mugs.

"So tell me something, Leo. What's your favorite Dostoyevsky novel?"

"*The Brothers Karamazov.*" Leo switched on the electric kettle and turned to Beth with a half smile.

"Now that's strange. I would have thought you'd go for *The Idiot*."

Beth saw Leo's shoulders sag.

"And I'd guess, if you were trawling through pop fiction, you'd come out with *The World Is Full of Married Men*. Was that Jackie Susann or Jackie Collins?"

"I don't know." Leo turned back and poured the water unsteadily.

"Jackie Onassis maybe?"

Leo shook her head in evident exasperation.

"Am I witnessing a sense of humor failure here? In one so young?"

"I'm tired, Beth. That's all."

"You *look* tired. You look exhausted."

The telephone rang and Leo handed Beth her cup of coffee, then ran into the living room to answer it. Within a few seconds, she was back.

"Who was that?"

"I don't know. They hung up."

"*They* hung up? Team telephoners?"

Leo gathered together a spoon, some sugar and a pitcher of milk and set them in front of Beth. The phone rang.

"Team telephoning. A new Olympic sport," Beth commented as she watched Leo run off again. By the time she'd noticed the bottle of whiskey and the pack of cigarettes on the counter, Leo had returned.

"Another hang-up," Leo announced.

"Your intended smokes and drinks, does he?" Beth motioned to the whiskey and Marlboros.

"That's exactly how Dad referred to Nick. My intended. Meg calls him 'that man.' His name is Nick. And yes. He smokes and drinks. In the morning he takes Ecstasy and at night he goes in for crack."

"That should spice up family gatherings. Don't get it, Leo. Some little kid must be playing a game."

"It might be Nick," Leo said.

Beth picked up her mug and trailed after her sister, watching as she lifted the phone, listened, and put it down again.

"Kids get bored on Saturday mornings and think it's hysterical to hang up on people," Beth commented. "Meg and I used to do that. We played all sorts of tricks. Once we called about twenty cab companies and sent them all to the house across Chestnut Street from us at the same time. Poor Mrs. Jenkins had to explain to all these irate drivers that she hadn't ordered them. We were watching from our window, laughing our heads off. Bad girls."

Leo smiled and sat down, thinking: I bet I know whose idea *that* was. The phone rang.

"Put the answering machine on, for Christ's sake."

"It's not working."

"Then let *me* get it," Beth said, quickly reaching for the receiver. "Fuck off and die, brats," she snarled into the mouthpiece. "Too late. Whoever it is hung up before hearing my words of encouragement. I think you should take it off the hook for a while."

"I can't. Nick might call."

"Why don't you call him? Oh no, of course ·you can't. He's with his *wife*. I thought he was supposed to have left her. Why isn't he here with you?"

"He can't just abandon—" Leo cut off and answered the telephone. "This is ridiculous," she said after replacing it. "What am I supposed to do?"

"I'll tell you what you're supposed to do. A: You finish college. B: You travel around the world for a while. C: You begin a career in translating for the UN or U2 or whatever you want to do with your skills. D: You wait until you're old enough to have a long-term relationship. You play the field, find out what great sex is all about. And then tell me. Oh shit. This is relentless. Take it off the hook for a while, will you? At least let me finish what I'm saying. If it's whathisname, he can call back.

"Good. Now where was I? I've told you what you should do. What you shouldn't do is get involved with an older married man, and live unhappily ever after."

"I'm already involved, Beth. You don't understand."

"I understand perfectly. Look at you. You have circles under your eyes that look like the black holes of Calcutta.

You're palpably miserable. If Ned were in love with you—"

"Ned?"

"Whoever. If he really cared about you he'd be here."

"Beth. Please. I can't deal with all of this now." Leo placed the phone back on the hook and it rang immediately.

"Hello? Who is this? Hello?"

Beth grabbed it from her hand.

"Go play in traffic, pervert," she screamed and hung up. "You're going to have to deal with it, kiddo. So you might as well start now. Dump him fast. Dump him this morning, if you can get a hold of him. I know how tough it was for you growing up. I know that you're angry—"

"I'm not."

"I know that you're angry and that right now you're acting out that anger in a way that might seem acceptable to you by entering into this doomed relationship—"

"I'm not angry, Beth."

"I know that you must think that you're in love—" she stopped as the phone started. "Jesus H. Christ. This is telephone harassment—let me get it again.

"Whoever this is, you need a shrink. I'll give you *my* number and—what? Yes, she's here. Who is this? Nick Booth. Well, Nick Booth, I'm Beth Preston. We're having a slight problem with the telephone here. Someone has been calling and hanging up continuously. It wasn't you? Actually, you weren't on our list of suspects, Nick Booth." Beth made a face at Leo and mouthed the word *dumb*. "Here she is."

"Hi," Leo said softly. "How are you?"

Beth began humming "When the Lovelight Starts Shining in Your Eyes," an old Supremes number. Leo tried to wave her away, but she took no notice and launched into "Baby Love."

"Of course I understand." Leo had turned her back on her sister and was speaking as quietly as possible. "Absolutely. Of course you should be with Thea. I'm fine. When do you think—"

Beth could hear a twinge of panic in Leo's voice.

"Oh, great." Relief replaced that panic. "Because we're supposed to go out to dinner tonight, remember? But if you can't, don't worry. I understand. Right. I'll see you later, then. But if you need to stay with Thea, don't worry. Really. I understand. Me too. Bye.

"He had to take his daughter to her ballet lesson," she explained, turning back to Beth. "And then he's going to take her out to lunch. He's coming over later this afternoon."

"Of course. I understand. He can't be with you when you most need him, but that's all right. I understand. Really. He can let you down whenever he chooses with whatever excuse, but, hey, that's fine. I understand. Don't worry."

"That's not fair, Beth. She's his daughter, not an excuse."

"So she comes first, right? Tell me something. When are you ever going to come first in this situation?"

"It's not a competition."

"Don't kid yourself. What would happen if you had an accident and had to go to the hospital but his beloved little daughter had a school play at the same time? Don't you wonder whom he'd choose to be with?"

Leo frowned. The phone rang. She picked it up. "Hello. Hello? Is anyone there? Oh, God." She hung up. "I think I'll take it off the hook now. Whoever it is will give up eventually."

"Nick Booth was with his daughter at the ballet class?"

"Yes. Nick was."

"Then this isn't some little kid calling, Leo. It's his wife."

"No." She rubbed her forehead. "I'm sure she wouldn't do something like that."

"He's told her about you, yes?"

Leo nodded.

"Well, he was probably stupid enough to tell her your name. So it's the little woman calling to annoy you. You should get your number changed. Better yet, change your life. Like I said, get rid of him. This is trouble, Leo. She's going to want revenge, and you'll be the target."

"No." Leo stood up, started pacing around the room. "You can lecture me all day, Beth. It won't make a difference. We were meant to be together forever."

"Don't you think his wife thought that when *they* were about to get married? She's walking down the aisle like a lamb to the slaughter, thinking: we're meant to be together forever. So then they're together for however many years and it starts to fray at the edges. Because it turns out that forever is a long, long time. You can't sustain passion, Leo. That's the definition of the word. It's fleeting."

"How do you know? You've never been in love."

"Whoa. Directing the anger at me now, are we?"

"Well, it's the truth, isn't it?"

"No," Beth replied. "It's not."

"You're kidding!" Leo rushed over to Beth, sat down beside her and grabbed her hand. "Who? When? Where? Tell me everything."

"Someone I met a long time ago."

"Do I know him? I don't believe this. You've been hiding this from all of us. Who is it?"

"Nobody you know. The only reason I'm telling you now is because I understand what it feels like to be obsessed with someone. That's all. It's no big deal."

"What happened?"

"What happened in my life is not the point. Nothing happened."

"Oh God, Beth. How awful. How long were you together? Where is he now? Was he married?"

"No, he was *not* married." Beth pulled her hand away. "Just because all my sisters fall for assholes doesn't mean I do. You live in such a fairy-tale world, Leo. I mention casually that I was once in love and you latch on to it as if it were somehow world-shattering news, as if I'd announced I'd shot JFK for the fun of it."

"But it makes such a difference. It changes everything."

"No. It does not. It doesn't change the fact that you have fallen in love with a man much too old for you, a married man with commitments who won't be able to love you the way you deserve to be loved, whose wife is sitting in her house right now probably dialing this phone number, whose child will doubtless hate your guts."

"Did you say all this to Meg when she was with Charlie?"

"No. Stop trying to make parallels out of completely different events. Meg was older. Meg didn't need protection."

"And I do?"

"Absolutely. You do. Of course you do."

"From what? From whom? From life? From Mom, from Dad? Are we going to play that old record yet again? Or should I really be protected from *you?*"

"Leo? What's happened? You know I'm not the person to take this out on."

"Then stop trying to run my life."

"Sweetheart, you're confused. That's understandable—"

"Could you leave me alone, please, Beth? Just this once? Or I'll say things I shouldn't."

"I get it. You're angry with me because you know I'm right."

Leo sighed. Beth could see tears surfacing in her sister's eyes.

"Fine, I'll leave you alone. The truth hurts, as they say. You need some time to think things through. You're not yourself at the moment. Honestly, you scared me there for a second with all that misdirected rage. As if I had anything to do with your current mess."

"I want to go to Dunkin' Donuts," Leo whispered, wiping her eyes with the palms of her hands.

"Great. Fabulous. Go to Dunkin' Donuts. Cheer up. Binge out. God knows you need to eat." Beth put her arm around Leo and smiled. "And maybe you'll meet some guy, some perfect, suitable guy while you're sitting on those revolting pink stools at the counter and Nick Booth will fade from your memory with the first bite of an old-fashioned cruller."

Leo's shoulders began to shake. Beth thought her sister might be on the verge of an emotional breakdown until she heard Leo's laughter.

"You see, kiddo. I can make you feel better. I know what you need. I know how to make you laugh. Although I don't understand quite why that was so hilarious. I'll talk to you later. Okay?"

"Sure," Leo replied, in the midst of another giggling fit.

Standing up, Beth patted Leo on the head, then took her mug, went to the kitchen, and put it in the sink. On the way out, she stopped and took a slug of whiskey from the bottle, then slipped a couple of Marlboros from the pack, placing them behind her ears.

"The operator said the phone's off the hook. That's why it's been busy all morning." Amy took a sip of her coffee and frowned. "Why has she taken it off the hook?"

"Maybe she wanted some uninterrupted time with Nick." Jimmy arranged the pillow behind him and sat up straighter in bed. He reached over and placed his thumb on a spot between Amy's eyebrows. "You frown so much, you're getting serious lines."

"I know," she smiled. "We all have them. All four of us. We make faces all the time and it shows. If you think mine are bad, you should see Meg's. She looks as if someone tried to carve hieroglyphics on her forehead. That's why she always has bangs—to cover them up."

"Did you know that in England they call bangs a fringe?"

Amy nodded, her frown returned. Jimmy and Rachel had gone to England on their honeymoon.

"You should go there sometime," Jimmy continued, oblivious. "*We* should go. I'd love to see it again. It's a beautiful country."

"My mother died in England, remember?" she said

sternly, thinking: that should shut him up on the subject of Merrie Olde Englande.

"I'm sorry. I wasn't thinking." He paused. "On the other hand, my father died in New York City and I go there pretty often. If you start to avoid the places where people you loved died, you'll end up leading a very limited life."

"Dad never told us exactly where she died, though. I don't know why we never asked, but we didn't. We just know she had a car crash somewhere in England. So if I went there, I'd be thinking she died on every road and every street I traveled on, and that would be disconcerting."

Actually, I'd be wondering where you and Rachel had gone, whether you were re-creating your honeymoon days with a different wife. I might as well start calling you Maxim. And Rachel Rebecca.

Amy got out of bed, pulled an oversized T-shirt saying "I Didn't Do It" over her head and brushed her hair. The morning had been so perfect; a lazy Saturday winter's day spent in bed reading the newspapers and drinking coffee. If this conversation about England hadn't started, Amy thought, they would have made love for the first time in what seemed like ages. But Rachel had ruined the atmosphere. Well, that was no big surprise. Rachel had a habit of creeping in on special moments and screwing them up.

The idea of going to England was a joke anyway. They couldn't afford it. Rachel managed somehow to take a huge chunk of Jimmy's salary. He was not only paying child support, but also mega maintenance. It made no sense, given the fact that Rachel was capable of working and supporting herself. But she'd maneuvered it so that Jimmy felt obligated to pay for her idle life.

Patrick, of course, hadn't contributed a penny to Amy and Charlotte, and Amy was forking out school fees, as well as paying for half of the rent on their apartment—that seemed the decent thing to do. Why should Jimmy be stuck with her bills? Besides, by paying her own way, Amy thought she was exhibiting moral superiority over her predecessor.

Jimmy accepted this financial setup readily; what he
hadn't done was congratulate Amy on her financial independence. He simply took it for granted. Never once had
he said how relieved he was that she wasn't like Rachel in
this respect. Often Amy wondered what it would feel like
to be Rachel and not have to work. She enjoyed her own
job at the lab, but trying to organize her work life and her
home life, as well as take care of all Charlotte's needs,
inevitably produced conflicts. Her time was so split by her
commitments that she could be neither the perfect mother
nor the award-winning scientist.

By nature, she'd never been one of those ladies who
lunch—her interest in maths and sciences had set her apart
from much of her female peer group from schooldays onward. Yet there were moments when she envied the freedom of those women whose husbands "looked after" them.
Not to have any financial worries would be a pleasant feeling.

Having just written checks to pay for her share of the
rent, heat and electricity bills, she couldn't afford a flight
to Florida, much less Europe.

Amy avoided looking at herself in the mirror as she
brushed the hair she now hated. She was tired of being
reminded that she was the least desirable sister in the family. Meg and Leo both had Mark's dark good looks while
Beth was a carbon copy of Victoria—Victoria before
Steven's death, when she was one of those vivacious
blondes who are supposed to have more fun. Amy felt she
might be classified as vaguely pretty or reasonably attractive, but she had never had the adjective "stunning" applied
to her; people didn't turn their heads in a restaurant when
she entered, except when she was with her sisters, or, in
the old days, when she was with Patrick.

Other women always twisted around in their seats to get
a glimpse of her dark, curly-haired, athletic husband. Patrick was too good-looking to resist. What does he look like
now? Amy wondered, then answered herself immediately:
he looks stunning. He'll always look stunning.

Amy, when she got dressed up, was aware that she always just missed. Unlike Meg, who invariably dressed impeccably and frequented makeup counters as often as alcoholics visited their local bars, Amy was at a loss when it came to fashion. She might have the right dress but the wrong shoes. Or the right skirt and blouse, but the wrong jewelry. "Just missing" seemed to be an intrinsic part of her character. When she ran a bath, she could never get it the right temperature; when she decided to go see a popular movie, it would have disappeared from the screens the day before.

An overall perspective was lacking from her life, she knew. On airplane trips, when she sat beside the window, she'd look down as they flew above Boston and try to figure out where they were, recognize landmarks. As far as she was able to perceive, though, the plane could have been flying over Detroit or Rome. She couldn't pick out a single familiar building or road. Fellow passengers, rows in front and behind, would say: "Look, there's the Prudential Building" and she'd squirm and stare and fail to find it. Often she felt as if she were tuned into the wrong frequency on a radio, that if she could only twist the knob, or press the seek button, she would be able to locate the channel that would pull her life together into a recognizable whole pattern. As it was, she sensed that she was traveling along a series of parallel lines that refused to converge.

"Earth to Amy." Jimmy was clicking his fingers beside her right ear. "Hel-lo."

"Sorry, I was somewhere else."

"What do you want to do about lunch?"

Lunch. Dinner. Food. Routine. "Women are given habit to replace happiness," Beth had said recently. "That's Pushkin. *Eugene Onegin*. You see, Ames, men have always known how boring everyday life is for women. But did they do anything about it? No. They *want* us to be bored. Because they know that *someone* has to be bored, so it might as well be women."

"I haven't thought about it. Maybe some tuna-fish sand-wiches."

"Fine."

Amy watched her husband get dressed. He had an im-mutable routine. First the boxer shorts, then a pair of socks, followed by trousers and topped off with a shirt, buttoned from bottom to top. After he'd finished tying his shoelaces, he'd straighten up and comb his hair, looking in the mirror with a self-conscious squint of the eyes. He's cute, she thought, as she studied his boyish features and lean body. Cute, and—the word "predictable" came to her unbidden.

When they'd first been introduced, through a mutual friend, Amy was convinced she'd met Jimmy before. He'd seemed so familiar, she'd spent at least a half an hour trying to place where she'd seen him. When it became clear that they'd never formally run into each other, she decided that she'd noticed him on the subway or street and lodged his face in her memory bank.

Despite this initial instant recognition, as time went by and they began to see more and more of each other, Amy realized that she'd forget what Jimmy looked like whenever she was away from him. His features faded and she was left with a hazy blur, an indistinct, though pleasant, im-pression of him. Whereas Patrick's face had been indelibly etched into her brain from the moment she'd seen him sticking his thumb out on the side of the road.

Patrick had dressed as haphazardly as he lived; clothes were always strewn over their bedroom and often she'd have to tell him his shirt wasn't buttoned properly.

Why was she thinking so much about Patrick at the mo-ment?

"Amy!" Jimmy was thrusting the telephone receiver at her. "Wake up, will you? It's Leo."

"Leo. What a relief," she smiled, grabbing it from him. "What's happening? I've been trying to call for ages. I've been worried about you."

"What's to worry about? Nick's wife had a fit last night and he went to be with her. Now he's with his daughter.

Beth's been reading me the riot act. Someone's been calling and hanging up the whole time. It's fun and games here, believe me."

"I'll come over right away."

"No. Listen. I've got some things to do. And Nick's coming later this afternoon, then we're seeing you for dinner, right?"

"Right."

"Beth suggested that I pick a suitable boy at—catch the irony here—Dunkin' Donuts." Leo began to laugh. "To replace Nick, that is. I promise you. She couldn't understand why I found that so hilarious. Can't you just picture it? Me spending my entire life haunting Dunkin' Donuts, picking up every guy that comes through the door? The serial doughnut slut?"

Amy laughed and relaxed. She knew that as soon as they were alone together, she'd be able to tell Leo everything she'd been thinking in the last ten minutes, and she was equally certain that Leo would help her sort through her jumbled emotions. If anyone in their family should have been a shrink, it was Leo.

It sure as hell wasn't Beth.

Chapter Seven

NICK WAS SLUMPED in a chair, the bottle of scotch at his side. "I don't understand why she wants to hang on to a dead marriage," he mumbled. Leo had to strain to hear his words. "It's been effectively dead for years. On a life-support system. Outside elements, the machine of society, pushing the breath in and out of the body. But brain-dead and heart-dead. Why not put it out of its misery?

"We've discussed it before, you know. Divorce. She's brought the subject up and we went as far as finding a lawyer and then, I don't know, it lost momentum. She'd be working too hard, or I would be. We didn't have the time. Or the inclination, I guess. Enough of an inclination to go through with the procedure. But it's not as if we were blissfully happy. I don't understand."

"Maybe she's worried about Thea."

"It can't be good for Thea to hear us screaming at each other."

"I can't imagine you screaming," Leo said.

"Oh no?" Nick cocked his head to the side. "You don't know me, Leonora. If I played you a videotape of Jackie and I shouting abuse, you'd think *Who's Afraid of Virginia Woolf?* should be reclassified as a comedy."

"You're exaggerating."

"No. No, I'm not. Some people, when they're together, act like poison on each other. At first you don't notice, of course. You're in love, there's this passion. What you don't see is that it's a sad passion. Rooted in insecurity. And soon the slow-acting poison begins to take effect. I mean both of us are poison, by the way. I'm as bad for her as she is for me. Taken separately, we're not terrible people, but put us together and we cause this reaction.

"As each day passes, the poison builds. Whatever elements combine to create the deadly mixture become more and more entrenched in the system. Pretty soon every comment that comes out is steeped in it, you know. The bile can't be contained. It's not a pretty sight. Or sound."

Leo shook her head and frowned.

"What did you fight about?"

"Does it matter? Anything. Nothing is too sacred, or too puerile. There was a time when I gave up. I mean, I stopped fighting. I played Gandhi. And that made her absolutely furious. My opting out of the battle made it seem as if I had no part in it, do you see? That it was all her poison, none of mine. It goaded her to new heights of outrage. So I decided to enter the fray again. For the sake of our marriage. Do you understand?"

"I understand that it sounds miserable. I don't understand why you both didn't get out of it a long time ago."

"Misery loves company."

"That's not an answer."

"No. Maybe it was our pride. Maybe neither of us wanted to admit publicly what a mistake we'd both made. Or else I had some old-fashioned belief that you have to play the hand you're dealt, especially if you've dealt it yourself. Plus I didn't believe, I really didn't, that it was possible to be happy with another person. I looked around at other marriages and they all seemed desperately flawed—not as bad as mine, I'll grant you—but not happy."

"So . . ." Leo sat, her arms wrapped around her knees, hugging them to her chest. "Do you think we can be happy?"

"I wouldn't have asked you to marry me if I didn't. Leonora, listen. I'm going to make one of my speeches, so bear with me, please.

"I know what people must think. I've been through it all in my head, listening to my critics. I can almost hear your sisters' voices saying the obvious: he's in a midlife crisis, he wants to be young again, so he's feeding off a child. A selfish older man indulging himself at a beautiful, trusting girl's expense.

"I've lacerated myself with the possible truth of all that. Am I ruining you for my sick pleasure, robbing your youth in the hope that it will regenerate me? If that were the case, though, wouldn't I feel young when I'm around you? Well, I don't. Your age makes me feel older, if anything. I don't want to go toss Frisbees on the beach with you, I don't want to go out and buy a convertible Porsche and take you to rave parties and pretend I'm hooked on Snoop Doggy Dogg—don't laugh, okay?

"I've spent such a long time studying you, trying to ascertain if the age gap is going to jump up and start baying for blood; days and weeks and months of looking for every possible impediment to us as a couple. And I'll tell you honestly, I've been hoping to find them, to give up this dream because of the pain and misunderstanding it will cause, the inevitable traumas. Nights like last night, for example. Days like today when I couldn't be with you.

"I've come to the conclusion that age isn't the issue, though. Because I've seen you in moments when you're older than I am. Wiser, certainly, but also carrying burdens far beyond your years. I don't know if it's linked to your family, your childhood, the deaths and despair lurking in the background of your past, or if it's innate and would be there whatever had occurred while you were growing up. You have a strength, Leonora, and an understanding beyond your years.

"You keep saying your sisters took care of you. Well, the way I see it, you took care of them. You're the person who held your family together and you still do. Everybody feels safe with you. I know I do. What I hope is that you feel safe with me. If that's the case, we *can* be happy.

"I won't mind if you do things appropriate to your age, with people of your own age. I won't be jealous or possessive. Well, I might be jealous," he smiled. "But I won't be possessive. I trust you. You haven't given me my youth back, but you have given me hope. Belief.

"How's that for a long-winded speech?" He reached for a cigarette.

"I don't know—" Leo frowned. "I always assumed you loved rap and grunge music. I mean, that was one of the reasons I agreed to marry you. This is a shock." She laughed, leaned over and kissed him. "First of all, I'm not a child, Nick. Or a girl. I'm not so sure about my supposed wisdom and strength, but I know we can go through whatever it takes to be together. We have to." She drew back, hesitated for a moment.

"What?"

"Do you think she—do you think Jackie might be making those calls to me?"

"I don't know. Honestly. I tried to calm her down last night, but she was not in the mood for reason. I wouldn't put it past her. It might be a good idea to get an unlisted number."

"Would she—I mean she wouldn't come here, would she?"

"No. I think she's angry that I found someone first, that's all. She'll realize soon enough that this is a good thing for both of us. She's got a life of her own. In a week she's off to Europe on some television project." He grunted. "Another one of our disagreements, actually. She's trying to get a program together on child murderers. There was that one in England, remember, where the two young boys killed a two-year-old? She's going to do some research on that. I said the whole subject was macabre, and that a television program wouldn't enlighten the public, only satisfy a ghoulish, voyeuristic bent in people. How she thinks she can sell it to a public service station, I don't know. We're not talking *Masterpiece Theatre* here."

"Will Thea be with us while she's gone?"

"I have to think about that one." Nick sighed. "Complications. So many complications."

"Are you too tired for dinner tonight?"

"Not with Amy." Nick took Leo's hand and squeezed

it. "But I think I'll need a month at a health farm before I meet Beth."

"These are wrong." David was holding up a package of chocolate chip cookies. "We like those big soft ones. The Pepperidge Farm kind."

"Oh, sorry," Meg grimaced. "I'll remember next time."

"Right," he said, reaching into the bag, pulling one out and taking a bite that spread crumbs flying on the rug beneath him. "These suck." He stalked off, yelling at Josh: "Get off my case, scumbag."

"Teenagers," Meg sighed and rolled her eyes.

"Spoiled dickheads," Beth replied. "You're frightened of them, aren't you, you little wimp?"

"No," she replied, and then again, more emphatically, "No. There's no point in being a wicked stepmother, that's all."

"So you turn into a pushover instead. Don't tell me—" Beth put a hand over her eyes. "Let me guess. You've bought them both their own computers, their own glitzy name-brand mountain bikes, you're playing the ply-them-with-presents-and-they-might-like-me game." She whisked her hand away. "Am I right? Am I psychic or what?"

"Anyway, as I was saying, Dad goes into this fishing analogy you won't believe, something to do with artifice and being attacked from beneath and above and—"

"Meg. Save it. We're talking about your situation here. Charlie leaves you to go off and do some male bounding on the rugby field—"

"Bounding?"

"Well, they're leaping around, aren't they? Trying to prove how athletic and un-heart-attack prone they are? Anyway, you're left holding the kids who treat you like shit and go on a riff about fucking chocolate chip cookies and you sit here and take it. I can't believe it."

"They're nice boys, really."

"They're smart boys. Doing the classic children of divorce routine, playing one parent off another and raking in the goodies as a result. What's the bet they go back to Helen and tell her about all the perks in this house so she has to compete and buy them better stuff herself. They're going to end up eating caviar, playing with NASA computers and owning Harley Davidson motorcycles before they're both fifteen."

"You don't understand."

"People keep telling me this. I don't understand love. I don't understand children, stepchildren, marriage—I don't understand. Wrong. I'm the only one with any perspective in this family."

"Josh!" They heard David's scream coming from upstairs. "Stop it. You're hurting me."

Meg wanted nothing more than to escape from her own house, leave Beth and Josh and David and head out for any destination where she could be alone and in peace. If some researcher on fantasies had come to her door, Meg would be able to tell all her wildest dreams without the slightest blush. They had nothing to do with sex. They all involved escape. She pictured herself alone on a bus to Miami, alone on a plane to Denver, alone on a boat surrounded by the fjords of Norway.

"What you have to do, Meg, is take some control over your life. Don't let other people tell you what to do."

"What do you think we should do about Leo?" Meg asked, aware of a guilty feeling stealing up on her; she was sacrificing Leo to get Beth off her own back. She could never tell Beth that she fantasized about leaving Charlie and striking out on her own. The word divorce was synonymous with failure. Admitting failure to Beth was not a prospect Meg relished.

"I tried to talk some sense into Leo this morning," Beth sighed. "I think she listened, but whether she'll act on it or not after she sees loverboy again, I don't know. The best strategy may be to confront Dick or Mick or whatever his name is and show him how much harm he's causing."

"Behind Leo's back?"

"Well, for Christ's sake, not in her presence."

"Do you think that's fair to her?"

"Meg. You're losing it. You're full of fear. What has the Chuckster been doing to you? Do you think you always need someone else's permission to speak? Do you hold your hand up and wait for him to call on you every time you want to say something?"

Actually, that's pretty close to the truth, Meg thought.

They heard a thud upstairs, then David's scream, which rapidly turned into a howl of agony.

"I better go sort those two out," Meg said. "I'll be back soon."

Five minutes later, Meg walked back down into an empty living room. She called out to her sister, but Beth had vanished, leaving the new Boston telephone directory splashed across the sofa cushion.

Oh, shit, she thought. *Has she found Nick's number? Is she going to call his house? No. She can't do that. What if his wife answers? What might Beth say to her? Oh, shit. What is she up to? Whatever it is, it's not harmless.* Meg, imagining what havoc Beth could wreak, put her head in her hands and saw, on the rug beneath her, a stray cigarette. It wasn't her brand, she didn't know where it could have come from. But she was certainly going to smoke it. As she leaned down to pick it up, her forehead bashed into the side of the glass coffee table. Straightening up, she wiped her hand on her head, looked at the blood on her fingers, shoved the cigarette in her mouth and lit it.

"Things are spinning out of control," she said to the air.

"Get out of my room, fuckhead," Josh yelled.

Beth paced. The Cowboy Junkies were singing "Misguided Angel" as she strode around the perimeter of her apartment.

She'd redecorated it recently. The walls were all white, the curtains white, the furniture black. The few objets d'art she possessed—two antique vases and three Oriental lamps—provided what color there was. She'd thrown out any paintings or posters she'd collected, having decided she didn't like being distracted by art.

The phone company hadn't delivered the new directory to her yet. But she always carried a pen and paper in her purse, so it had been easy to copy the number from Meg's new book. Every year she looked for a new listing, every year she came up with nothing. Finding it now was a shock to the system. Of course, it might not be him. Chances were that it wasn't. S. Manning. The S could stand for Sarah or Susie or—God forbid—Steven. The odds were weighted heavily against her.

So why was she hesitating? Make the call, find out it wasn't his number, hang up, have a drink and relax. No problem.

What if it was him?

She headed over to her desk, rooted around the bottom drawer and pulled out the Boston College yearbook. Opening it to the page with his picture, she picked up the telephone receiver and dialed, before allowing herself any more time to consider.

A male voice answered on the third ring.

"Is this Stuart Manning?"

"Yes."

Beth closed her eyes.

"My name is Mary Mulligan. I was in your year at BC. We're having a little reunion and thought you might be interested in attending."

"You're joking," he laughed.

"No. No. I'm not." She checked the picture of Mary Mulligan again. A good-looking girl. If Stuart remembered her, he wouldn't be averse to a call. Unless they'd been an item once. Oh God, had she picked the wrong person to impersonate? Some ex-girlfriend he couldn't stand?

"Well, thank you very much for the invitation, but I'm afraid I'm not interested in reunions. How did you find me, by the way?"

"You're in the telephone book."

"But I haven't been in the country for years. What is this? Is BC so hard up for money they troll through the book every year for old graduates to hit up?"

"No, of course not. We're not looking for money, Stuart. Just a little get-together, that's all."

"Really?" he paused. "Who else is coming?"

She thumbed through the pages, selecting names at random.

"Wait a minute—" he stopped her. "John Sherry is dead, for Christ's sake. He was mugged and knifed on graduation day. Everyone knows that. It was a cause célèbre. Is this some kind of scam? What the hell is going on?"

"This isn't a scam. Look, I'm sorry. I'm not Mary Mulligan. I've never been to BC. There's no reunion. I should have said who I was from the beginning."

"Well who are you?"

"Beth. Beth Preston."

Silence. He didn't speak. She could sense him searching through his memory to locate her name and coming up blank. He didn't remember her.

"I don't know anyone called Beth Preston."

"Yes you do," she said urgently. "You gave me a lift home from the supermarket about eighteen years ago. My sisters, too. Our mother had left us there, remember? I was twelve. You said—"

"Oh, God. Wait a minute. There were four of you, right?"

"Right. Absolutely. Four of us. But I was the one you talked to. I was in the front seat."

"You had blond hair."

"I still do," she said with relief.

"I can't believe this. Beth Preston. I remember. You were left there in the cold. All these kids, just abandoned. I didn't know what to do."

"You did the right thing. You were perfect."

"I don't believe this." He sounded genuinely stunned.

"I've never forgotten you."

"Oh."

What had changed in his voice? Something. There had been pleasure in it before, when he'd recognized who she was. But on the last sentence his tone had become hard and flat.

"I thought it would be nice to see you again, to find out what's happened in our lives since that meeting."

"I don't think so, Beth. It was nice to hear from you, though. A surprise."

"But it would be even nicer to see you." She was aware that she was flailing now. "It's amazing that we live in the same city, that you've come back to Boston. Where have you been, anyway?"

"Away."

"Well, I gathered that. You don't need to be so vague, you know. I'm not some crazy person. I know the reunion bit was a little off the wall, but I wasn't sure if I should introduce myself right off the bat."

"It would have been simpler if you had."

"I know." She grabbed the pen beside her and started to punch it into a pad of paper. "Don't you remember what you said to me?"

"When?"

"Back then," she almost shouted with exasperation. "In the car, when you took us home. You said that I was going to break a lot of hearts, but I should remember that I broke yours first."

"That was true," he said. "You were an incredibly cute little kid. Brave, too."

Well, hey, I'm cute now too, she wanted to say. "I don't understand. Why don't you want to meet?"

"I don't see the point."

"The *point?* I've spent years trying to find you and you don't see the point?"

"You've done what?"

"Jesus." She was now on the verge of tears. "I wanted to find you—I trusted you. I cared about you. Is that so bad?" In all of her daydreams this conversation had been wonderful. How could it possibly have gone so wrong so quickly? How could she be pouring her heart out to him within minutes?

"No," he said hastily, with a touch, finally, of compassion. "Of course it's not bad. But it's not possible, either."

"Why not?"

"Beth. Can't you leave it alone? Take my word for it. Trust me again. It's not a good idea."

"Are you a criminal?"

He laughed.

"Listen. I have a very nice memory of you. Thank you for reminding me of it. It's touching. I'm glad you thought I helped you. Let's leave it at that. Good-bye, Beth."

He hung up.

The bastard hung up.

Amy and Jimmy's apartment in Cambridge consisted of the first two floors of a three-story wooden house on Bellis Circle. It had been renovated, so the ground floor was on two levels—the hall, kitchen, dining room and study on the entrance level, and, down a few steps, a spacious living room with an old-fashioned fireplace. Amy always had a variety of flowering plants in every room, and had managed to incorporate Charlotte's toys into the general scenery, so they looked welcoming without creating clutter. The only object that seemed out of place was a plastic model of the brain sitting on the desk beside the telephone.

When the doorbell rang, she shot a quick, nervous look at Jimmy and went to answer it.

"Hi," she said, giving Leo a kiss, then stepping back to shake hands with Nick. He was holding out a bottle of wine, so she took it from him with a smile. "You didn't have to bring anything," she said.

Don't stare at him, she told herself. You've got all night to check him out.

"Beware of Greeks bringing gifts?" he smiled back. He had impossibly deep eyes, she thought immediately. He looked ancient.

"Oh God, did Leo tell you about that?"

"Yup," he nodded. "I've heard most of the Beth stories. I think."

"No way," she heard Jimmy say behind her. "There is no end to Beth stories. Come on in. Which one is this, then?"

As they walked in and down to the living room, Amy diverted to the right and put the bottle of wine in the kitchen, listening, as she did, to Leo explain.

"Beth had a very rich boyfriend once. He did something to irritate her—I can't remember what exactly, but before that he'd asked her to go to Greece with him for a week— all expenses paid, first-class travel, the whole bit. Have you heard this one, Jimmy?"

"No." He shook his head.

"Anyway, whatever the guy had done to piss Beth off, he didn't know about, so he assumed the trip was going ahead as planned.

"Beth fixed up some special stationery with a Nestlé logo at the top, and typed out an offer of a free trip to Greece on it. All expenses paid, et cetera. Then she went into her local store, dumped out half a tin of Nestlé's Quik mix into a plastic bag she'd brought along, stuffed the piece of paper with the offer into the can and put it back on the shelf. She'd put her home number on, of course, so a couple of days later she gets a call. From an eighty-year-old woman who has never been abroad in her life and can't believe she's won this free trip.

"Beth explains to her how to get a passport and what clothes are right for Greece at that time of year. She takes the ticket her boyfriend has given her to TWA or whatever airline it was and says she's got some terminal illness and won't be able to take the trip, but wants to give her ticket to a friend. The helpful guy behind the counter changes the ticket over to the old lady's name.

"On the day of the flight, Beth picks the woman up, chauffeurs her to Logan, where she's supposed to meet the boyfriend, who is still completely in the dark. She gives the old lady a wad of money, leaves her to check in, then finds her boyfriend. She proceeds to inform him that she's not going with him to Greece, but is sending someone very special in her place. He goes ballistic, obviously, but she stands firm and says she will never speak to him again unless he treats this person with respect and gives her a great time in Greece. She takes him over to introduce him to the eighty-year-old, tells them both to beware of Greeks bearing gifts and disappears."

"Not true." Jimmy shook his head. "Not even Beth could do that."

"But she did," Amy said as she came down into the living room. "The old woman had a blast. She called Beth when she got back and said she'd never had such a good time in her life and what a wonderful man Nestlé had sent to help her through the trip."

"The guy played along with this?" Jimmy asked.

"He wanted to see Beth again. So he did, yes."

"Unbelievable. *Did* he see Beth again?"

"Absolutely," Leo answered. "He got lots of points for being so nice to the lady. I think he bought himself a couple of months with that one."

"A couple of months?"

"That's a long time for Beth," Amy smiled.

"Do you believe this family?" Jimmy turned to Nick.

"I'm beginning to, I'm afraid," Nick replied.

"What if the guy had abandoned the old woman? Left her to fend for herself? Then this wouldn't be an amusing anecdote at all. It would be cruel." Jimmy sounded indignant.

"Beth said that she wouldn't have gone ahead with it if the woman hadn't seemed like she could take care of herself. And she gave her enough money to have a very comfortable week. Where she got it from, I don't know. She probably borrowed it off Dad. Anyway, Beth said the old woman could have stayed in a hotel the whole time if she'd wanted to."

"That's not the point, Amy." Jimmy glared at her.

"I *know*. I'm not saying what she did was right. We were just telling you what happened. That's all. We don't have to spend all evening talking about Beth's scruples, do we?"

'No," Leo answered quickly. "We don't."

"So, Nick. You're the *Globe*'s theater critic?" Jimmy asked, switching to a breezy, conversational tone.

"Yes. I'm taking a couple of weeks off at the moment, though."

He crossed one wiry leg over the other, tapped his foot in the air. He had thinning dark hair, a lean frame. There's a touch of Sam Shepard in him, Amy decided. All angles and exposed bones. He looks like an underfed cowboy who has seen too many roundups.

"I'm afraid we don't get out to the theater," Jimmy said. "So we don't read the reviews."

"It's embarrassing," Amy added. "We both read trash, too. Leo's the intelligent one in the family."

"Come off it, Amy. You're a neuroscientist. I don't understand the first thing about your job," Leo protested.

"It's science. So it's straightforward, mathematical. Scientists don't have to think about the deeper meanings in life."

"But you do if you're studying the brain," Nick said. "You have to try to get to grips with consciousness. What's deeper than that?"

"Consciousness may be memory, pure and simple, and memory is a function of the brain, and neural functions are scientific, so we're back to square one—science."

"That's a depressing thought." Nick smiled as he said this. "Do you two mind if I smoke?"

"No, not at all. Oh, God. We haven't offered you anything to drink. What would you like?"

As Amy went back up to the kitchen to fix the drinks, she heard the front door open. Peering into the hall, she saw Zoey enter, toss down her bag and head toward the living room.

"Hey, Amy," she called out. "Dad. You'll never guess what's just happened." She was wearing a pair of lime green jeans, and a lemon yellow sweatshirt; with her strawberry hair topping it off, she looked like a fruit sorbet.

"Zoey!" Jimmy jumped to his feet, rushed over to give her a hug. "What are you doing here?"

"Sorry." The girl stopped as she caught sight of Leo and Nick. "I didn't know you had guests. Hi Leo."

"Hi Zo. We don't count as guests. You know that. Come sit with us. This is Nick. You don't have to shake hands with him, don't worry. How are you?"

"*I'm* fine." Zoey flopped down on a chair and Amy quickly poured a Coke and added it to the tray she brought down.

Zoey had the expectant expression of someone who was dying to tell big news.

"I don't want to interrupt anything," she said apologetically.

Jimmy smiled proudly at his daughter, a look that Amy caught. Okay, she wanted to say. I know that Charlotte interrupts conversations all the time. I know. But she's *younger*.

"We were just talking about consciousness," Nick said. "And I was about to ask if scientists believe in the soul. You've come at exactly the right time."

"What's happened, Zoey?" Amy asked.

"Well, let me put it this way. I'm going to be the proud possessor of a new stepfather. Anyone have a cigar?"

"What?" Jimmy sat forward. "Rachel's getting married?"

"You got it. His name is Alex. Very hunky. Hot stuff on the dance floor. Looks like a recent graduate of West Beverly High—someone who'd hang out at The Peach Pit with Brenda and Brandon. Which makes sense since he's just twenty-six years old."

"She's marrying some guy *ten years younger than her?*" Jimmy looked stupefied.

"Hang on." Amy was aware of a deluge of different emotions engulfing her. Jimmy's stunned amazement seemed a little *too* stunned—his mouth was literally open, as if a low-budget, ditzy movie director had said: "More shock. We need to see some *serious* shock here." While

Zoey was playing the young Tatum O'Neal: clued-in kid who can't be fazed by anything. At the same time, the tempo of Nick's foot tapping had upped and Leo, she could sense, was desperate to launch into a defense of age difference in happy couples.

"How long has this been going on? How long has Rachel known him?" she asked.

"About five minutes. You can say one thing for Alex. He's not afraid of commitment," Zoey laughed. Everyone else was silent. "Lighten up. It's not a tragedy. They met at a party. They fell in love. They're getting married. Maybe Rachel will calm down a little." Zoey never referred to her mother as anything but Rachel. "Well, okay, that's doubtful. Oh. I forgot to tell you. The party was last night."

"Well then." Jimmy sat back. "It's just another one of Rachel's harebrained escapades. It won't come to anything."

"I'm not so sure, Dad. I've never seen her like this. I mean, I've seen her in lust before, but she's got a weird glow to her eyes, a kind of Waco, Texas, look to her."

"What does Alex do?" Amy asked.

"He *looks* like he should be a personal trainer to Janet Jackson, but in fact he's a doctor. Specializes in asthma. Go figure."

Leo laughed.

"You seem remarkably unconcerned, Zoey," Nick commented.

"There's not much I can do about it. Besides, I like him. He was all shy and embarrassed when he and Rachel told me about their plans. Looking for my approval. Rachel's boyfriends are usually the scum of the earth. Not nasty or abusive. Just plain dumb. Alex is pretty smart, actually. It's like he knows he's getting into trouble on this one but he can't resist it and he's taking some huge leap of faith. Probably the way you felt, Dad. At the beginning."

Amy watched the blush appear on Jimmy's face.

"The thing about Rachel," Zoey continued, "is she's *fun*. She went up to Alex at this party and asked him to dance and suddenly he turns into a megastar on the floor. John Travolta before he got into *Pulp Fiction*. Maybe normal people think asthma doctors don't dance so he doesn't get much of a chance to strut his stuff. I don't know. But Rachel certainly makes things happen."

"I have to go see about dinner," Amy said, getting up. Leo followed her to the kitchen.

"I know, Amy, I know. How many times have we said that about Beth? She makes things happened. But *we* make things happen too. In different ways, that's all. And they're just as valid as all this fun and excitement."

"Really? Why do we start off the evening talking about Beth and then spend the rest of the evening talking about Rachel? You know everyone is fascinated by this story. Jimmy's dying to know all the details. Nick's probably curious, too. Where do *we* fit in? Can you picture me getting Jimmy out on the dance floor and causing a sensation?"

"No. And I wouldn't with Nick, either. That's not the point. Look, we've had this conversation so many times and we never get anywhere with it. Yes, Beth gets a lot of attention. Yes, so does Rachel. But *we* are as guilty as everyone else, because you know as well as I do that we love to tell our Beth stories. It doesn't mean that we have to compete. Beth and Rachel are like characters in a book, and the problem is, they're stuck on the pages; they can't change, they can't lead normal lives. Maybe they feel oppressed knowing that they have to keep doing wild and crazy things to satisfy everyone's expectations of them."

"I'm oppressed by having to think about them at all. They're like vampires. They're draining my blood. I wish Jimmy would tell Rachel to fuck off."

"When have we ever told Beth to fuck off?"

"Okay. You're right." Amy pulled a casserole out of the oven and slammed it on the counter. "This is probably overcooked. Thanks to Rachel."

"So what do you think of him?" Leo asked, with a cautious smile.

"Nick? Oh God, of course. I'd almost forgotten what

this dinner is all about. I'm sorry Leo. I like him, I really
do. He seems genuine and caring. And he obviously has a
sense of humor. Which is crucial in this family."

"He does," Leo nodded. "Definitely."

"And you two clearly love each other."

"It is obvious?"

"Is Lisa Marie Presley Jackson screwed up?"

"Okay, okay. It's obvious," Leo conceded happily.

"He looks so sad, though, sometimes. Nick. He looks
like a tragic hero. He reminds me of someone. I can't quite
place it yet, though."

"Liam Neeson maybe?"

"Get out of here—" Amy pushed Leo gently on the
back. "I'm going to try to fatten you two up a little with
this lousy, overcooked meal."

As she placed the food on the dining room table, Amy
was able to stare at Nick covertly. He was sitting at an
angle and below her direct gaze, but she could see his expression, and, again, she felt she knew that look intimately.
Leo, beside him, her face in profile to Amy, was listening
to Zoey. Amy shut out the words they were saying from
her mind and concentrated on Nick. How was it that he
seemed old and yet so young and vulnerable simultaneously? Who did he remind her of?

Leo. Amy could almost hear her mind click as the connection was made. Leo on the day of their mother's funeral.

Jesus, she thought. They could be twins—the eight-year-
old girl and this forty-year-old man. Leo in the back of that
black limo, looking pale, drawn and haggard. Amy remembered the thought she'd had at that time: this is how she'll
look when she's sixty. But she still looks like a child as
well. How strange.

They had the same color hair, the same facial structure.
Amy watched as Nick turned his head; now both he and
Leo were in profile to her. The similarity between them
was so evident she couldn't believe she'd missed it before.
The only major difference was eye color. Leo's were dark
brown, Nick's dark blue.

Nick began to laugh at something Leo had said, and with the laughter his face was transformed. His cheeks filled out, his eyes brightened. The lines disappeared from his forehead.

Amy quickly turned her back to him. He wasn't Leo anymore. No. She saw a photograph of a laughing child on her mother's dressing table. Steven. And this time the eyes matched too.

"Supper's ready," she called out, thinking: *I don't even want to begin to consider what all this might mean.*

Chapter Eight

"WHAT IS THIS, Father-Daughter Day or something?" Beth peered past her father, looked out the door to the street. "Have you left a redhead waiting there? No? Not this time? What's happened to your treat 'em mean, keep 'em keen M.O.? Don't tell me you've been a nice guy and allowed her to go home when you made this visit? Or is she hiding beneath the steering wheel?"

"Hello, Beth."

"Hi Dad."

"Would you consider offering me a glass of wine?"

"Why not?" Beth shrugged. "Come on in. Take the weight off your feet. Tell me your problems. I'll send you the bill later."

"How much do you charge per hour?"

"Not as much as a hotshot lawyer. White or red?"

"Red, please."

Mark sat down in the black leather armchair, crossed his legs and then his arms.

"So—" Beth poured the remains of a bottle of claret into two large glasses. She handed Mark a glass, took her own over to the sofa facing him, sat down, tapped the tips of her fingers together and said: "Would you like to start with your childhood?"

"I wanted to talk to you about Leonora."

"What's to say?"

"A great deal, don't you think?"

"No. I'm coping with it."

"In what way, exactly?"

"In the appropriate way."

"Which is?"

"None of your business."

"Beth. You're being childish."

"And you're being what? Paternal? Bzzz. Wrong answer. Try again."

"I'm *trying* to understand what's going on," Mark sighed. "If, before you're willing to talk with me, you need some form of mea culpa for your childhood, I might as well leave now. You can be as scornful and derisive of me as you want, but it won't help Leonora."

"Tell me something, Dad. Since we're having a heart-to-heart. Why haven't you remarried? I've always been curious about that."

"Once was enough."

"I bet it was."

"You've taken that comment the wrong way, Beth. You continue to misunderstand my relationship with your mother. I loved her. You know, she had almost as sharp a sense of humor as you do. The first time we met—we were still kids at dancing school together—she gave me such a hard time I thought I'd be very happy never to come near her again, no matter how pretty she was. Then I saw she was joking and it didn't take me long to find out that behind her wisecracking facade was a truly sensitive girl."

"Mmm hmmm. When did you discover her fragile nature? Somewhere between the waltz and the fox-trot?"

"Listen to me, Beth. Victoria *was* funny. She *was* sensitive. She *was* beautiful. I know you never saw her that way, you never knew her before, but I did. It's impossible to describe the loss of a child. You would never understand the pain of it until you become a parent yourself. It goes against nature to be standing at your child's grave. It's a horror of inconceivable proportions. It *can* make you crazy."

"If you're asking me to honor the memory of someone I never met—the Victoria you knew, well, think again. I mean, people say Beirut was once a lovely city. I'm not planning a visit."

"Is that all you can say?"

"Yup."

Mark bowed his head. When he raised it a minute later, a tougher expression was in his eyes.

"Let's get back to Leonora."

"Leo's marriage, you mean. I think it's terrific. It's right up there with Meg and Charlie's as a shining example of possible domestic bliss. Or domestic blitz. Take your pick."

"Please—" Mark shook his head. "Please don't tell me this man of Leo's is anything like Charles. I don't think I could stand another pompous bastard in the family."

"Well, that's one subject we're entirely in agreement on." Beth sipped her wine, stared at her father. "All right," she said after a long pause. "I haven't met him. I assume he's an idiot, and I'm sure I'm correct. He's too old. He's married. He has taken advantage of her. Of course I blame you for this predicament."

"Of course you do."

"Maybe if you'd spent a little time with her—"

"I *did* spend time with her. I spent time with all of you. As much time as I had available. You seem to forget that I had to support you all, that I had work to do."

"And women to conquer."

"Listen to me very carefully, Beth. Yes, I saw other women. I needed—" He stopped, uncrossed his legs. "No. I refuse to justify my actions to you. You don't understand because you don't want to understand. I'm a convenient scapegoat for you. I always have been and I always will be."

"So go ahead, then. Explain to me what Leo is doing with a man closer to your age than hers. You take no responsibility for that, do you?"

"I don't know." Mark stood up, began to pace around the room with his hands behind his back. He was retracing the path she'd taken that afternoon before calling Stuart. "I wonder if Steven's death has something to do with it."

"Steven?" Beth let out a shout of exasperation. "Steven again? Jesus. Talk about scapegoats. That kid has been a scapegoat for centuries. And now he's taking the rap for this?"

"You know perfectly well his death had a profound effect on our family. On your mother—"

"Not that again." Beth snorted. "We had this conversation twenty seconds ago."

"You don't know what Victoria went through—"

"Get this through your head, Dad. I don't *want* to know. I don't want to hear how lovely Mom was. I don't want to hear those stories you pull out sometimes about your golden honeymoon in Morocco or how much everyone, even the gas station attendants and the waitresses and the garbagemen, loved Mom before she accidentally killed Steven and went nuts. I listened to stories about Steven all my childhood. The last thing I want to do is to listen to stories about how great and fun Mom once was. I'm an adult and I don't *have* to listen to anyone."

Beth realized her voice had reached screaming level, but didn't bother to lower the volume.

"Leo's romance has absolutely nothing to do with Steven. I can't believe you tried to pull him out of the bag again. I've listened to excuse after excuse, all having to do with poor little Steven's accident. That's why Mom cracked up. That's why you were so fucking useless. It doesn't wash, Dad. If Steven were involved in this, Leo would be about to marry a baby, not some middle-aged Lothario."

Mark stopped in front of his daughter, right underneath her ceiling light. She could see the few gray strands in his hair. Picture of a distinguished lawyer, she said to herself. I wouldn't be surprised if he'd had the gray touched in to lend the crucial air of gravitas.

"I hate that vicious look in your eyes, Beth. It's so unnecessary and futile. I hate the way you scream like a child having a tantrum." He paused, regarding her with evident despair. "You know, there are moments in a book or a movie when the entire direction of the plot changes because of a missed opportunity. Someone leaves a message on an answering machine that gets wiped off and never heard, or a letter is delivered to the wrong house and its contents are never read by the person it was destined for. Things go astray and life takes a different turn because of a simple twist of fate. That's what I feel has happened in our relationship."

"Have you ever sent me a letter or left a message for me you think I haven't received?" Beth asked, glaring up at him.

"I wasn't intending to be taken literally."

"Oh. We're into metaphors and allegories, then, are we? I'm surprised you didn't mention fishing. Well, I take my life literally. What actually occurs or doesn't shapes my feelings. The facts count. What would you suggest? That I see a psychic to understand what your emotions really were and are? Maybe then I can have a little chat with Steven too. And Mom. Family therapy around the crystal ball. Fabulous."

"Too good and too pure for life in this world," Mark muttered, turning his back to Beth and heading for the door.

"Don't think I didn't hear that, Dad," she yelled at him. "Beth in *Little Women*, right? That's how she's described when she dies. Don't give me that shit."

The front door closed and Beth was left, sitting on the sofa, gesturing wildly in an empty apartment.

When the telephone rang, she grabbed it, screamed "Fuck you and the horse you rode in on," then slammed it down.

"Where's the goddamn coffee, Meg?"

Charlie was scouring the cupboards, pulling jars out, dumping them on the kitchen counter, swearing all the while.

"We've run out. I'm sorry. I'll go out and get some now."

"By the time you've gotten back I won't want it anymore."

"Then I'll get some tomorrow morning."

"Fine. I'll have a Coke."

Meg brushed her hand back through her bangs, quickly

let them fall again. She opened the refrigerator door and made a face.

"We're out of Coke, too."

"Jesus, Meg."

Why? she asked herself. Why is everything my fault?

"The boys drink a lot," she said defensively.

"Don't blame it on the boys. You leave half-opened cans all over the place. Why can't you ever finish one, do you know?"

"They go stale so quickly. The fizz runs out and I can't bear to drink Coke without the bubbles."

"For Christ's sake. It's not champagne."

Coke. We're arguing about Coca-Cola. This can't be the sum total of our relationship, can it? Whether I'm capable of finishing a can of Coke or not?

"I know it's not champagne, Charlie. Listen, I'll get some Coke tomorrow too."

"What am I supposed to drink now?"

Acid. Drink some acid.

"I don't know. How about—" The doorbell rang and Charlie went off to the hall, saying over his shoulder, "That'll be Helen."

"Helen?" The swinging door closed on her and Meg found herself looking wildly around the kitchen for someone to talk to.

Helen? What's Helen doing here? It's Saturday night. She doesn't pick up the boys until tomorrow afternoon. Has she come over to do the dishes or something? Meg stared at the plates on the kitchen table, effectively clean already, as the boys and Charlie had gobbled up Helen's chicken casserole. If Charlie knew she was coming, Meg asked herself, why didn't he tell me? *Whose house is this, anyway?*

She could hear Josh and David calling "Mom" in excited voices. Meg quickly took the dishes, dumped them in the machine, put everything Charlie had taken out in his manic search for coffee back in the cupboards and began to wipe the counter with a sponge.

"I've heard of cleaning up before the cleaning woman

comes," she mumbled. "But cleaning up before the ex-wife sees the mess? This is ridiculous."

"Meg!" Charlie was shouting. "Come on out."

If there had been a back door to the kitchen, Meg thought, she would have escaped and gone to some local bar and ordered three shots of tequila. She wasn't in the mood to see Helen. She really wasn't. Her head still hurt from bashing it against the table in the morning.

"Oh Helen, hi," she smiled as she walked into the living room, wiping her hands. "What a nice surprise."

Helen, Meg noticed, looked over at Charlie with a conspiratorial grin. What the hell was going on?

"I asked Helen if she'd come collect the kids early, darling," Charlie said, moving over to her and putting his arm around her shoulder. "In case you've forgotten, it's our anniversary tomorrow."

"Oh God, no." Meg brushed her hair back in a frantic gesture and saw Helen suddenly staring at her, frowning.

Okay, okay, I'm a lousy wife. You were the perfect wife. You would never forget an anniversary. Go ahead. Shoot me.

"No, I mean, I hadn't *forgotten*, no. I just thought we weren't going to do anything special. That's all," Meg finished, she knew, sounding lame.

"Well, we *are*." Charlie tightened his grip on her shoulder. "I've planned a few special events."

"I'm taking Josh and David so you two can have some time on your own," Helen explained. There was anxiety in her voice, Meg could hear it. Of course there was. For the first two years of Charlie and Meg's marriage, Helen had avoided Meg as if Meg were a hit woman who had a contract out on her. Helen always dropped the kids off outside the door, never setting foot in the house. According to various friends of Charlie's, she refused to mention Meg's name in conversation with them, and, Meg found out through surreptitious means, Helen extended this policy to Josh and David. When the boys were at home with their mother, their stepmother didn't exist.

Meg had felt like a nonperson, someone who had been "disappeared" courtesy of a South American fascist government. That attitude had changed one afternoon when Helen had a flat tire outside the house and thus was forced to come in and ask for assistance. She'd been polite and distant then, chatting guardedly, but from that day on, Helen had begun what seemed like a relentless campaign to make friends with Meg.

Now Helen was at the point where she was bringing over casseroles and colluding in an anniversary surprise.

It was a little much, Meg thought. Pretty unnatural for an ex-wife to be quite so accommodating. She had to admit that she preferred the old order of things, when she didn't have to see Helen.

"Gosh. This is great. How nice of you. Would you like a glass of wine or something before you take them back?"

"A glass of water would be fine." Helen turned to Josh and David. "Get whatever you need together, will you? And Charlie, would you mind taking a look at my car for a second?" She handed him a set of keys. "It seems to be having difficulties starting."

"No problem," Charlie said.

What would he have said to me? Meg couldn't help but wonder. "Take the car to the garage, I don't have the time." No, Meg cautioned herself. Don't get on Charlie's case because he's being nice to Helen. This is all about his anniversary surprise for *me*.

"I'll get you some water," Meg said. Helen followed her into the kitchen.

"You've been hurt," Helen whispered as soon as the swinging door closed shut.

"What?"

"Your head."

"Oh. Right." Meg put her hand to the bandage underneath her bangs. "I hit it on a table this morning. Really stupid of me."

"I understand."

"Sorry?" Meg filled a glass with water from the tap. "Ice?"

"I understand."

"Oh. Thanks. I was reaching for a cigarette on the floor. I know I shouldn't smoke. It's a terrible habit, but I've really cut back and I'm going to quit but it's just so hard—"

"The first time was the worst for me." Helen put her hand on Meg's shoulder.

"I didn't know you smoked. I've tried patches, hypnotherapy, acupuncture, everything. How did you manage to do it finally?"

Charlie came through the door, threw the keys to Helen and announced "It started right up. I don't think anything's wrong with it but maybe you should get it checked out tomorrow."

Who's paying for that?

"Right. Right. I will," Helen said hurriedly, backing away from Meg. "I better get the boys moving."

"Thanks, Helen," Charlie said.

"Yes. Thank you, Helen," Meg added, still holding the glass of water Helen hadn't touched.

Charlie followed his ex-wife out and Meg could overhear them saying good-bye. When the front door closed, Meg went to join her husband.

"I hadn't forgotten our anniversary, you know. We've just never celebrated it before. What makes number three so special?"

"You do," he answered, hugging her. "I thought you deserved a treat."

It was amazing how easily he could make her happy when he tried. A few nice words, thoughtful gestures, and she was suddenly blissful.

"So what have you planned?"

"Well, the plan for tonight is obvious. Then I thought we'd have a quiet Sunday morning reading the papers and drinking a bottle of champagne. After which, I've invited a few people over for lunch."

"Really?" Meg felt herself stiffen. "What people? What lunch?"

"The food's not important. I can go out and buy something tomorrow morning."

"I thought we were supposed to relax and drink champagne tomorrow morning, not worry about lunch and food shopping."

"I said *I'd* do the shopping. Christ, I'll cook the lunch if you want."

Sure. Some chance of that.

"What people?"

"Mike and Mary. John and Sally."

"Mike and Mary?"

"Yes. Mike and Mary." He stepped back, shook his head. "What's the problem, Meg?"

"You *know* my problem with Mike and Mary. They hate me."

"I thought you were over all that."

"All what? The fact that they talk about Helen nonstop? And when they're not talking about Helen, they're talking about Josh and David, asking all about them and never once, not *once* asking me anything about myself or my life. Mike is patronizing. Mary is practically Helen's best friend. Why should they come to our anniversary party?"

"Because they're my friends. And you're reading them all wrong, as I've told you before. They feel that they can talk about Helen because they believe that you don't have any insecurity on the subject. It's a tribute to you that they feel they *can*. If they knew how paranoid you are about my past, they'd be horrified."

He still looks good. Meg thought. *Strong and tall and fit. He still sounds the same. What's happened? Why does he irritate me so much? And why can't I just shut up? Give him a huge anniversary kiss and tell him how wonderful he is? Because he called me paranoid.*

"I'm not fucking paranoid. I don't want to hear about Helen all during lunch, that's all," she said, feeling the anger gain momentum. "What's paranoid about that? It seems normal to me. I give in to you all the time. I had them to my wedding and you knew I didn't want them there and what did Mary do? Mary, wonderful, fabulous Mary. Your best friend Mary—" It was at its peak now, Meg could feel it. The anger was unleashing itself like a multiple orgasm. "Mary sat there at the dinner afterward and cornered Beth and started talking about Helen's virtues—at *my* wedding. That's all she could talk about. Helen this. Helen that. I call that seriously tactful, don't you?"

"Meg. Jesus. Calm down. You're losing it."

"It was lucky Mary picked Beth. She started in on how Helen is such a good cook and such a perfect mother and such a fabulous gardener—"

"Meg. Stop this. You're irrational."

"And when she asked Beth whether *I* had a green thumb like Helen's, Beth said 'No. Meg's like me. She prefers to be *sent* flowers.' "

"You're getting things way out of proportion."

"It was my fucking wedding."

"It was *our* wedding. I'm sure Mary didn't mean it the way it sounds. You know you can't trust Beth's version of events."

"On something like this I can. Definitely."

"This is pointless. You're not listening to me. You haven't given Mike and Mary a chance. You were against them from the beginning." Charlie made a move to the side, as if he were avoiding an oncoming tackle.

"If they'd been nice to me from the beginning I would have been fine. Don't you remember that first lunch with them when they informed us that children are maimed for life in a divorce? How was that supposed to make me feel?"

"I'm not having this conversation any longer. You're ruining our anniversary with this incredibly childish behavior."

He turned his back on her and she could see he was shaking with rage. So was she. She wanted to scream at him, tell him he should take her part, understand *her* feelings. Instead, knowing full well from past experience that it was up to her to understand *his* feelings if she wanted this evening to end in anything but disaster, she forced herself to calm down. The fury she had experienced scared her anyway. She had never been a fighter; she hated arguments at the best of times. The eve of their anniversary was the worst time to have a fight that she knew she'd inevitably lose.

"Okay. You're right. I guess I did overreact. We'll have Mike and Mary tomorrow."

"Will you be civil to them?"

Her stomach began to churn again. She needed a cigarette.

"Have I ever been anything else? Of course I will. I'll ask Mary how to grow poison ivy. Or belladonna. How about that?"

She saw his relaxed face as he turned back to her.

"How about coming upstairs? Now."

"I'll just go and have my nighttime cigarette in the kitchen and then I'll be up. Okay?"

"My wife the nicotine addict," Charlie said, kissing her on the forehead.

"Don't worry. I won't smoke at lunch. I'm aware of how health-conscious Mike is."

"I know he can be a real pain at times. But he's an old friend."

"I like him, really. He's very bright. I wish he liked me, that's all."

"He does, idiot. You've got to get a little more confidence. You put yourself down too much. We'll have to work on that."

And when we've finished with my self-confidence, will you start on my pronunciation?

As she walked to the kitchen, she called to Charlie on his way upstairs.

"I didn't know Helen used to smoke."

"Look who's talking about Helen all the time," he laughed. "Anyway, she didn't. Helen's never had a cigarette in her life."

* * *

Leo got out of bed, made herself a cup of coffee, returned to the bedroom and sat in the chair by her dressing table, watching Nick sleep. She liked to study the different movements his face made, his unconscious tics and the occasional smile that surfaced briefly and then disappeared into the night. The traffic beneath her window sounded like waves, a steady flow of rhythmic noise with a siren breaking now and then like an angry roar of the sea.

There were moments when everything in life made sense, and this was one of them. She wanted both to savor and share it. So she had a silent conversation with her mother and Steven, telling them all her thoughts; a habit she'd developed over the years until it became an important part of her life. She found that she could communicate with them as if they were sitting beside her.

They weren't always with her, nor could she summon them at will. That was why she believed in them. Leo had never told anyone else about these sessions with her dead brother and mother; not so much from a fear of people thinking she was crazy, but a superstition that if she acknowledged their existence in public, they would then go away.

"Amy really liked Nick. But you know that already, don't you?" She had just finished saying this when the doorbell buzzed.

Beth on some kind of wild midnight visit, she immediately thought, and trudged to her intercom wearily, annoyed at the interruption. She's probably found some guy off the street she thinks is perfect for me and has dragged him along for a postmidnight first date.

"Hello."

"I'm here to see my husband," a voice crackled back. "Let me in."

Leo stood in shock, her hand suspended by the "entry" button.

The buzzing started again, an insistent blare. Leo

slumped down onto the floor and sat motionless. The buzzing didn't stop.

"What's going on?" Nick flicked the light switch in the
living room. "Who is it? Jesus. It's one A.M. Who the hell
is there?" He was standing in a pair of striped boxer shorts,
looking like a punch-drunk featherweight boxer.

"It's Jackie," Leo said.

"Oh shit. I don't believe it."

Jackie must have been leaning against the buzzer, for it
went on without any break.

"She's going to wake up the neighbors," Leo said, trembling. "I don't think she's going to go away."

"I don't want her coming in here."

"Neither do I. But I don't think we have a choice."

"Leonora," Nick said softly as he watched her get up
and press the entry button. "I'm so sorry about all this."

"I've got to put on some clothes." Leo rushed to the
bedroom, pulled out a pair of sweatpants and a T-shirt from
her dresser, got dressed, then realized that she'd put the T-
shirt on inside out.

"Damn," she swore, struggling to reverse it without taking it off again, aware that she couldn't stop shaking. Hearing a loud knock on the apartment door, she rushed out.

"Please," she implored Nick, who had remained standing
in the same spot. "Put some clothes on too. It's not right.
I mean, it looks awful."

"Leonora—" he started to protest.

"Please, Nick."

As soon as he headed to the bedroom, Leo went to open
the door, expecting to come face-to-face with a malevolent
gargoyle.

What she saw was an elegant, perfectly coifed, expertly
made-up tall blond woman, dressed in a tailored dark blue
suit, white blouse, and red, white and blue scarf.

"Leonora, I presume." The woman spoke in a deep
voice.

"Yes. Hello." Leo held out her hand to shake Jackie's
and was met by a cold stare of appraisal.

"Been out jogging, have we?"

"No. I mean, I was just having a cup of coffee. Would you like one?"

"I'd prefer a scotch. I assume Nicholas has a bottle here. In his new home."

"Yes. Of course. I mean, yes, I have some. Come in and sit down, I'll get you a drink."

As she went into the kitchen, she heard Nick's voice and then Jackie saying: "Nicholas. You should have told me."

"Told you what?" He sounded exactly as he had when Leo had first approached him in Dunkin' Donuts. Aggressive and angry. She'd forgotten how scary that voice was.

"Told me about your leanings. Of course I should have guessed. All those years at an all-male boarding school. Your lover may have the word 'female' written on her birth certificate, but you couldn't get closer to a young boy if you tried."

Leo spilled the scotch she was pouring.

"Get out, Jackie." Again, that awful voice.

"And I thought you wanted to be civilized. Oh, thank you Leonora. How kind. You see, Nicholas. Some people do have manners."

"What do you want?"

"A little chat. What a cozy little place this is." Jackie gave the apartment the same cold stare as she'd given Leo. "And how sweet. Family pictures?" She strolled over to Leo's desk, studied three framed photographs. "Sisters or friends?" she asked, picking one up and turning to Leo.

"Sisters."

"I never had one myself. And you have three. *Embarrasse de richesse*. Look at that blond hair. What does *she* do?"

"Beth's a therapist."

"Oh, really? Perhaps I should send Thea to her."

"Thea doesn't need a therapist." Nick's face was twitching, but his eyes were motionless.

"All children of divorce need therapists. How about you, Leonora? Are you a child of divorce? Do you know what it feels like, or are you one of the lucky ones who have never experienced your family being wrenched apart?" Jackie kept hold of the picture in one hand, her scotch in the other.

"My mother died."

"Well, that's convenient, isn't it? I'm sure Nicholas wishes I would do the same. Disappear graciously. No fuss, no muss."

"I will physically throw you out of here if you don't leave now."

"There's no need to threaten me. Is there Leonora? Leonora? Is something wrong with your ear? You look like you're about to pull it out of its tiny socket." Jackie walked over to the sofa, sat down, placed her drink on the side table, the photograph on her lap. "Sit down, sit down." She waved to Nick and Leo. "Make yourselves comfortable." Neither moved; they stood, forming, in effect, a triangle, with Jackie at the point.

"I thought I'd give you two lovebirds a talk on the facts of life. We all know how, in the first flush of romance, people go a touch crazy. They forget about reality, don't they? And if that reality is potentially nasty, they think they can simply wish it away. So it's time for me to give a speech. Has Nicholas given you any of his speeches?" She turned to Leo. "He used to give them to me at the beginning. I found them endearing.

"Oh, dear. Have I hit a soft spot, Leonora? That frown. Nicholas, you really should have changed your routine. Anyway, here's *my* speech.

"I'm not going away. I'm not going to disappear. I refuse to be patronized or tolerated or discarded. And I will use everything in my power to make your lives miserable. There. Short speeches are always the best, don't you think?"

"Does 'everything in my power' include Thea?" Nick's tone had turned from belligerent to weary.

"That's for me to know and for you to find out, as they say." On the last word, Jackie rose, walked over and handed the photograph to Leo. "Sin casts a long shadow. Good-bye, Leonora."

When the door closed behind Jackie, Leo felt as if she'd been caught up by a tidal wave and thrown on the beach with a vicious, ferocious slam. Every part of her body ached.

"Leonora. Oh God, I'm sorry." Nick approached, his arms out to embrace her, but she backed away instinctively.

"I'm tired," she whispered. "I need to sleep."

"Leonora. Listen to me, please. Will you?"

"Don't." She shook her head. "Don't call me Leonora anymore. Just don't."

"We have to talk."

"I can't."

"We *have* to."

"You know the worst part?" Leo was looking off, out the window, her voice a monotone. "The worst part is the speech business. That's the worst. You gave her speeches. You give me speeches. You know something? Beth was right."

"Right about what?" he asked gently.

"I can't." She refused to meet his eyes. "It hurts too much. And at the same time I know that's not the worst part. The worst part is that she might use Thea, hurt Thea. Turn her against you. I *know* that's the worst part. But it doesn't feel like that to me. It should but it doesn't. So what kind of person does that make me? I can't do this. I just can't do this."

She heard the sound of Nick striking a match. She heard him inhale.

"We have to fix this," he said. His voice was shaking. "Now. Or something unbearably precious will be lost forever."

"Forever is a long time," Leo stated sadly and went to lie down.

Chapter Nine

BETH OPENED HER eyes, looked around the room, then closed them. Sunday morning was closing in. Hard. Hangovers hadn't occurred to her when she'd had the apartment redone. The white was too dazzling, the black too depressing. What she needed was a cool, calm color to soothe her aching head. Interior designers should all plan hangover rooms for occasions like this. Plus, she'd forgotten to take any aspirin the night before. Which meant she *had* to get up, negotiate the trip to the bathroom, find the Excedrin and try not to throw up when she swallowed two.

Red wine followed by white wine followed by vodka. She got out of bed, put one hand over her eyes and stumbled into the bathroom. The damned walls were closing in on her. It was one of those times when she knew, if she had to get in the car to drive, she wouldn't be able to differentiate between the accelerator and brake. At least she could go back to bed with a bottle of Perrier and wait it out. No clients to see, no phone calls to make, nothing to do except wallow in the lousy feeling of nausea, exhaustion and eye-searing pain. Maybe she should call Amy and see if she could arrange a quick prefrontal lobotomy.

Groping for the Excedrin bottle in her bathroom cabinet, she found herself looking straight into the mirror. Blotched skin, ravaged eyes, deranged hair.

Victoria.

Beth steadied herself against the towel rail.

This was the last thing in the world she needed. Stuart had dismissed her, her father had walked out spouting inanities, and now she was haunted by some bloodshot vision of her mother.

By all rights, Victoria should have been an alcoholic.

She looked like one; every morning she was the picture of a walking hangover. The fact that she didn't drink was irrelevant. It only made things more difficult. If Victoria had been a heavy drinker, Beth could have been the child of an alcoholic; she could have joined Al-Anon and gone to group meetings to discuss the effects of alcoholism on the family. The craziness would have been labeled and everyone would have understood. "It's a disease," they'd say, "a disease that can be treated." Not an amorphous, terrible, despair for which there was no cure. Except, of course, some Lazarus-like raising of Steven from the dead.

"Go away," she said to the woman in the mirror. "I don't want you here."

It took an unaccountably long time to open the child-proof bottle, shake out two aspirin, bend over the sink tap and force them down.

Victoria had gone away to England never to return—alive, that is. Beth could still summon up the feeling of supreme happiness she'd experienced when the cab had driven up to take her mother away. The unprecedented air of relaxation that descended on the house as soon as Victoria was out the door was liberating. Beth could have written a fulsome thank-you letter to whichever Garden Club honcho had convinced her mother to go to London. Nothing else would have moved Victoria; her only link to real life being this stupid group of dragon society ladies who were wrapped up in rare species of roses.

Before Steven's accident—or as Beth referred to it, B.S.—Victoria had been wild about flowers. She'd been an active Garden Club member, gone to all the flower shows in all the different cities, and participated vigorously in discussions of peonies, pansies and poinsettias. That was one of Mark's more annoying refrains on those occasions when he tried to describe to his daughters what Victoria had been like before Steven's death—her creativity with flowers. She was, apparently, a genius, fashioning amazing displays out of the most unlikely combinations. Roses with carnations and sunflowers. Lilies with tulips and nasturtiums. All Beth could picture was her mother as a lousy actress playing Ophelia in the mad scene, scattering flowers at Gertrude's feet.

After Steven, well, after Steven, Victoria had given up on just about everything, but some vestige of floral fanaticism made her continue to attend the meetings, albeit in a desultory fashion. The other members were probably desperate to kick her out, but couldn't bring themselves to, what with the Tragedy. So they took her along to the Chelsea Flower Show in London. The day they were due to come back, they lost her. Or she lost them. She disappeared. Mark received a frantic telephone call, so off he went in search of his wife.

Six days later he brought her back in a coffin.

Mark was adamant that his daughters not see their dead mother's body, which was fine by Beth. What would be the point in that? Mawkish sentimentality, fake tears: she'd had enough of that at the funeral. All Victoria's "old friends" who wept designer tears. Well, these supposed buddies had given up calling the house a long time before Victoria's exit from it. Most probably they were as sick of hearing about Steven as Beth was.

At least Fate played an apposite part in this drama. Steven killed by a car, Victoria killed in a car crash. All very symmetrical.

Beth struggled to her kitchen, grabbed a bottle of Perrier out of the fridge, fought her way back to the bedroom and collapsed. The best cure for a hangover was sex.

Her bed was conspicuously empty.

Why had Stuart refused to meet her? It made no sense. He'd cut off the possibility as if it had presented a threat to him, but why? She'd waited all these years to find him, and now, here he was, miraculously in the same city, and she wasn't supposed to see him. It was absurd. Even more absurd that she'd accepted his rejection as final. That's why she had drunk herself into a stupor. Not because her father had been the usual asshole he was; she could cope with that. But because she believed her dream of twenty years had vanished with one phone call.

Beth raised herself on one elbow, reached for the bedside telephone and dialed the number she had now memorized.

"Hello." A female voice.

"Hello." Beth paused, her addled brain racing. "I'm selling kitchen equipment to newly married couples and I was wondering if you'd be interested—"

"Sorry," the voice interrupted. "I've been married for years and I'm not interested."

"In kitchen equipment?"

"Isn't that what you said you're selling?"

"Yes. But I do encyclopedias for the children, too. You know how important knowledge is for growing minds. How about a set for the kid? Everything they need to know about aardvarks, everything they need to know about life."

"How about giving me a break? It's Sunday morning. What did you say your name was?"

"Lorena," Beth replied. "Lorena Bobbitt."

"Well, thanks but no thanks, Lorena." The woman hung up.

Beth crawled back under the covers.

Stuart had married some humorless wimp.

Served him right.

The creep should have waited for her.

Halfway down the stairs from her bedroom to the kitchen, Amy stopped. There was a person huddled in the chair in the corner of the living room, dressed in a flannel shirt and blue jeans, arms wrapped around knees, face staring off into the gray morning light.

"Leo," she said, descending quickly. "What are you doing here?"

"I couldn't sleep. I had to leave my apartment. I left Nick there. I didn't want to wake you up, so I used the key you gave me. Am I intruding? I'm sorry."

Leo looked like someone two months into a disastrous Polar trek.

"Don't be ridiculous. I'm glad you came here. God, you're freezing. Let me light the fire and get you a cup of tea or coffee. Then we'll talk."

"Thanks."

Amy placed newspaper, kindling and logs on top of one another, lit a match to them, went up to the kitchen and made two mugs of tea with milk and sugar as quickly as she could, then settled down in front of her sister.

"You're shaking," she said. "What's happened?"

"It's Nick. No. It's Jackie, his wife. She came over last night—"

"You're kidding."

"No. She wanted to tell us that she was going to get nasty about the divorce. That was bad enough. I mean, you should have seen her, she was all dressed up. She looked so pulled together. Incredibly chic. She was wearing high heels. But then—" Leo bit her lip.

"But then what?"

"Then she said something," Leo twisted around in her chair. "You're the only person I can talk to about this."

"Have a sip of tea first."

Leo took the mug and cradled it to her chest.

"From the beginning, when we met, Nick used to say 'I'm going to make a speech' to me and I can't explain why, but it was a private thing between us. At least I *thought* it was. But he used to say that to her too. So I don't see what the difference is. Between me and her. We're the same person. We have different faces and we're different ages, that's all. He's used the same line on both of us. So what's this whole thing all about? That's what I can't figure out. I thought we were different. I thought *I* was different. What a joke."

Amy was quiet. She remembered Leo's face when she'd first told the story of meeting Nick. She remembered Leo's face at dinner the night before.

"Tell me something, Leo. You know your last boyfriend,

John? Did you ever tell him you loved him?"

"Well, yes, I did. A few times. It wasn't the same as Nick. I mean my feelings weren't the same. John was sweet, but—"

"But you used the same words to him as you did to Nick, didn't you? You've told Nick you love him, haven't you?"

"Yes, but that's different."

"Why?"

"It's a different kind of love. And I see what you're getting at, Amy, but it doesn't wash. Everyone uses the phrase 'I love you.' It's a standard way of showing affection. Saying 'I'm going to make a speech' is different. It's personal. Okay, it doesn't sound that personal, but it was for me. It was part of our whole relationship, somehow."

"You know about neural networks in the brain, right?"

"A little."

"Well, I won't make this technical. Synapses fire, connections are made along certain paths. If you picture the brain plotted out on a map, what happens is that, as time goes by and memories build, certain routes are used more than others. It's like, when you come here in your car, you normally take the same streets, the ones that will get you here the quickest. You'd deviate only if there were a traffic jam or something special you wanted to do along the route. Are you following me?"

"I think so." Leo sat up a little, took a sip of tea.

"That's what happens to thoughts. They tend to take the same track. And the more that track is taken, the more likely it is to be used again. Nick used the phrase that he's used before, one in his long-term memory. You think it's not specific to you, but it may be specific to the emotion he feels. The love."

"The same love he felt for Jackie."

"Love can be both general *and* specific. You know how Dad sometimes calls us by the wrong names? He might call me Beth and you Meg?"

Leo nodded.

"Does that upset you?"

"No. I know he knows who he's talking to, he just gets mixed up with all the names occasionally."

"Right. That's my point. He has the same general feeling of love for all of us, but we know that he sees us as individuals even if he confuses our names. Memory isn't located in one area of the brain, it's distributed. And Nick, when he feels love, brings out a phrase that he's used before, but which, in this context, is specific to you. He's not thinking of Jackie when he says it."

"So how many other times is he repeating himself? Is everything he says to me something he said before? To her? It makes me feel sick."

"Words and phrases aren't the problem, though, are they? Not really. You wish he'd never loved anyone before you. That's what this is all about. And that's impossible."

"I wish he loved me *differently*."

"No, you're lying to yourself, Leo. You wish he'd never loved Jackie—period. I know how you feel. I wish Jimmy had never loved Rachel. I can't stand the fact that he did. But at the same time, I know that I loved Patrick. I did. And both those loves are specific to the person, don't you see?"

"I'm not sure."

"I'll make a confession to you now. There are moments when *I* get confused. I start to make coffee for Jimmy and I put in two spoons of sugar. That's how Patrick liked his. I can get halfway across to Jimmy with the cup before I realize what I've done. Do you think he should walk out on me if I told him the truth?"

"No. But that's not the same. Coffee's not the same."

"You can't get past the fact that Nick once loved Jackie, can you?"

"She was so awful—so condescending. So brutal. She made me feel like a piece of trash."

"Which was exactly what she wanted."

"I guess so. But Nick was almost as bad. You should have seen how *vicious* he looked. Both of them. They were people I wish I didn't know."

"It all sounds like a great excuse to get out."

"What do you mean?" Leo's head snapped up.

"The horse fell at the first hurdle. It's limping. Shoot it and put it out of its misery. Get rid of him and lead an easy life."

"Amy? Why are you doing this? I thought you'd be sympathetic."

"I am. But you're the one who has taught me about how people should react in situations like this. Reverse our positions, Leo. Tell me what you'd advise me to do in the same circumstances. I find out that Jimmy's once said the same intimate thing to Rachel as he has to me. Do I cut and run? *You* tell *me*."

"I'd say—" Leo's voice faltered, she stared into the fire.

"You'd say?"

"If you love him, you should stay with him. But Amy— she calls me Leonora. That's what he calls me. I can't stand it."

"Then tell him to call you Fred."

"Amy—" A smile flickered across her face.

"And you can call him Ethel."

"Amy—stop. I'm miserable, remember. I'm not supposed to laugh."

"Or you can call him Betty and he can call you Al."

It happened, as it often did when Leo and Amy were together. They began to giggle and soon the giggling took off into raucous laughter, the two of them overcome by waves of mirth, which might subside momentarily but then be sparked off with another fit. Occasionally they tried to analyze it, when they calmed down. It wasn't the same kind of humor as Beth's; more often than not it was based on a reference to television shows, pop songs, movies, or silly memories of childhood. Meg and Beth would look at them in wonder if it occurred when they were around, as if to say "we don't get it." Nobody else *did* get it.

When Amy finally heard the knocking on the door, she gathered herself together.

"Who's *that?*"

"It's Nick," Leo said, immediately sober. "I don't think I can face him right now. Not yet."

"I'll deal with it," Amy answered. "Don't worry."

"I hope you don't mind an early morning visit. I'm supposed to be shopping, but I needed a break."

"Meg." Amy motioned her in. "Leo's just come over too. This is great. What can I get for you?"

"A new life. No—just kidding. Some coffee would be terrific. I need a hit of caffeine. Leo—God—what's happened? You look like you've been up all night."

"I stayed up late and woke up early," Leo replied. "So I thought I'd wake up Amy for company."

"Where's Jimmy?" Meg scanned the ground floor.

"He's still asleep. He can sleep through anything. Especially on a Sunday," Amy called from the kitchen. "We could have a rave party and he wouldn't budge from the bed."

"Well, I *am* having a party." Meg headed for the fireplace and stood in front of it. "A lunch party. So I can't stay long. Leo—have you been crying?"

"Amy and I got into one of our laughing jags just now."

"Oh. That explains it. You two are seriously strange, you know. What was it this time? Some scene from *Happy Days* remembered?"

"*I Love Lucy,*" Amy said, bringing Meg her coffee. "And then a Paul Simon song."

"I can't figure out why television didn't rot your brains completely. You two never stopped watching that crap."

"So what's the party in honor of?" Leo unfurled her legs, wiped her eyes with the back of her hand.

"Don't ask. Our anniversary. Number three. Guess who's coming to lunch? Mike and Mary."

"Oh no," Amy sighed. "Not them again."

"They're not *that* bad. Not really. I have to make more of an effort, that's all."

Amy and Leo exchanged a quick glance.

"Dad came over yesterday. Then Beth," Meg announced.

"To talk about me?" Leo asked immediately.

"To talk about you and Nick."

"What did they say?"

"I'm not sure, actually. Dad gave me this speech about fishing—"

"Does everyone in the whole world have to give speeches?" Leo moaned.

"And Beth vanished before she'd said anything at all, practically. Something weird is going on with her. I mean, something even weirder than usual."

"But she must have said something about me and Nick before she left. I need to know what she's up to, Meg. I know you don't approve either, but I can't handle it if Beth and you are planning some kind of campaign against me I don't know about."

"Leo—" Meg's voice rose to a hectic pitch. "I'm *not* against you. You always lump me in with Beth. This whole crazy family is split down the middle. Me and Beth, you and Amy. Since when? That's what I want to know. You two go off into corners and giggle your heads off over some private joke, just the way Josh and David always go off together. I'm the stepmother, right? I don't count. And now you're making me feel like the wicked stepsister in Cinderella. Plotting against your marriage to Prince Charming. I was a little shocked when you first told me about it. Maybe I went a little overboard. But I am *not* Beth." Meg grabbed a cigarette from her bag and scratched a match so hard it flew out of her hand.

"Okay—it's okay. I've got it," she said, picking it up from the floor. "Jesus, I'm so tired of defending myself when I shouldn't have to, I can't tell you. I don't finish Cokes. I don't buy enough coffee. I don't like Mike and Mary. I don't do the right things with the boys. Shit. I can't even light a match. If I could just be alone. I want out."

"Out of what?" Amy asked gently.

"Out of—out of this whole fucking mess." She strode off, up the stairs to the door. Leo nodded to Amy and followed Meg. Before Meg could twist the doorknob, Leo had put her arm around her.

"Don't go. Please. Come back and sit down and talk. Tell us what's going on in your life. I'm really sorry for jumping down your throat. I'm feeling paranoid at the moment, that's all. Nick's wife came to my apartment last night and it was a nightmare. Come and sit down. You need to unload."

"You're not paranoid, Leo. None of us are paranoid. I hate that word. We're all a lot stronger and saner than anyone gives us credit for, including ourselves. I'm just beginning to realize that. Anyway, I can't sit down. I've got to go shopping. We're having this goddamned lunch."

They were standing in front of the window by the door, looking out onto the street.

"A few more minutes won't matter. Come on, Meg. I didn't tell you my big news. And, before you go nuclear, no, I'm not pregnant."

"What big news?" Meg asked without moving. She was staring out the window, her eyes fixed on the street.

"Beth was in love once. She told me yesterday. Now that's *huge* news, isn't it?"

"Amy?" Meg called over her shoulder. "Amy, can you come here for a second?"

"We can sit down and talk about it in the living room, Meg. The three of us," Leo coaxed.

"What is it?" Amy asked, approaching her sisters.

"I've just told Meg that Beth was in love once upon a time. I mean *really* in love."

"I don't believe it," Amy exclaimed.

"Well, there's something else you're not going to believe either," Meg said, pointing out to the street. "That man over there, beside the fire hydrant. Isn't that Patrick?"

"Terrific. Great. I arrange for us to have a whole morning to ourselves and you leave me sitting alone for hours. Very thoughtful, Meg. A wonderful anniversary gesture."

"I'm sorry. Really." Meg stood holding a plastic bag in one hand, a bottle of Mrs. T's Bloody Mary Mix in the other. "I dropped by Amy's. Leo was there too. And we saw Patrick on the street outside. It was such a shock."

"Patrick?"

"Patrick. You know—Amy's first husband."

"So?"

"So she hasn't seen him for years and he was standing right outside her house and then he just disappeared, walked off. We couldn't believe it."

"And as a result you forgot about our anniversary and our lunch. Tell me something, Meg. Who is your family?"

"What do you mean?"

"I mean, when you hear the word 'family' who do you think of? What's your first reaction?"

"My sisters."

"I thought as much."

"That's not fair. You're my husband. They're my blood."

"Now I know where your loyalty lies."

"Please don't make me feel guilty. You don't understand."

"Oh, but I do. What's in the bag?"

"Eggs and bacon. I thought we could do a kind of brunch. With Bloody Marys. It's Sunday. People have brunch on Sundays."

"What an inspired choice."

"Charlie, please. I don't want to argue. I've apologized. What else can I do?"

"You could, possibly, forget your sisters for one minute. You could remember that I exist. You might even consider that I was worried about you. You've been gone for hours. You might have called and told me where you were."

"I'm sorry. But Leo had a terrible experience too—her new man's wife showed up at her apartment last night and—"

"I'm going to get changed now."

Charlie turned his back on her and stomped upstairs. Meg put the bag and bottle down on the floor, fumbled in her overcoat pocket and pulled out a pack of cigarettes. The doorbell rang just as she'd lit one.

"Sorry we're so early," Mike said brightly. "I wanted a while alone with Charlie to give him some information I've just gleaned on other candidates up for the presidency."

"I can help you with lunch," Mary added, walking through the door, shaking a fresh layer of snow from her coat.

I can afford a decent apartment. I can do it without taking any alimony. What time do the real estate agents open on Monday mornings?

"Gosh, you look so *chic*, Meg. I suppose you wouldn't dream of wearing an apron, would you? Helen and I used to take turns doing Sunday lunches. We wore the most ridiculous aprons. I'm an expert on roast potatoes now, thanks to her. Oh, I almost forgot. Happy Anniversary."

Chapter Ten

A BLIND WOMAN walking down the street with her guide dog headed straight into the low-hanging branch of a tree. She stumbled with the impact, almost fell, mouthed a swear word, reached down and clobbered the dog.

How was the dog supposed to know? Amy wondered as she witnessed this scene. The dog's eyes are trained at ground level, watching out for traffic, other pedestrians. How was the dog supposed to know the branch was going to be there?

But there's always a branch out there and you're either the blind woman or you're the dog. Reality bites.

"So whose side are you on in the great brain debate? Edelman or Crick?"

"I'm not sure I'm on either." She turned from the window to face Patrick. He was leaning against the door in her tiny office, wearing jeans and a heavy dark blue fisherman's sweater. "At the moment I'm too involved in the specifics of schizophrenia to pay much attention to the infighting."

Don't let your voice even flicker, Amy told herself. You're taking this in your stride.

"Schizophrenia. Aren't you wandering onto Beth's patch?"

"How do you know Beth's an analyst now?"

Patrick shrugged.

"Actually, Beth's not really an analyst," Amy continued, proud that she was managing to sound so matter-of-fact. "She doesn't have the training. She's a therapist. Anyway, neuroscientists and neurobiologists have a better chance of understanding the causes of schizophrenia than any psychiatrists do. Do you know how long it took psychiatrists to realize that clinical depression was chemically based?"

"A long time, huh?"

"A long time."

I'm not going to smile.

"You've got the heat on too high in here." Patrick hadn't moved an inch. He looked as he had always looked—obviously handsome and deceptively languid.

"I know."

"I'm surprised you don't fall asleep."

"What were you doing outside my apartment yesterday morning?"

"Checking it out."

"And?"

"And, it's a nice place."

"I'm so glad you approve."

"Uh-oh. Are you going to yell at me now?"

"What are you doing here, Patrick?"

"Just visiting."

" 'He who binds himself to a Joy/Does the winged life destroy/He who kisses the Joy as it flies/Lives in Eternity's sunrise.' "

" 'He who binds *to* himself,' not 'binds himself to.' " Patrick corrected her.

"That's right. I should remember, shouldn't I? Seeing as how it was your good-bye note."

"What else could I say? William Blake said it better than I did."

"Do you think I should read that to Charlotte every night? Or just when she asks where her father is?"

"Guilt trip time? Sorry, Ames. I'm not booked on that flight."

"What do you want? What are you doing here?"

"Do you still go to Celtics games?"

"Sometimes," she spoke cautiously. Beware, Amy, she told herself. Beware ex-husbands showing up out of the blue.

"I was in L.A. last week and they televised the Lakers-Celtics game. I stared at the screen waiting for crowd shots,

hoping to catch a glimpse of your face. I got eyestrain trying to find you."

The phone on her desk rang and Amy reached for it
automatically.

"Hello," she said. "Could I call you—"

"Cheerio." Patrick waved. He winked. "See you later."

"Amy? Amy?"

She recognized her father's voice speaking into her ear.

"Dad," she answered softly, staring at the empty doorway. "What do you want?"

"I don't *want* anything. I called to see how you are."

"Oh. I'm fine."

"You don't sound it."

"I'm tired, that's all." Amy laid her head down on the
desk, placing the receiver a few inches away.

"Have you spoken with Leonora lately?"

"I saw her yesterday. She's fine. She wants to be left
alone. We all want to be left alone."

"I can't hear you, your voice is muffled."

How am I supposed to handle this? How am I supposed
to react? That's the most romantic thing anyone has ever
said to me. Could it be true? Was he really looking for my
face in the crowd? Why did he vanish? What's going on?

"I can't hear you, Amy. This must be a bad connection.
Hang up and I'll call you again."

She raised her head, picked up the phone, spoke clearly.

"Someone's just come into the office. I've got to go
now."

She hung up, put her head back down on the desk and
began to cry.

The woman sitting on the sofa opposite her was a class act,
which was more than could be said about most of her clients, Beth thought, especially at the first session. Most beginners were nervous, shy, unsure of where they should sit,
what they should say. This one had a surprising air of confidence. She'd headed straight for the end of the sofa closest

to Beth's chair, sat down and settled back easily, studying
Beth with a cool gaze.

"You were lucky I had a cancellation at such short notice," Beth remarked. The woman nodded. She looked as
though she'd had a cancellation, too. Of a modeling appointment.

"So, Eve, what brings you here?"

"I need some help. Not for myself, but for my sister."

"Yes." Well, that's a bad start, Beth thought. And I expected this one would be brighter than the others. Mas-
querading her own problems as her sister's is a tired ploy.

"My sister's young, in her early twenties, and she's
started a relationship with a much older man, a married
man. I've tried to reason with her, but she doesn't listen.
I'm concerned. I don't know what to say, how to get
through to her. I thought you might be able to help."

Synchronicity. Carl Jung *was* right. Beth leaned forward,
intrigued. This was uncanny.

"What's your family background?"

"Our mother died. There are four of us. Sisters, I mean.
I feel I should be a mother figure, but this man, Carl, has
taken over, he's running my little sister's life. And he's
ruining it."

"Your mother died? You have three other sisters?"

"That's right."

"I can't believe it."

"Excuse me?" Eve looked baffled.

"I know this isn't professional," Beth said quickly, "but
I have to tell you. I'm in exactly the same position. Exactly.
I shouldn't be telling you this, but the coincidence is extraordinary. *I* have three sisters, *my* mother died, *my* youngest sister is involved with an older married man. This is
unreal."

Eve sat in stunned silence.

"You don't, by any chance, have a brother who died?"

"A brother?" Eve shook her head. "No."

"Well, that's a relief. You would have been my doppel-
gänger. As it is, it's too close for comfort. I have to be

honest. I don't think I'm the person you should talk to. It's too close to my own experience. I've already crossed lines that shouldn't be crossed."

"Oh, no. Don't say that. Please. If we have so much in common, it will be much more beneficial. You understand already. I didn't come for help for myself, you see. I mean, I'm sure I'm part of the problem somehow, but I don't want to focus on myself, I want to help Andie. My sister."

"I'd be more than happy to talk with you. But not on a client/therapist basis. Perhaps we could meet outside the office."

"Why not here? I won't intrude on your professional hours. If we could meet at the end of the day? Or in the morning, before your first appointment?"

"All right. That sounds reasonable. Eve—how did your mother die?"

"Cancer. How about you? How did your mother die?"

"In a car crash. In England."

"Did it affect your sister badly?"

"Leonora? Yes. More than the others, the rest of us. She was younger, eight years old. She's the most sensitive, the most vulnerable one. That's why this romance is such a tragedy. She's looking for security. Looking for love in all the wrong places. She's still a child at heart. Much too trusting."

"And the man she's involved with, what's *he* like?"

"An asshole."

"Does the rest of your family disapprove?"

"Most of them. One of my other sisters is sympathetic, but I'm sure she knows it's wrong, really. How about you?"

"About the same."

"I can't get over this." Beth shook her head. "This is *seriously* bizarre."

"I know," Eve smiled. "It must be fate. I've been trying to think of ways to break up Andie and Carl, but I keep coming up empty. She's completely infatuated."

"*I've* thought of confronting Nick—Leonora's man— and telling him what a horrible thing he's doing, how manipulative he is, but I suppose he won't listen any more than Leo will. He's on to a good thing and he knows it. Why would he listen to me?"

"I don't think he would," Eve agreed. "But you must know what makes your sister—what makes Leonora—tick. Where her susceptibilities lie."

"Oh. Leo's susceptible, all right. She hates causing any-one pain. She's got the proverbial heart of gold. So I know she must be feeling guilty about Nick's wife. And even guiltier because Nick has a child, a daughter." Beth picked up a pen by the table beside her and tapped the end against her forehead. "Leo dealing with a stepdaughter at her age— it's ridiculous."

"They're planning to get married?"

"Oh sure. True love leads to the altar, remember. Fairy tales come true. Aren't you married?"

"No."

"But you're wearing a wedding ring."

"I *was* married. A long time ago."

"Bad news?"

Eve laughed.

"Not good news, no."

"How about your sister? Andie? Does her man have any children?"

"Afraid not. I've tried to get my father involved, but he hasn't been particularly helpful. He's in international fi-nance so he's away a lot. What does your father do?"

"He's a lawyer. Preston, Pembury and Saltonstall. You know, Boston Brahmins at work together."

"Really? Don't tell me you went to coming out parties and have a fabulous summer house and tons of money?"

"Yes to the summer house, but no to the coming out parties. Not my scene. As for the money, in our case, the old bluebloods squandered it in about two seconds flat. They spent half of it wandering around Europe pretending they were aristocrats and the other half building wonderful mansions their progeny have to work their asses off to keep up. My grandfather didn't do a day's work in his life. My father does nothing *but* work."

"It sounds as if you have a privileged lifestyle, though. Your sister must not have to worry too much about money. It sounds as if she's had an easy time in life."

"I don't know. All in all, it's a con, this WASP business. All it means is that the parents think they have to send their children to private schools, think they have to buy Brooks Brothers or Ralph Lauren clothes, join expensive country clubs full of their sort of people, keep the second house going. So they go broke."

"You sound angry."

"I just hate the hype. It's as if we're supposed to walk off the pages of an Edith Wharton novel. None of that plays anymore, except when Scorsese films it. But my father still buys into it. He cares about his image. He has this proper Bostonian air to him, he's a member of the Somerset Club, all that crap. My father cares about his reputation, about our family's reputation. As if it mattered.

"God—" Beth flung the pen away. "I should be paying *you* for this hour. Sorry about that. I get carried away on certain topics sometimes."

"Don't worry, really. It's fascinating. I'm so glad we've met. You've helped me enormously already."

"Really? I don't see how."

"Trust me. You have."

Eddy was running toward her in staccato steps, flailing his hands in the air, his head rocking from side to side. "It's the end," he wailed. "It's all over. It's finished." He grabbed hold of her hand, his feet churning up and down in place. "It's finished."

"What's finished, Eddy?" she asked gently.

"It's all over." He held his hands out, flapped them at his sides.

"Calm down, Eddy. Everything's okay."

No one knew exactly what was wrong with the boy. The headmaster had once mumbled the words borderline autism, but Meg thought it must be something else entirely. Autistic children hated physical contact. Eddy ran to her arms whenever he had the chance. On Monday afternoons, when she left school an hour early, Eddy would rush from the playground and hang on to the side mirror of her car, pleading "Don't go. Don't go," trotting beside her car like a faithful dog.

Strangely enough, the other children never teased him. Perhaps they respected his sense of urgency. Anything could set Eddy off into panic. A siren in the distance. The bell that rang at the end of a period. Another child's absence from class. There were so many signs presaging doom in his little mind, prompting the Eddy mantra: "It's all over. It's finished."

"Come on, Eddy. Everyone's going to play a game of soccer now."

"Can I play?"

"Sure."

Eddy's version of soccer was to run wildly over the field, hitting the ball in any direction. Meg could never get him to join one team or another. He was a rogue element. Again, Meg was amazed that the other kids tolerated his antics. Beth's theory on this was that every group needs one crazy person to make the other members feel safe. Meg had refrained from asking whether Beth felt Victoria's craziness had made their family group feel safe. She would have had to endure hours of haranguing while Beth figured out a way around that one.

Taking Eddy's hand, she delivered him to Mr. Richards, the soccer coach.

"See you tomorrow," she said. "I'm leaving now, Eddy. It's Monday afternoon. Don't come follow my car, okay? I'll be here tomorrow."

"Okay, okay, okay." He rushed headlong into the field of play, running in circles.

"Try to keep him from following my car, will you? It's dangerous."

"I know," Adam Richards sighed. "I'll do my best."

Meg went back to her classroom, shouldered her bag, grabbed her coat and headed for the parking lot, taking occasional backward glances to make sure Eddy was still attempting to play soccer. She smiled as she saw Adam's effort to pin the boy down. He'd put him in as goalie. Eddy stood in the nets for approximately ten seconds before he ran to the other end of the field and threw himself at the ball, picking it up in his hands, clutching it to his chest and taking off with the others rushing after him, screaming his name.

The kid's in hot pursuit of the millennium, Meg thought. A miniature Nostradamus.

She stopped when she saw the woman standing beside her car. What the hell was Helen doing here? Had someone been hurt? Charlie? Josh? David?

"Meg," Helen called, waving to her. "Don't worry. Nothing's happened. I just thought I might grab you for a quick drink."

A quick drink? It was four o'clock in the afternoon. Helen—secret smoker, secret drinker?

"The boys are over at friends' houses. I had some time, so I thought I'd come into town and look you up. Do you have to get home right away?"

"No. I was going to go to the gym on my way back." Oh, God. She'd done it again. Helen was many pounds heavier than she was. Mentioning a gym—was that an in-your-face comment to make to an ex-wife? "But there's a nice bar next door to it. I've always wanted to go there, see what it's like."

"Great. Where is it?"

"Commonwealth Avenue. Around BU. If you follow me, I'll show you a good place to park where you don't have to feed a meter."

As she led the way to the bar, checking in her rearview mirror to make sure Helen was behind, Meg remembered one of her father's favorite expressions: "Comparisons are odious." Sure, Dad, she thought as she looked back at the Mercedes convertible Helen was driving. But I can't help

making them. Here I am in my six-year-old Toyota while
Helen buzzes along in her fancy sports car. Paid for by
whom? My husband. Who was once her husband. She gets
the house, the racy car, and a nice fat alimony check every
month. I get the pleasure of Charlie's company and tedious
lunches with old friends of hers.

"Stop it, Meg," she chastised herself, hitting the steering
wheel with the palm of her hand. "This isn't about money.
Money can't buy you love. Love is all there is. Imagine."
She searched with her left hand for the tape box and, at the
next traffic light, pulled out an old Beatles cassette, shoved
it into her tape machine. "Baby You Can Drive My Car,"
Ringo sang. She pushed the eject button immediately.

Parking on the street behind Healthworks, she waited for
Helen to pull into the space next door. How cozy, she
thought, watching as Helen locked the Mercedes with one
of those remote-control gadgets she'd never owned herself.
Our cars can bond while we're at the bar. Maybe mine will
benefit from the propinquity. But how can she own such a
snazzy car and dress herself in rags? This time Helen was
clad in brown corduroy trousers and a Halloween orange
wool sweater, complete with one gaping hole under the left
armpit. No makeup. No jewelry. A pair of dirty sneakers.
The brief snowfall of the day before had melted and they
trudged through the slush together in silence, Meg wondering all the while what this drink was in aid of. Did Helen
want *more* alimony? Or was she going to criticize Meg's
handling of Josh and David?

"Here we go," Meg said, opening the door to the Italian
bar. "I pass by this place all the time and wonder what it's
like inside."

"It's nice." Helen surveyed the dark room, divided into
eating and drinking areas. The bar was on the right, with
stools and a couple of tables, the restaurant on the left.
"Authentic Italian. At least it *looks* authentic."

"What would you like?"

"A Bloody Mary."

Meg ordered two Bloody Marys from the bartender,

waited as he fixed them, then carried them to the table where Helen had ensconced herself.

"I asked *you* to come for a drink. I should have gotten these," Helen said.

"No problem." You can pay, Meg wanted to add. "It makes a great change from the treadmill."

"God, I should be working out. I can't seem to get the energy to go to a gym."

"Once you start it can be addictive."

"I'm sure."

Meg sipped her extra spicy Bloody Mary and smothered a cough. Helen fiddled with the celery stick in hers, twirling it in circles.

"So? How are the boys?" Meg pulled her cigarettes from her coat pocket, scrabbled for matches in her bag and lit one.

"They're fine. You know, on each other's backs the whole time, but fine, really."

"Do they argue when they're with you, too?"

"Are you kidding?" Helen picked up her drink, took a large swallow. "Those two were born to fight."

"That makes me feel better—I thought it might have something to do with being at our house."

"Oh, no. I can't stand it. Sometimes Josh actually hurts David. I don't know what to do about it."

"Do you think I can help in any way?"

"I don't know." Helen stared into her drink, seemingly preoccupied with the floating slice of lemon.

"Well, if there's anything I can do, just tell me. I'm really fond of them, you know. They're great boys."

"Thanks." She glanced up with what reminded Meg of a Shy Di look. "How are things between you and Charlie?"

"Fine," Meg said at once. "They're fine."

"Oh. I thought maybe—"

"You thought maybe *what?*"

"I don't want you to misinterpret my motives here, Meg. I'm concerned, that's all."

"Concerned about what?" She couldn't keep the edge

out of her voice, it was impossible. What right did Helen have, what possible right did she have to pry into her relationship with Charlie? This conversation was so far out of line it was ludicrous. Obscene.

"He hit me too."

"What *are* you talking about?"

"Charlie hit me too."

"Charlie's never hit me in my life. What *is* this?"

"The bandage on your forehead. That silly story about reaching down for a cigarette. I assumed—"

"You assumed wrong. I can't believe this. And I don't believe you. For the sake of the kids I'm going to pretend this never happened, okay? This conversation didn't occur. I've always wanted to say this and now I will. Get a life, Helen."

Meg ground out her cigarette, stood up and walked out of the bar.

"Jesus," she muttered as she strode into the next-door gym. "What a nightmare woman. How twisted can you get? I haven't been fair to Charlie. Maybe he's not perfect with me because he's had such a bad experience with her. Maybe all he needs is more time. Maybe I should cancel those appointments to see apartments. Helen's trying to break us up. That's a joke." She flung her membership card at the woman behind the desk and stomped off into the changing room.

Chapter Eleven

SHE SAT CROSS-LEGGED on the floor, encircled by letters. There must have been fifty of them, delivered to her door an hour ago. Or was it two hours ago? Leo had lost track of time. Nick was visiting his mother in Wellesley; he had been gone since noon. The package arrived at three, addressed to her, with a note inside saying: "Hope you enjoy these as much as I did: Jackie."

She'd carried it into her living room, staring at this mass of correspondence, all addressed to Jackie. Thin white envelopes. Nick's painfully neat handwriting. She'd taken them out, spread them around her and sat looking at them. Occasionally, she'd pick one up, stare at it, put it down again.

When she'd arrived back from Amy's the day before, Leo had found Nick waiting for her. He must have been chain-smoking since she'd left; the apartment was saturated with a foggy, noxious cloud. And he'd looked the way she felt—shattered. They'd talked then. At six, after five hours of intense discussion, she'd taken a nap. He hadn't. He'd been at her side when she woke up, ready to talk more. As if they were dealing with the Cuban Missile Crisis, she thought later. That's how serious, how desperately serious, the conversation had been. Point by point, they went through it all. Jackie's visit, her reactions to it, his reactions to it; every emotional nuance was plumbed to the depth.

"I tend to talk in paragraphs," he'd said. "It's an old habit and one I've always been a little embarrassed by. People have short attention spans and I feel I have to warn them when I'm going to launch into a long spiel. I say 'I'm going to make a speech now' to all sorts of people. My parents made a joke of it ages ago and now I do it as a kind of reflex action. I do it at work, even. It's a phrase I use, that's all. It wasn't a special phrase between me and Jackie. I didn't know it was a special phrase to *you*."

She'd nodded, relief mixed with a tinge of sadness. Why had it meant so much to her? She didn't know, couldn't explain, except to say it was part of her sense of them as a couple, this phrase.

And then they'd moved on. To Thea. How he could keep his daughter's love. Would Thea feel that a rejection of Jackie was also a rejection of her? What could he say to set her straight, assure her of his love?

Leo was amazed by how much she herself had to say on that subject. Being a daughter. What a child needed from parents. She couldn't recollect ever going into the emotional consequences of her mother's death in such detail.

"I felt abandoned," she said. "Even though I had Amy and Meg and Beth, I felt such loss, as if a black hole had appeared in my heart. Grief is so isolating, partly because no one has the same relationship to the dead person; everyone has a different frame of reference, so it's impossible for anyone to share fully another's feelings.

"I could see things in my mother the others couldn't. She had a sense of humor. Beth would say something completely wacky and my mother wouldn't laugh or smile, but she'd get a little spark in her eyes. I was the only one who saw it, but I swear it was there. I felt a closeness to her that didn't make sense on the surface. She didn't pay any more attention to me than she did to the others, but I felt it nonetheless. And I loved Dad's stories about her—the way she was before Steven died. He said they always wanted to leave parties at the same time—that they'd invariably look across the room and nod to each other simultaneously and then make their excuses and leave. They were that much in synch. I thought it sounded so romantic." Leo reached out and touched the back of Nick's neck, then leaned into him and kissed him on the cheek.

"At her funeral, at the graveside, when we were all standing there, waiting for some flowers to be delivered,

Beth said something to the minister that made him smile. He tried to hide his mouth with his hand, but I'd seen the smile.

"And I remember thinking, even at eight years old, 'Mom would like this.' I was confused and desolate and I didn't understand what had happened—I mean I didn't understand exactly what death meant—but I remember that moment clearly. I knew that Beth had said something funny. I thought: if only Mom were here, she might actually laugh and then Beth would laugh, we'd all laugh and everything would be okay. Everything would change.

"I was always convinced that that's all it would take. One moment when we all understood one another, one moment when my mother would break out of the trap she was in and join the rest of us. But it never happened.

"Now I'm the one making speeches." Leo smiled. "It's contagious."

"I don't know whether parents, whatever the circumstances of their lives are, ever get it right," Nick said sadly. "My own mother and father were so strict that when I started counting up my presents under the tree one Christmas Eve, they went berserk. They said I was being greedy and selfish and then they gathered up the presents on the spot and took them to a charity place and gave them away. It taught me a lesson, I suppose. I wonder, though, whether that lesson was on how to hide my selfish instincts, not how to get rid of them."

Leo fingered the letter closest to her knee. Had Nick written to Jackie in the same way he had talked to her all yesterday? Had he been as intimate, as revealing? Should she read one? All of them?

They were postmarked twenty years ago. What had he been like then? He would have been just a couple of years younger than she was now. If she could divorce herself from the emotional content, she might be able to learn more about his character, what had shaped him back then. *If* she could divorce herself.

She slipped a white piece of paper out of the envelope.

"Darling Jackie," it began, "I can't believe I've been away from you for so long—" The words sliced through her. She cut back, ripping the letter into pieces.

One by one, Leo picked up the other envelopes and re-placed them in their package. She stood up, lifted it and carried it like an unexploded bomb to her hall closet, put-ting it at the far end, next to an old pair of boots. Then she gathered the remnants of the letter she'd started to read, put them in an ashtray and set fire to them.

If she told Nick about the package, he'd be furious with Jackie. The battle between them would escalate. If she didn't tell him about the letters, it would be the first de-ception of their relationship.

A few years ago, she'd been walking down Boylston Street when she'd spotted an old school friend across the road. "Dana," she'd yelled, charging toward her, waving. A taxi's worn-out brakes screeched to a halt half an inch from her, the driver screaming: "You stupid bitch, look where you're going. You should be dead." Engulfed by shame, she'd kept her head down and gone over to Dana, who grabbed her arm, squeezing it fiercely.

"Leo," she'd shrieked, "Leo. You almost got killed. What were you thinking?"

Passersby were staring at her. "Jesus, some fucking stu-pid girl," she heard a man mutter.

"I was so happy to see you again, I *wasn't* thinking," she'd answered, a wave of adrenaline panic coursing through her.

She hadn't seen the taxi coming then.

She hadn't anticipated Jackie now.

Amy wasn't listening. She was looking at her daughter, consumed with a feeling of love mixed with such pain it was almost unbearable. Charlotte was babbling away about her day at school, some science project that involved worms, bugs and frogs. Talking so fast it would have been hard to understand her even if Amy had been paying close attention.

She's constitutionally unable to keep anything to herself, Amy thought. Everything that goes into her little mind pours right out again, without any filter. She doesn't worry whether anyone else is interested in what she's saying, she doesn't care if she gives herself away with this endless enthusiasm. She puts herself, her feelings, on permanent display, hoping for what? Reciprocity. An equal, fervent response. Which ninety-nine percent of the time she doesn't get. Because she wears everyone down.

Her friendships are intense and short-lived. No one can stand the pace, not even other seven-year-old-kids. When they back off, she's bewildered, uncomprehending. "Why won't Emma invite me over anymore?" she asks and Amy wants to say: "Because you're in her face. You never let up." Instead she offers a poor excuse Charlotte blinks at. She doesn't have the heart to dampen her daughter's overwhelming exuberance. She knows she should say "Charlotte. Keep yourself to yourself a little more. Hide a little." But she doesn't.

Every person has boundaries, Amy knows, and Charlotte persists in invading them. She doesn't allow others any space. The kind of person who comes up to you at a party and stands much too close.

The kind of person who drives Jimmy crazy.

What would she do now if I told her her father is in town? Amy asked herself. She'd jump up and down and get wildly excited and beg to see him. Patrick—a fantasy figure of a father. Amy had told Charlotte that Patrick was an explorer of sorts, someone who had to roam the world on his own. It was as close as she could get to the truth, and Patrick's exotic postcards from foreign countries played right into it. Morocco, Russia, India—Charlotte had all his birthday greetings posted up on her wall. Amy remembered a time she'd been over at Beth's and heard a line in one of the romance-gone-wrong songs Beth played continually: "This has to be the best one yet/A singing telegram from you in Tibet." Whoever wrote those words must have known Patrick.

It was pointless to say anything to Charlotte—at least right now. Amy didn't know whether Patrick wanted to see their daughter. He hadn't even mentioned her name in their brief conversation. For all she knew, he could have vanished again.

"Cutting up the worms was the really rugged part . . ."

So she shouldn't worry too much that she hadn't told Jimmy about Patrick either. It wasn't as if she had *planned* not to tell him; she just hadn't, that's all. An instinctive reaction. Why bother Jimmy if Patrick wasn't going to be a factor in their lives, if he were going to fly off somewhere almost immediately?

"They were squirming and stuff, but they don't have any brains, do they, so there wasn't much guts or gross stuff coming out . . ."

What would Patrick think of Charlotte if he did see her? She was a lovely looking girl with slightly curly dark hair and bright blue eyes. A little on the small side for her age, but athletic like her father. Charlotte's inability to keep still for more than a few minutes at a time reminded Amy of Patrick. She wasn't a hyperactive child, she didn't run around screaming, but she always had to be doing *something*.

If they watched TV, Charlotte would pick up any object she could find and start tossing it from hand to hand, until the motion became so distracting Jimmy would begin to squirm and Amy would have to ask her to put it down. At which point Charlotte would turn her attention to the television show and begin to ask questions. "What's going to happen next?" she'd query and Jimmy would say, in an elaborately controlled tone of voice: "Why don't you just watch and find out?"

Patrick's brand of continual movement had been dynamic, not noisome. His form of energy had spurred people on. "Let's drive to Virginia," he might say on a dull winter's weekend. He'd round up a few friends and off they'd go. Those were the salad days, the time before Charlotte arrived, when freedom was not just a possibility but a way of life. Charlotte's energy was the flip side of her father's coin. It depleted the people around her, as if her spark could be maintained only by draining everyone else's battery.

Would Patrick understand her character, be endeared rather than put off by her boundless eagerness? Or would he have preferred a daughter like Zoey? Someone self-possessed and cool?

Charlotte idolized her stepsister. Whenever Zoey was around, she would follow her as if she were her favorite pop star, plaguing her with questions and talk. Zoey tolerated her graciously. Once she even lent Charlotte a much-coveted sweater. It hung down like a dress on Charlotte, who refused to take it off for days. Until, inevitably, she spilled a glass of Coke all over it. Amy had washed that sweater at least fifty times, but there was a lingering, defiant stain.

"Oh well," Zoey had said, "It wasn't my favorite anyway. I stole it from Rachel, actually. And she's bound to forget she ever had it. Sometimes I think she has Junior Alzheimer's. You wouldn't believe how much she forgets."

A generous response, one that confirmed Amy's growing affection for her stepdaughter. But not one shared by Jimmy.

"Amy," he'd said. "I don't think Charlotte should borrow Zoey's clothes. Or use her computer. She's bound to break it and then we'll be in another situation like this one. Zoey will have to be nice about it and that's not entirely fair to her. I think it would be a good idea generally if Charlotte let Zoey alone more."

"Has Zoey complained about her?" Amy asked, trembling.

"No. Not exactly. She doesn't have to, does she? It's obvious."

It's obvious. My daughter is a pain. Yours is perfect. Amy thought of Beth's nickname for Steven: Do No Wrong. Zoey could do no wrong in Jimmy's eyes. But then Zoey wasn't around enough to do much wrong even if she chose to. She breezed in and out like a visiting VIP; she wasn't there on a day-to-day basis. There were times Amy wished she could blame Zoey for something with an easy conscience. She would have liked to turn to Jimmy and criticize his daughter just to even the score a little. But Zoey was guiltless.

Over the two years they'd been married, Amy had tried to resign herself to the unequal nature of affairs in their house when it came to their respective children. She could just about handle the fact that she was, in effect, a one-parent family, that Jimmy would never treat Charlotte as anything other than an irritating appendage. After all, she often found herself thinking, he didn't beat Charlotte, he wasn't a tyrant or a monster—he was civil, if distant.

Charlotte probably didn't pick up on the times she annoyed her stepfather so; Amy was the one attuned to Jimmy's silent judgments. *She* was the one who suffered when she'd see him turn away from Charlotte in mid-flow, a look of supreme boredom on his face. It was a situation she had to learn to live with, that's all. She could keep her bruised maternal feelings under control.

Except.

Except for the times when they'd visit friends who had kids and Jimmy would be so *interested* in these other children. He'd sit and talk with them, play games, give them the kind of devoted attention that merited exclamations of "What a wonderful stepfather he must be for Charlotte" from the mothers and fathers of these terrific offspring. On the way home, in the car, he might say "What a bright little girl Harriet is," or "He's got an unusual mind, Freddie, for a boy of seven."

Amy, hearing these hymns of praise, would clench her fists, stare out the window and think, Why? Why can't he treat Charlotte like that? Is she *so* impossible?

"Maybe it all has something to do with the fact that Charlotte is another man's child," Leo had stated once. "She's a constant reminder that you slept with another man. Jimmy might have more of a problem with that than you think."

"But Zoey is a constant reminder that Jimmy slept with Rachel. And I like Zoey. What's more, I *tell* Jimmy how fond I am of her."

"Men are more proprietorial when it comes to sex," Leo

said. "I remember when I took a biology class once, the male teacher announced that the *real* difference between the sexes was one fact and one fact only—a man can't ever be sure whether a child is his or not. A pregnant woman is positive that she's the mother, but a father can never be absolutely sure."

"Except in these days of DNA testing."

"Okay. But how many men go in for that? How many would actually put it to the test? He was saying that there's always a lurking doubt, an unconscious one, but it's there nonetheless. So maybe they're more touchy about their wives' previous sexual history than a woman is about a man's. I'm sure Jimmy has difficulty coming to terms with your marriage to Patrick."

"No. He doesn't."

"He *says* he doesn't. But I bet he looks at Charlotte and thinks of Patrick."

"Not Jimmy. No. He looks at Charlotte and thinks—shut up and leave me alone."

"Mommy? Are you listening to me?"

"Of course I am, sweetheart," Amy reassured her. How nice it would have been to have someone around who could share her love for Charlotte, someone who understood her foibles and loved her all the more for them. Someone she didn't have to feel defensive with when the subject of Charlotte came up in conversation. Her sisters loved their niece, especially Leo, who could sit down with Charlotte for hours, listen patiently and ask relevant questions, but what Amy really wanted was a man, a father for her daughter. Was Patrick coming back to fill that role? To bind himself to his daughter?

Fat chance, Amy thought. He looks the same, he talks the same, he is the same person who left six years ago. What if he offered Charlotte his love and then vanished again? Amy's tears at the time of Patrick's departure had been sufficient to keep the Wailing Wall watered for decades. She wasn't going to watch her daughter sobbing the way she had. No way.

She wouldn't tell Charlotte about Patrick's arrival. She wouldn't tell Jimmy, either. For years she'd wished that Patrick might show up to teach Jimmy what it felt like to have an ex-spouse hanging around. Now, when it came to it, she knew Patrick's appearance meant nothing but trouble. For everyone.

"Looking good, kiddo," Beth said, leaning across the table at the Casablanca in Harvard Square. "The tousled hair, whaler-back-from-the-sea image suits you."

"Thanks. You're looking great too. 'Time writes no wrinkle on thine azure brow/Such as creation's dawn beheld, thou rollest now.' "

"Rollest? As in shake, rattle and?"

"Not exactly, Beth."

"Are we talking Shakespeare?"

"No. Byron. 'Age cannot wither her, nor custom stale her infinite variety'—*that's* Shakespeare."

"Aha. Can we skip the poetry for a while, Patrick? It reminds me of school. I want to know what you're doing back in town. Playing Humphrey Bogart to Amy's Ingrid Bergman? Lovers meet after years apart, struggle with their feelings, then sacrifice themselves to a greater ideal. Are you going to end up with Claude Rains? Is there a world war going on I don't know about? What's the plot here?"

"There isn't any plot. I wanted to see Amy, that's all."

"Is that why you called me? Do you want me to arrange a meeting?"

"No. I've seen her once already. I went to her office this afternoon."

"I see. And?"

"And I saw her."

"Right. You saw her. End of story. Come on, Patrick, dish the dirt."

"There's not any dirt to dish. We had a brief conversation. I left."

"Was there blood on the walls?"

"Nope. No blood, sweat or tears. She looked fantastic."

"Are you still in love with her?"

"Of course I am. I always will be."

"But—"

"But marriage and I don't mix. It's a crazy institution."

"Are you planning to see Charlotte?"

"Yes."

"I don't think that's a good idea. Not if you're going away again."

"I might stay in Boston for a while." Patrick pushed the sleeves of his sweater above his elbows.

"Doing what?"

"Whoa. Third degree."

"Well, what did you expect? You walked out on my sister and my niece without any warning, you left us to pick up the pieces—and there were a lot of them, let me tell you—and now you're back spouting poetry, sounding as if you'd taken an advanced course on how to be enigmatic."

"Of all the people I know, Beth, I'd expect you to be the one who understands that life doesn't have to arrange itself in traditional patterns." He took an elastic band off his wrist, stretched it close to the breaking point, tossed it on the table. "I'm not the 'Hi, honey, I'm home' type. I don't want to join any PTA groups. If it were up to me, I wouldn't want Charlotte to have the kind of education everyone else sets so much store by. She'll forget ninety-nine percent of what she learns at school, she'll go on to college and forget what she's learned there too, and the odds are she won't get a job anyway. Money for nothing. A waste of valuable time."

"What? Should she be hitchhiking around the world?"

"It might be more valuable in the long run."

"Wake up and smell the decaf, kiddo. A seven-year-old girl left alone for more than twenty seconds would be molested, raped and chopped up into little bits. I wouldn't call that a valuable experience."

"I'm not suggesting she go out on her own," Patrick said with evident exasperation. "I'm not suggesting she travel the world with me. All I'm saying is that it's possible for

me to see her without damaging her life just because I'm
not Major Dad. People are more flexible than you give them
credit for."

"Patrick. I'm on your team. I always have been. You fit
into our family perfectly—until you left. But you can't
keep moving the goalposts. Amy's married to someone
else. Okay, the guy looks like André Agassi minus the earrings, the long hair, the designer stubble, the talent; he talks
with all the intellectual flair of Pete Sampras—but she's
made a choice. She has a career, a life. If you come back
into the picture, you're going to tilt the frame."

"Is that such a bad idea?"

"That depends on your motives."

"I don't have any motives."

"Sure."

"Beth—" Patrick picked up the rubber band, shot it at
his ex-sister-in-law. "Trust me."

Helen was lying. Lying through her teeth. Charlie had never
hit her. He wouldn't do something like that. Meg had seen
him with the children enough times when he'd lost his temper. He'd yelled, certainly, but he was a softie at heart.
He'd never hit them. He'd never hit anybody.

Meg remembered the first time they'd met, at a dinner
party hosted by one of the women who worked at her school,
Emily McClain. Emily was engaged to a law professor at
Harvard and wanted to have what she described to Meg as a
"grown-up" dinner party with "grown-up" people.

"But I need a friend there with me," she'd said. "I've
never done any formal entertaining. You can be an exception to my grown-up rule."

Deciding not to take this as a criticism, Meg had cheerfully
gone along and found herself in the midst of some of the most
boring people she'd ever come in contact with. By the time
she'd sat down at the table, she was looking at her watch wondering how early she could leave without being rude.

Positioned between two men, both of whom immediately
zoomed in on the women on their other sides, Meg was left

in a social no-man's land with no one to talk to and nothing to do. During the first course, she alternated between staring at her plate and trying unsuccessfully to join in on the conversation to her left. During the main course, she stared at her plate some more and then listened in silently to the conversation on her right. The man was telling the woman a story of how he was snubbed by the maître d' at an expensive, upmarket restaurant.

"I'd called in advance, reserved a table by the window, but when we got there, this creep refused to seat us at the table I'd booked. Obviously he was looking for a bribe, or else he thought I wasn't important enough to get the prime table. We had a God-awful fight. I'd promised my wife I'd take her to that restaurant and sit at that table for our anniversary, you see. And he was saying I couldn't. So I slugged him and walked off."

"Really? Did he call the police?" the woman asked, obviously impressed by this macho tale.

"No. At least not to my knowledge. I hit him on behalf of all the people who get bad treatment at all the pretentious restaurants those snobby food critics have orgasms over."

"Excuse me," Meg interrupted, forcing her way into the conversation.

"What?" The man turned to her, acknowledging her existence for the first time that evening.

"You're not telling the truth."

"I'm not? In what respect?" he arched his eyebrows. Meg could see the beginning of a smile.

"You didn't hit him."

The smile spread. He shifted in his seat, turning to her. "How do you know?"

"I just do."

"Well." He rolled his head around as if he were doing exercises to loosen the tension in his neck. "Well. You're right. I've told that story before and no one has ever picked me up on it. What makes you so perceptive?"

"I don't know," Meg shrugged.

"Tell me something you *do* know, then. Tell me what you're doing at this party."

He peppered her with questions, all the while seeming to weigh her answers as if they held the key to something infinitely important. The next time Meg looked at her watch, it was two o'clock in the morning and they were the only ones left sitting at the dining room table, engrossed in conversation.

"Don't—" he admonished. "Don't look at your watch. It doesn't matter what time it is."

"But I have to work tomorrow. I have to get some sleep. And I think everyone else must have left—we're being rude."

"You can't go. I need you. You're the only person in the world who can keep me out of trouble."

She was dazzled and daunted by him simultaneously; confused by her attraction to him, slightly scared by these surprisingly intimate words.

"No. Really. I've got to go."

"Can I bring the glass slipper to your school tomorrow?"

"It won't fit," she said, mustering all her rational thoughts. "You're married, aren't you? Oh my God. Where's your wife now?"

"She's at home. With a cold. I'm not being crass, Meg. I'm not suggesting an affair. I just want to see you again, that's all."

"Yeah, right," Meg could hear Beth saying. But she was tired of listening to Beth.

"Okay. If that's all, I suppose there would be no harm in seeing you again."

He put his hands up in the air.

"No harm at all. I promise. We've got so much to talk about."

They did have a lot to talk about, as it happened. They talked nonstop through five lunches. They talked all the way to her apartment, after the sixth lunch. They stopped talking, however, as soon as they got inside.

Charlie was a big man. Wide-shouldered, tall, with a forceful face and confident brown eyes. He looked less like the academic he was than the rugby player he also was. Meg was always amazed when she heard him talk seriously about the law, for he had such a physically imposing presence, it was difficult to believe he had an equally weighty brain. As soon as Charlie made a decision in life, he followed it through, never wavering from his course. "I don't have time for soul-searching," he'd once said to Meg. "If you know what you want from life, why spend time asking why you want it? Trust your instincts."

Yes, Charlie was ambitious. Meg knew that. And yes, sometimes he could steamroller people if they got in his way. But he was not a violent man. He would never hit a woman. He would never hit his wife.

Meg glanced over at her husband as he watched the evening news. Should she tell him what Helen had said?

"This country's legal system has gone to hell," he commented. "O. J. Simpson is going to walk, you know. Well, maybe he won't walk, but he won't get the chair. Not that I believe in capital punishment, but if you have a law, you have to apply it to all people equally. That man is unequal under the law just because he happened to have athletic talent once upon a time. It's a disgrace."

"I love you," Meg said.

It's possible. I can make this marriage work. I can have my family after all. Anything's possible.

Charlie rolled his eyes and hung his shoulders.

"Oh God," he sighed. "Does that mean I'm supposed to come over and shower you with kisses? I'm too tired, Meg. I've got too much on my mind. Some other time."

Meg reached over and took a handful of papers from the table beside her. Assignments she'd given to her class. "Write a story, any story," she'd said, and now was as good a time as any to look at the results.

"Its al overr," Eddy's story began. Meg immediately put it down. She wasn't in the mood. She was too tired. She had too much on her mind. There were at least four apartments that sounded worth looking at.

Chapter Twelve

BETH STOOD IN stunned disbelief as the ball whizzed by her. She had served the perfect serve, rushed to the net in an intimidating, confident run and then been passed. It wasn't supposed to happen. She'd lost the point, which meant she'd lost the set and the match. This definitely was not supposed to happen.

Robin, the annoyingly gracious victor, smiled sweetly and said "Bad luck." Of course it had nothing whatsoever to do with luck. Beth had blown it, well and truly, for the first time in their weekly competition.

"I guess it had to happen sometime," Robin continued, walking toward the back of the court. "You just had an off day."

Beth knew perfectly well what she was supposed to say: "No. You played beautifully." The truth was, however, exactly as Robin had phrased it. She'd had an off day. If she'd been playing up to par, Beth would beat Robin every time they played until the end of eternity. To lie to Robin in some gesture of good sporting behavior would be to patronize her.

"How about a drink?" she asked. That proposal was as sporting a suggestion as Beth could muster. In fact she would have liked to avoid Robin's company until she'd thrashed her 6-0, 6-0 the next week.

"Sorry, no can do. I've got a date."

" 'No can do'? Where'd you pick that one up from? One of your assertiveness training courses?" Never, Beth swore to herself, never have alcohol before a game of tennis. That's what had thrown her off; two glasses of white wine with Patrick.

Robin blushed and mumbled something about "it's just an expression."

"So who is this hot date with?"

"An old boyfriend. I went out with him years ago and he suddenly called me up out of the blue."

"You can't step in the same river twice, you know."

"I wasn't planning to wade into any rivers, Beth. Every time I open my mouth, you jump down my throat. Sometimes I feel sorry for your clients."

"So do I."

They both laughed at that and Beth felt a little better about life.

After she'd showered, changed and driven home listening to Iris Dement singing Easy's "Getting Harder Every Day" nonstop for the twenty minutes it took to get to her apartment, she felt a lot better about life. Robin's aberrant victory might serve a purpose. How many more weeks would she have shown up knowing that she didn't have a prayer of winning? They'd been playing for six months now and there would have to come a time when Robin gave the game up as hopeless. Not now, however. One win would keep her going for another six months at least. Beth's Monday evenings were safe for a while.

Invariably, she and Robin would go out for a drink after tennis and end up having dinner. Doubtless the old flame's arrival back on the scene wouldn't last for longer than a week and that routine would also revert to the norm. Robin's attempts to keep a man interested were sadly similar to her efforts to return a ball hit deep to her backhand.

Beth switched on the light by the door, tossed her tennis racquet and sports bag on the sofa and went to look for any messages on her machine. There were none. She thought of calling Meg and Leo to tell them of Patrick's arrival in town, but decided that this piece of information could wait. Patrick had always been her particular friend; she understood him better than the others, better even than Amy did, when it came down to it. If the truth be known, she'd been surprised when Patrick married Amy. Not only because he wasn't the marrying type, but also because Amy wasn't capable of handling his capricious nature.

From a young age, Amy had coped with the Preston family vicissitudes by being relentlessly practical. When set with any task, she'd perform it without questions, which was why she'd done so well at school. Amy was the type of girl who always did her homework, was always where she said she'd be; someone scrupulously responsible. She had even taken over the cooking, the cleaning, the family chores without any resentment; all of which left Meg and Beth herself free to lead their lives as if their mother had been a functioning human being.

Beth should have felt immense gratitude toward her younger sister, she knew. But she didn't. Amy had taken over Leo as if Leo belonged to her. And sometimes Amy had refused to join in on Beth's humorous escapades. She didn't say anything, but Beth could feel her disapproval, a tacit condemnation of Beth's attitude toward life. Not that Amy understood Beth's attitude toward life any more than she did Patrick's; for, strangely enough, given Amy's belief in science, she didn't like to experiment. She was rooted in a day-to-day existence consisting of rules that she took seriously. Her only breakout had been when she married Patrick, and that had been doomed from the start.

When Patrick ran away leaving Amy holding the baby, Beth had made an offhand comment—something along the lines of "Now you can be one hundred percent scientifically sure that oil and water don't mix"—and from that point on Amy had never looked at her straight in the eyes. Even now, seven years later, Beth knew that Amy tended to avoid her whenever possible. Of course it had been an insensitive thing to say, Beth was fully aware of that, but it had just slipped out and Amy shouldn't have had quite such a sense of humor failure. After all, it was the truth. But that was exactly what was at the heart of all the problems in their family—the refusal to recognize and deal with the truth.

Meg was a past, present and future master of the art of

self-deception. All the children in her classes were "little angels," her two stepsons were "nice" boys, her husband was "wonderful." Meg's take on reality was simple: wishing will make it so. Wear the right clothes, look pulled together, say the right things at the right time and you'll be fine and dandy.

No wonder Meg was a nervous wreck. She spent all her time trying to sidestep the nasty parts of life; as a result she couldn't move forward. She was stuck in an emotional warp, afraid that, if she stood up for herself or complained once, the whole structure she'd so carefully built would come tumbling down on her head.

After Victoria's death, Meg had set out on a hopeless quest to win Mark's esteem. Beth watched as her sister tried to make all the right moves. She'd stay up waiting for Mark to get home from his work or his women, then attempt to talk to him about "his day." These little chats would always end up with Mark yawning discreetly and saying: "Sorry, Meg, but I'm done in. I'll talk to you tomorrow." Well, tomorrow and tomorrow and tomorrow crept in its petty pace from day to day and the promised intimate conversations never happened.

On Mark's birthdays and Christmas, Meg bought complicated fishing gadgets that she should have known would be of no interest to her father; he liked fishing the old-fashioned way. He'd smile wanly as he opened the package, say "thank you" in that over-polite way of his and pack the present back in its box. Beth would have felt sorry for Meg if this wooing of Mark had not been quite so stupid. It was based, as was all Meg's subsequent stupidity with men, in her inability to come to terms with the truth.

Mark was not interested in being a father. He might take his daughters on desultory fishing trips occasionally, but the male mechanism that drove him had nothing to do with family life. Work was what mattered, work and sex. It was what mattered with ninety-nine percent of men, whereas what mattered with ninety-nine percent of women was men. How many times had Beth sat down with female friends, supposed career women from all walks of life, who, when given free rein in a conversation, would inevitably turn the subject matter to men? This oppressed class of women spent a large proportion of their lives figuring out how to please their oppressors. They giggled about clothes and makeup and dates as if they were still teenage schoolgirls. And then they'd go back to work and play at being macho females. Schizoids. That's what women were these days. Split personalities on the rampage.

Meg was no exception. Sure she had her job at the school, but it didn't fulfill her, not really. She needed a man to define her and as the years rolled on, she took any definition that came her way. The last and most absurd of which was Charlie.

Once she had gotten it through her head that Mark was not going to change, that he wouldn't suddenly start to rain affection and concern down on her pretty head, Meg looked elsewhere for comfort. She went through a series of boyfriends, all of whom she declared to be "fabulous, wonderful, just right." She did everything in her power to placate and please. Whatever hobbies they possessed, she would launch herself into with a passion. For four excruciating months when she was twenty-one, she tried to learn how to play the clarinet because the man in question liked Dixieland jazz. She would have volunteered to become a clone of any guy she dated. And this behavior, of course, made them run away as fast as their hairy legs could take them.

As soon as these picture-perfect relationships fizzled out, Meg made it a badge of honor to remain friends with the erstwhile lovers. They were all still "fabulous and wonderful," they just weren't "right" for her. At the core of this determined desire to please a man, any man, was, Beth knew, Meg's desperate wish not to be left alone. She had a game plan in life, a simple one. She wanted to cocoon herself, wrap herself in the protective coating of wife and mother. She wanted to play happy families. As if there were such a thing.

"Look, Meg," Beth had advised her years ago. "Face

facts. You know the first line in *Anna Karenina*? 'All happy families resemble one another, but each unhappy family is unhappy in its own way?' Well, I'd like to ask Tolstoy if there is such a thing as a happy family with a child over the age of three in the equation."

Meg had dismissed her with some comment about rampant cynicism.

And now Meg was married to the Galloping Egoist.

Meg and Amy and Leo all believed that Beth didn't like men, she knew. But that wasn't the case. She liked men well enough. She just hated the fact that they were boringly predictable. And Beth's true horror in life was not, like Meg's, being left alone, but being bored.

Beside her bed, Beth had a framed quotation from Kierkegaard's *Either/Or:* "How terrible is tedium—how terribly tedious." It was always interesting to see which men commented on it and which didn't. One guy had even gone so far as to turn it facedown before he began his amorous attentions. No one expressed any pleasure at seeing it.

There were times when she wished she could have been a lesbian. But if men were good for anything, they were good for sex, and she'd never been physically attracted to a female. All she asked for, all she wanted, was to be surprised. Yet each encounter with a man was depressingly like the last. They were interesting for a short span of time, that being while they were trying to get her into bed. As soon as she had sex with them, they began to pale, one by one, into some variation of a typical male.

If she treated them like dirt, they loved her; if she treated them nicely, they made little speeches about their inability to commit, assuming that she was desperate for them to commit, or else they proposed marriage within seconds, assuming that she was desperate to get married. The "new age" ones cooked dinner for her, told her about their "feelings" and were even more boring than the old age ones who wanted her to cook dinner for them while they avoided talking about their feelings. All of them wanted twenty-four-hour ego massage; some hid this more successfully than others. But the end result was the same. They were boring, boring, boring.

Sometimes she'd call Robin, tell her what was happening in a relationship she was having and then predict exactly what was going to happen next. What he would say, how he would say it, down to the last word and physical gesture.

"You could make a fortune if there were some way to bet on male behavior," Robin had once joked. Beth spent the next ten minutes figuring out if it were possible to take her talents in this field to Las Vegas and clean up.

Even Patrick, Beth reflected, who was seriously attractive and had a flair for life, was predictable. Predictable in his unyielding urge to be unpredictable. He might try to scorn the rules of society, but in the process he made his own set of rules for behavior that were just as rigid: don't settle down, don't get trapped, keep moving. No way would Patrick stay in Boston for more than a few weeks. Beth would have bet her life on that.

Stuart was different. She'd known that from the moment she got in his car. He was her twin, the one man who would understand. He would never be predictable or boring. He'd touched her core that afternoon and he was the one she wanted. Now someone else had him. Well, whoever she was, she didn't deserve him. Of that much Beth was certain. What she didn't understand was how the earthquake that had sent her reeling even at that young age could have left Stuart unmoved. How could he not have remembered her? How could he turn down the chance of seeing her?

Beth thought of calling him again, then discarded the notion. She didn't want to hear the wife's voice, and what else could she say to Stuart, if he answered? Still—why on earth had he moved to Boston? Didn't that say something? Perhaps he'd repressed that car ride all these years and some unconscious stirring of the memory had brought him back to Boston again. To see her.

Perhaps not. She'd been a child. He remembered her as a child. A kid who had sashayed into his life and out again without making any impact. And all this time she'd been living in the kind of dream world she criticized Meg for inhabiting. What if Stuart were like Charlie? The odds were high that that was the case. After all, what man wasn't, at bottom, transcendentally tedious? Finding Stuart to be like all the other men she knew would be more of a disappointment than never seeing him again. At least this way she could keep her feelings for him intact.

It was time to practice what she preached and start distinguishing between fantasy and reality. There was no possibility of creating one of Meg's little happy families. With Stuart or anyone else. Living life alone was far preferable to living with the kind of compromises she saw her sisters making every day.

Leo. She had to get Leo out of the mess she was in. So far she had done almost nothing to help. One short conversation did not a game plan make. Aggressive action was called for, and clearly Meg and Amy had both opted out, so it came down to Beth, as any decisive action had always come down to Beth. *She* was the one who had approached Stuart in the parking lot, *she* was the one in charge—a natural-born leader. A natural-born killer, some of her old boyfriends might say, which was fine with her. They were natural-born victims.

Nick Booth had moved out of his house, but his wife must still be ensconced there. Beth could call her. Pretend to be doing a survey of family values in the nineties and ask pertinent questions. Gauge Mrs. Booth's mood, her personality, and what attitude she was taking to this upheaval. Given enough information, Beth could then proceed in developing a strategy. It wasn't the best of ideas, but it might help.

She dragged out the telephone book, looked up Nicholas Booth and found the number and address. He lived in Cambridge, not far from Leo, as it transpired. Sitting down with a pen and paper, she made out a list of questions, starting with the obvious ones and moving on to the knockout blows like: what is your attitude toward divorce? She'd

start out the conversation by announcing that she was doing
research work for the Tiny Tim Center of the Human Spirit.
Who could refuse to answer an institution with that title,
especially so close to Christmas?

After two rings, she heard the answering machine kick
in. "Hello. This is Jackie Booth. Thea and I are unable to
come to the phone at the moment. Nick Booth has abandoned his family and is busy screwing his teenage mistress.
Leave a message at the beep."

Beth found herself staring at the telephone in her hand
for a moment before she hung up. That was some kind of
message. Jackie Booth was going to make big trouble if
that was anything to go by. Leo was in deep shit.

Jackie probably would have told the Tiny Tim Center to
fuck off, so it was just as well Beth hadn't gotten through.
Hearing that message was definitely grounds for a glass of
wine. Beth stood up, went into her kitchen and pulled a
bottle of Muscadet out of the fridge. She'd have to watch
her growing propensity for drinking on her own, but this
time she could forgive herself.

Jackie was definitely the one calling and hanging up on
Leo. God knows what she would do next. At the same time
as breaking up this romance, Beth would have to protect
her youngest sister from the revengeful actions of Mrs.
Nicholas Booth. That voice had been brutal. That voice had
been——Beth stopped as she was about to put the corkscrew
on the top of the bottle. She went back into her living room
and pushed the redial button on her phone.

The message came through again. She smashed the receiver back down.

"I don't fucking believe it," she said, and then said it
again.

Clever little bitch. What a nasty, clever little bitch. How
had she managed it? Easily enough, it would seem. She'd
found out somehow what Beth did for a living, where she
worked, and made the appointment. Not difficult. But then
Jackie had fed her an outrageous story and Beth had swallowed it hook, line and sinker, like one of her father's hun-

gry little fish. She was probably still laughing at Beth's credulity. Beth reviewed the conversation and felt the anger rise and buck as she recalled all she had told "Eve." About her family, about Leo. Beth had handed this woman rounds and rounds of ammunition, willingly. Pleased that someone was so interested. Beth had acted just like all the men she knew—ask me a few questions and I'll tell you my life story.

She knew she could be accused of many things in her life, but rank stupidity had not been one of them, not before this moment.

Well, Jackie Booth, aka Eve, was not going to get away with it.

This was personal now.

She dialed Leo's number.

"Hi, kiddo, am I interrupting something?"

"No." Leo sounded tense. "We're just having a pizza."

"Well, I won't keep you long. I'm sure you and Nick have a lot to talk about. But I wanted to invite you two to dinner. On Thursday, let's say. At Locke-Ober. A celebration. Kind of an engagement party, I thought. I'll get Amy and Jimmy and Meg and Charlie too—maybe even Dad—a family affair. My treat."

"Beth. Why would you give us an engagement party when you disapprove of our relationship?"

"Because I don't disapprove. I think it's fabulous. I think Nick is fabulous."

"You've never met him. Come on, Beth, what is this really about?"

"I don't have to meet him to think he's fabulous. *You* think he's fabulous and I'm sure you're right and I think you two should get married and if it doesn't work it doesn't work and you can get divorced and who cares about that anymore?"

"Are you drunk?"

"Leo. Relax. Okay, I was dubious, I admit it. But I've changed my mind. And if you have any problems with Meg or Mark or anyone else, I'll help you, I promise. I'm behind you one hundred percent."

"I don't understand."

"There's nothing to understand, kiddo. But listen, you may need help with Nick's wife. I mean, if she starts to play up on you, if she tries to make your life miserable. I'm sure she's a scheming, manipulative bitch, and I wouldn't put anything past her."

"Why are you sure that Nick's wife is scheming and manipulative?"

"Most wives are, aren't they? I mean they've traded in their independence for a man so they get bitter and twisted."

"Amy and Meg aren't bitter and twisted."

"Oh, fine. Okay. Amy and Meg aren't, you won't be. Fine. I don't care. Stop picking on me over every little point when all I'm trying to do is to help."

"Beth. Call me again tomorrow, will you? And if you say the same things then, I'll believe you. I think you're on Ecstasy or something."

"No, I'm not on anything, Leo. I'm your older sister being supportive. Trust me, for Christ's sake. Just trust me."

Beth hung up and went back to her bottle of wine. She could worry about the morality of supporting Leo and Nick in their romance later. Right now she had another agenda. She had arranged to meet "Eve" again on Friday afternoon. Now *that* was not a tedious prospect.

Chapter Thirteen

"So I came by to get a little food from you guys because you always have great food and God knows Rachel doesn't and I want to eat something before the concert or I'll faint and embarrass myself afterwards."

Zoey sounds just like Charlotte, Amy thought, listening to her stepdaughter. And, because her face is so excited, she *looks* like a little girl too, despite the fact that she's dressed to maim.

"I can't believe Alex knows him." Zoey was hopping from foot to foot.

"You can't believe Alex knows who?" Jimmy asked, struggling to be patient. He wasn't used to his own child being so enthusiastic, Amy could tell. It made him nervous.

"Brad Roberts."

"And who is he when he's at home?"

"Come on, Dad. You're not *that* old. What a sad way of talking. Brad Roberts is the lead singer in the Crash Test Dummies. You know—'God Shuffled His Feet.' "

"God shuffled his feet?"

"It's a fantastic song. You must have heard it."

Jimmy shook his head.

"I like 'Afternoons and Coffee Spoons,' " Amy said. "He's got some interesting lyrics. How does Alex know him?"

"You wouldn't believe the people Alex knows. The guy has hidden depths. I think he met Brad in Canada or something. And—can you believe *this*—Alex once met Kurt Cobain too. I mean, the radical factor on that one is astronomical. Anyway, Alex is taking Rachel and me to the Crash Test Dummies concert tonight and then backstage to meet Brad. What am I going to say to him?"

"Why don't you just shuffle your feet?" Jimmy asked. Amy could see the disappointment descend on him when Zoey didn't laugh.

"Do I look all right?" she turned to Amy.

"You look great."

In a black mini skirt, white tank top, ripped leather jacket and lace-up boots, Zoey was dressed like a seasoned teenage groupie.

"Where's Charlotte?"

"In her room, doing her homework."

"Well, I'll grab a chicken leg and go say good night to her. Then I've got to get back to Rachel's and make sure she doesn't do her usual take-five-hours-to-get-dressed routine. I don't want to be late. Not tonight."

"Of course not," Jimmy muttered as he watched her head off to Charlotte's room. When she was out of earshot, he glared at Amy and said "Why didn't you say something?"

"Say what?"

"Tell her she shouldn't be going out on a school night, for Christ's sake."

"Jimmy. You know she *always* goes out on school nights and she still manages a B plus average. You've never complained before. Why now? And why expect me to do it?"

"If she didn't go out so much she might have an A average."

"Why don't *you* tell her that?"

"I can hardly tell her that when Mr. Cool Alex is the one taking her to this damn concert. What would that make me sound like?"

"What would it make *me* sound like? The wicked stepmother. Besides, I've never seen her so excited."

"Exactly."

"Jimmy. If I understood what this argument was about, I might be able to have it. But I don't, so I won't."

"Bye guys." Zoey skipped through the room, waving her chicken leg. "I'm out of here. Charlotte's crashed out, by the way. I thought she might be dead for a second there. I don't think I've ever seen her so still. That may be because I've never seen her asleep. I'll give your regards to the band."

The front door slammed.

"I can understand if you're jealous of Alex," Amy said softly, "but don't take it out on Zoey."

"What? I'm jealous of someone because he's met some zombie who shot himself and became a teenage cult hero? I once met someone who knew someone who once met Jimi Hendrix. Big deal."

"Oh, so you know who Kurt Cobain is?"

"I know who he *was*." Jimmy brushed the hair back from his forehead, drummed his fingertips on the table. "I think I'll go see how Charlotte is."

"Well, that's a first," Amy mumbled.

"What?"

"Nothing."

"Fine. I've got a headache. After I've seen Charlotte I think I'll crash out myself."

"Great. A family of crash test dummies."

That was the most absurd conversation I've ever had with him, Amy thought as she stared at his retreating back. Why can't he admit that he's jealous of Alex? If we could talk about it rationally, it might help. As it is, he's lashing out at me with all that anger and I'm the one who least deserves it. And suddenly he decides to pay attention to Charlotte. But when? When he knows she's asleep. Terrific.

"He doesn't love us," she said out loud. The release she felt actually speaking the words surprised her. "I made a big mistake. He only cares about Zoey and Rachel. He's not attracted to me. He hates Charlotte. I've made a mistake. I am *so* pissed off."

She felt herself relaxing slightly. Why? Was Beth right, did expressed anger actually help a difficult situation? Maybe. Maybe Beth was right about everything, after all. That would be a turn up for the books. Amy had spent the past six years trying to put down anchors while Beth sailed willfully into gales. And look at the outcome: Amy, twice-

married, working in the lower echelons in neuroscience—
hardly a well-paid career—sitting in her house admitting
that she'd screwed up on yet another major life decision.
Beth, happily single, raking up the bucks from willing clients, watching as everyone else's life collapsed. Or something like that. Amy shook her head to try to clear it, but
the thoughts wouldn't budge. Beth was happy. Beth hadn't
made any major mistakes. Maybe she'd left a gang of unhappy people trailing in her wake, but she was content in
herself. She could say exactly what she wanted to say to
anyone, their father included.

How many times in their teens had Amy stood by cring-
ing as Beth laid into Mark with vicious, wounding remarks?
She'd toss her blond hair, fling some insult at him, walk
off and leave Amy and Meg and Leo to try to make peace.
Meg tried the hardest and always failed. She'd heap compliments on her father that he brushed off with exasperation. Amy and Leo, after witnessing Meg's failure, retreated
upstairs to watch television together. And Mark, whatever
time of day or night it might be, walked out of the house.
Beth would poke her head into Amy's room after an hour
or so, unfazed.

"So Dad's flown the coop again," she'd snort. "The consummate chicken."

It never seemed to bother Beth that she was the one
who'd driven him away. If Amy had the nerve to point this
out to her, she'd smirk and say: "If he doesn't like to reap
the whirlwind, he shouldn't have sown it in the first place."

Amy and Leo would then exchange a knowing glance
and keep their mouths shut. That was always the best policy
when in Beth's presence.

So—Amy thought, as she heard Jimmy close the door
to Charlotte's room and move down the hall to their own
bedroom—so maybe honesty is the best policy and I should
go to our room and confront Jimmy and tell him how much
I resent his attitude to Charlotte and to me. Tell him he has
to change. He has to love us as much as he loves his first
family. Or else.

Absolutely. And then tomorrow I can discover exactly what is the chemical cause of schizophrenia, develop a drug to cure it and win the Nobel Prize.

Amy stood up, preparing to go and check on the sleeping Charlotte. After she'd tucked her daughter in, she'd talk to Jimmy and try to work things out without issuing any kind of ultimatum. Of course he must be jealous of Alex's relationship with Zoey; that was understandable. If Patrick had shown up with a wife-to-be who took Charlotte to concerts and introduced her to famous stars, Amy would be consumed with envy. Jimmy's reaction was a human one and it was her job to help him come to terms with it.

For reasons she could never explain to herself afterward, Amy stopped in midstride and changed direction. Instead of going straight to Charlotte's room, she walked to the front hall and pressed her forehead against the freezing windowpane, gazing out into the night.

The figure sitting on the wall across the street, blowing clouds of air visible under the street lamp, waved at her and beckoned. She threw on an old jacket hanging from the coatrack and stepped out, closing the door quietly behind her.

"The Person from Porlock," Patrick said, grinning, as he came up the front steps. "Asking you out to play."

"Are you stalking me?"

"I guess you could call it that." He sat down on the top step, patted the empty space next to him. "Come on, play hooky. Freeze your butt off beside me."

"Okay. I will. For a second." She tried not to look at him. She didn't want that physical tug.

"What does Charlotte want for Christmas?"

"Jesus, Patrick. What am I supposed to say to that? A father?"

"I'd like to see her, Amy. I know that decision should be up to you, so I'm asking you now. Can I?"

"I don't know." Amy shook her head. She saw his profile and closed her eyes. This was too difficult, much too difficult. He was far too attractive.

"Do you think I'd ruin her life?"

Amy concentrated on the sliver of the moon above her. It looked like the end of a fingernail after a French manicure. Meg had a French manicure mania. Beth teased her about it mercilessly.

"Is that really what you think?" Patrick persisted.

During the first year after Patrick had disappeared, Amy, when she wasn't crying, had rehearsed a showdown with her husband. It would take place whenever he came back. She would sit him down opposite her and grill him until she got the truth concerning what had gone wrong, why he had left. She would be rational throughout, of course. Coherent and in control, approaching it like a scientific experiment, step-by-step.

The only problem with this scenario was the fact that Patrick hadn't come back. Until now. And now she felt as if she'd been woken up in the middle of the night to find a stranger standing over her bed. She was so panicked, no words could escape her mouth. She looked down and saw the bulky army boots she was wearing. Why did she have to have those on *now?* Now, when Patrick was finally here. She should have been dressed in some femme fatale outfit. Instead she was clad in these damned boots, old corduroy trousers and a sweatshirt of Jimmy's. And she still had the secretarial haircut.

"Ames—" Patrick put his hand to her cheek and pressed it gently. "I don't want to hurt Charlotte. You know that."

"I don't know anything." Amy shook her head again. She felt a welling in the pit of her stomach. Then the floodgates burst. "I don't know a fucking thing. Why did you leave? Why didn't you tell me you were going to leave instead of writing that stupid note? I get contacted by your lawyer about a divorce, you send Charlotte pretty little postcards and you never tell me. You never tell me anything. Was our sex life lousy or something? Were there things I wasn't good at in bed? Had you met someone else? Were you just plain bored? Did you hate me? What? What did I do wrong? Just tell me what the hell happened."

Patrick removed his hand from her cheek and put his arm around her shoulder.

"Nothing happened, Ames. You didn't do anything wrong. I couldn't stay, that's all. You know me. I couldn't have settled down into a routine life with a routine job, I—"

"I don't want to hear this shit. I really don't."

"What *do* you want to hear, then?"

"I don't know." Amy wasn't crying but she was shaking, trembling all over. "Nothing, I guess. There's nothing you can say that will ever make me feel better."

"I could tell you about some of the miserable times I've had," Patrick said smiling. "That might cheer you up."

Amy couldn't check a small laugh.

"Should I tell you about the time I was thrown in jail in Delhi? You'd love that one. I *really* suffered."

"Patrick. Please. Don't make me laugh. It's not fair."

They sat in silence for a few minutes. I'll get pneumonia, Amy thought. I'll die because of a clandestine talk with my ex-husband.

"You know what Beth said when you left? She said 'Now you can be a hundred percent scientifically sure that oil and water don't mix.' "

"Sounds like vintage Beth. I had a drink with her earlier."

Of course, Amy thought. I should have known.

"What did she say? Did she tell you how much disdain she has for Jimmy?"

"Jimmy?"

"My husband, Patrick."

"Oh. No. All she said about him was that he looks a little like André Agassi."

"Really? I suppose he does. Without the long hair and the earrings and the beard."

"Something like that. You're both way behind the times, though. He's cut his hair off—probably for Brooke Shields. Do you think she's a modern-day Delilah?"

"As my stepdaughter would say—care factor?"

"Sorry. I know we're supposed to be having a serious

conversation." Patrick shrugged. "Maybe I'm a little nervous. Beth told me that you'd built a new life for yourself and I shouldn't ruin it."

"Beth never thought I was good enough for you. She never thought I was interesting enough."

"Beth doesn't know you, that's all. And she never understood us. She thinks she has X-ray vision, but her perception is so focused she's blinkered peripherally. As a result, she misses out on a lot."

"I've never thought of it that way."

"Well, you should, Ames. I'm surprised you haven't overcome your Beth problem by now. Take her as she is. Just don't listen to anything she has to say because it's distorted. She's got so much anger and resentment, she's paralyzed. So she runs around trying to paralyze everyone else. At least that's the way she used to operate. And my bet is, she hasn't changed. But listen, I don't want to screw up your life, I really don't. Beth might be right about that."

"You have a right to see your daughter," Amy countered.

"Even though I bolted?"

"You're not a horse, Patrick. You're Charlotte's father and you have a right to see her. If I'm honest I'd say that I want to show her off to you. She's kind of frenetic, but she's lovely. Truly lovely. She deserves to have a father's attention."

"Wouldn't your husband—wouldn't Jimmy mind? Would he resent me for invading his territory?"

"Jimmy doesn't—Jimmy isn't possessive of Charlotte."

"Is he possessive of you?"

"No."

"So he wouldn't mind us sitting out here talking like this?"

"I don't think so. Maybe. I'm not sure."

"Where is he now?"

"In our room. He's got a headache so he went to bed early."

"I see. Propitious for me." Patrick pulled his hands to

his mouth and blew on them. "But listen, before we both go into shock and develop hypothermia from exposure to these sub-zero temperatures, I should tell you that I got a job bartending at the Casa B this afternoon and I'm staying with a friend up on Beacon Hill. Here's the number—" He pulled a piece of paper out of his pocket and handed it to her. "Call me. We can arrange a time for you to bring Charlotte by if you meant what you said."

Standing up, he pushed his hands deep into his coat pockets.

"If you change your mind, let me know. Whatever happens, I'd still like to see *you*, Ames. We have a lot of catching up to do." He cocked his head to the side and grinned. "And by the way, for your information, if I were still your husband I wouldn't let a little thing like a headache send me to bed without you."

Amy continued sitting on the step long after Patrick's figure had disappeared from view. Her brain was racing in so many different directions no coherent thought could emerge.

Neural physiologists had done experiments differentiating the areas of the brain that respond when a person talks silently to himself from the ones that leap into activity when a person is actually spoken to by others. This had been helpful when studying schizophrenia, for a common characteristic of schizophrenics is auditory hallucinations. When a schizophrenic "hears" voices talking to him, which part of the brain is firing? Recently researchers had been trying to establish scientifically what anyone with common sense would guess: that an auditory hallucination sets off the same part of the brain as the one that is fired when someone is talking to himself, that the "voices" are actually the schizophrenic's own inner voice. A man Amy worked with had taped a schizophrenic speaking, distorted the tape and played it back to him. Instead of saying, as a normal person would, "What have you done to my voice?" the man had claimed that the voice on the tape was the "devil."

As she tried to sort through all the voices clamoring for

attention in her brain, Amy wondered whether she could distinguish her own. As yet, no neuroscientist had been able to locate the place in the brain where the "self" resides. They knew where "will" was, but "will" was an entirely different entity to "self." Or was it?

When she heard the sound of her own teeth chattering, it took her a minute to recognize that this wasn't some auditory hallucination. It was a purely physical response to freezing temperatures. She rose and went inside the house. Walking straight to Charlotte's room, she kissed the top of her sleeping daughter's head, whispered "I love you" and nestled her into her sheets and blanket.

The night-light in the shape of a frog cast a low glow and Amy remained sitting on Charlotte's bed, gazing at the walls covered with Patrick's postcards, the little girl's dressing table, the toys piled in the corner. You could chart a child's life through its toys, Amy reflected. They were almost more revealing than snapshots. There were the Lego blocks Charlotte had gone crazy over when she was four, there were the stuffed frogs she'd had a passion for at five, there were the dinky musical instruments she'd developed a mania for at six—all abandoned now, never used or played with. Charlotte had moved on to Barbie dolls. Amy couldn't wait for this phase to end; Ken and Barbie seemed to her figures that, if they came to life, would be scarier than any of the horrors in the *Nightmare on Elm Street* movies. Finally, Amy's eyes stopped on a xylophone shoved against the far wall. Patrick had brought that home a month after Charlotte was born.

"You're crazy," Amy had laughed when he opened it proudly. "Charlotte can't play with that thing now. She won't be able to for a while yet."

"Well, then, for the first time, you can accuse me of thinking of the future," he'd replied.

And the next morning, he had woken Amy up by tapping her on the ribs with the rubber-ended sticks, singing "Hey Jude" as he played up and down her rib cage.

Amy kissed Charlotte again, stood up and left the room,

shutting the door noiselessly behind her. For a moment she leaned against the closed door, but she was no nearer any logical thought process than she had been since Patrick wandered off into the night.

Jimmy was asleep on his side of the bed. At least she wouldn't have to lie to him. Not yet. After changing, brushing her teeth and putting a conditioning cream on her face, she climbed in beside her husband.

I feel like an adulteress, she thought, staring up at a ceiling she couldn't quite make out in the dark, starting an inner dialogue she knew would lead into regions best left unexplored.

Have I betrayed Jimmy?

I was close, so close to following Patrick when he left, catching up with him and saying: "Take me with you. Wherever you go, take me with you. Don't leave me again."

Okay, I didn't, but it's the thought that counts, isn't it?

If Jimmy told me that he was on the verge of running off with Rachel again, what would I say? Would I forgive him because he hadn't actually done it, or refuse to forgive him for even considering it?

What do I do now?

Do I let Patrick see Charlotte or not?

Am I falling in love yet again with my irresponsible, hopeless first husband?

Did I ever fall out of love with him?

Jimmy shifted slightly beside her.

Should I wake him up and tell him everything? Tell him about Patrick?

No, Amy decided. It wasn't his business. It was hers.

Chapter Fourteen

"IT SOUNDS CRAZY, I know, but I'd rather have Beth against us than with us."

"Why?" Nick stopped massaging Leo's feet and moved up the bed to sit beside her.

"Because you'd understand everything I've told you about her if she's on the rampage. But now, when you meet her, she'll turn on the charm and you'll look at me as if I were a head case. Then you'll try to explain to me how much I've misunderstood her over the years."

"Is Beth that potent a seductress?"

"When she chooses to be, yes. I've seen it all before. I watched Patrick fall under her influence. He laughed at everything she said. It used to kill Amy."

"And you think I'm just as easily taken in?"

"Oh, Nick. *Everyone* is. Even I am. You watch. When we go out for this dinner, I'll sit there and laugh with her too. I'll forget all the times she's been brutal to people I love and I'll melt—along with you and all the others."

"Does that include Charlie?"

"Beth never sets her sights on Charlie. His mere presence offends her. But he'll go along with her as well. He doesn't get what she's talking about, all her jokes fly right by him, but he pretends to understand."

"And Jimmy?"

"She sort of tolerates Jimmy. He doesn't say much, and sometimes he looks at her as if she'd recently been released from the Betty Ford Clinic, but most of the time he simply watches and listens with a bemused expression on his face."

"So what do you want me to do? It sounds like I'll be in trouble with you whatever my response to Beth is."

"You're right." Leo picked up a pillow and hugged it.

"You can't win. And I can't figure out what's happened to change her mind about us. It sounded as if she'd have a minister come to the table and marry us right there in the restaurant if it were possible."

"I wish it were."

"I don't think Jackie would be too pleased about that prospect. Or Thea."

"Leonora—" Nick grabbed the pillow from her, turned her face to him. "Jackie is *my* problem. So is Thea. Let me handle them."

"You told me you'd given my number to Thea. Why hasn't she called you?"

"Thea is reserved. She lives in a world of her own; even I don't have access to it. And it's been that way since birth, not since I began seeing you. I adore her, but she's very remote. From her mother too."

"Does she like her ballet classes?"

"No," Nick grimaced. "They're a concession to Jackie who once harbored hopes of being a prima ballerina herself. It's not worth the friction it would cause Thea to give them up."

"What *is* Thea interested in?"

"Her friends. She has a gang of friends at school, always has had. The teachers often tell us how popular she is and I, for one, find that hard to reconcile with her character when she's at home. The older she gets, the less time she spends with us. She's always off with friends. When she *is* at home, she spends most of her time in her room by herself, or talking on the telephone to her buddies."

"She doesn't bring them back to your house?"

"No. She goes to theirs." Nick's grimace deepened. "This is making me sound like a terrible father. All I said last night about being frightened of losing her—it was true, but what I didn't say is that I feel I've lost her already. You know, I've never seen her cry."

"Never? Not even when she was a baby?"

"No, not even then. We took her to the doctor, actually. We thought something was terribly wrong with her because she never cried. He told us she was fine and that we should count our blessings." Nick paused. "There have been occasions when I've even entertained the idea of spying on Thea. Going to her friend's house while she was there and watching her through a window to see what she's really like. That's pretty sick, isn't it?"

"No." Leo shook her head. "It's sad."

"So tell me what I'm supposed to do, will you? How can I get through to her?"

"I don't know. There's the fantasy scenario, of course. She sees how happy we are together and she comes out of her shell. I become her new best friend."

"Well, you're a hell of a lot closer to her age than—"

"Stop right there, Nick. What you're talking about has nothing to do with age, and you know it."

"All right. But at least you might be able to tune in to her wavelength a little more effectively than I can."

"And if I don't? What if she hates me?"

"She won't."

"Nick, I've watched Meg with her two stepsons over the years and I've seen how difficult a relationship it can be. They loathed her at first; they refused to speak to her, treated her like dirt. It's been better recently, but it's been a long haul. Even now, they're a hell of a lot nicer to me than to Meg. She must be a constant reminder to them of the pain they went through when Charlie and Helen split up. I'm not sure they'll ever really get over it.

"Why should Thea like me? She may not feel she's had a happy home life, but that doesn't mean she welcomes a rupture to the status quo. And the fact that I am so much younger than you is more likely to hurt than to help. You know, sometimes I think Beth was dying for Dad to get remarried so she could focus all her anger on a stepmother. It's a natural instinct, I think, no matter what your relationship has been with your mother."

"It will work out. If we both try hard and have a lot of patience."

"But we're starting out with all these strikes against us.

That's what worries me. When two people get married, there's supposed to be an aura of happiness surrounding the event, all these well-wishers hoping for the best. Who will be at *our* wedding? If Thea's there will she be sulking in a corner, shooting me evil looks? Will Jackie turn up and cause some scene? It seems such a terrible way to begin a new life."

"Am I robbing you of a dream wedding, Leonora? Am I taking away all your fantasies?" Nick reached over and grabbed her hand. "I am, aren't I?"

"Sometimes I feel unclean. That's all."

"And I've made you feel that way."

"The circumstances have. I thought I could handle the complications. But when it comes down to it, it's a lot more complicated than I ever imagined."

"Do you want to call a halt to it? Is that what you're saying? I thought we talked this all through yesterday. I thought we were all right."

"I don't know." Leo pressed her hand into Nick's. "I thought we were too. But I still have some of the same reservations. I mean, you must have loved Jackie. I know you did. And I know you tried to explain to me what went wrong, but I keep thinking—if it went so wrong with her, when you didn't have any of these problems to begin with, when it was straightforward, what will happen with *me* when things get tricky? And they're bound to get tricky, Nick. This isn't going to be smooth sailing. It's going to be rough. Really rough."

"There's one major difference. You and I can talk. Jackie and I could only shout."

"Would you write me letters if I went away?"

"What?"

"Would you write to me if I went away?"

"If you went away? Where are you going?"

"I don't know. But I think it might be a good idea. I think I need some time to myself."

"Oh God, Leonora. I'm losing you again. We began by talking about Beth's so-called engagement party for us and now you're planning to leave me. I don't think I can stand this." He took his hand away and began to hit his knee. "Don't do this. Please. Jackie's leaving to go to England at the end of the week. She'll be out of our way for a while, at least. And then you can meet Thea and judge for yourself how difficult she will be. Don't rush to any judgments. You *might* get along. Jackie might find Mr. Perfect in London and run off to the South of France with him. Anything could happen. Don't go away because you foresee some kind of disaster. You're not psychic, you know. Just give me a chance. Remember, I'm the one who tried to leave you before and you brought me back. Let me bring you back now. It's only fair."

"I don't know what's fair to anyone anymore. Nick—" She put her hand on her forehead as if she were feeling for a fever. "After Jackie left that night, I was upset and confused. Now I'm just confused. I remember how unhappy you looked that first time I saw you at Dunkin' Donuts. I don't want to be the cause of that same kind of pain. And I really don't know if I'm strong enough to go through what we're going to have to face together. Why can't you leave Jackie and be on your own for a while, see what it's like not to have a woman in your life?"

"How long is 'a while' Leonora? Weeks? Months? Years? I don't want to be on my own. I want to be with you. What if I get run over by a bus when I'm in my 'waiting' period? How would you feel then? You don't understand how little time is left—you're too young, you don't know that time is finite."

"I'm perfectly aware that people die." Leo threw the covers off and got out of bed. "Saying that *you* might is a ridiculous form of emotional blackmail." She went and took her dressing gown from the hook on her bedroom door, and wrapped it around her. "I'm beginning to feel claustrophobic in this room. We seem to have spent the last two days in here talking about nothing but 'us.' Going around in circles. What's happened to normal life, Nick?"

"It's on hold for the moment, that's all." He reached for

a cigarette. His face was creased, his lips formed a thin line of misery.

"Let's get out of here. I feel like I'm in a foxhole, waiting for the bombs to drop. Let's get out."

"It's past midnight," Nick protested.

"I know."

"Where do you want to go?"

"Come on," she said, walking over to him and grabbing his hands, pulling him up. "I'll show you a slice of my past. We'll put on some warm clothes. I'll find a flashlight."

"You'll end up killing me, you know that?"

"Maybe." Leo stood on her tiptoes and kissed him. "Maybe not."

Nick peered through the window at the empty sentry box on his right.

"What's that for? To keep out undesirables?"

"Absolutely. Look at the sign hanging over there: 'The Country Club.' Not any old country club, but *the* Country Club. This place is ritzy. They don't want any run-of-the-mill people coming in here. Only fee-paying, socially acceptable members."

"That's right. I used to hear about it. In my day they didn't accept Jews or blacks, I remember. Don't tell me you're a member of this place."

"No. But my parents were. I don't know if Dad still is. I should ask him sometime. We used to come here in the summer to swim. We didn't think in political terms in those days, all we thought about was the pool. That's where we're heading now. There's a golf course to the right and left of us. In the daytime you have to be careful driving or you'll get a golf ball through the window. Head around to the right here. That's the main clubhouse on the left. We used to have dancing lessons in there."

"You can dance? I mean old-fashioned dancing?"

"I'm a whiz at the waltz. I have many hidden talents, Nick."

"You have many talents, indeed, Leonora. Some aren't so hidden. Where do we go now?"

"Drive up that little hill and we'll park here. The pool's in front of us, over there. But that's not where we're going."

"Thank God for that. I thought you were going to tell me you are one of those people who swim in Arctic temperatures for the fun of it. Another hidden talent."

"Nope, come on. This is where the flashlight comes in."

Leonora got out of the Honda, zipped up her parka, pulled a woolen hat over her head and put on a pair of mittens.

"Wrap up. It's going to be freezing and we've got a ways to go."

"And I've got promises to keep. And miles to go before I sleep," Nick murmured.

"You sound like Patrick. He always used to quote poetry."

"I suppose I should be flattered," Nick said, buttoning up his jacket. "But I'm not sure I want to be compared to the rogue Patrick. He strikes me, from what you've said, as being solipsistic to the core."

"Patrick may be a lot of things, but he's not *anything* to the core."

"Which is his problem?"

"Which is the problem of everyone who comes into close contact with him."

"Boy, you can be razor-edged sometimes, Leonora. I wouldn't want be on the other end of that kind of judgment. Sliced to ribbons."

"No, listen, I like Patrick. But he's one of those men you take one look at and think: either I fall in love and throw myself over a cliff for this guy, or I treat him as a friend only and live a happy life."

"I thought Amy was more sensible than to get involved with someone like that."

They were walking down a path, Leonora leading Nick and pointing their way through the dark with her flashlight.

"Watch out—there's a bunker right here. Amy doesn't want to be sensible all the time and I don't blame her. Patrick was a kind of escape for her—a way out of the family, out of all the responsibilities she'd taken on. Out of everything, including her own feeling that she's not exciting enough. Amy has never understood just how wonderful she is. And Patrick was romance incarnate, until he left. Look—see that wooden building through the trees—we're almost there."

"Almost where? Did you conduct Satanic rituals in the middle of the golf course? What's that building doing there?"

"We're off the course now. Into the lovely dark and deep woods. And that's the skating house. Come on—I'll show you."

Nick stumbled after Leo as she plowed through the woods, training her light on the building in front of them. He could make out the vague shape of an extended log cabin.

"Looks like Abe Lincoln country here. Where are we? In a different century?"

"Yes. That's exactly where we are." Leonora grabbed him by the arm and propelled him forward to the cabin. "See the room on the left—that's where you put your skates on. And over here to the right is where we used to have skating parties on Friday nights. I bet they still have them." She dragged him through a wooden door frame, into a room in the middle of which a few benches were scattered.

"See that huge fireplace? We'd huddle around that, drinking hot chocolate after we'd been skating for hours. And over there—" She pointed to the far corner. "They're still there. I don't believe it. Those big green wood chairs with runners. You can take people out on the ice in them. Wrap up tiny kids or people too old to skate and take them out for a turn in one of those. Like a wheelchair on ice."

Nick stamped his feet to get his circulation going and looked out the window of the cabin.

"Is that where you skated?"

"Yes. You can't see it clearly in the dark, but it's a beautiful pond. And they have lights to illuminate the skating area in the night. You could skate in the days of course, too. There's a makeshift ice hockey rink at the far end of the pond. But it was unbelievably fun at night."

Nick took the flashlight from Leo's hand and turned it on her face.

"Look at you—pure joy. Did you fall in love here for the first time? Is that what's making your eyes shine so?"

"No. If you want to know, the first time I fell in love was with one of the lifeguards at the pool. This place is so special because—"

"Hold on. I want to hear about this lifeguard."

"His name was Michael. Incredibly attractive. Tan, blond, the whole bit. I was twelve and pretty shy. All the teenage girls who hung around used to go up to him in their bikinis and flirt with him and I'd watch from a distance. I guess he was eighteen or so. He seemed ancient to me—of course nowhere near as ancient as you are. You're supposed to laugh at that, Nick, not wince.

"Anyway, once I was sitting on my own by the diving boards, watching him perform these acrobatic dives. You know, doing three somersaults in the air before landing perfectly, all that—I thought he could have been an Olympic gold medalist. After one of these dives, he came out of the pool, shook himself off and walked up to me. 'Hey, I hear your name is Leonora. My sister's Leonora too.' I nodded and smiled. He walked off.

"That was the extent of my passionate first love. He never said anything else to me and I never dared talk to him. By the next summer, he'd gone. My heart was broken for about three hours."

"I'm glad to know how enduring your love is."

"I'm not going to acknowledge the gibe. The point about this place"—Leo retrieved the flashlight from Nick, shone it around the room—"is that everyone was always happy here."

"Weren't they just as happy cavorting around the pool, flirting with hunky lifeguards?"

"No. The atmosphere was different at the pool, more competitive. Here it didn't matter if you could skate well or what your figure looked like—after all, we were swamped in winter clothes. There's something wonderful about being outdoors in the cold, I think. It brings people together. We all laughed a lot. Also, there were so many days we couldn't skate, when the pond hadn't completely frozen over. We'd have to call first and ask if the skating was on, so the enjoyment was never guaranteed. That made it even more special. And this place *is* out of another century. See—" she directed her light at the walls. "Look at those black-and-white pictures of old skaters. Women in long skirts. Men skating with them, their arms around their waists. They look—I don't know what the right word is—I guess I'd say 'dashing.' Nothing has changed. No video games or CD players. Just the pond and this log cabin. That's all anyone ever needed."

"You and I should come here sometime and skate," Nick said, putting his arm around her waist. "We can be dashing together."

"I'd love that. I haven't been here since I was fourteen. I miss it."

"Why did you stop coming? Did you start to object to the politics of this club?"

"I wish I could say I did," Leo sighed. "Because I do. Even though the admittance policy has changed considerably—as you can imagine. No, I stopped coming purely from embarrassment. One Saturday morning I came over on my own—took the bus and then walked here, and I was surprised that no one seemed to be here. I hadn't called first, because I'd been skating the night before, and the temperature, as far as I could tell, was still cold enough to keep the pond frozen. So I put my little white skates on, laced them up and set off across the pond happily. About forty feet out, I began to hear some creaking noises, like the ones you hear in an old house at night, but I didn't pay any attention. Not until I heard this voice over a mega-phone, a male voice, shouting at me to get the hell off the ice. It wasn't thick enough. It was cracking under my weight.

"He was shouting at me, screaming, telling me to come back immediately. 'You're on thin ice,' he kept yelling. 'Get back now.'

"I turned around, terrified, and crying. Put my head down and skated as quickly as I could back to this cabin, scared at every step that I was going to fall through. When I finally got back, he was glaring at me, this man. I don't know who he was, I didn't recognize him. I rushed to take my skates off and get out of here. I never came back. Until now."

Nick sat down on one of the benches, took a cigarette and lighter out of his pocket.

"Why do I think you're trying to tell me something with that story, Leonora? Is that what this trip was all about?"

"What do you mean?"

"Come on, you start off by describing this place to me as some version of paradise"—he bent over and lit the cig-arette—"and then end up by saying that you were effec-tively thrown out of paradise for skating on thin ice. No—sorry—you *chose* to leave paradise because you had skated on thin ice. Which is exactly what you think you're doing with me, isn't it? Skating on thin ice."

"Maybe you're reading too much into it."

"Maybe I'm not."

"I *thought* I was answering your question, not giving you a parable to apply to us. But if you think there was some subconscious motive in this trip, you might be right. I've remembered things recently that make me realize that I rush into potentially dangerous situations without thinking properly sometimes, that's all."

"Dangerous situations? Does that category include mar-riage to me?"

"I didn't say that. But if you insist on talking about us and our marriage, okay. I'm not sure exactly why we're getting married. I don't understand why we shouldn't live together for a while."

"We *are* living together. We'll live together until my divorce comes through."

"I meant after that."

"I see."

"When you proposed to me, I said yes without thinking."

"I suppose I had the old-fashioned notion that people who love each other the way we do should get married at the first possible opportunity." Nick dropped his cigarette on the floor, ground it out with his shoe. "Getting married is a risk, I know. A risk I want to take. You want to live together until the right time arrives for our wedding—fine. But I'm worried that your idea of the right time is like your memory of this place. A perfect time, when everyone is happy. Perhaps those perfect times can exist in a place like this when you're a little girl skating along happily, but I'm not sure those ideal times can happen in the kind of world we live in. There is always going to be a risk, Leonora, and complications. Of one kind or another. Are you going to balk like this at every problem?"

"No. Don't you see how many problems there are now, though? What if we did get married as soon as possible and crashed and burned as a result? I'd always think that we had gone too fast, that if we'd waited, we might have had a better chance. It's my fault, I know. I'm too impulsive and it scares me."

"Too impulsive? That's one of your qualities I most admire. You have great instincts and you run with them. What's wrong with that? All right—don't bother to answer. I can see that you're determined to be careful now. And I know I can't afford to be dogmatic about this, Leonora. Nor do I want to be. I'll wait, if that's what you want. And if you want to go away by yourself for a while, I'll wait for you to come back." He grimaced. "I don't have any choice."

"Do you think I'm being unreasonable?" Leo sat down beside him, took off her mitten and reached for his hand.

"No. Not in the least. I think I've probably been out of my mind to believe this would all go off as I hoped it would."

"Why won't you look at me, Nick?"

"You're pointing that flashlight right in my eyes. I couldn't see you if I tried. I'm like the proverbial rabbit caught in the proverbial headlights."

"Sorry." She lowered the light. "Is that better?"

"Well, now I'm not blinded, but I'm freezing. Let's leave."

"I'm sorry, Nick."

"Don't apologize for being more grown up than I am. And don't worry, I won't be peevish and petulant for more than five minutes." He stood up, coughed. "So what are we supposed to do about this engagement party, then?"

"We don't have to do anything. I want you to meet all the family together. We don't have to tell them we're not getting married right away. What I've said doesn't mean we're not going to—just that we'll wait a bit. And I want you to know that I wasn't planning this. That's not why I brought you here. It just happened that way."

"Shit happens." Nick shrugged. "It could have been worse. You could have told me to take a walk out on that pond and carefully carved a hole in the ice around me as I was listening to you reminisce."

"Nick. Please don't be angry."

"I was *trying* to be funny."

Leo bent down, retrieved the cigarette butt from the floor, put it in her jacket pocket.

"Leave things as you found them, as my father used to say," she said, standing up.

"He didn't manage to leave your mother as he found her, did he?"

"You can never leave a person the way you found him or her," Leo said softly. "Not if you make any kind of impact on their lives. You can hope only that you leave them for the better. In Dad's case, he didn't have much of a chance. Don't judge him until you've met him, okay?"

"Okay. I didn't mean to be nasty with that comment. I'm the last one to criticize another person's marriage. It was"—Nick smiled feebly—"an impulsive remark."

"There are much better ways to be impulsive," Leo stated, returning his smile. "Let's go back to bed and get warm." As she set off, she paused, looking over her shoulder at Nick. "Sometimes all I wish for in life is that you'd never been married before."

She saw him hang his head and shake it.

"At the moment *I* wish I'd never developed a passion for Dunkin' Donuts coffee. I think they spike the stuff with some kind of crazy love potion, I really do. The way I feel about you isn't normal. From now on I'm going to drink herbal tea and develop a Buddhist philosophy. Are you ready for a speech about illusion versus reality?"

"Keep drinking the coffee," Leo said, shining her flashlight into the trees.

Chapter Fifteen

THE WORLD HAD turned upside down, Meg decided, and she was the only person who hadn't turned with it.

There was Beth, happily chatting with Nick as if they'd been friends for years; there was Amy, who seemed to have lost ten pounds in two days, decked out in a low-cut, glamorous dark blue velvet number, looking like a beauty rather than brains expert; and there was Mark, beaming with pleasure, presiding over the proceedings as if he had transformed himself into a latter-day Spencer Tracy figure in *Father of the Bride*. Leo, it's true, still *looked* the same, but her demeanor was so mature it was almost frightening. Meg hadn't seen her put her hand to her earlobe once. Or frown, for that matter. Jimmy was uncharacteristically voluble and kept cracking jokes, while Charlie sat in a seeming stupor.

At least she knew the reason for Charlie's silence, Meg thought. He'd announced to her in the car, on the way to the restaurant, that he'd found out his chief rival for the presidency of Harvard was a hotshot from California. A female hotshot with all the right qualifications.

"They'll appoint *her*," he muttered darkly. "First female president of Harvard. What a coup in these politically correct days. She's a shoo-in. I made some calls to colleagues in California. Apparently she's a nightmare. A nightmare woman." Meg had long since figured out that any female Charlie didn't think worth daydreaming about was a "nightmare woman."

"I'm sure," Meg tried to console him, "that whoever gets the job will be the best qualified person."

"We're *equally* qualified, Meg. But she has the ace up her skirt. You know what Freud would have been talking about if he were alive these days? In this country? Vagina envy. Who wants to have a penis and balls now? What are they there for? To get kicked."

"I think you're overreacting."

"Wait and see," he said glumly. "I'm dead in the water. A dead white male."

Charlie was doing a great job of brooding, Meg concluded, as she watched him pick at his food, although no one else seemed to notice. Beth was too busy grilling Nick about his wife. A strange topic to be pursuing on first acquaintance, but Beth was relentless. Where did Jackie grow up? Where had she gone to college? What did she do now? How did she get her job? Meg saw Nick look over to Leo once or twice during this interrogation and get a half-smile and a little go-with-the-flow shrug in reply. When Beth pressed on with "Tell me, though—what's Jackie most frightened of?" Nick looked truly ill at ease. "I don't know," he answered. "Her shadow, I suppose. Like all of us."

Meg laughed dutifully at one Jimmy's Newt Gingrich jokes, but was still eavesdropping on Beth, who leaned back in her chair, took a large gulp of wine and said: "Don't evade the question, Nick Booth. You must know. So why not tell your future sister-in-law?"

"Nick—" Meg quickly put in. He was on her left, Jimmy on her right. Nick needed her a lot more than Jimmy did. "Tell me. Are you a fisherman like Dad?"

Her father, sitting between Leo and Amy, must have been paying peripheral attention to Nick as well, for his head snapped up at this question, and his gray eyes zeroed in on Nick, waiting for his reply.

"When I was younger I fished a lot, yes. It's been a long time since I picked up a rod, though."

"We'll have to get you started again," Mark said, his voice traveling easily across the round table.

"Our father is a master angler," Beth cut in. "He knows *all* the angles. And exactly how to use his rod."

Meg saw Amy roll her eyes at Leo. Life was getting back to normal.

"Mark." Charlie deigned to speak. "Have you heard of a woman named Harriet Harwood?"

"No." Mark shook his head. "I can't say that I have."

"Oh." Now he was staring at his plate again. Meg wanted to murder him. This was a family dinner, a family dinner in Leo's honor and all Charlie could think of was himself. The rest of the table stared at Charlie, waiting for him to go on, but he was silent.

"Isn't Harriet Harwood the cause célèbre at Stanford? I think I read an article on her in our paper a while ago." Nick commented, looking at Charlie, who was to the left of Beth. "Do you know her?"

"No. I don't know her. I don't want to know her."

"She's in the running for the presidency of Harvard," Meg explained. "Charlie is a little worried that she might get it because she's a woman."

"What's wrong with that?" Beth asked, turning to Charlie. "Should she be disqualified because she's a female?"

"I never said that," Charlie barked. "I don't think she should get preferential treatment, that's all."

Beth put her hand on Charlie's arm, pulled it away quickly.

"Oooh. Sizzling male. Touchy subject. What do you think?" She eyed everyone else in a circular sweep. "Should we have a huge argument here about male/female rights and end up breaking chairs over one another's heads in this bastion of Boston, the oldest, most respectable restaurant in the city? That would be fun. Or should we politely retreat from the fray and ask each other anodyne questions? What's your favorite color, Jimmy? Don't tell me, it's plaid. Christ, where's the wine waiter when you need him? Sorry—him or *her*."

"He's right behind you, Beth." Mark sighed.

"Well, thank God for big favors."

"Do you enjoy working at the *Globe*?" Mark asked Nick.

"Now *there's* an original question," Beth snorted.

"Beth. Please. Tonight was your idea. There's no need to be difficult."

"Tonight *was* my idea, Dad. And I had hoped for some intelligent, fun discussion. Remember when you sent us to dancing school? The old dragon who ran the show used to tell us that we had to ask our partners where they went to school, how many brothers and sisters they had, what sports they liked—we'd have to fit in all these riveting questions before the music stopped. And then she'd quiz us to see if we'd done our bit. 'Freddie goes to Dexter, he has one brother and he just adores football.' Spare me."

"I used to hate that place. I could never do the cha-cha-cha," Amy laughed, looking at Mark. "I used to crack up every time she would start with the 'One-two-cha-cha-cha.' I can't believe you sent us there."

"Leo was the only one who could actually dance." Meg began to laugh as well. "I used to step on these guys' feet the whole time. When it was 'ladies' choice' the boys scattered as far away from me as they could get."

"It was antediluvian, Dad. What made you sign us up for that, anyway?" Leo smiled across at Nick, then turned to Mark.

"I suppose it was fairly ridiculous," Mark admitted. "I guess I sent you there because I'd gone. In fact, I'd quite enjoyed it. It was one of the few ways you could meet girls in those days. It's where—" he stopped.

"It's where you met Mom," Beth filled in the sentence for him. "And for that reason, if none other, you should have ditched the whole idea."

Oh Christ, Meg thought. Two minutes. They'd had maybe two minutes when the general conversation had been reasonable.

"Fishbone!"

Meg swiveled in her chair when she heard this cry, wondering if someone were choking at the next table. What she saw was a woman approaching *their* table, a young man a few steps behind her, her arms outstretched, a huge grin on her striking face.

"Hey, what are *you* doing here?"

Now the woman had her hands on Jimmy's shoulders and was leaning over, kissing him on both cheeks.

"Rachel." Jimmy stood up awkwardly, his napkin falling on the floor. "Hello."

Rachel. The ex-wife. Meg studied her closely, silently remarking on how dissimilar she was to Helen. She seemed full of confidence, bursting with energy. Tall, big-boned, with a large nose, a pre-Raphaelite shade of red hair and traffic light green eyes, Rachel was a force to be reckoned with, Meg could tell. She looked like one of those women who might say "Come on, let's go settle a new frontier" and inevitably convince anyone in her vicinity to trail along behind her.

Immediately after taking Rachel in, Meg glanced over at Amy who was sitting with a strangely beatific expression on her face, watching the scene develop. Was this why Amy had dressed so seductively tonight? Meg wondered. Because she knew the old competition was going to show up? No—Rachel's appearance was clearly a surprise.

"Jimmy—this is Alex." The young man stepped up beside Rachel and Meg found herself drawing in her breath. He was startlingly handsome. "Alex—this is Jimmy." They shook hands. "First husband meets second husband. I suppose this is a historic occasion."

"Second husband?" Jimmy asked, looking up at the taller man.

"We got married this afternoon," Alex answered, smiling. "It's nice to meet you."

"Does Zoey—was Zoey—" Jimmy's voice faltered.

"So what's with the Gypsy outfit, Rachel?" Beth waded into the conversation. "Are you reading palms on your wedding night to earn enough for a Caribbean cruise honeymoon? I'm not sure the management of Locke-Ober would approve. But you can start with me and see how far you get."

Caught off guard by this verbal thrust, Rachel took a small step back, glaring at Beth with overt hostility. Meg could see a flicker of a smile cross Amy's face and Meg smothered a laugh herself. It was such a relief when Beth picked on other people's appearance, especially as there was always at least a kernel of truth in her comments. Rachel's garb was unusual, to say the least. She *did* look like a Gypsy with her dangling gold earrings, multicolored shawl, long black skirt and voluminous blouse, over which hung an array of gold necklaces.

"Don't tell me *you* are Amy," Rachel said in a tone that was supposed to be scornful, Meg realized, but came out as slightly fearful instead.

"No." Beth pointed across at her sister. "The beautiful one over there is Amy."

"I'm pleased to meet you at last, Rachel," Amy said, sitting perfectly still. "First wife meets second wife. A historic occasion."

"I'll do the rounds of our family for you, Rachel and Alex," Beth said. "My father, Mark, is there beside Amy— no don't get up, Dad. I know how polite you like to be, but if we all stand up, it will look like we're playing some complicated jack-in-the-box game. I think we can be informal. Right. And that's my sister Leo, beside my father. Jimmy, you know. Then my other sister, Meg; Leo's fiancé, Nick, myself, and here to my left, Meg's husband, Charlie. Now you can ask us all what school we go to and what are our favorite sports."

"Excuse me?" Rachel looked flummoxed. She put her arm around Alex's waist.

"An in joke," Beth replied breezily, reaching for her wineglass.

"Jimmy, it's very nice to meet you," Alex spoke. "I'm sorry about the surprise. We should have told you before, but it was all pretty spur-of-the-moment. The wedding, I mean. It was a surprise to Zoey, too. We picked her up from school, brought her with us to the ceremony, and I think she was going over to tell you about it tonight. Since you're here, she must have missed you. You have a lovely daughter. I'm proud to be her stepfather."

"And I'm proud to be her stepmother," Amy chimed in.

"I wouldn't mind having a stepfather who looked like that," Beth remarked, nudging Nick.

"Are you two having dinner here?" Mark asked.

"Yes," said Alex. "Our table is in the corner. I think it's time we went to eat. I'm starving," he grinned. "Sit down, Jimmy. I'm sorry we've interrupted your family get-together. Come on, Rachel. It was nice to meet you all."

Rachel hesitated, looking as if she wanted to say something more, but then smiled at her new husband.

"Okay, Doc," she said. "Lead on."

"Doc?" Beth queried, keeping her eyes on Alex as he made his way across the room.

"Yes. He specializes in asthma," Amy answered.

"Bad career choice. Just looking at him takes a healthy person's breath away. Think what he'd do to an asthmatic."

"He seems very nice," Leo commented.

Jimmy bent down to pick up his napkin. When he surfaced, he looked as if Tom Cruise had conducted a beneath-the-table interview with him for a part in his vampire movie; all the blood had drained from his face. His eyes were vacant and unfocused.

"Nick"—Mark picked up his wineglass—"I'd like to take this opportunity to welcome you to our family. I'd stand up and make a toast, but I don't have any speech prepared. All I can say is that you're a very fortunate man to have Leonora's love and a somewhat less fortunate man to be saddled with the Prestons en masse. As you have doubtless gathered already, we have quite a few fractious moments when we're together. I hope you can see beyond that to the underlying love we share."

Meg saw her father give a specific look to Beth that translated into an order: keep quiet on this or you'll be sorry. Surprisingly, Beth obeyed. Meg had anticipated a remark such as "Even X-ray vision wouldn't help him on that one, Dad." Beth's silence struck Meg as more ominous than the usual comeback. "So," Mark continued, obviously relieved, "let's drink to your happiness. Yours and Leonora's."

"Absolutely." Beth raised her glass. "Well said, Dad."

Meg, Amy and Leo looked at one another in amazement, while raising their glasses. *This* is the real historic occasion, Meg thought: Beth praising Mark.

"Thank you. I can't tell you how much we appreciate your good wishes," Nick addressed Mark. "I know you must have reservations about our—about our relationship. It is very generous of you to welcome me to your family in this way."

There was a sadness in Nick's voice that Meg couldn't fathom. His face was undeniably attractive, but at the same time gaunt and drawn. Something was wrong; something beyond the obvious problems of the age gap and his impending divorce. Those dark blue eyes of his had a thin film of misery covering them, and although he had spoken what sounded like the right words in response to Mark, he hadn't said them with conviction. It was as if he were playing in a game that he knew he was going to lose, Meg concluded. And it was a game he passionately wanted to win.

"Thank you, Dad," Leo said solemnly, leaning over to kiss their father on his cheek.

Silence had never been a problem in the Preston family. Normally, if there were a gap of more than two seconds between speech, Beth would fill it. Now, inexplicably, silence descended upon the table and refused to budge. Everyone seemed to have retreated into their own private world, like bears in hibernation. And there was no sign of spring.

Jimmy sat scratching his nose, his gaze continually wandering off to the corner of the restaurant. Leo tugged at her earlobe. Mark twirled his wine in his glass. Amy raked the tablecloth with her fork. Charlie trained his eyes on the ceiling. Nick pulled out a cigarette and lit it. Beth studied the people at nearby tables. And Meg thought she might explode with tension.

"Patrick's in town," Amy announced, placing her fork carefully on the side of her plate. Her words, seemingly directed at Mark, were loud enough to be heard around the whole table.

"Patrick?" Mark lifted his chin, turned his face in Amy's direction, while his eyes sought Jimmy. All eyes at the table swiveled to Jimmy. Except Amy's.

She nodded.

"Mmm hmm. He wants to see Charlotte."

"Really?" Mark moved his chair back a few inches. "Is that a good idea?"

"He's her father." Amy replied, a defensive edge to her voice. "She deserves to have a father's love. Every child deserves a father's love."

"Hear, hear." Beth clapped. "My sentiments exactly."

"I think we should go now, Amy," Jimmy said, his face turning from white to red in seconds. "Get back to the baby-sitter."

"Jimmy." Beth looked at her watch. "It's only ten o'clock. Is your baby-sitter five years old?"

"Shut up, Beth."

Everyone flinched at Jimmy's words. This was unwise bravado, Meg thought. She found herself leaning forward, in an effort to shield Jimmy from what she knew would be a terrible onslaught from Beth.

"Jimmy." Beth threw her hands up in the air. "How churlish of you. Do I take it that you hadn't previously been apprised of the aforementioned Patrick's presence in Boston?"

"Do I take it that you were *previously apprised?*" Jimmy snarled back. Meg had never heard Jimmy speak in anything but calm tones. Clark Kent had gone into the telephone booth and emerged with a new suit of rage.

"Of course you were apprised," he continued, spitting out the words. "You were *all* apprised. Everyone at this table." He skewered each person with a look of frenzied loathing. "In this Masonic family everyone is apprised of everything. Everyone except the person who *should* be apprised." With each "apprised" his tone took on another layer of scorn.

Meg caught a fast glimpse of Charlie nodding in sympathy.

"James, please," Mark intervened, sounding as if he were talking to a mentally unbalanced client. "Calm down. *I* didn't know anything about Patrick."

"*You're* not a sister. You're like the rest of us men. Barely tolerated."

"I would have told you, Jimmy," Amy said, rather blithely, Meg thought, considering the circumstances. "But you were so caught up in the saga of Rachel and Alex—"

"Excuse me, Leo and Nick." Jimmy stood up, threw his napkin on the table. "Excuse me, Mark. I'm leaving."

"Wow. Dramatic gesture. High dudgeon. Are you going to stalk off indignantly now?"

"I have taken your supercilious shit for three years, Beth. I have been polite. I haven't responded to your supposedly funny barbs and I've watched quietly as you relegated me into the leagues of boring people you have to endure. After all, I work in insurance, right? Beneath contempt. That's fine. But you're not beneath contempt. Not beneath my contempt, anyway."

He didn't stalk, but walked slowly off, away from the table, through the restaurant and out of their sight.

"Ames—" Leo reached over and grabbed her sister's hand. "Shouldn't you go after him?"

"Rachel has probably been spying on us the whole night. Let her go after him."

"Amy. Please. This can't be right." Leo was obviously distraught. "I don't know what's behind all this, but it can't be right to let him go off like that."

"Why not? He doesn't care, not really. He doesn't care about me or Charlotte."

"I've got a good idea. Why don't we call Patrick up and get him over?" Beth waved at the wine waiter. "That would be fun."

"Jimmy's right. You're a pain in the ass." Charlie's speech was slurred.

"Why's that, Charles? Because I say what everyone else is too afraid to say?"

"I think it's time to call a halt to all this." Mark stopped the approaching wine waiter in his tracks. "We've had sufficient wine, thank you very much. Now—" He turned back and addressed the table at large. "I don't know how I let this evening get so out of control. It's unseemly and squalid. My apologies, Nick. Why you decided to drop that bombshell on Jimmy in the middle of a public dinner, Amy, I will never understand—"

"That's the problem, isn't it, Dad? The public part. God, you must have been relieved when Mom put herself in purdah. You didn't have to deal with the consequences of her craziness publicly, did you? She hid in the house and you hid in public."

"Beth—" Meg was surprised to hear Nick's soft voice. "People struggle for the right response to any difficult situation. Sometimes they succeed in finding one, sometimes they don't. You seem to think that your father didn't suffer as you did. Do you really think that you know him well enough to make that assumption? Do you believe that your own response to your mother was perfect?"

"My response is none of your business." Beth tossed her blond hair.

"You're right. But your father's response is none of my business either. I think that's what he's trying to say. The matter is a private one—between you and him."

"Well, Nick Booth"—Beth drew back in her chair—"you're the only person who has said anything sensible all night. I'll refrain from digging up family ghosts." She stuck her hand out to grab her glass of wine but missed it.

Meg saw that sometime in the last few minutes, Mark must have surreptitiously requested the bill, for he was now pulling out wads of cash and placing notes on a silver salver. Presumably he hadn't wanted to prolong the dinner any longer than necessary, so was avoiding the bother of a credit card. Feeling, finally, a twinge of relief, Meg looked over at Charlie, who resembled a heap of smoldering ashes. He had reached the same level of uncoordination as Beth, and Meg knew that Charlie drunk was Charlie difficult. The evening had been a disaster for everyone concerned, she decided. The only way to salvage this wreck of a night was to end it. Silence again enveloped the table, but this time it was welcome.

"We're off," Mark commanded. Fortunately, no one protested. The general melee of rising from the table and gathering coats masked the gloom of the Preston family retreat from Locke-Ober. Amy cast one glance over her shoulder in the direction of Rachel's table but didn't stop walking toward the exit. Beth stumbled once but quickly recovered. Leo had one hand on Amy's arm, one on Nick's; she looked as if she were supporting the weight of the world. And they all followed Mark like little ducklings heading for a pond.

"Shit," Beth yelped, when she stepped into the night. "It's freezing."

A man unlocking his car ten yards away turned to stare.

"What's your—" Beth suddenly stopped, reached out to Meg to steady herself and screamed "Stuart!"

He didn't respond, turned back to his car.

"Stuart. Wait!" Beth yelled again, rushing toward him.

"Excuse me?" The man seemed terrified by the specter of this blond apparition running at him.

"Oh, shit!" Beth stopped, did an abrupt about-face, headed back to the group, shaking her head. "It wasn't Stuart."

"Who the hell is Stuart?" Charlie asked. The air seemed to have restored his balance.

"Stuart is our guardian angel," Beth replied. "Stuart saved Meg, Amy, Leo and me."

"Stuart?" Meg looked over at Amy and Leo. Clearly they had no idea who this Stuart was either. "Who is Stuart?"

"Nobody remembers. Nobody remembers anything important," Beth wailed.

"Beth. Did you bring your car here?"

"I can't remember. I remember only important things."

"Fine. I'll drive you home, then. You can try to remember the unimportant detail of the whereabouts of your car tomorrow morning." Mark took his daughter's arm.

"Is your car still here or did Jimmy take it?" Leo asked Amy.

"We came in a taxi," Amy said. "We didn't want to worry about parking."

"We'll take you home, Amy." Nick shook Mark's hand, then Charlie's, before giving Meg and Beth a short hug. "I'd like to find out who Stuart is sometime," he said to Beth, a half-smile on his face. "I may need a guardian angel myself."

"Stuart's mine," Beth scowled at Nick. "Keep your hands off him."

"No problem." Nick raised his palms in the air, and backed off. "We better get going." He began to walk in the direction of Tremont Street, Leo and Amy beside him.

"There's something special about that man," Meg confided to her father. "I probably shouldn't say this, but I think he'd be a great husband for Leo."

"We'll talk about it later, Meg," Mark replied. "Right now I've got to maneuver Beth into my car somehow. And I think it would be wise if you drove Charles. He's a little the worse for wear himself."

"What?" Charlie, a few paces away, approached Mark, Meg and Beth.

"I was just saying good night, Charles." Mark sighed. He looked old, Meg thought. Old and worried. "It's inadvisable, I think, to have too many family gatherings. I may be out of town for Christmas."

"Oh, Dad—" Meg began to protest, but then was hit by the look of dismissal she so remembered from her youth. "Good night." She gave Mark a quick kiss on the cheek. "Good night, Beth."

Beth did a little dance on the pavement and waved gaily.

I wish *I* was drunk, Meg thought as she walked with Charlie to their car. I would love to wake up tomorrow morning and not remember any of this.

"Someone should give Beth a good belting," Charlie said as he sank back into his seat. Meg froze as she was about to turn the key in the ignition.

"A good belting? There's no such thing as a 'good' belting. What are you talking about?"

"She was drunk, she was being a pain in the ass. Someone should have shut her up."

"Physically shut her up?"

"Jesus, Meg. Don't sound so stricken. I've heard you complain about her enough."

"That's not the point."

"What *is* the point?"

"There's no excuse for hitting anybody."

"Can we get going? I'm freezing and I'm tired and I've got a lot of work to do tomorrow."

"You can't think it's ever right to hit someone."

Charlie put his face in his hand in an exaggerated gesture of weariness.

"This evening has been a nightmare. All I want to do is get home and sleep it off. I don't think it's right to make me sit here and argue the ethics of violence."

"I don't want to argue, Charlie. I just want to know—" Meg paused.

"You want to know what?"

"I want to know—" Why couldn't she articulate the words? What was stopping her?

"You're getting as incoherent as Helen used to be."

Meg turned the key; the engine started. After she'd stripped the gears once, she drove off in the direction of midnight.

"I thought you said that Beth was charming." Nick put his free hand on Leo's knee. He was driving slowly, talking

softly. "I could use a lot of adjectives to describe her behavior, but charming isn't one of them."

"No. Not tonight. She *can* be, though. I think it's Dad's
presence that flicks some switch in her. Do you think we
should have gone in with Amy when we dropped her off?
I'm really worried about her. I don't understand why she
told Jimmy about Patrick in that way, I really don't. And
I usually understand everything Amy does."

"Perhaps it was a retaliation of a kind. You know, Rachel showing up must have been a shock to her. It's strange
that they'd never met before."

"I know. But still. I don't get it. I mean, Amy's always
been worried that Jimmy still cared for Rachel, and now
that Rachel's married, I would have thought Amy would
be relieved."

"She may not have liked the look of blank shock on
Jimmy's face. He was obviously upset by the news."

"Yes. But something was wrong before all that. Amy
was in a strange mood from the beginning. Oh God, I hope
she's not falling for Patrick again. That would be awful."

"It would certainly complicate matters. I like Jimmy. I
think he's got a lot going on beneath the surface, that he's
an undervalued man. And I liked your father. He's very
distinguished, isn't he? He coped pretty well with the whole
situation."

"Well, he's used to Beth. I wonder who Stuart is."

"Don't we all. The mystery man. Beth said he saved all
of you. What does that mean?"

"I have no idea. She was so drunk she could have been
fantasizing."

"Does she usually drink that much?"

"No. I mean, I've seen her pretty drunk before, but not
falling down drunk like she was at the end tonight. I'm
worried about her too, now. And I'm worried about Meg.
Each time I see her she looks more miserable."

"Charlie wasn't exactly a happy camper, either."

"Great party."

"Great party," Nick nodded.

"I can't believe that Beth listened to you when you told her the conversation between Dad and her should be private."

"I don't think Beth actually likes hurting your father; she feels compelled to do it, that's all. She doesn't know how to stop herself, but if anyone gives her a good reason to stop, she'll listen."

"It's more complicated than that."

"I'm sure. But sometimes it's a good idea to forget all the complications, the nuances, and approach things as if they were simple."

"I love you, Nick."

"Will you marry me?"

"Oh, God." Leo looked out her window at the Charles River. "This really is too complicated."

"No, it's not." Nick squeezed her thigh. "It's simple. One of these days you'll realize that."

"I'm perfectly capable of taking care of myself." Beth unhooked her seat belt with some difficulty.

"I'm sure you are. But I insist on seeing you to your door."

"Old-world politesse?"

"Common courtesy." Mark was holding the car door open for his daughter.

"Well." She brushed away his offer of an arm to help her, and careened out onto the sidewalk. "You must feel like King Lear, Dad. Surrounded by ungrateful children. Sorry—*one* ungrateful child."

Mark ignored this remark and kept close to her side as she stumbled her way to the front door of the apartment building.

"You're not planning to work tomorrow, are you?" he asked.

"What's tomorrow? Friday? Yes. Friday. Yes, I'm going to work. I have an important appointment with a woman named Eve."

"I don't think you'll be up to it."

"Oh, but I will." She searched in her handbag for keys, finally found them. "Look—I can turn the key in the door, Dad. I'm fine. I owe you for dinner, I know. It was supposed to be my party."

"Beth—" Mark took hold of her arm before she could disappear through the door. "I'm worried about you."

"How sweet. You come home late and you come home early. You come home, babe, when you're feeling small."

"What?"

"Lines from a song, Dad. Now will you let me go? I need some sleep."

"Beth?" he asked her as the door closed between them. "Who's Stuart?"

"This happened once before, when I came to your door. No reply," he heard her sing as she vanished from his sight.

Some people eat when they are anxious, Amy said to herself. And some people sleep. There was Jimmy, lying on their bed, dead to the world. That was the way he dealt with trauma—he made himself unavailable. He must have come straight home, paid the baby-sitter and collapsed into bed. Yes, she could wake him up now and try to talk about what happened that evening, but it would take him a while to come to grips with consciousness and she wasn't sure she wanted to talk about anything anyway. The conversation was predictable. She would apologize for springing Patrick's arrival on him in the restaurant, and then, within minutes, he'd introduce the topic of Rachel and her marriage to Alex. Too much of her life had been spent listening to people she loved talking about the people they loved; first her mother, now Jimmy—both captives of the past.

Patrick lived in the present.

Patrick rarely slept.

Right now Patrick was probably mixing a margarita at the Casablanca.

Amy closed the door to their bedroom as softly as she could, took off her high heels and crept downstairs, to the telephone. She called information, listened to the number she requested, memorized it, hung up, picked up the receiver immediately and pushed the right buttons.

"What's up, Ames?" he'd asked as soon as he came to the phone. She hadn't given her name when she'd asked for him. He just knew.

"Would you like to see Charlotte on Saturday morning?"

"Absolutely. What time?"

"I'll bring her over at ten."

"Fantastic. You've got the address?"

"No."

She memorized the numbers and words he spoke.

"Patrick? Tell me something. Do you talk about me to your girlfriends? Am I some sort of ghostly presence in their lives?"

Amy could hear him collect his thoughts. He was giving this question careful consideration. Behind the silence Bonnie Raitt was singing: "I need you at the dimming of the day."

"I don't, Ames. No. You know, when people talk about their past romantic relationships they are usually trying to package them in such a way as to make them either entertaining or illuminating. I don't believe in reducing love to anecdotes. But I do believe in ghosts."

"So do I."

"Do you think ghosts have brains?" Patrick asked in a Boris Karloff whisper.

Amy laughed.

"They're probably the only creatures that do. Humans have been deluding themselves since creation."

"Well, then, neuroscience for a living is one big con, isn't it?"

"I'm beginning to think so."

"I've got to go now, Ames. Some schmuck is signaling for a light beer. Good night."

"Good night, Patrick."

Amy found a blanket in the hall closet, carried it to the sofa in the living room and stretched herself out. For many years, as a child, she'd slept in her clothes. Only when she'd first gone to a friend's house for the night had she realized that there was a whole different set of apparel for bed.

She didn't want to take her velvet dress off. For once, she'd gotten her appearance right. If Patrick had come into Locke-Ober, he would have been pleasantly surprised. That was how she should dress every day—as if she might run into Patrick.

She wasn't going to take off her makeup either. Why bother? As she turned over onto her stomach, she could feel how much weight she'd lost in the last couple of days.

"Screw diets," she remembered Beth saying once. "The only failsafe way to lose weight is to fall in love." Beth had always been thin. Was she permanently in love? Amy closed her eyes. Beth actually running after a man, whether drunk or not, was a sight to see.

So who the hell was Stuart?

Chapter Sixteen

BETH PUT HER hands to her temples, rubbed gently in a circular motion. She was having problems focusing on Jackie/Eve, who had chosen to wear a dazzling blue suit that hurt Beth's eyes and who was busy spinning out the ridiculous tale of her supposed sister Andie and Andie's supposed lover. Cut the crap, Beth wanted to say. Yet she managed to refrain from speaking and smiled sympathetically in the creep's direction.

"Where does Andie go to college?" she interrupted.

"Wellesley."

"Well, she must be bright, then. At least it's not some rinky-dink place for no-brainers like UMass."

Score one, Beth said to herself as she watched Jackie's face crumble. At least she could remember some of the information Nick had given her last night. UMass was Jackie's alma mater.

"My sister Leo is incredibly intelligent too. She's at Harvard. Do you know how high you have to score on the boards to get into Harvard?"

"No." Jackie crossed one leg over another, pulled her skirt down a little to cover her thighs. Creeping cellulite? Beth wondered. Varicose veins? Women in their forties must start to panic, no matter how attractive they might be. Time to hit her vanity soft spot.

"We're lucky Leo went to Harvard, you know. She was approached by a scout from the Ford modeling agency during her senior year of high school. They wanted to make her into the next Kate Moss, but Leo decided not to go that route. She's not into the superficialities of life."

"I see."

"Given her looks, I'm amazed she has such brain power

as well," Beth sighed. "Some people have all the attributes."

"What's happening with her relationship with that man—what's his name? Nick? Is it going well?"

"No."

"No?"

Beth watched Jackie try hard to hide her pleasure at this news. The corners of her mouth twitched, her hands gripped the sides of her chair in anticipation.

"It's all over between them now."

"Really?"

"Mmm. He's gone back to his wife. Which I must say is a relief to all of us."

"He's—? When? I mean is this very recent?"

"Not very. He went back a couple of days ago."

Squirm out of this one, sweetheart. I want to see you try.

"How do you know? I mean, couldn't your sister be lying to make you *think* he's gone back? Andie did that once, I remember."

Good old Andie.

"Nope. I was over at Leo's apartment when Nick left, a actually. She was unbelievably distraught. I heard her telephone him at home later. I was so worried about her mental state during this conversation that I grabbed the phone from her and I ended up—can you believe this?—talking to Nick's wife. She sounded very nice, I have to say. Concerned about Leo, but obviously relieved that Nick was back."

"I don't think that's possible."

"Really?" Beth now tried to hide a smile. "Why not?"

"I just don't think—I just think they're lying to you."

"Well, that would be subterfuge on the highest level. I don't think Leo could have faked that emotion. She was clearly beside herself. I had to give her a Valium. If the whole scene were a scam, that would mean they'd gotten someone to impersonate Nick's wife. Really, they wouldn't have to go to such lengths. I'd find out soon enough that they were lying. What would be the point?"

"I don't know."

"Exactly. Anyway, Leo's not the kind of person who could lie. So—tell me more about Andie. Now that my problem is solved, I'd like to help you with yours."

"You actually talked to his wife?"

"Mm hmm."

"What was her name?"

"I'm not sure. Something like Juliet, I think. I remember it had a J in it somewhere. Maybe Marjorie. Why do you want to know her name? What difference does it make to you?"

Jackie's face tightened. Her eyes blinked as if she'd just rubbed soap in them. Beth enjoyed seeing the composed facade unravel. It helped her hangover.

"I have to get going now," Jackie said, grabbing for her purse. "I have some work to finish before I take off for England."

"Oh, really? And we were just beginning to chat. What a shame."

Something about Beth's tone had stopped Jackie in her tracks and Beth observed the same bolt of recognition she remembered receiving a few minutes after hearing Jackie's voice on the answering machine. Putting her hand over her mouth, and leaning forward, Beth whispered "got you" to herself as she watched Jackie's face express hatred, then mortification, then hatred again. Hatred was definitely the emotion she'd settled on.

"Very funny," Jackie spat out, with a withering look to accompany the words.

"*I* thought so."

"You're just like your sister. A stupid little deceiver."

"Oh, no, Mrs. Booth. *You* get the prize for deception, I'd say."

"Concealing my identity from you is hardly on the same level of immorality as breaking up a marriage, is it?"

"My sister is not immoral."

"How would *you* label her actions, then?"

"I'd say she happened to fall in love with a very nice man who happened to have made a huge mistake when he married first time around. What did you do, Jack? Drug him, blindfold him, handcuff him and lead him to the altar?"

"You're a fucking bitch."

Beth smiled. She stood up, went over to Jackie and patted her shoulder.

"Thanks. By the way, when you majored in makeup at UMass, didn't anyone tell you blue eyeshadow and eyeliner is a very bad idea for a blonde, even a highlighted one? I'd take it off before I went to England if I were you. You'll never get that date with Prince Charles."

Points for not slamming the door, Beth thought as she watched Jackie Booth exit her office. If she'd known what it would do to my head, she would have seized the opportunity. Perhaps now Jackie will change targets and concentrate on me rather than Leo. Perhaps she'll give up altogether. Whatever the case, at least I've proved I'm not the gullible dumbo she must have taken me for. We're even after two rounds. Let's see who comes out fighting in the third.

Helen stood in the doorway, flanked by her two sons.

"Well," she said, as she did a little hesitant shuffle from foot to foot, "they're yours for the weekend, Meg."

"Why don't you come in for a cup of tea or coffee?" As soon as she'd issued this invitation, Meg regretted it. Josh and David brushed by her, knapsacks in hand, and headed straight for their rooms upstairs. The day before, Meg had found a bottle of vodka beneath Josh's bed. She knew she should talk to Helen about this, but she hadn't said anything to Charlie yet. Instead, she'd left it where she found it, deciding that a three-quarters full bottle of vodka in her stepson's room did not constitute a crisis. She could start worrying when she found it empty.

"I want to apologize," Helen said as she followed Meg

into the kitchen. "I know I upset you the other day. I didn't mean to. Really. It was stupid of me to say what I did."

"Are you telling me that you were lying?" Meg grabbed two coffee mugs, but didn't make any move toward the kettle. She didn't want to have this conversation. She didn't want to talk to Helen ever again. Some alien had invaded her body and mind and was forcing her to go through this charade of polite behavior.

"No." Helen squirmed into a chair by the table, then half-rose from it. "Do you need any help?"

"I think I can manage two cups of coffee on my own." Saying this didn't spur Meg on to any movement, however. She stood with the coffee mugs and stared at the kitchen cabinets.

"Meg? Are you all right?"

This was the fourth time that day she'd been asked the same question. Aside from meetings with the parents of some of her pupils, work had passed by in a listless blur. She couldn't remember driving home.

"You can get the coffee." Putting the mugs down on the counter, she went over to the chair opposite Helen's and sat down heavily. Perhaps someone had spiked her coffee this morning with a general anesthetic. Perhaps she'd unconsciously drunk the bottle of vodka underneath Josh's bed herself. She could hear the television come on in the living room next door. If only she could go join Josh and David and watch with them. A twenty-four-hour stint in front of MTV might be just what her numb brain needed.

"Do you take milk and sugar?" Helen asked.

"Yes, please. One sugar." This is nice, she thought as she watched Helen bustle around the kitchen. Someone is waiting on *me* for a change. Maybe I should tell Charlie that Helen is moving in and becoming our housekeeper. That would solve all sorts of problems.

"Charlie's worried some woman is going to get the presidency," Meg said dully.

"Would you like me to make you some toast or something?"

"No thanks." She reached out and took the coffee Helen proffered. "He can't think of anything else."

"He can be pretty single-minded sometimes." Helen settled in across from Meg.

"I don't think I understand people with one-track minds."

"Well, I've often thought that it's fine for a man to have a one-track mind if that track happens to be you," Helen commented.

"It *was* me. For a while."

"I know. It was me once. For a while."

Helen had a nice wry smile, Meg decided. It wasn't smug.

"Do you know how hard I tried to make Josh and David like me?" The aliens had changed the program. They'd stopped the "polite" button and pushed "confess."

"I can imagine."

"I don't think so. You don't know how much they hated me. Nothing I did was right. They used to look at me as if I were the trash someone had forgotten to put out. They wouldn't touch anything I cooked for them. And then they'd snuggle up to Charlie. They were all over him. 'Daddy this, Daddy that.' They got all his attention. I was jealous. So jealous. I *knew* that they needed all his attention, but there was none left over for me. I used to freeze up inside every time he hugged them, called them pet names. I used to wonder why he couldn't love me like that. I wanted to trade places with them, really I did. They were a family unit. I was an outsider."

"But it's changed now, hasn't it?" Helen put her elbows on the table, rested her chin on her right palm.

"In a manner of speaking. Now most of his attention goes to his work. The rest of it to the kids. So I'm still an outsider. Josh and David aren't the ones who think everything I do is wrong anymore. Charlie is."

Helen was silent. Meg studied her carefully. She was dressed in blue jeans, a black turtleneck and a gray Gap sweater. She looked like someone who'd be a good traveling companion. If there were a flat tire on the car, Helen would fix it—without moaning or patting herself on the back. She wasn't the kind of woman Meg would ever choose for a friend, yet an unholy alliance was beginning to form between them.

"You want to know why I'm telling you all this, don't you, Helen? I don't have any idea. You're the last person I should be talking to right now. I don't even know why I invited you in."

"Maybe you think I'll understand. Because I've been in the same position."

"Have you?"

"I used to dread Charlie coming home from work. He'd walk in the door and find fault. The place was a mess or I hadn't changed a burned-out lightbulb, or I'd forgotten to get the kind of bread he likes. It could be anything. He didn't understand what it was like to bring up two boys. I know that sounds like the typical housewife whining, but I felt so alone sometimes. And misunderstood."

"Then why wasn't it a relief when he left?"

"Why was I so hurt? Do you want me to count the ways?" Helen shook her head ruefully. "First and foremost I'd been rejected. For someone younger and prettier. At a certain point in a marriage, you think you can relax. You can let yourself go a little—or, in my case, a lot—and not have to worry about it. You think you can trust your partner. You don't believe that when he comes back home and you're slobbing around in sweatpants, picking up kids' toys, that he's just been with someone glamorous. It's the same old story, the same old song. I was stupid and I trusted him. So I was betrayed *and* rejected. And as far as I knew, he could be an entirely different person with you. Someone fun and funny and happy. As far as I knew, you must be doing everything right and I was still doing everything wrong."

"I always thought *you* were the one who did everything right." Meg sighed. "The cooking, the gardening. You seemed like the perfect wife."

"Meg. If I'd been the perfect wife, why would he have left me?" Putting her hand on Meg's arm, Helen squeezed it gently. "Maybe we should both stop thinking that we have to be perfect."

"You don't hate me?"

"Oh, I did. Absolutely. Just the thought of you tormented me. I *knew* that the boys were giving you a hard time and I delighted in it. I wanted you to suffer. I was as obsessed with you as some women are with men. On the day I knew you were getting married, I drove by the church. I wanted to run you over. Luckily, I didn't know what time the ceremony was and I gave up at about three o'clock. I heard later the ceremony was at four. You had a close call." Helen took a long sip of her coffee. "Later, I'd fantasize about you and Charlie breaking up, divorcing, and then, of course, Charlie coming back to me, the prodigal husband."

"He told me that you'd never fall in love with anyone else." Meg reached behind her, opened a cabinet and found her pack of cigarettes she'd hidden in the back, near a silver tray.

"Did he really?"

"He said that you're a one-man woman."

Helen emitted a quiet chortle.

"Well, he may have been right about that at the beginning, but he's wrong about it now. For a long time, years, I guess, I blanked out any bad memories. I thought our marriage had been blissful. So I was in mourning for it. I kept thinking I could resurrect it. There was no way to resurrect it with you in the picture, so I tried to blank you out of my mind. I promised myself never to mention your name. That didn't mean I didn't think about you the whole time, though.

"The strange thing is, about a year ago, I woke up in the middle of the night and I thought: I don't love him anymore. Like Saint Paul on the road to Damascus. I had a real revelation. I thought: he's the father of my children; he has a place in my life. But I don't love him anymore. I can't tell you how happy I was. Suddenly I remembered the bad times. How awful I'd felt about myself in those last years of marriage. I realized that I didn't need him. It was absurdly simple, so I didn't trust the feeling for a while, but then it didn't go away. What can I say? It felt as if I'd been let out of jail. That's when I stopped thinking of you as the bitch from hell. It didn't stop me from wanting to punish you, though. You were still the enemy."

"But I'm not now?"

"Meg, I don't think we'd ever be friends, exactly. Too much has happened between us. I wanted to get to know you better because of the boys. I thought it would be better for them if we were seen to be on good terms. Now—well, I'm not sure. I'd like to help you, but I don't want to be dragged back into Charlie's life *too* much, if you see what I mean. If you and I spend all our time talking about what it's like to be married to Charlie—well, we're both in trouble. I have a life of my own now. I know you don't think that, but it's true."

"I'm sorry about yelling at you at the bar. I misinterpreted what you were doing. I'm sure you *do* have a life. Have you fallen in love with someone else?"

"No. But there's someone on the scene potentially. I'm not sure, though, that I particularly want a man in my life right now. It's incredibly liberating to live without one. I'm sure I'll change my mind. At the moment, though, I'm enjoying my newfound freedom. I married Charlie when I was twenty. I haven't had much chance to play. And I'm not forty. Yet." A slight blush rose on Helen's face.

"Did he—did he hit you often?"

Helen stood up, went and deposited her cup of coffee in the kitchen sink. When she returned to her chair, she perched on its edge, as if she were preparing to leave at any moment.

"Three times. He wasn't a classic wife batterer. All those times, I'd had too much to drink and I was being what I'd guess you call confrontational. Some rising anger in me surfaced about the way our lives had turned out—how he had gone from strength to strength while I was stagnating at home. I didn't think he appreciated what I'd done for him and I'd have too much to drink and it would all come out. In a hysterical way, I guess.

"I'd scream and shout and then he'd smash me. I suppose he thought there was no other way to shut me up. He never apologized for it. He believed he was right to do it. 'It's impossible to reach you in any other way when you're drunk,' he'd say. Since they happened over a period of fourteen years, those three times seemed like aberrations and I'd forget about them. When I saw you with that bandage, I felt like some recovered memory person—it all came flooding back. I could feel the pain and the humiliation of being hit."

"He hasn't hit me."

"No. And he probably won't. I *was* an ugly drunk."

"That's no excuse for hitting you."

"No." Helen shook her head. "It isn't. However, there are a lot of things that happen in a marriage that there are no excuses for."

Meg stared at the smoke rising from her cigarette.

"I was obsessed by you too, Helen," she said. "I felt as if we were involved in a competition. So if Charlie was annoyed by something you'd said to the kids, or something you'd said to him, I'd be secretly thrilled. You were my invisible enemy. I used to listen into his side of phone calls to you and hope that they'd end in a fight. Really—I'd sneak up outside his study and stand by the door, trying to make out what was going on in the conversation. As soon as I could tell he was about to hang up, I'd creep away again like some spy in my own house.

"I'd have these really sick thoughts. What would happen if Charlie died? Would people treat you as the grieving widow, or me? Would you be in the front pew with Josh and David and Charlie's parents while I sat somewhere else? *You* are the mother of his children, *you* spent all those years together. Where did I fit in? Somewhere in the background?

"You know, for the first two years of our marriage, most

of my mental energy went toward winning over Josh and David and the rest of it I spent trying to win my undeclared war with you. Charlie and I as a couple, two people together, seemed irrelevant. It was all these other relationships that counted."

"You don't have to worry about me anymore, Meg. I'm not a factor. And the kids are starting to like you. I'll help with that. I promise."

"I know." Meg lit another cigarette from the butt of her last one, blew the smoke out without inhaling. "What I don't know is how I'll feel without all these other factors to concentrate on. It's like when Communism collapsed. The enemy's gone. Doesn't that mean you have to start examining yourself?"

Amy watched as the woman behind the counter wrapped the bra and underpants in pale pink tissue paper. *I can't afford these*, she'd thought as she signed the Visa bill, *but I'm buying them anyway.* They went with her freshly waxed legs, and her recent facial. All luxury items indulged in when she should have been buying Christmas presents. Who looked at legs in the dead of winter? Who cared about fresh skin when the raw cold would bite into and redden it within minutes? Who, exactly, did she want to wear this underwear for?

She wasn't about to strip down when she took Charlotte to see Patrick, although she knew the intangible bonus that could be derived from wearing a sexy bra whether anyone else saw it or not. It would make her feel desirable.

"You want to know what the definition of love really is?" Beth had said years ago, after watching a video of *Love Story*. "Love means never looking over the guy's shoulder for someone more interesting on the horizon."

Tomorrow morning was Amy's walk into the horizon, she knew. She was heading straight for the figure there, not deviating from her path. And Jimmy wasn't getting in her way; if anything he was giving her good reason to speed up the pace.

This morning, he'd woken up, dressed, made himself a cup of coffee and left without so much as speaking to her. She'd been prepared for a long harangue about her behavior last night; she'd even been able to come up with a number of reasonable self-justifications. But he'd vanished before she'd been able to give them, not even saying good-bye as he passed her on the sofa.

Well, if he didn't want to know what was going on in her mind, she didn't want to know what was going on in his, either. How easy it was to move from being an intimate to being a stranger in someone's life. A few days of non-communication and she felt as if she were living with a new roommate, not a husband of two years' standing.

Making her way from Bonwit Teller's to the Park Street subway station, Amy chided herself for not calling Leo. Normally she'd be in touch with Leo at least once a day, but at the moment she wanted to avoid her sister's searching questions. Leo would want to protect her from Patrick. Right now protection was not what Amy required. Right now all she wanted was to use what time was left in her lunch hour to get to the box office at Boston Garden and buy three tickets for the Celtics game next Wednesday. Patrick would skip work for the night, she knew, if he had a chance to go to the game. Father, mother and daughter enjoying an evening of basketball together—a family outing. What a strange and exciting prospect that was.

Sitting down and wedging her new purchases carefully behind her feet, Amy considered the other people surrounding her on the subway car. They all looked tired, yet determined to get wherever it was that they were going. Was anyone on a similar journey to hers? Out to try to buy back a family with tickets to a sporting event?

The man directly opposite to her, wearing a Boston Red Sox baseball cap, jeans and a dark green sweatshirt, had a slightly bemused expression on his face. He looked at her, blinked, looked away. Just as she had thought she recognized Jimmy the first time she met him, Amy felt a strong twinge of familiarity pass through her seeing this man. He appeared to be in his early forties. He looked like someone who might have had a bit part in television sitcom. "Retrieve," Amy commanded her long-term memory, but it refused her bidding. Perhaps he was someone she'd once worked with. She could see that he took a sideways, covert glance at her before he got off at the next stop. He, too, seemed to be wondering if he knew her, but that may have been because she'd been quite blatantly staring at him for the past couple of minutes.

Amy continued to search her memory as she exited at Boston Garden and made her way to the Celtics box office. It was his profile that had ignited the thought that she'd seen him before. A small mole on the upper left-hand side of his cheek. Why was there a lingering feeling of fear when she recollected it? She deviated from the main road to take a shortcut through the parking lot where she used to go after the games to try to get the players' autographs. Once Larry Bird had signed her T-shirt. Patrick had insisted, when he found out, that she wear that T-shirt on the night of their wedding. "You're not going to believe what proximity to a sporting genius does for me," he'd said. How right he had been.

Halfway across the parking lot, she stopped. She'd forgotten the Bonwit Teller bag, left it on the subway. All that effort, all that money, gone. She couldn't afford to go back and replace the absurdly expensive bra and panties, she couldn't believe she'd been so stupid. The tears came, slowly at first, but then with a frightening momentum. Why had she bought them in the first place? Why was she going to get these tickets now? The whole idea of Patrick coming back into her life was ridiculous. It would never happen. She should go home, make things up with Jimmy and continue to live her life as she'd lived it before. A life of maintenance. At some point in her existence, she had traded in her dreams for the simple notion of maintaining the status quo. Nothing exciting was ever going to happen to her again.

Standing in the middle of the parking lot, Amy heard

herself sobbing. She looked around to make sure no one could see her and then sat down on the hood of a Chevrolet and gave in to it.

"Excuse me. Are you all right?"

Through the blur of tears, she could make out a short, fat man with a concerned frown on his face. She had no idea where he'd materialized from.

"Yes. I'm all right. Thank you."

"Can I do anything to help?"

"No. Thank you." She shook her head.

"Well, I don't think it's a good idea to be by yourself like this in the middle of a parking lot, young lady. Even in broad daylight."

"No." Amy stood up. "It's not."

Excuse me sir, but my sisters and I have lost our mother . . .

Whose voice was that?

Beth's.

A cold winter's afternoon. A parking lot. Star Market. Chestnut Hill.

Stuart was our savior.

"Are you sure you're all right?" the little man asked again.

And when she'd been in the backseat of his car, Amy could see only his profile.

"I have to call my sister," Amy announced, hurriedly shouldering her bag. "I have to get going."

"It's not as bad as it seems now, you know. Cheer up."

The kindness of strangers, Amy thought as she rushed off to find a phone booth. Maybe she should spend her life in parking lots.

"How old was I?"

"You were a baby. You wouldn't remember anything. But I'm sure that was the guy's name. Stuart."

"Mom left us alone in a parking lot?"

"She thought she had seen Steven, so she forgot about us and followed him. That's what Beth and Meg told me afterward. Anyway, Stuart—I think it was Stuart—drove us home."

"Mom thought she saw Steven? Oh, God. That's awful. That's so sad. Beth thought she saw Stuart last night, and now you think you just saw Stuart on the subway? These strange sightings are beginning to sound genetic. You can remember what he looked like after all these years?"

"I don't think I saw *him*. He had a similar profile, that's all."

"Well, it's all very bizarre, but I can't concentrate on this right now. I'd rather talk about what's happening with you and Jimmy."

"But Leo, don't you see? I think Stuart is the one Beth's in love with."

"Some guy who gave us all a lift twenty years ago?"

"Right. It makes sense, if you think about it. She must think of him as a knight on a white horse. He rescued her, the princess."

"Is that what Patrick is to you now? A knight coming to rescue you?"

"No. Hold on, I have to put some more money in. Okay. I want Charlotte to meet Patrick, that's all. Is there anything wrong with that?"

"You're the one who's been so upset about Jimmy's feelings for Rachel. Do you think you're clear about your own feelings for Patrick?"

"Are anyone's feelings ever clear?"

"Amy."

"All right. Maybe I'm a little conflicted. I'll admit that. But I'm not going to jump into bed with Patrick, if that's what you're worried about."

"I'm worried about you."

"I've got to go now. I'll be fine, I promise. I won't do anything stupid."

"So you want me to call Beth and ask her about Stuart?"

"Absolutely. If he's the mystery man in Beth's life, she's even crazier than we thought. It's like being in love with a ghost. It's like Mom."

"Stuart may not be a ghost, Ames. He may be alive and well and walking around Boston, or taking subways."

"No. Stuart drove off into the sunset twenty years ago. He's Beth's impossible dream. Call me later, will you?"

"Of course."

Just as Leo had hung up and was about to dial Beth's number, the phone rang again.

"Is my father there?" a voice asked.

"No, he's not. Thea?"

"Yes." This affirmative was said in an emotionless tone, one that made it difficult to take the conversation any further.

"I'm Leo. Or Leonora. Whichever you prefer."

Now there was no response at all.

"I'd like to meet you sometime. If that makes sense to you."

"Is it supposed to make sense?" Thea didn't sound like her mother, or Nick. She had a flat, almost midwestern accent.

"I'm not sure."

"Would you tell my father that I called? And that my mother is going to England tomorrow night."

"Where will you be staying while she's away? You're welcome here."

"I'll be with friends."

"I'm sure your father would like to see you." Leo was aware of the desperation in her voice.

"Right."

"Do you have a number he could contact you at?"

"Gosh, no. Sorry."

The word "sorry," if pronounced in a sneering tone, could sound a lot more hurtful than "fuck off," Leo decided.

"Well, if there's some emergency—"

"What are you? A nine-one-one operator?"

"No, I just wanted—"

"Look. You don't care about me, I don't care about you. Just tell my father I called, okay?"

There goes the best-friend scenario, Leo thought as she tried to untangle the hopelessly knotted telephone wire.

"Okay. I'll tell him you called."

Leo listened to the dial tone for a few minutes before putting the phone down. At least Thea had made the effort *to* call. She hadn't disappeared without informing Nick that she would be gone. There was some sense of responsibility in that dead voice of hers.

In a way, Leo was relieved not to be meeting Thea immediately. She wasn't ready for her. Jackie inspecting her, looking her up and down, had been enough. A fourteen-year-old's appraisal might be even more brutal, especially if Nick were on the sidelines, hoping for the best.

"I'm not ready to be a stepmother," she said out loud, imagining Nick sitting across from her. "Maybe I *am* too young."

No. She'd made a stand on the age difference and she had to stick to it. Age didn't matter. Christ, her own mother hadn't been prepared to be a mother even in her thirties. She'd left them all standing in some parking lot.

Leo was beginning to hate the telephone, but picked it up anyway and dialed Beth's number.

"Is this good news or money?" Beth answered.

"It's me, Beth. I wanted to ask you something."

"Shoot."

"Is Stuart the one who drove us all home after Mom had left us in the parking lot?"

"You remember? You can't possibly remember. You were too young."

"I'm *always* too young," Leo sighed. "Just tell me, is that who Stuart is?"

"Yes."

"And is he the one you were in love with?"

No reply.

"Are you still in love with him? Is he in Boston?"

"Leo, sweetheart. I've got to go now. Sorry."

Beth had never dodged a question in her life. She must be seriously in love, Leo decided.

Again the dial tone buzzed in Leo's ears. She replaced the receiver, walked over to the hall closet, peered in at the box of Jackie's letters. If she took them out, read them all now, she knew with a certainty she couldn't explain that her relationship with Nick would be over. "To read, or not to read," she said quietly as she stared at the floor of the closet. Then she heard Nick's key turning in the front door.

Chapter Seventeen

"YOUR FATHER'S KIND of cute," Rachel said. Thrusting both hands into her purse, she came out with a pink pill-shaped object and a pair of nail scissors. Amy watched her as she quickly snipped the end off the pink pill, squeezed the contents into her palm and then slathered a transparent gooey substance over her cheeks. "A good-looking guy for his age. Kind of distinguished."

"Mmm. That's what a lot of people say." It was difficult not to stare at Rachel's suddenly shiny face. "Is that glitter you've put on?"

"Oh, no. It's a special sort of moisturizer. If I put it on five times a day it really boosts my skin tone."

"I see."

"Anyway, like I said, I came here to talk about Zoey and now I'm telling you what a hunk your dad is. Typical. It's like this teacher I once had in school. She could never stick to the subject, just kept wandering off all over the place. Miss Gambee. She was supposed to be teaching math. We loved her."

Amy stared at Rachel in astonishment. She'd been amazed, ten minutes previously, to find Rachel ringing her doorbell and completely flabbergasted when Rachel greeted her with a bear hug and kiss on the cheek. The lightning transformation from noncommunication to best buddies didn't ring true. She'd ushered this uninvited guest inside, however, and stood by as Rachel heaped compliments on the decoration, plunked herself down on the living room sofa and started to talk in a way that reminded Amy so much of Zoey she found it difficult not to warm to her. Rachel was ditzier than Zoey, that was for sure, but she had Zoey's relaxed attitude and sparkling eyes. Now this blatant admission of the need for magic moisturizer hit a chord of empathy in Amy she couldn't check.

"Maybe I shouldn't be saying this, Rachel, but you seem different than you were last night." That comment, Amy thought, should be nominated for the greatest understatement of the year.

"Sure. I mean meeting that sister of yours was a trip. Okay, maybe my outfit was a little on the statement side but I would never call it 'Gypsy,' you know? Mad Moroccan, maybe, but not Gypsy. So I wasn't too pleased with her and I was on the defensive."

Rachel was dressed in skintight black leather pants, a white diaphanous blouse and the same boots and leather jacket Zoey had worn to the concert. From Mad Moroccan—whatever that was—to Motorcycle Mama? Rachel obviously liked making all sorts of statements with her clothes.

"But you've always been so cold on the telephone," Amy said, still reeling from the sudden warmth directed at her. Would Rachel be quite so friendly if Jimmy had been home?

"I know," Rachel groaned. "It's like I couldn't see why you should figure in this whole deal. I mean I didn't choose you for a friend, did I? I pretty much got landed with you as a step-wife or whatever two women are called who've been married to the same man. And so I thought, well, fuck that for a laugh. I don't *have* to deal with this woman, do I? Fishbone and I are friends. Period. I don't need a brain surgeon in my life. What would we talk about? Besides, I got a kick out of saying 'Is James there?' in that superior voice. I don't get to use that voice too often."

Amy saw Rachel squint, relax, then squint again.

"Besides—" she hesitated.

"Yes?" Amy was curious. Rachel looked decidedly nervous.

"I'm one of those people who doesn't think about someone else's position unless I'm in it myself."

"What?"

"I mean, I didn't think about you. I mean, what you might feel about me and Jimmy being friends still. I didn't care. I didn't think it was any of your business. Then this morning this little bitch calls up looking for Alex and it turns out she's his old girlfriend and I thought—what a pain in the ass. I wanted to kill her. And I thought—hey, Amy probably wants to kill me. You know? That's kind of how these things work, isn't it?"

"Kind of."

"I guess if I'm real honest I have to say I was pretty jealous of you for a while there. You had Fishbone and I had this series of jerk-off men. Zoey used to come back and tell me how normal and happy you guys seemed. That bugged me. I was out there in Singletown, trying to figure out if there's one straight, available man left in this world who won't make you split the cost of a pizza when you go out, while you two were nice and cozy together. It's not like I have a career, either. Not like you. My career is men and God knows I wasn't getting any promotions.

"Anyway, one guy I dated for about two seconds—he was a shrink. He said I had some unconscious something, like some desire to break you two up when he heard me calling this place at three in the morning to talk to Jimmy. Usually I don't go in for that psychobabble stuff, but he was pretty smart. A real asshole, but smart."

Amy noticed Rachel wince slightly as she remembered this man.

"Anyway, now, what with Alex and everything, my whole life has changed. And I know you must hate me. I don't like the idea of someone walking this earth hating my guts. I start thinking about it and it gives me the creeps. I'm used to being popular. Some people think I'm kind of crazy but they still like me. Not just men, either. I hate those women who only have men friends. My girlfriends are a huge part of my life. So this is the deal. I'd like you to like me."

"You want me to like you?" God, who actually *asked*

someone to like them except six-year-olds on their first day
at school, or Sally Field at the Oscars?

"Yeah." Rachel brightened, flashed a dazzling smile in
Amy's direction. "Is there something wrong with that?"

"I don't know. I guess not." Amy regarded her former
rival carefully. Rachel appeared to her like a huge puppy
dog wagging its tail, waiting for a pat. She needed Amy's
approbation in a way Amy found surprisingly touching. No
wonder she'd called Jimmy at all hours. Rachel was one
big sponge trying to soak up any love or friendship on
offer. Now the concept of Rachel carting Zoey around with
her everywhere made sense to Amy. Rachel *did* need a
mascot. Rachel, Amy was beginning to realize, needed all
the help she could get.

"I like you already, actually," Amy reassured her.
"You're remarkably honest about yourself."

"Whatever. Anyway, that's great that you like me.
That's really good. You see the thing is, I need to talk to
you about Zoey, too. And it's better if we talk as friends.
I'm still not so clear whether I want Alex's old babe to be
friendly with me, because basically I'd like to kneecap her,
but I'm doing a lot of yoga these days and that's supposed
to help center your thinking, so I'm sure I'll figure out
pretty soon what my take on her should be. She sounded
like she was two years old or something. Alex said their
relationship wasn't serious, but you never know with guys
sometimes. They don't tell you things. I had this boyfriend
once—"

"Rachel. You said you wanted to talk to me about Zoey?
Is she in trouble?"

"No. I am. Have you got a Diet Coke around anywhere?"

Amy rose, found two cans of Diet Coke in the fridge.

"Don't bother with a glass," she heard Rachel call. "I'll
take it from the can."

Returning to her seat opposite Rachel, Amy opened both
cans and handed her one.

"Cheers," Rachel said, clinking her can against Amy's.

"I'll tell you what the program is here." She spread her leatherclad legs, leaned back and threw one arm over the top of the sofa. "The way it is now, I've got Zoey most of the time, right? And that's been great because I love her to death, I really do. She's a sweetheart, and, if you want to know the truth, she's kept me on the straight and narrow. I mean, she's a sensible kid and sometimes I've got a wild streak and she keeps me reined in a little, you know?"

Amy nodded.

"Anyway, she's fourteen and I think it's time she lived a more settled life. She's got to start thinking about college, because she's a lot brighter than I ever was and she should take advantage of that. So she shouldn't hang around with me so much anymore. I mean, I probably shouldn't have taken her to a lot of the places I've taken her to already, but then again, I think she's learned a lot from that.

"But I'm not going to sit here and bullshit you about my commitment to higher education. It's like this." Rachel took a swig of Diet Coke and leaned forward. "I had Zoey when I was twenty-one. Fishbone and I were getting along okay. It's not as if we had fights or screamed at each other. But something was missing. Something big was missing. I couldn't put my finger on it. I know I *thought* I was in love with him when I married him, but I was so young, what did I really know? We'd been dating on and off since I was thirteen and people assumed we'd get married—you know childhood sweethearts and all that stuff—and we did. It's funny how sometimes the way other people see you is the way you decide you should be. But it's not really you, you know?"

"Yes," Amy responded immediately. "Yes, I do know."

"So when Zoey was about four years old, I went a little crazy and I ran off with a total asshole and that was the end of my marriage. Which, frankly, was just was well, because Jimmy didn't love me. He was kind of intrigued by me and he liked me, but he didn't love me. *That's* what was missing. And I didn't love him, either—which makes for a huge gap in the fabric of life, if you think about it.

We had just sort of ended up together. And neither of us knew how to get out of it. Until I bolted. Like I said, I ran off with a complete loser. And my scorecard after him hasn't been too impressive either. A whole lot of strike-outs."

"Until you met Alex."

"You got it. Until I met Alex. I can't begin to tell you how much I love that guy. I wake up every morning so happy I can't believe it."

"So—" Amy hadn't touched her Diet Coke. She was riveted by Rachel's story. "You want a chance to be with Alex without Zoey around all the time."

"Don't think I haven't asked myself a lot of tough questions, Amy. Like: am I threatened by the fact that Zoey is a great looking teenage girl and Alex is only twenty-six? Or, is her presence in the house a reminder of how old I am every time I look at her? That kind of thing. And if I'm totally honest, sure, maybe some of that kicks in on a gut level. But there's more to it. I need time alone with Alex. We need time alone together. Jesus, we didn't even get to go on a honeymoon because the whole marriage thing was so spur of the moment he couldn't get time off work. Which is crazy, I know.

"Anyway, I don't want Alex to have to play the father role, not yet. I know he's great with Zoey. She adores him, but it's a lot to ask from someone—you know, to take on a wife and a kid in one fell swoop. The truth is, I'm scared shitless of losing Alex. And right now, all my attention is directed on him. It's not fair to Zoey. I can't give her what I gave her before.

"If we could just switch things around, so that she is based here and comes to see me occasionally—like she always came to see you guys. If that were possible—" Rachel paused, crumpled her empty can of Diet Coke. "I know it's a hell of a lot to ask. But I also know you've been a great stepmother to her. I should have thanked you for that before, but I didn't, because of all that jealousy shit I told you about before. Which was dumb. Anyway, obviously I wouldn't take any child support from Jimmy anymore, no more alimony of any kind, which should help a little on the financial side of things. I'm just asking you and Jimmy to think about it. I made sure Fishbone was working late tonight so I could talk to you on your own first. You'd be the one who'd have to make the most changes in your life if Zoey came here. I think Fishbone would be happy with it. It's you I'm not so sure about. Like—what's in it for you, you know?"

Amy considered that question. The answer depended upon so many unknowns, she couldn't process it properly. A week ago, she would have said "yes" to Rachel's suggestion without any hesitation. A week ago Patrick was somewhere in California.

"Mom. Can you play a game with me?" Charlotte ran down to the living room, stopped when she saw Rachel. A huge grin spread over her face.

"Charlotte. This is Zoey's mother. Mrs.—"

"Rachel. Hi, sweetheart. What's happening?"

"You look like Zoey." Charlotte stared at her intently. "Only older."

"Brutal kid," Rachel smiled. "But cute. Zoey's told me a lot about you."

"Can you play a game with me, Mom?"

"Not now, darling. Later. When Zoey's mom has gone, okay? We need to talk for a while. Can you go back to your room?"

"There's nothing to do."

"Well, I promise I'll do something with you in a little while."

"What am I going to wear tomorrow?" Charlotte asked, hopping up and down.

"We'll talk about that later."

"But I have to wear something special for my father. I don't have anything special. What's he going to be wearing?"

"I don't know, darling. It doesn't matter, really. We'll find something for you later, I promise."

"Will he take me bowling?"

"You know, I met Fishbone in a bowling alley when I was twelve," Rachel chimed in. "He's a mean bowler."

"Who's Fishbone?" Charlotte asked. "That's a funny name."

"Fishbone is Jimmy. Your father."

"Jimmy's not my father. He's my stepfather."

Rachel looked at Amy, puzzled.

"I'm going to meet my real dad tomorrow morning. I hope we can go bowling. I went bowling with my friend last Saturday. It was cool."

"Zoey told me Charlotte hasn't seen her father since she was a baby," Rachel addressed Amy. "That's why I figured she must think of Jimmy as her dad."

"That's right, she hasn't seen her father," Amy replied. "But he's in town and she's going to see him tomorrow."

"Wow." Rachel turned to Charlotte. "You must be pretty excited."

"Why do you call Jimmy 'Fishbone'? He doesn't look like a fish. That's such a weird name."

"Charlotte. Please leave us alone for a few more minutes. Then we'll play a game and I'll help you choose your clothes for tomorrow."

"But Mom."

"Charlotte."

"Mom. There's nothing to do."

"I'll let you watch the TV in my bedroom, okay?"

That did it. She scampered away without another word.

"I've always believed in bribing kids myself," Rachel said, watching Charlotte run off. "The great thing about bribery is that it works."

"I can't imagine Zoey ever being difficult."

Rachel chuckled in a deep, quite masculine voice.

"Zoey has her moments. Not that I should be telling you that right now. When I'm asking you to take her."

"Rachel, I have to think about it. Maybe I'll have an answer for you tomorrow," Amy added, seeing the dismay cloud Rachel's face.

"Sure. That's fair. You must have a lot on your mind, what with Charlotte meeting her dad and everything."

"Yes. She got so excited when I told her I thought she'd have some kind of fit. She's calmed down a little now, but it's a big day for her, obviously."

"Is he a nice guy, Charlotte's dad?"

"I think you'd like him."

"Hey—we have the same taste in men, I guess. So it makes sense."

"I suppose it does." Amy was surprised to find herself smiling. Within the space of twenty minutes, she'd grown fond of Rachel, almost protective of her. How could her deep-rooted hatred evaporate so quickly? Partly because Rachel had admitted to feeling jealous of her. She couldn't think of anyone who had ever been jealous of her before; it made her feel guiltily pleased. And partly because Amy could understand now why Jimmy remained close to his ex-wife. Rachel was the kind of person who, once having become a part of someone's life, wouldn't want to leave it. She probably still sent birthday cards to the "asshole" shrink she'd dated for "about two seconds." Amy could sense that the bond between Rachel and Jimmy had more to do with their teenage dating years than their adult selves.

"You know, sometimes I think that someone has decided to give me the best present in the world—Alex," Rachel said in a tone of disbelief. "And I keep thinking that whoever the someone is who gave me the present will change his mind and take Alex away. So all the time, I feel like I'm living on a knife edge. It's going to kill me unless I relax a little. As it is, I spend half my days trying to keep myself in good shape. It's unbelievable all the shit you have to do to keep up your appearance when you get older. I figure that after a woman turns thirty she is like twenty years older than a man of the same age. Like, I'd feel safe if I were with a guy in his fifties. With Alex, I feel scared shitless."

Amy thought of Leo. By Rachel's calculations, Leo had

chosen someone of the perfect age. Maybe she wasn't so far off the truth.

"But you're looking great, Rachel. And besides, age and physical appearance aren't everything."

"That's what I keep trying to tell myself. It doesn't wash, you know. Not when you're with someone like Alex who makes women's heads turn when he walks into a room."

"My first husband, Patrick, used to do that too. He still does, actually."

"Really?" Rachel raised her heavily penciled eyebrows. "What does Jimmy think about him? I mean Jimmy's a nice-looking man, but he's not a head-turner. Is he jealous?"

"I'd say he's more jealous of Alex than he is of Patrick. He's got a slight problem about Zoey liking Alex so much."

"Well, that problem would be solved if Zoey came here to live, wouldn't it?"

"I suppose it would,"

"Hey—" Rachel threw her hands in the air. "I'm not trying to pressure you. The choice is yours."

"I'll think about it. I promise. And I'll let you know tomorrow afternoon."

"Okeydoke."

So *that's* where Jimmy got some of his more feeble expressions—Rachel. She sounded as if she were permanently stuck in a teenage vocabulary warp.

After Rachel gave her another bear hug to say good-bye, Amy asked the question she'd never dared ask Jimmy.

"Why *do* you call Jimmy 'Fishbone,' Rachel?"

"You know, I've been calling him that for so long, I can't remember."

Boy, Amy thought. If you only knew all the possible reasons I ran through in my mind for that nickname, all of them involving strange sexual practices.

"Oh, wait a minute." Rachel stopped as she got to the front door. "I remember now. It's been so long since it happened, I'd completely forgotten. But now that I think about it, I made some kind of sick fish stew for Jimmy once and he got a bone caught in his throat. Like he didn't have to go to the hospital or anything. The bone escaped, but the name stuck."

That was one of the obvious explanations Amy had discarded as soon as she'd thought of it.

It's time to move from studying schizophrenia to an in-depth analysis of paranoia, Amy decided.

Beth put the rest of the mail aside and tore open the brown paper wrapping on a small rectangular parcel. At least, she thought, it's not a bill. There was no return address on it and she didn't recognize the writing. When the ninety minute audio tape was revealed, she sighed. A fucked-up client wanting to talk to me without paying for it, she decided. Probably someone too scared to tell all her sexual fantasies to me in person. This will either be unbelievably boring or something I can sell to a pornography shop.

She fixed herself a small green salad, patted herself on the back for pouring water into her glass rather than the wine she craved, slipped the tape into her stereo system, pushed "play" and then sat down to eat and listen. The sound of muted applause and then an acoustic guitar filled the room. Beth recognized the tune immediately: Bonnie Raitt and John Prine's duet "Angel from Montgomery." One of the best songs in the history of humanity. She got up and retrieved the bottle of wine she'd passed by. It was heresy to listen to this song without some form of liquor in your hand.

As the song finished, Beth waited for whatever was going to come next. Nothing could top the opening, she knew, but she was incredibly curious to find out what followed. Out came Steve Earle's gravelly voice singing "My Old Friend the Blues." Whoever had made this tape certainly knew Beth's taste in music. She retrieved the brown wrapping paper, studied the writing intently, but couldn't recognize it. All she had for a clue was the postmark: Boston. While she racked her brain for a possible sender, Steve

Earle segued into Iris Dement singing "Let the Mystery
Be."

This was some mystery, Beth thought. But it wasn't one
she could simply accept. She had to find out who was responsible. None of her patients could possibly know anything about her penchant for country music. Not one of her
old boyfriends could possibly come up with such a perfect
blending of songs. Or she'd be with him now.

As one song followed the next, she searched for clues
in the lyrics, but kept drawing a blank. The mystery tape
compiler had ended Side B with a killer. Emmy Lou Har-
ris's "From Boulder to Birmingham," which had to be the
saddest, most romantic song on record, a song full of yearn-
ing, despair and heartbreaking love.

"Christ," Beth said to the empty wine bottle when the
music stopped. "Whoever the fuck sent this knows how to
make me cry."

There had to be a follow-up to this tape. It couldn't be
a random Christmas present, it was much too personal for
that. Someone out there was making a first move. One that
negated the possibility of a response. She had to sit back
and wait for the next.

In her second year at college, Beth had received a bunch
of flowers with no note attached. She'd spent the next week
scouring the campus for wonderful men who might have
been the anonymous flower-giver, but after a while she forgot all about it. Six months later, another delivery of flowers arrived with no note. This, she thought, was a cool
move. Six months between flowers meant the guy had remarkable self-control and a decent attention span.

That evening she attended a party given by her French
professor. Everyone had a lot of wine and did their best to
speak the language intelligibly. At the end, a nerdy boy
who always sat in the front row of the class came up to her
and handed her a huge envelope, then scurried off. When
she opened it, she found pictures of sunrises and sunsets, a
lot of execrable poetry professing undying love and a confession: "I sent the flowers." Beth threw the flowers in the

trash, and told the nerd at the beginning of the next French class that she appreciated the gestures but not the feeling behind them. He hung his head, wiped his hands against his trousers and disappeared from the classroom forever. She never felt guilty about it. After all, what nerd needs to speak French?

Nerds could easily send flowers. But they couldn't make a tape like that. Only a dream man could send a tape like that.

And the only dream man in existence was Stuart.

Stuart knew everything there was to know about her without having to be told.

It had to be Stuart. That's why she hadn't recognized the writing. Stuart had found her address in the phone directory, made the tape late at night while his horrible wife slept upstairs, and sent it off.

Beth stopped herself from picking up the phone and dialing Stuart's number. Instead, she went over to her CD and tape collection and began to make her own selection of songs. She'd send him a tape back. The mother of all tapes. Stuart was hers.

"All I said was that he might need some extra help, some psychological help. They couldn't have objected to that."

"They did." Mr. Armstrong's voice was sympathetic, but firm. "They called me and said that if Eddy was considered abnormal by the staff of the school, they didn't want him enrolled in the school anymore."

"I didn't say he was *abnormal*," Meg protested.

"I know, Meg. I'm not blaming you. I'm informing you of what's happened. Eddy won't be a pupil at our school."

"Do they think he's like all the other children? They must see that he's different. No parents can be that blind."

"There are all sorts of parents, Meg. Some send their child to a psychiatrist if he comes home from school saying he's had a bad day. Others refuse to acknowledge obvious problems. Eddy's parents didn't like what you told them."

"It was a normal teacher-parent meeting. I *also* told them

how fond I am of Eddy. I can't believe they'd pull him out like that. He'll be so upset. He won't understand at all. Haven't they thought of what it will do to him?"

"I did all I could to talk them out of it, but failed. And I'm sorry to call you on a Friday evening, but I thought you'd want to know. I've seen how he follows you around the school. Perhaps it *is* for the best. He may have become too attached to you."

Meg knew that if she didn't finish the conversation now she'd begin to cry. It was not a good idea for a male boss to hear a female employee crying—no matter how caring the profession.

"Well, thank you for calling, Mr. Armstrong."

"I know it's not your fault, Meg. And I'm sorry that it has happened. But these things do happen sometimes. Try to enjoy your weekend."

"Thank you, I will," she said. "And you enjoy yours as well."

Meg put down the receiver, conscious that Josh and David had been listening in to her end of the conversation. She probably shouldn't cry in front of them, either, but she couldn't help herself. Eddy was lost to her. Eddy cared a lot more about her than her stepsons did.

David took one look at the tears running down her cheeks and bolted from the kitchen. "Dad," she heard him scream to Charlie, who was in the shower upstairs. "Dad. Meg's crying."

"David's an asshole," Josh pronounced. "You want to be left alone, don't you?"

Meg came very close to saying "David *is* an asshole" and throwing her arms around Josh.

"You're in trouble at your school, right?" Josh scratched his neck, regarded her with evident interest.

"Sort of. Right."

"Yeah. I know the feeling. When you're in trouble at school, you don't want everyone on your case. You want to be left alone."

Meg nodded.

"Uh oh. I hear Dad's heavy footsteps on the stairs. He's going to be pissed as hell that he's been called out of the shower. Maybe you should say you have your period. Women use that stuff as a defense in legal cases now. So Dad would understand it."

How did the male species get this way? Meg asked herself.

As Charlie came in, dressed in a bathrobe, his hair still dripping, Josh got up from the kitchen table, walked by Meg and surreptitiously palmed her a cigarette and lighter on his way out. Her first thought, as she received these objects, was "Christ, he's drinking *and* smoking." The second was sheer, overwhelming gratitude.

"What's going on? What's the matter?"

"I'm sorry," Meg apologized, wiping away her tears.

"Has someone died?"

"No. It's one of the kids at my school—Eddy. His parents have decided to take him out because of something I said to them today."

"And?"

Meg lit Josh's cigarette.

"And he's one of my favorites. So I was upset. David didn't need to call you down here."

Charlie's inner struggle was visible to Meg. She knew he was deciding between being sympathetic and being seriously annoyed by her weakness. His facial muscles clenched, then made an effort to relax.

"Do you want to talk about it?"

"Yes, I do," Meg confessed. "But you might want to get dressed first, and dry your hair."

"I'm all right. Come on, sit down." He led her to the table. They sat in the same positions she and Helen had been in earlier that evening.

"What did you say to the kid's parents?"

"I told them he needed some outside help. Eddy's not like the others. He runs around in circles and waves his hands and keeps talking about the end of the world. I'm not sure what's wrong with him, but I know he needs some kind of psychiatric assessment."

"His parents didn't want to hear that."

"I guess not. But I told them what a wonderful child he is. I wasn't being negative, I really wasn't."

"I'm sure you weren't."

This is all I want, Meg thought. Someone to listen to me, someone to tell me I'm doing a reasonable job. Someone to acknowledge that I'm a decent person.

"The point about Eddy is that he's not exactly normal, but he's an extraordinary boy. Sometimes he says things that take my breath away. He pointed to one of the other teachers yesterday and said "She's got ignorant hair." And one time he said to one of the other kids: "The shape of your head is like a melting igloo." Most of the time he's running around like a wild, frightened, doomed little baby, but there's a lot more to him. He reaches out and grabs my heart. I can't stand the thought of him not being there on Monday. It's not fair to him, either."

"Right. You know there's a wild card candidate now. A dark horse."

"What?"

"Well, we all thought it was between me and Harridan Harriet. That was bad enough, but now some idiot from Georgia is coming up on the rails. Some Forrest Gump type. Shit-for-brains, but a good administrator apparently because you can't help but love him. Like your kid. So everyone who was torn between me and Ms. California now solves the problem by going South. That way no one's feathers get ruffled. It's not male versus female anymore, it's time for Mr. Nice Guy who, from what I hear, can't even translate the 'Veritas' Harvard motto."

"I guess there's nothing you can do about that."

"Exactly. Like you and your little problem."

"I wouldn't say there's much of a similarity."

"No? Well, I suppose the difference is that you lose a pupil, whereas I lose a job."

"You don't *lose* a job, you just don't *get* a job."

"I *lose* a job I deserve, Meg. A job that would help keep this show on the road and help me pay alimony I can't afford while my ex-wife lives the life of Riley."

Meg wished she could roll back the tape and return to the time when these words would have been another skirmish won in her war with Helen.

"I took care of that woman financially for all those years and now I'm being taken." Charlie shook his head. One last drop of water flew off onto the table. Money was the one subject guaranteed to elicit Charlie's wrath toward Helen.

"Didn't she help take care of you by looking after the kids? Maybe she feels taken too."

"How can she feel taken? I'm supporting her, for Christ's sake. She's leeching my blood. Our blood. She's a perfectly healthy woman. She should get a job and support herself."

"I suppose so." As she said these words, a feeling of disloyalty to Helen engulfed Meg. The confusion this created made her nervous.

"Anyway, are you all right now?"

"I'm fine." Meg managed a weak smile.

"I'm sure you'll find another little kid who will grab your heart."

How about *our* little kid? Meg wondered. But I can't ask that, can I? I know the response I'll get.

"I never asked you last night. What did you think of Nick?" Given that Charlie obviously felt he'd done his bit on the Eddy dilemma, and Meg felt she would go crazy if she heard another word about the Harvard presidency, a change of topic seemed the best way to continue this husband and wife conversation.

"He seems like an okay guy. Way too old for Leo. But a nice man. What did you think?"

"I liked him."

"Probably because he's a smoker like you. You smokers stick together. A dying breed. Listen, can you do me a favor while I go get dressed? Will you call your father and see if he has any information on this Forrest Gump character?

His name is Andrew Wybourne. Georgia Tech."

"I doubt Dad would know anything."

"Well, give it a try, anyway. I need all the information I can get."

"Sure," Meg replied, thinking of Eddy. She would have liked to kidnap him, take him to Montana or someplace safe, just as, all those years ago, she'd wanted to run away with Leo. Why hadn't she then? Why didn't she now? What exactly did she have to lose?

"Meg?"

"What?"

"The look on your face then was frightening. Are you sure you're all right?"

"I've got my period."

"Oh." Charlie nodded, and reached out to pat her hand. "I see. That explains everything."

As soon as Charlie had gone back upstairs, Meg went into the living room, found a pen and a piece of paper and sat down to work out exactly how much money she needed to survive on her own.

How strange, Leo thought, to run away from home and end up at your father's. She hadn't planned to come to Mark's when she'd left her apartment. All she had known was that she had to get out. Nick was driving her crazy. She'd told him Amy's story about Stuart and he had spun out of control, refusing to believe that any mother could leave her children abandoned in a parking lot. He'd gone on at such length and with such vehemence, she'd wondered whether he was really talking about his own relationship with Thea.

Whatever the underlying psychological truth, Leo knew she didn't want to hear another word about Victoria's mangled mothering. She was beginning to feel like some kind of freak. There must have been some other children who'd been abandoned at some point in history. She wasn't the only one. Besides, as she pointed out to Nick, the story had a relatively happy ending. They'd arrived home safe and Beth had met Stuart, the love of her life. Nick responded by insisting that Leo was heavily into denial.

"I'm so sick of this," Leo had countered. "Everyone always puts their own interpretations on *my* childhood. Beth thinks I'm angry, you think I'm in denial. *I* think it was all right. In fact, *I* remember being pretty happy. But no one listens to me." She'd left then. Picked up her coat and bag while he was in the kitchen fixing himself a drink, and slipped out on the sly. Now she was sitting opposite her father, watching his familiar gray eyes as he talked about his latest legal case.

Mark knew when not to probe. He'd welcomed her in without asking why she'd come, settled her down with a glass of wine and launched into an account of his day that he must have known she was only half listening to. It was soothing, finally, to hear someone talk about a relatively mundane subject. Leo felt her shoulders loosen.

"Leo." Mark was shaking her awake. "You dropped off. You must be exhausted. Would you like to spend the night here?"

"I'm sorry, Dad. You weren't being boring. I haven't had much sleep lately."

"Do you want to talk about it?"

"I'm tired of everyone trying to take care of me. It's exhausting."

"By everyone, do you mean Nick?"

"Nick. Beth. Being the baby of the family can be a pain sometimes. I know everyone is trying to help, but I don't need to be helped."

"What do you need?"

"I don't know. I used to think I didn't need anything. Then I met Nick and I knew I needed him. But I think he's trying to be my father. I've already got a father."

"In a manner of speaking, Beth would say. Only on a genetic basis."

"Beth has a different relationship with you than I do."

"Well, if I had to present my case in court, prove that I'd been a good father to you all, I'd have a hard time convincing any jury."

"God, Dad, you sound as guilt-ridden as Nick. He feels he's not close to Thea, which is part of the reason, I'm beginning to think, that he's taken up with me. Beth might think I'm looking for a surrogate father, but it may be that Nick's looking for a surrogate daughter. Meanwhile you're telling me you haven't been a good father. *I* think you've been a good father. Doesn't that count?"

"Of course it does. But you've always been lenient in your judgments of people."

"Leo the pushover?" She squirmed in her chair. "The trusting, innocent one? I'm fed up with that label."

"It fits, however."

"No, it doesn't. I happen to like most people I meet. That may mean I'm indiscriminate, it may mean I'm stupid. It doesn't mean I'm some little innocent baby."

The telephone rang, but Mark let his answering machine take the message. A female voice said "Mark? Don't hide behind your machine. I know you're there. It's Friday night. You haven't called me in three days. If that's your shitty way of telling me you don't want to see me anymore, I want to tell you something. *I* don't want to see *you* anymore either. And by the way, your ego is the only big thing about you. Good-bye."

"Dad—why didn't you pick it up?"

"Because she was right. It *was* my shitty way of telling her I don't want to see her anymore."

"I always thought you were a gentleman."

"I try to be," Mark smiled. "But when presented with a certain type of female, any gentleman can turn into a full-fledged bastard. I met her a week ago and forgot myself. The momentary lapse has caused me a lot of problems elsewhere lately."

"Do you have a *regular* girlfriend, Dad? You never tell us anything."

Mark didn't respond to his daughter's question.

"I have to say," Leo pressed on, "I was surprised to find you in alone on a Friday night. That woman sounds seriously pissed off."

"Well, Leonora, you've been sounding seriously pissed off tonight, too. I'm willing to grant that you're not a baby, but I want to know what's happening in your mind. Why are you sitting here with me and not with Nick?"

"I told Nick about Mom abandoning us all in that parking lot and he went so berserk I couldn't handle it anymore. I had to get out."

"Victoria abandoned you? In which parking lot?"

"The one in Chestnut Hill, by the Star Market. Didn't you know?"

"No," Mark shook his head forcefully. "No, I didn't know."

"Well, I didn't know until today either. I was a baby at the time. Amy told me about it."

"I wish someone had told me then. If she abandoned you, how did you get home?"

"That's where the mysterious Stuart comes in. Apparently he's the guy who gave us a lift home and Beth has been in love with him ever since."

"Stuart? That's Stuart? Some person who gave you a ride home? I'm very confused here, Leo. Did Beth know Stuart before he gave you a ride? Why haven't I ever met him?"

"Stuart was a stranger Beth approached in the parking lot. And ever since, she's been in love with the *idea* of Stuart, not Stuart himself. I don't think anyone knows where Stuart is. Beth picked him up in the parking lot, he dropped us off at home and then drove away."

"I'm still not sure I understand. Your mother left you, but where did she go? Do you know?"

"She thought she saw Steven. It's terrible, Dad. She thought she saw him, so she followed him."

"Oh, Jesus." Mark began to pace around the room, shaking his head all the while. "Why didn't anyone tell me? It might have helped."

"I don't see how it would have helped."

"It would have," Mark said so softly Leo could barely hear the words. "Believe me, it would have." He paused and then turned on her. "What the fuck were your sisters thinking of, not telling me?"

She'd never heard him say the word "fuck" before.

"Dad, calm down. You're as bad as Nick. It's not that huge a deal. We got back safely. Mom was just a little crazier than usual on that occasion, that's all."

"That is *not* all, Leonora. Not by a long shot. If I'd known—"

"If you'd known you couldn't have done anything radical to change the situation, aside maybe from putting Mom in a nuthouse. And if you'd wanted to do that, you would have done it long before the parking lot incident."

"You don't understand. You don't understand the ramifications."

"Dad, I *lived* with the ramifications, remember?"

Mark turned his back. He was ramrod straight, as always, but she could sense an anger in the upright posture. Was *she* making him angry?

"What happened to the boy?" he asked with a voice so full of misery, it made Leo tremble.

"What boy?"

"The boy she mistook for Steven."

"I don't know. I guess as soon as she realized he wasn't Steven, she stopped following him and came home. I know Amy told me she was home when we got back with Stuart."

"So Amy would know all the details?"

"Well, Amy was only about seven or eight. Meg would know more. Or Beth. I mean, that incident must be indelibly imprinted in Beth's memory if she's been carrying a torch for a complete stranger all these years. Actually, I'm surprised she never mentioned it to me before. You know how she likes to bring up Mom's inadequacies. Maybe she wanted to keep her crush on Stuart a secret."

"Where is Beth now?"

"At home, I'd guess."

Mark moved to the telephone, picked it up and dialed.

"It's the goddamn answering machine," he said after a few moments.

Leo was silent, considering her father. Normally so sanguine, he was displaying signs of nervousness she couldn't account for. There was sweat on his forehead—this from a man who could play three sets of tennis without producing a drop of perspiration. Yes, he could have been thrown by this story of Victoria's behavior, but Victoria's behavior had never been anything but bizarre. Mark had been, if not cavalier, at least seemingly unruffled by it in the past. Why should this particular tale of woe so upset him?

"Leonora." Mark approached her. "Would you mind very much if I had some time to myself right now? I don't want to be inhospitable, but I need some time on my own."

"Why is everyone going so crazy about this?" Leo blurted out, surprised at how hurt she was by her father's dismissal of her. "Mom used to forget to pick up Meg and Beth at school the whole time. You and Nick are making me feel as if *I* should be in a state of nervous collapse too. As if this were some benchmark incident in all our lives. But I don't see how this story changes anything, except maybe that I feel sorrier for Mom than I did before. Is there something I don't understand? I've always been glad you didn't send her off to some mental institution. We may have been an odd family, but we managed. And Mom was part of that family. Am I wrong?"

"*I* was wrong, Leonora. Perhaps Beth was right the other night. Perhaps I was too influenced by what people might say if I put Victoria away somewhere. I thought I could handle her. So I didn't get her the help she needed when I should have. Oh, I took her to a psychiatrist, to quite a few psychiatrists. They all recommended hospitalization. She didn't want to be hospitalized, and I respected her wishes. At least that's what I thought I was doing at the time. In fact all I did was to choose the easiest and therefore the worst option. I've known that for quite a while now, but that story of yours just proves it beyond a shadow of a doubt."

"Dad—don't beat yourself up about this. You couldn't—"

"Oh, but I could. I could have helped and I didn't. I have blood on my hands, Leonora."

"You're overreacting."

"I'm being honest. If I were to be entirely honest I'd go further than that. I'd say that by not getting her the help she needed, I was punishing your mother for a crime she didn't commit. Because, you see, I blamed her for Steven's death. Or at least some part of me did. How can you be so careless as to run over your own child? Oh, I never said anything—I was sympathetic and came out with all the right phrases when it happened—but she must have known my darker thoughts. Steven was so—so special. I loved your mother so much, but not enough to help her when she most needed it. I couldn't face her erratic behavior afterward. I was angry at her for not going back to her normal self—as if she had a choice. I was selfish and I caused unbearable heartache and mayhem as a result."

"Dad, honestly, I think you should calm down. We're all okay. The four of us are probably closer than most sisters. We may have the occasional problem, but doesn't everyone? I know Beth can be difficult, but she's bright and she's funny and in her heart she's very loving. You don't have any blood on your hands. You didn't cause Mom's car crash. We're not maimed for life. You should forgive *yourself* now."

"Leonora." Mark walked over to her and put his hand on her shoulder. "You should be with Nick. He seems like a fine man."

Leo looked up at her father and saw a finality in his face that scared her. He was at the end of some rope she couldn't identify.

"I'm not going to leave until you promise me that you're all right."

"I'm all right. I've lived with all this for a long time now. But I'll feel a lot better if you go back to Nick and make things right between you. He can look after you properly. Right now, I can't. And despite all your protestations to the contrary, you need to be looked after. Everybody does."

As Leo gathered her coat and bag, she caught sight of a photograph on a table in the corner of her father's living room. A wedding picture. Victoria and Mark smiling happily for the camera. Beside it was a picture of Steven, laughing his baby's laugh. She'd seen these pictures thousands of times, but they had never struck her with such sorrow as they now did. She wanted to take them both and cradle them in her arms, bring her happy parents and her happy brother back to life. Instead, she kissed her father on the cheek and started her journey back to Nick.

Chapter Eighteen

CHARLOTTE WAS BOUNCING up and down on her chair as if it were a trampoline. Amy watched her with dismay, silently begging her to settle down. Patrick was leaning against the wall, eyeing his daughter with curiosity, directing questions at her that Charlotte answered in monosyllables.

"She's brighter than she seems," Amy wanted to tell Patrick. As if he were the headmaster of a school interviewing Charlotte for admittance. Relax, she told herself. Patrick's the one who has to prove himself here, not Charlotte.

"So school's okay?" Patrick asked.

"Yup." Charlotte thudded onto the cushion, bounced up again.

"What do you like most about it?"

"I dunno."

"Who's your best friend?"

"Emma. But sometimes Emma doesn't invite me over to her house when she has Cassandra and sometimes Cassandra is mean to me so I don't understand why Emma invites her over and not me. Cassandra can be nice, but she's never invited me over and she had a party at McDonald's and Emma and everybody went but I didn't."

Perfect, Amy thought. Charlotte goes from monosyllables to mindless chatter. What must Patrick think of me as a mother?

"Cassandra," Patrick repeated thoughtfully. "Prophetess of doom."

"That's exactly what our teacher, Mrs. Duggan, says sometimes when Cassandra's done something bad."

"Do you ever do anything bad?"

Charlotte stopped bouncing. She stole a quick look at her mother, smiled shyly.

"Come on," Patrick urged, "You can tell me."

"Once Mrs. Duggan told us she'd lost her watch so I came back early from lunch break and changed the clock on the wall of our class so she'd think it was later than it was and let us out early."

"Did it work?"

"Yes," Charlotte said proudly. "We got out twenty whole minutes early."

"You didn't tell me about that," Amy said. Charlotte frowned.

"Well I did something like that when I was around your age." Patrick moved to Charlotte's chair and knelt down beside her. "We had a substitute teacher once because our teacher was sick. And I rearranged all the chairs and the desk in the classroom after lunch so the new teacher would be confused and think she'd gone to the wrong room."

"Did it work?" Charlotte looked at him, wide-eyed.

"Yes." Patrick glanced over at Amy and winked. "I guess we've got trouble in our blood."

"Did you ever do anything bad, Mom?"

Amy sighed.

"No. I was a goody-goody."

"Your mother got in trouble when she married me."

"Why?" Charlotte stared at Patrick, then at Amy.

"Because I'm a bad influence. I turn goody-goodies into troublemakers."

"Why?"

"I don't know," Patrick shrugged.

"Is that why you went away?"

"Yeah." Patrick ruffled the top her head. "That's why I went away."

"Oh." Charlotte blinked her eyes a few times. "That seems kind of dumb."

He laughed.

"You've got my number, Charlotte. Kind of dumb. How

about going out onto Boston Common? Would you like that?"

"Sure," she said. "I guess so. But don't try to show me the swan boats. I've seen them zillions of times. They're boring."

"I agree. They bore me too. Listen. I've got a better idea. Why don't we go bowling. Your mother whispered to me when you came in that you like bowling."

"I'm pretty good at it."

"So am I. Let's hit the bowling alley, okay?"

"There's one near Fenway Park."

"Great. Your mother can drive us there."

"Am I allowed to bowl, too?" Amy asked.

"Jimmy's first wife met Jimmy at the bowling alley. She calls him Fishbone," Charlotte announced.

"Does she now? That sounds kind of dumb to me."

"Me too," Charlotte smiled. She reached her hand out to touch Patrick on his shirtsleeve.

That's done it, Amy thought, watching her ex-husband and her daughter. They've bonded. And all because of Rachel's nickname for Jimmy.

"Come on, Ames." Patrick grabbed her hand. For a moment the three of them were linked physically and Amy felt the tears come to her eyes, the same sort of tears she'd cried when Charlotte had been born. "Let's get over to Fenway Park."

"Patrick—" Amy took a deep breath and then dived into dangerous territory. "Charlotte's in a school Christmas play on Monday morning. Would you like to come see her?"

"Absolutely. What part are you playing, Charlotte?"

"One of the wise men."

"Very apposite," he commented.

"I hate my costume."

"Then don't wear it. Don't wear anything."

Charlotte giggled. "You really *are* a troublemaker."

"You bet I am. And a great bowler, too. Let's go."

Charlotte dragged Amy back as they were heading out

the door and pulled her down so she could whisper in her ear.

"He's fun. And he's really handsome."

"I know," Amy whispered back, pulling a comb out of her bag and giving both her hair and Charlotte's a quick run-through. "I know."

"This is a stupid place to go Christmas shopping. Why didn't we go to Quincy Market? At least they've got a Sam Goody there."

Whine, whine, whine, Meg thought. David's turning into a real moaner.

"Oh, shut up," Josh barked. "We've never been to this mall. It might be great. Besides, Quincy Market is full of tourists. It's a rip-off."

"This place may be a rip-off too."

"Just shut up."

"Stop elbowing me. It hurts."

"Boys," Charlie said. "Try to be civil for the car ride, will you? There's no point in fighting."

"Well, there's no point in going to this mall. There's not going to be anything good there."

Right, Meg thought, looking out the car window. I know what I'm not supposed to say. I'm not supposed to say: "David, you think it's going to be bad because I'm the one who suggested going to it. If your father had suggested it, we wouldn't be hearing this crap." So I won't say it. And I certainly won't tell anyone in this car that the reason I suggested going to the Chestnut Hill Mall was only because I wanted to drive by the Star Market parking place and try to remember what Stuart looked like. And the only reason I want to remember what Stuart looked like is that Amy called me last night and told me Beth is in love with him. If I admit my reasons, Charlie will do a U-turn on the spot and head for Quincy Market.

"What would you like for Christmas, Meg?" Josh asked.

"Anything," she answered. Josh was fast becoming her secret ally. Why was that? Did he know she hadn't ratted on him about the vodka and cigarettes? Was he trying to buy her silence by being friendly? If so, his tactic was working. At this precise point in time, she felt incredibly fond of her older stepson, and had absolutely no idea of how to convey that feeling to him.

"Remember what you gave her last year?" David sneered. "One slice of cheese. Excellent present."

"It was very nice," Meg said defensively. "It was Brie, my favorite."

"Yeah. One slice. Overwhelming."

"So. What did *you* give her, Dave? A hairband. She never wears hairbands. Hairbands are for completely sad people."

There it was. The Star Market. Meg pressed her face against the window, stared as they whizzed by. Stuart had blondish hair. Blondish hair and a nice voice. He'd said something about California. That was the sum total of her memory regarding their rescuer. What had he done to earn Beth's undying love? He'd been there when she needed him.

"Don't call me Dave."

"Boys. What do you two want for Christmas?" Charlie asked.

"A sound system," David replied.

"You already have a sound system, *Dave*."

"It doesn't have two tape decks, so I can't record anything, *Josh-u-a*."

"You want two tape decks? Well, that sounds like a reasonable request," Charlie said in the special intimate tone he reserved for his sons.

"Dad. You don't have to give us everything we want, you know."

"Shut up, Josh," David screamed.

"Fuck you, asshole."

It hadn't happened at all as Leo had expected. Thea had shown up out of the blue, walked into the apartment as if she'd been there hundreds of times before and was now sipping a cup of coffee with all the panache of someone who normally haunted Parisian cafes. This fourteen-year-old hadn't bothered to dissect Leo with a withering look. She didn't have to. Her presence itself, the way she managed to ignore her surroundings, was withering enough. Why had she turned up after saying she wouldn't? The answer was simple: money.

"Twenty dollars is fine," Thea announced. "I'm afraid I spent the money Mom gave me yesterday, and we're going to a movie tonight. I didn't want to borrow from friends."

"Of course not." Nick nodded his head. He looked as cowed by Thea as Leo felt. She was tall for her age, thin, with an ethereal face set off by cold, blue eyes. Dressed in black leggings, a black sweater that came down to her knees and a black scarf, she looked like she was about to pull a Jean Paul Sartre play out of her bag and start explaining existentialism.

While Nick went to the bedroom to get his wallet, Leo debated which opening lines she might use to begin a reasonable conversation. "How is school?" was one. "Which movie are you going to tonight?" was the other. She decided to remain silent.

"Thank you," Thea said as her father returned and handed her a twenty-dollar bill. "I'll go now."

"No, please. Stay for a second. You haven't finished your coffee," Nick pleaded.

Thea didn't move, but her face reflected that she was making a huge sacrifice. Nick began to wring his hands like some Dickensian character, while Leo racked her brain for anything to say to break the now horrible silence in the room.

"Nick says you go to the same school as my sister's stepdaughter," she finally managed. "Her name is Zoey. Do you know her?"

"Zoey?" Some light filled Thea's eyes for an instant.

"Yes. She's your age. Red hair—"

"I know what she looks like."

"Are you in the same class?"

"We're the same age. So we would be in the same class, wouldn't we?"

"Are you friends?" Leo asked, pressing on despite the snide dismissals.

"Zoey is a star." The voice was dead, but the eyes weren't.

"I met her the other night," Nick joined in. "I thought she was great."

"Great?" Thea spat the word out as if it were a foul piece of gristle.

"My sister Amy is very fond of her," Leo added.

Jesus, Leo thought. We are both *courting* this girl. We'll do anything to get a positive reaction from her, to score points. She's even more powerful than Beth.

"Zoey's another kid with divorced parents who shuttles from house to house." Thea fixed Nick with a haughty glare as she delivered this line.

Nick rubbed his mouth with his hand. Leo could see that he was trying desperately hard not to reach for a cigarette.

"Did you know that Zoey's mother has just remarried?" Leo was curious to discover exactly how well Thea knew Zoey, whether she could find a way out of the dead-end street Thea was presenting them by talking to Zoey later and getting some inkling from her of what was going on in Thea's head.

"No, I didn't know that," Thea admitted. But there was finally an edge to her voice, an edge of sadness.

"His name is Alex. We met him the other night. He's a nice man, a doctor."

"Right." Thea stood up. "I've finished my coffee. I'm going now."

"We're in all weekend," Nick said anxiously. "You can come visit any time."

"Good-bye, Dad. Good-bye—" she nodded in Leo's direction, "I can find my own way out."

Beth examined the house across the street. It was run-down, seedy. Stuart was living in squalor. That was a depressing truth. When she'd deposited the tape through the mail slot of the door, she hadn't been able to see anything inside, but the outside was enough. In *Sleepless in Seattle*, Beth reflected, Meg Ryan embraced Tom Hanks on the top of the Empire State Building, but she'd seen his beautiful architect's house on the water first. Lucky girl. If she knew he was living in a dump like this, maybe she wouldn't have made the trip to New York.

Stop being so materialistic, Beth told herself. It's Stuart's *spirit* that counts. Isn't it? Besides, Stuart wasn't the architect type. He'd probably been a junk bond tradesman who'd been nabbed for insider trading. That's why he had been so cagey on the telephone that time. He *was* a criminal, albeit a white-collar one.

The front door of the house suddenly swung open and Beth resumed her stakeout position—slumped in her seat, baseball cap pulled down over her head as far as it could go without obstructing her vision.

Stuart was instantly recognizable. No extra pounds padded his stomach, as far as Beth could tell from this distance, and the sandy-colored hair remained as distinctive as it had been that day in the parking lot. This was Stuart. The man of her dreams. Seeing him in the flesh didn't change anything, it simply added to her conviction that he was meant for her and her alone.

Stuart had her tape in his hand, and was looking up and down the street, presumably trying to see who had left it there. Beth dove under the steering wheel, waited for what she considered a safe period of time—two minutes—and resurfaced. He was still standing there, looking puzzled. Just as she was about to hide again, she saw that his attention was distracted. A woman had appeared beside him in the door. They began to speak to each other.

Okay, Beth thought. Time to check out the competition. She looked like some fucking cheerleader. Cute, blond, fresh-faced. Gross. A child squirmed between them now, a little blond boy with OshKosh jeans on. Stuart picked him up and threw him in the air once. The boy squealed with delight. Beth thought she was going to throw up if the director didn't yell "cut" soon. This glutinous little scene had to end.

The cheerleader grabbed Macaulay Culkin from Stuart's arms, tickled him, planted him on the ground, took his hand and set off down the street. Stuart was waving good-bye like some sap. When he finally stopped, he bent over and picked up the tape from the ground. He'd dropped it. The creep had practically trodden on her work of art while he'd been playing Daddy with that brat.

Beth started her car, backed with a crunch into the car parked behind her, mumbled: "Fuck it. Hit and run," and floored the accelerator.

At least he hadn't kissed the cheerleader good-bye, she thought as she took the corner way too fast. At least he'd have time alone to listen to her tape as the wife and the brat were out buying health food or whatever it was they were off to do.

Besides, he was cheating on Little Mrs. Perfect already. He'd sent Beth the tape. All was not innocent in the Garden of Eden. There was a snake lurking in the grass.

They had split up to do their separate shopping as soon as they'd arrived at the mall and now Meg was wandering through Brooks Brothers looking for a suitable shirt and tie for Charlie. There were plain shirts, striped shirts, polka-dot ties, striped ties. Her eyes were beginning to tire of the bland choices on offer. Maybe this year she should buy Charlie something different.

Meg wandered out of Brooks Brothers and straight into Josh.

"How's it going?" she asked.

"I haven't found a wax effigy of David to stick pins into. Otherwise, I've done Dad. And Mom. And you. So pretty good." Josh was carrying three bags in his right hand. One sported the label of Victoria's Secret. Had he been buying lingerie for his mother? Or Meg? Or an undisclosed girl-friend?

"Do you feel like taking a break for a few minutes?" he asked.

"Yes. Definitely. There's a bar over in the corner there. I think it's called Charlie's, if you can believe it. I might be in need of a quick drink. And I'll buy you a Coke," she added hastily when she saw his face light up.

"All right. Are you going to go ballistic if I have a cigarette?"

"Josh. I know I should, but I won't. This time. Special Christmas shopping dispensation, okay?"

"Fine."

Ushered to a booth in the smoking section, Meg and Josh both pulled out packs of cigarettes from their pockets and placed them simultaneously on the table.

"When did you start?" she asked.

"A month ago," he answered, grabbing a Marlboro. "I can quit any time."

"Mmm," Meg said, reaching for her Merits. "So can I. A screwdriver and a Coke please," she said to the waiter. When he asked for her ID, she produced her driver's license with a smile.

"The older I get, the happier I am when someone asks for my ID. I know they have to card *everyone*, but I can still dream about being mistaken for an underage drinker."

"You look okay for your age, Meg."

"Thanks, Josh."

They puffed away, Meg wondering whether this would be a good time to bring up the subject of the hidden vodka bottle, as they were on their own and in neutral territory.

"So. Are you going to leave Dad?"

"What?"

"Are you going to leave Dad?"

First Helen stuns me with tales of Charlie's violence over a Bloody Mary, Meg remarked to herself. Now Josh comes up with this question as I'm waiting for my screwdriver. I shouldn't sit in bars with any of Charlie's family. Never again.

"Why would you ask that question? What makes you think I'd leave?"

"I dunno. It seems like anytime you want to talk to Dad he tells you he's too busy, so you shut up and go away and I figure you must be getting tired of that. You're playing by his rules the whole time."

"That's not entirely true."

"No?" Josh shrugged. "Maybe not. It seems like that. But I'm not around that much. Maybe when we're away he has the time to talk to you, but I figure by then you've lost track of whatever it was you wanted to say and you probably end up listening to him and his problems."

"Well, he's got a lot on his mind right now with this Harvard presidency business. And he's the one who pays for most things to do with our life, so he has a right to be listened to."

"I don't get it," Josh blinked and leaned back in his chair. "You don't have any rights because you're not making as much money?"

"I didn't say that."

"I thought women had *all* the rights now. Lots of women would go ballistic if they weren't listened to, no matter how much money they did or didn't make."

"Do they teach you feminism at school?" Meg looked at the approaching glass of vodka and orange juice with relief. She definitely needed a drink.

"Nah. They don't have to teach it, it's everywhere. Like one of our women teachers got pregnant by one of the men teachers and the man had to switch schools because he wasn't going to marry her and she went apeshit and the headmaster had to take her side."

"I see. I don't see why that means you think I'm going to leave your father, though."

"I just felt like asking, that's all."

"Would you like me to leave?" she asked tentatively.

"No." He shrugged his shoulders again. Josh, now that she thought about it, shrugged a lot. "I wouldn't blame you.

That's all. Dad can be pretty insensitive to women. I'm not sure he likes women."

I'm not sure he likes women.

Meg felt the room around her dissolve into blankness for a moment as she focused on these words. She struggled to pull her thoughts together in some coherent form.

"Are you saying that because of the way he treated your mother?"

"Can I have a sip of your drink?"

"Sure," she answered quickly. He was no longer a fourteen-year-old boy but someone who held the key to her world. Her calls to the real estate agent, her careful working out of what money she needed, all her steps in the direction of a separation had been like a game she was playing in her own mind. Each move had been satisfying, but she'd never truly admitted the fact that the game could become real one day, that she'd actually leave Charlie. Sitting in the bar, listening to her stepson, Meg became acutely aware that this was not only a possibility, it was fast becoming a certainty.

"The way he treated Mom is pretty much the way he treats you," he said, after taking a long pull from her glass.

"Oh."

Charlie doesn't like women. I don't think I like Charlie.

"He's different with David and me. I don't know if that's 'cause we're his children or 'cause we're boys." He reached for her glass again.

"Josh. Are you drinking a lot?"

"Nah. Just sometimes. You found the bottle of vodka, didn't you?"

"Yes."

"Thanks for not saying anything. Dad would go on a rampage telling me how I had to keep a straight head to get into law school. As if I cared."

"I wanted to wait until I'd talked to you about it."

"Don't worry. It's just a phase I'm going through—the drinking and the smoking."

"A phase you're going to grow out of?"

"I dunno." Josh shrugged. And then he said with a be-atific smile that strangely reminded Meg of Eddy: "Some-times I hope not."

"I'm glad you didn't do what some grown-ups do all the time."

"What's that?" Patrick asked.

"You didn't let me win on purpose. I mean, you beat me. Lots of grown-ups let you win and that means they think you're stupid and you don't know they're letting you win."

"I wouldn't do that, Charlotte. And I don't think you're stupid."

Amy handed over their bowling shoes to the Charles Manson look-alike behind the counter.

"I wish you'd let *me* win," she said. "I wouldn't mind if that meant you thought I was stupid. I would have en-joyed beating you on any terms."

"I bet you would have," Patrick grinned.

Shit, Amy thought. Shit, shit, shit. I'm totally turned on at noon in a bowling alley. I want to reach out and grab his ass. Oh shit.

"Here. I'll pay," she said as Patrick went for his wallet. "My treat."

"Thanks," he said. "I appreciate it. I'm broke. As usual."

"No great tips at the bar?"

"Afraid not."

"Well, I'll treat you to lunch, too, if you've got the time."

"We'd see time dawn together if I were able. But sorry, Ames, I have to get going now."

Don't ask him, Amy. Do not ask him what's more im-portant than us. Don't try to pin him down.

"Do you need a lift anywhere?"

"Patrick the eternal hitchhiker? No, I'm fine."

"Do you have to go?" Charlotte asked in her most ba-byish voice.

"Yes I have to go, Charlotte. But I'll see you again soon."

"Oh, that reminds me. Wait here—" Amy rushed over to one of the bowling lanes, tore a sheet from the scorepad and wrote the name of the school, its address, and the time of the play in huge letters on the back. "We'll see you there on Monday."

"Great," Patrick picked Charlotte up, gave her a kiss on the cheek, deposited her back on the floor and grabbed her left hand with his. "Always remember, Charlotte. Shake hands with your left hand, not your right. The left is closer to the heart."

"But no one else does that," Charlotte looked confused.

"I know no one else does that. You're different. You're special. You're a wise woman. Stay close to the heart at all times."

Amy closed her eyes. She wanted to stop time from moving, hijack this moment and keep it forever.

"Bye, Ames," he said gaily. "We've got a fantastic kid."

And then he was gone. This time, though, he wasn't gone for good.

"Is Jimmy coming on Monday too?" Charlotte asked as they walked out of the building, holding hands.

"I don't know, sweetheart. Would you like him to come?"

"Could Zoey come with him?"

Zoey. Amy had yet to tell Jimmy about her meeting with Rachel. When she'd informed him the previous evening that she was taking Charlotte to see Patrick this morning, he'd gone into a nonspeaking sulk. The jealousy she used to yearn for as a sign of his love now made it easier to break away from him. Another night sleeping apart ensued. And another silent morning. Would he want to come to Charlotte's play if Patrick were there? Probably not.

But, Amy countered her growing sense of guilt, Jimmy wouldn't have wanted to come anyway. He would have attended under sufferance. So why should she worry about not asking him?

"Zoey will be at her own school on Monday. I think it's better if Patrick came and Jimmy didn't, don't you?"

"I guess so," Charlotte answered thoughtfully. "Am I supposed to call Patrick 'Dad' now?"

"Do you want to?"

"Maybe later," she said. "Maybe after the play."

"Is this Leonora Preston?"

"Yes," Leo answered.

"You don't know me, Leonora. And this is a strange phone call, but my name is Stuart Manning and—"

"Stuart? *The* Stuart?"

"*The* Stuart? Hardly. I met you once when you were a baby."

"In a parking lot."

"Yes. In a parking lot."

"Stuart. God, I can't believe this. Where are you? Everyone's been talking about you."

"What do you mean?" he asked gruffly. "Who has been talking about me?"

"My sisters and I. You're our hero. Our savior."

"That's not true." He retorted quickly. "I gave you a lift once, that's all. Your sister Beth called me last week to remind me of it. I remembered all your sisters' names then, of course, because of the *Little Women* connection. I tried to find Meg and Amy in the phone book, but they weren't listed, under Preston anyway. And then I remembered the baby—you. You weren't called Jo, though, so it took me a while, but I dredged through my memory and came up with Leonora. It's an unusual name, so it stayed with me. It was easy to find you."

"But I've got an unlisted number now."

"I know."

"So how did you get it?"

"I have a friend."

"A friend in the telephone company or in the Mafia?"

"Both, and many in the C.I.A., too."

"Right. I deserved that, I guess. If that was a joke." Leo

found herself trying to imagine what Stuart looked like, but the only picture she could summon was a man in chain mail jousting in front of a cheering crowd.

"It was a bad joke. Listen, I know I shouldn't be bothering you, but you were the only Preston sister I could find."

"But you said Beth called you."

"I know," Stuart sighed. "That's what I'm calling *you* about. I'm worried about her. I think she may be dangerous."

"What?"

"Look. I told you this was strange. I've just moved to Boston and the first thing I know, your sister calls me out of the blue and asks to meet me. I mean, I drove you home that day. Fine. But I never expected to get a call from her twenty years or so later. It's a little weird, don't you think?"

"Maybe she wanted to thank you."

"She wanted to *meet* me. Anyway, I said that it wasn't such a great idea. Later, after I'd thought about it, I figured I'd been a little harsh. It was an innocent call. I'd overreacted. So I found her number and called her back, but before I could say one word, she screamed 'Fuck you and the horse you rode in on' into the receiver and hung up."

"Oh no," Leo groaned. "You've got to understand Beth. She does things like that sometimes."

"Well, it didn't sound too sane to me. And then this morning, I got a tape pushed through my door. A tape with all this country music on it. I racked my brain trying to work out who could have put it there, but you see I don't know anyone else in Boston. I came here because I'd gone to college here so I know the city, but I didn't contact anyone from BC. No one knows I'm here. Only Beth.

"It's a very romantic tape. I think she may be obsessed with me and that's worrying. I thought you might be able to help. And now you tell me everyone's talking about me. It's not healthy. I gave you all a ride home. *That's all I did.*"

The panic in his voice began to make Leo feel very edgy as well.

"We know that's all you did, and we're very grateful for it. Beth may have a 'thing' about you—"

"I don't want her to have a 'thing' about me—"

"She wouldn't hurt you, if that's what you're thinking. She's not some kind of Glenn Close in *Fatal Attraction*."

"I know she put this tape through my door."

"All right, maybe she did. But that's not so bad, is it? It's not as if she'd boiled your pet rabbit."

"I want her to get off my back."

"Stuart. I'm sorry if she's annoyed you so much. I'm sure she didn't mean to."

"I don't think she's stable."

"She's *not* crazy." Who *is* this guy? Leo thought. What a paranoid man.

"Could you please tell her to leave me alone?"

"Absolutely, Stuart. And don't be concerned. Everyone will stop talking about you now."

She heard a long intake of breath on his end of the line.

"Leonora, listen. I know I must sound harsh, but I have my reasons."

"Well, Beth has plenty of reasons to stop contacting you. She's got tons of men chasing *her*."

"She was a seriously cute little kid." His tone had softened. He sounded almost wistful. "I don't mean to be cruel. The 'fuck you and the horse you rode in on' routine got to me. Then the tape. It's full of wonderful songs. *Too* wonderful."

"Beth has great taste in music."

"She does."

Another long pause.

"I know this is going to sound strange after everything I've just said to you, but if you or your sisters are ever in trouble again, let me know. Maybe I can help."

"I don't understand. You said you wanted Beth to leave you alone."

"I know, I know, and I meant it. I don't want her to

focus on some image of me she has that isn't real. That can cause a lot of pain. But I do care about all of you. I admit I'd forgotten about that day in the parking lot until Beth phoned me, but when I remembered, I could recall every single detail. Anyone else could have given you all a ride, but I'm the one who did. And I'm the one who drove away. I was involved and I chose to step out of the picture. All I'm trying to say is that I feel some kind of responsibility. Not to Beth specifically, but to all of you. Not that you'll ever need me again now that you're all adults, but here's my number. Do you have a pen?"

Leo grabbed the pen she'd just been using for translation work and copied Stuart's number down on her message pad.

"Stuart? Now it's my turn to ask you a strange question."

"Okay. Shoot."

"Were you on a subway yesterday at lunchtime?"

"No. Why?"

"Amy thought she saw you."

"Christ. Your whole family is nuts. Maybe I should take back my offer."

Leo was beginning to like him.

"Too late. I've got your number."

"What happened to your mother?" he asked.

"She died fourteen years ago."

"I'm sorry."

"Thank you. I guess you must have seen her at her worst."

"She wasn't in terrific shape, no. Anyway, if you can disabuse Beth of this obsession, or 'thing' or whatever you call it she has for me, I'd be very grateful."

"It would help if I told her you're married."

"I'm not, but that's probably the best idea. Feel free to lie."

"I can't do that."

"All right. Tell her I'm a recluse. Tell her anything you think will work that's honest."

"Why don't *you* tell her?"

"I have this feeling she wouldn't pay any attention."

"Why do you think she'd listen to me?"

"I'm not sure. The four of you seemed so much a unit. And you've got a persuasive voice."

"We are a unit. We always have been."

"Then you see I was right to call you, but I apologize for interrupting whatever you were doing on a Saturday afternoon."

"That's all right. I was translating *Dead Souls*. I needed a break. Besides, it's nice to hear the voice of our savior."

"Don't start that again," Stuart laughed.

I'll figure out a way, Leo promised herself after they'd said good-bye. I'll make sure he and Beth meet each other. That will be the best Christmas present I can give her.

Chapter Nineteen

"I TOLD YOU, Leo. *He* sent *me* a tape. That's why I delivered one to him. I can't believe he called you. He must be crazy."

Beth was fast approaching the raving stage. She tossed her hair furiously, clenched her fists and snarled. "He thinks I'm stalking him. He's got delusions of grandeur."

"First of all, I don't think he sent you that tape. You said there was no return address, no identification. Why did you assume it was from Stuart?"

"He was the logical choice."

"Beth. Logical? Someone you met once, twenty years ago?"

"All right. Okay. Maybe I jumped to conclusions. But I was sure in my heart. I *felt* it was from him."

"Well, now you know that it wasn't. So you have to see how he might have been a little upset to get an unsolicited tape through his door. *After* having been told to fuck off."

"I didn't know I was saying that to *him*."

"I know, Beth." Leo soothed her. "But Stuart doesn't know you. He wouldn't understand."

"What's to understand? Dad had just visited and done his usual routine on me. I was pissed off."

"Stuart doesn't understand your belief in the cathartic power of expressing anger. He's not one of your clients, remember?"

"He should be. He needs some help."

"Okay. He *should* be. What I'm trying to say to you is that Stuart sounds very wary. As if something had happened to him once to make him permanently afraid of people invading his territory."

"No. You know what happened? His little cheerleader

wife found out about the tape and went haywire. That's why he called you. She went berserk with jealousy."

"He's not married. He told me he wasn't."

"Bullshit. I saw her. And their kid. I've talked to her on the phone."

"When?"

"I *saw* them yesterday when I dropped off the tape. And I talked to her last weekend when I tried to call him a second time. He's lying to you. He's a complete fake."

"I don't get it. He asked me to lie to you, to tell you that he *was* married so you'd get off his back. I refused because he'd already told me he wasn't married. So why would he lie?"

"He's a psycho. Shit. I made us all get in a car with a psycho. I'm surprised we're still alive."

"He didn't sound like a psycho," Leo said slowly, trying to sort all these facts out in her mind. "He sounded a little paranoid at the beginning of the conversation, but by the end he was really sweet, actually. I liked him."

"Yeah. You'd like Ted Bundy."

Leo stepped on her rising anger. Contrary to all her sister's beliefs, she knew it wouldn't help to express it right now.

"So you don't want to meet him."

"No, I do not. I made a huge mistake, okay? I thought he was God's gift to women. What I didn't know was that that is exactly what he thinks he is. I won't be bothering him and his little sweetheart anymore. You can tell him that."

"I think I'll leave it alone."

"I cannot believe he called you. The nerve. What a gutless wimp."

Leo didn't bother to point out the contradiction in the last two statements.

"So who *did* send the tape to you?"

"You want to know something? I don't give a shit. What's for breakfast? And where's Nick Booth?"

Leo looked at her watch.

"He's gone to a little diner where we always spend Sunday mornings. I'm about to join him there."

"Great. I'll come along."

"I'm sorry, Beth. Nick and I have a lot to talk about. On our own."

"Oh, fine. I know when I'm not wanted."

"Come on, Beth. Don't make me feel guilty. Or I'll throw something at you."

Beth laughed. Rising from her chair, she went and hugged Leo.

"How did you grow up so fast, kiddo? It's scary."

Thirty-five minutes later, when her doorbell rang, Leo checked her watch again and congratulated herself on her perfect timing.

"So," Meg said, settling herself into the chair Beth had vacated. "Where's Nick?"

"He's gone ahead to a place where we always have brunch on Sunday mornings. I'm meeting him later. Here— have some coffee."

"Thanks." Meg took the mug. "I need some caffeine."

"You look a little tired."

"I didn't sleep much."

"I could tell from your voice on the phone last night that something's wrong. It's been wrong for a long time, hasn't it? What's happening?"

"Oh, Christ." Meg's shoulders slumped. "I don't know. Nothing. Everything. My marriage is a little screwed up at the moment."

"Why?"

"It's hard to explain."

"Try."

"I guess I feel swamped. At the same time I feel utterly alone. That doesn't make any sense, I know, but it's the truth. I can't really cope with Josh and David, even on weekends. I really like Josh, but I don't know what my relationship with him is supposed to be. I know I'm not his mother, but am I supposed to be his friend, or another authority figure? And David just drives me nuts. So I favor Josh, which isn't fair to anyone. Charlie's all wrapped up in his career. I don't have anything that's *mine* except my job and that's been difficult lately as well. I *think* I want a baby. That's what I've always thought I wanted. But now I keep thinking what I really want is to leave Charlie. I've even been to see some apartments. I'm confused, Leo. Totally confused."

"Do you love Charlie?"

"Sometimes. I think I do. Then he says something that either makes me want to burst out crying or else chop his head off. I might love him, but I don't know if I like him. It's not healthy. That's for sure."

"It doesn't sound like you should be considering having a baby with him."

"I know, I know. Still—I can't quite let go of the idea. It's been so central to my life, even though I always knew he didn't want another child. I'm screwed up, Leo. I have this stupid plan—a last-ditch effort. I want to tell Charlie I'm pregnant just to see his response. If he's happy about it, then I can admit I lied but I'll know it's okay to go ahead and try to get pregnant. If he's pissed off, then I'll know he'll never change."

"Meg. I'm sorry, but that doesn't make any sense. You're not even sure you like him. You shouldn't be thinking about babies or pretending to be pregnant."

"You're right. I know. But I don't know if I can leave him. It's such a *huge* step, Leo. People talk about divorce all the time, but actually going through with one—all the fallout from it, I don't know. It scares me. I keep thinking that if I knew for certain he doesn't want a child, I'd be strong enough to leave. Whatever happens to me, I don't want to be married to a man who doesn't want my baby."

"You can't just take his word for it?"

"If I had taken his word for it, I would never have married him in the first place. I was one of those stupid women who believe they can change a man."

"I don't think anyone could change Charlie's mind about anything."

"I know. That's one of the things I loved about him at the beginning. His certainty. Now—" Meg bowed her head.

"The last thing I want to do is to push you toward a divorce. But I hate to see you so unhappy. Whatever happens between you and Charlie, you need to know inside yourself that you *can* make it on your own, Meg. Whether you leave him or not, you have to know that."

"I think I do know that already. I think I also know that I should leave him. I *think* all this, but I'm not *sure*, and I have to be sure. I need to give him one more chance. For my own sake. That's why I'm going to go through with this pretend pregnancy business, no matter how stupid it may seem."

"What if Charlie actually likes the idea of you being pregnant? Are you sure you'd like to stay with him even then?"

"That's a tough question." Meg raised her eyes to meet Leo's. "You're too young to ask such tough questions."

"You'd be surprised how much I've grown up," Leo said, frowning. "It's scary."

Amy arrived with Zoey and Charlotte in tow, fifteen minutes after Meg left.

"Charlotte," Leo said, wrapping her arms around her niece. "Could you and Zo do me a big favor? Before you take off your coats, could you please go to the deli farther down Huron Avenue and pick up some bagels for us all? And some cream cheese?"

"I know the place," Zoey said, grabbing Charlotte's hand. "Come on, Lot, I'm starving. Let's buy tons and tons of food."

"Here's some money." Leo handed over a twenty-dollar bill to Charlotte. "You're in charge. Don't let Zoey go too wild."

"Zombie is *always* wild with food." Charlotte looked at her stepsister with adoration.

"Zombie?" Leo asked, laughing.

"That's her nickname for me," Zoey explained. "Suddenly she's gone on a nickname kick. We'll be back in ten minutes or so."

"Great. Thanks, guys." Leo took Amy by the arm as soon as the girls had gone and drew her into the kitchen. "What's going on, Ames? What happened with Patrick yesterday?" She lifted herself up onto the counter. Amy took a seat at the table. They always took these positions whenever Amy visited. Leo couldn't count the times they'd spent hours conversing in the kitchen.

"Charlotte and he got on really well. That's all. We went bowling, like I told you."

"What happened between *you* and Patrick?"

"Nothing special."

"Amy. Christ. You're in love with him again, aren't you?"

"Maybe."

"Oh, no."

"Look. Don't do this to me. I didn't give you a hard time about Nick. I understood. You've always understood me. Don't stop now, when I need you the most."

"I understand, Ames. Of course I do. But I don't trust Patrick. I *like* Patrick, but I don't trust him. Not where you're concerned."

"He was wonderful yesterday. You don't know what it's like to see them together. How nice it is to be a real family. I think he loves her, I really do."

"Does he love her enough to stick around?"

"He's coming to her Christmas play tomorrow. The old Patrick wouldn't be caught dead at something as boring as a kid's Christmas play."

"Yes, he would. He'd go to one Christmas play just to see what it was like. What he wouldn't do is go to another one the next year. I'm not trying to lay a guilt trip on you, really I'm not. But what about Jimmy? Where does he stand in all this?"

"I don't know. We're not speaking at the moment. Actually, we haven't been speaking for days. I told him you wanted me to bring Zoey over here this morning. That's been the extent of our conversation. He didn't even ask about Charlotte's meeting with Patrick yesterday. That's how much he cares."

"Maybe he's hurting."

"Why are you taking his side?"

"I'm not." Leo shook her head forcefully. "I'm on your side. I always will be, whatever you do. But I think you love Jimmy. I think you're infatuated with Patrick. You've always been infatuated with Patrick. And you're letting the infatuation cloud your love for Jimmy."

"Would someone please tell me what's so wrong with infatuation? What's so wrong with *fun?* Patrick and I always had fun. I've missed it. I've missed him."

"You didn't exactly have a blast when he left you."

"I'm not saying I want to marry him again. I'm not thinking ahead. I'm taking things as they happen, that's all."

"While you're busy not thinking ahead, you might lose Jimmy—you know that, don't you? Are you willing to take that risk?"

"I'm tired of not taking risks."

The intercom buzzed.

"Amy—" Leo jumped down from the counter, went and put her arm around her sister's shoulder. "You do whatever you have to do. No more lectures from me."

"Thanks. I know I probably need a lecture, I know you're probably right, but I can't change the way I feel. So tell me. Why did you want Zoey to come along today?"

"She knows Nick's daughter, Thea. I need to get some information from her."

"You seem so focused. As if you were a general directing the troops."

"That's what I *am* doing. More or less. But my battle plan hasn't worked out so well," Leo frowned. "I had this absurd idea last night that I can make everyone happy, that I can solve everyone's problems."

"You've always tried to do that," Amy said as the apartment buzzer sounded.

"Have I?" Leo asked over her shoulder as she went to let the girls in. "I must be crazy."

"Charlotte," Amy called out from the kitchen when she heard the front door open. "Come here with the food and we'll fix a big breakfast for Leo and Zoey."

"What about us?" Charlotte asked, running in, laden down with bags. "I'm as hungry as Zombie is."

"Me too," Amy said, sighing. "We all need some sustenance."

"Zo—come into the living room with me for a few minutes, will you?" Leo asked.

"Sure." Zoey took off her designer-ripped blue-jean jacket, and followed Leo. "What's happening?"

"Remember Nick? You met him the other night when we came to dinner?"

"Sure. He looked a little like Clint Eastwood."

"Really?"

"Yeah. Not in *Bridges of Madison County*, but in *In the Line of Fire*. I could see him wrestling with John Malkovich on the elevator. But Nick looked like he might lose."

"I guess he might. Anyway, he's got a daughter, a girl who goes to school with you. Thea."

"Thea Booth? No shit?"

"Are you two friends?"

"We used to be. Best friends. For like two years."

"What happened?"

"She got into another group. She started hanging out with the depressed people."

"The depressed people?"

"Yeah. They're a year ahead of us. They wear black all the time and look sad."

"Why did she do that? Do you know?"

"I think—I think it had something to do with me, actually."

"What?" Leo asked nervously.

"Well, like I said, we were best friends. And then this

other girl, Caroline, came into our class and Caroline kind
of picked me out as *her* best friend. I was nice to her because she was new and everything and Thea—I think Thea
thought I'd ditched her. Girls get really caught up in that
stuff when they're twelve and thirteen. It's serious—who
hangs out with who, you know. Thea got pissed off and
went with the depressos. Once you go with the depressos,
there's no way out."

"What do you mean?"

"They're so heavy. No one has ever gone with the depressos and come back to us normal types. We're like light-
weights, you know. We care about clothes and boys and
music and shit. The depressos care about *life* and how bad
it is."

"But Nick told me all Thea's teachers say how popular
she is."

"Hey, she's got tons of depresso friends. The depressos
hang out and drink espressos together. The teachers like
them because they're so serious."

"Thea said that you're a star."

"Listen, we were like sisters. I think Thea's a star. But
she got hurt when Caroline came on the scene and instead
of talking to me about it, she just went her own way. It
made me sad, I can tell you. I miss her."

"Did she talk about her parents with you?"

"Sometimes. No offense, but she said they were a pain
in the ass. That's why we never went over to her house.
She said they were always fighting. She said she didn't
want to have anything to do with them. She couldn't wait
to be old enough to leave home."

"Do you think there's any way you could revive your
friendship with her now? I think she needs you—or someone who'll really understand. She's angry at Nick. And
me."

"So they're getting divorced, her parents?"

"Yes."

"Thea used to say she wished they *would* get divorced.

I can try to talk to her, sure. I can tell her all the great stuff about being a child of divorce."

"Such as?"

"Such as having a wickedly cool stepfather, a really nice stepmother, two houses to choose from, and lots of people feeling sorry for you. Such as when you don't do your homework, telling the teachers that you've left it at your other parent's house by mistake. Such as getting money from your mother *and* your father, so doubling your monthly allowance. Such as having a kid stepsister who worships the ground you walk on so you can get her to wait on you hand and foot. There are a lot of pros to this situation, you know. You just have to have the right attitude."

"You must have *some* bitterness."

"Nope." Zoey ran her fingers through her red hair. "Some of my friends have parents who stayed together. They're *really* fucked up."

"Why?"

"They have to be perfect. They don't have any excuses. It's a pain, let me tell you. If a child of divorce does well and is happy, she's a genius, a megastar. If a child from a regular family does well, she's just normal. Divorced parents are so frightened that they've screwed up their kids, they treat them like precious metals. It's fun to be golden. A whole lot better than being taken for granted."

Charlotte came in, carrying a tray of toasted bagels covered in cream cheese.

"Thanks, Lot," Zoey said, winking at Leo. "Now go get me a glass of orange juice, will you?"

Chapter Twenty

WHICH MOVIE WAS it? Meg asked herself, as she watched Charlie eat his breakfast. Something famous. The married couple start off eating their breakfast side-by-side, and move farther apart over the years until they are finally at opposite ends of a long table, not speaking to each other. She and Charlie hadn't reached that stage yet. They were still, at least physically, side-by-side. And all she had to do now was to tell him she thought she might be pregnant. "I might be pregnant." Four words that she didn't have the courage to speak.

"I might be pregnant," she kept saying to herself, over and over. "I might be pregnant." When Charlie reached across to get his newspaper, always his prelude to leaving the table, she knew she had no time left to practice.

"I might be pregnant," she mumbled.

He heard her.

"You *might* be pregnant?"

Meg nodded.

Charlie put the paper back down on the table. He stared at her with such intensity, she looked away.

"Nice try," he said simply, with a touch of amusement in his voice.

"What do you mean, nice try?" Meg tried to summon up outrage. It wouldn't come anywhere near her.

"On Friday you tell me you've got the curse. On Monday you tell me you might be pregnant. The female cycle doesn't work like that, Meg. Nice try."

"I lied on Friday."

"Oh, I see. Why do I think you'd be more likely to lie about being pregnant, or about possibly being pregnant?"

"I don't know," she mumbled again, abashed.

"Well, I do. You want to see what my reaction would be, don't you? And if I say 'hey, terrific,' you'll throw away your pills and do it for real. Am I correct?"

"*Would* you say that?"

"No. So don't throw them away."

"*I'd* take care of the baby, Charlie. It wouldn't interfere with your life."

"You have no idea what having a baby involves. It would interfere. With my life, with our lives."

"What if I'm miserable without one?"

"Are you telling me you're miserable now?"

"I'm unhappy."

Charlie pondered. When Charlie pondered, Meg knew he was weighing pros and cons up in his mind, very carefully. He never pondered for less than five minutes. She had to wait it out.

"I see," he finally said. Some scale had tipped. But in which direction? "It appears you're trying to blackmail me."

"What?"

"If I say I don't want to have a baby, you'll make a fuss and we'll have a crisis in our marriage that we'll have to talk about endlessly and that way I won't have time for my work. You're making me choose between my work and you just at the moment when my work is at a crucial juncture. You think I'll give in and say 'yes' to a baby so I won't have to take time out from work."

"Excuse me? Where did all that come from?"

"It's the truth, isn't it, Meg?"

"I couldn't even follow what you were saying. I'm supposed to be forcing you to make a choice, right? But I'm supposed to *know* you'll choose having a baby so you won't have to make a choice? I don't understand your thinking."

"I'm being logical."

"Just tell me—do you want a baby or not?"

"I've told you before. No, I don't. But if I have to have

one to stop you from being so silly, to keep you quiet, I will."

"To keep me quiet?"

"I want a peaceful life."

"With no nagging wife."

"Come on, Meg. You know me by now. I know you. We don't need to get into these kinds of arguments. We love each other."

"Oh."

"So you can have what you want. You've won. You've got your baby. Well—" Charlie winked. "You'll be on your way to getting your baby, starting tonight. Just don't expect me to do any of the dirty work when the deed's done."

He tapped her on the head with his newspaper, picked up his car keys from the table and walked blithely out of the house.

Meg remained seated, staring at the patterned grain of the wooden table.

I have too many clothes, she thought. *It's going to be hell moving everything.*

A few minutes later, on her way upstairs to pack, it came to her.

Citizen Kane. That was it.

Amy had saved a seat beside her in the tiny school hall. Her coat rested on top of the folding chair—a signal to ward off any potential butters-in. The place was packed. People kept coming up and saying "Excuse me, is this seat taken?" "It's about to be," she'd say, smiling apologetically and they'd back off. Five minutes before the play began, there was standing room only. Amy could sense the covetous stares at the one empty seat. She could sense the disapproval emanating from foot-weary parents. She didn't flinch. Patrick was always late. Doubtless he'd arrive just as the curtain went up. As long as he came in time to see Charlotte enter with the other Wise Men, she didn't care.

Joseph and Mary made it to the inn and were refused entry.

No Patrick.

Joseph and Mary bedded down chastely in the stable.

No Patrick.

Amy kept craning her neck toward the door.

The baby Jesus, in the form of a doll, arrived on the scene. Video cameras whirred.

No Patrick.

Get another script, Amy wanted to shout. Tell the Wise Men to wait a while.

Luckily, there was a brief pause in the action for a communal rendering of "Away in a Manger."

A host of angels fluttered around the doll.

Charlotte, dressed in a yellow shift, walked in, flanked by two other children. Time for another communal carol: "We Three Kings." Charlotte knelt down after the last note and placed what looked like a candy bar wrapped in yellow paper at the doll's feet. Amy's eyes swiveled from Charlotte to the door, back to Charlotte, back to the door. Her neck was beginning to ache.

Everyone on stage sounded happy about this miracle.

Amy wasn't.

Some child with glinting braces delivered a closing speech on the importance of recognizing other religions. Amy thought she might turn Muslim, if that meant she could swathe her face in a veil for the foreseeable future.

They all sang "Deck the Halls."

The man two seats away from her stared at her lifeless coat on the unoccupied seat as the applause echoed through the hall.

"I suffer from claustrophobia," she explained. He nodded, but not sympathetically.

Beth had arranged her office carefully. One chair for her, one sofa for her client. The chair and sofa were placed at right angles, allowing Beth to get an early take on new arrivals. The ones who sat on the far end of the sofa were the easy ones, whereas the clients who positioned themselves as close as they could to her chair were naturally aggressive. It was far more difficult explaining the value of aggression to naturally aggressive people. People coming for therapy wanted to change their lives, not be reinforced in their old habits.

There were pillows to be punched, lightweight objects to be thrown—for the beginners—and a row of increasingly heavy glasses on the side table. The next-door office, a theater ticket agency, complained of the noise of breaking glass. "What are you running in there?" the secretary often asked as they passed on the stairs. "An all-day Greek restaurant?"

Susie, cowering at the end of the sofa, threw a feeble punch at a pillow.

"Do you feel better?" Beth asked.

"No."

"Of course you don't. You didn't put your weight into it. You barely touched it."

"I'm not sure how this therapy is supposed to help me in real life," Susie whimpered. "I mean, I can't go around hitting people that bother me, can I?"

"No." Beth put on her patient voice. "You can't. But there's a part of you that would like to, isn't there?"

"Yes," Susie nodded enthusiastically.

"You're tired of being meek and humble, aren't you?"

"Yes." Her head now looked like the bobbing head of a fake dog in the back of a particularly tacky car. Would her eyes light up to signal right and left turns? Beth wondered.

"So I'm allowing you to be strong in this office. Here. You can get a sense of your own strength, you can begin to understand your anger. Physically. Accept your rage. Act it out. Then you can transfer the physical to your mental outlook. This is a symbolic procedure, Susie. One that you can use throughout your life."

"I see."

The office buzzer went off. Beth looked at her watch and silently cursed Chloe, her next client, for arriving early.

"Excuse me for a moment, Susie," she said. "I'll just get this. Hello?"

"Hello, Beth. This is your old friend Jackie."

"I've got a client, Jackie."

"I don't mind," Susie, overhearing the conversation, said quickly, gathering her coat and bag. "Really."

Beth put her hand over the intercom.

"You have ten minutes left, Susie."

"I don't mind. I'll go early."

She was halfway out the door.

"We're going to have to work on this, Susie. You shouldn't give up your rights so easily."

"I know, I know, I'm sorry," she replied. The door closed behind her. Beth turned her attention back to the intercom.

"What do you want, Jackie?"

"I have some information for you. Let me in."

Beth could hear Susie say, "Sorry. Have a nice day," to Jackie as she passed her at the door. Jesus, that woman needed *centuries* of help.

As she was deliberating whether to let Jackie in or not, Beth realized that Jackie had already gained access. She'd walked in as Susie walked out. Therapist shot dead by estranged wife. There wasn't room enough in the headline to explain the tangled relationships, Beth knew. The reading public would assume *she'd* been having an affair with Nick. What would Stuart think? she asked herself before remembering that she didn't care anymore what Stuart thought.

"I thought you were supposed to be in London," Beth said evenly when Jackie appeared in her office doorway. "What happened? Did they turn you back at immigration as an unsuitable alien? The Brits have always had good taste."

"No," Jackie smiled. Her mouth looked like a knife. "I discovered something when I was there that made me come back early." She took out mimeographed sheets of newspaper. "I thought this might be of interest to you. And, of course, to Leonora. I didn't stay to see her reaction. I didn't need to. But I'm glad to have seen yours."

"The skirt's a tad too short, isn't it Jackie? I mean, the

red and green suit is very festive indeed, but the skirt's a little too revealing."

Jackie didn't rise to the bait. She just stood there holding out the mimeographed sheets. Beth knew now that something explosive was being handed to her. Jackie was too cool, too calm. She knew she was winning. But with what weapons? Had Leo posed for *Playboy* in the nude without telling anyone? Was her youngest sister an international arms dealer? What could possibly make Jackie look so smug? Reaching out for the paper, Beth imagined Socrates grabbing the hemlock. Whatever happened next, it wasn't going to be fun.

It was a long article. Beth didn't understand what was going on until she got to the second page and found the highlighted paragraph. Four sentences. Beth reread them. She quickly went back to the first page, looked at the top to see which newspaper had printed this story. The *Sunday Times*. The English *Sunday Times*. Was Jackie bluffing, had she manufactured this newspaper, this story? No. Jackie wasn't dumb. Jackie knew Beth could check it out with a couple of phone calls. Beth willed herself not to sit down, but her willpower was no longer a functioning aspect of her personality.

"Do you need some help? Are you going to faint?"

"Fuck off."

"I was fairly certain you didn't know. But I wanted to see your face. Now I've seen it. Good-bye, Beth. Very nice to have met you."

"You can't fucking do this."

"*I* didn't do anything, did I?"

"You gave this to Leo?"

"I did. I've explained in an accompanying letter that if Leonora leaves my husband alone, I won't find myself compelled to take this information any further. But if she persists in her relationship, I'm afraid the truth will have to come out."

"Who gives a fuck whether the truth comes out? I couldn't care less if you went public with it."

"No? Think about it, Beth. Don't you think it might affect your job? Just a *tad?* I can't imagine wanting to be a client of yours, knowing this."

She pointed to the sheets of paper. "Can you? Merry Christmas."

Oh, Jesus, Beth wailed as the door closed behind Jackie. Her brain kept racing for exit doors, but couldn't find any. *We're all doomed now. All of us.*

Beth used to love barging into Mark's office, creating a spectacle of herself. Adorned with various punk haircuts in various hues, outrageous clothes, even a nose ring once, she'd sail through the soft-carpeted halls of Preston, Pembury and Saltonstall, on her mission to shock. It always worked. Once some legal aide had sidled up to her and asked where she'd had her hair done, but on every other occasion she was gratified to see slack jaws, wide eyes and expressions of horror.

"You're not really helping your case," Mark used to say. "They'll all feel sorry for me. You haven't accomplished what you set out to."

Oh, but she had. She'd brought him to the public's attention. She'd outed him. His underlings would talk about the boss's wild daughter in bars after work. They'd speculate about his home life. They might even whisper in corridors. A hint of impropriety would hang upon him. There would be a scratch on the sleek exterior.

Beth knew exactly what she was doing.

But now, as she made her way to the plush office in her sensible, working clothes, all she could think about was Leo. They weren't pleasant thoughts.

Mark's secretary wasn't at her desk, not that Beth would have paid any attention to any effort to halt her progress. Barging in, she saw Mark standing straight, talking on the telephone, looking out the window.

"Dad," she said.

He turned, motioned her to a high-backed leather chair.

"Dad. Hang up. This is important."

Mark made polite excuses to whomever he was conversing with. He placed the receiver gently back on its cradle. He politely asked his daughter if she wanted some coffee.

"Read this," Beth ordered, handing him the newspaper article. "You'll understand when you get to the paragraph highlighted in yellow."

He took a pair of glasses from his breast pocket. Another affectation, Beth found herself thinking as she watched him scan the pages. Like the gray in his hair.

He finished reading. He'd done exactly what she had—read the relevant paragraph twice over, then checked for the name of the publication. Like father, like daughter. No, Beth thought. Not.

"It's true, isn't it?"

He nodded. Not a goddamn hair out of place, she thought. Not one facial twitch. Why wasn't he a professional poker payer?

"I—"

"Cut it, Dad. I don't want to hear the whys and whens and wherefores now. Maybe later. I don't know. Maybe I never want to hear whatever paltry explanation you choose to give. I'm not concerned about you. It's Leo. Nick's wife gave this to me. And she's given a copy to Leo, too. I tried to call her from my office. No reply. I went over to her place. No reply. But she might be in there. I want you to come with me right now and break down the fucking door."

"Could Nick's wife have been bluffing? Perhaps she didn't give it to Leonora."

"Nick's wife doesn't bluff. I hate to think what reaction Leo will have to this. You know how sensitive she can be. I almost called the police. But I don't want the police in on this if we can help it. You know how difficult this story will be to explain."

"Let me try getting a hold of Leonora now."

"Go ahead. I haven't called for at least two minutes."

Mark snatched the telephone, dialed a number, stood waiting.

"No answer." He tapped his fingers on the desk. "Wait—Nick?"

Mark looked at Beth with relief.

"Nick, it's Mark here. Could I speak to Leonora please? No—oh—could you just check the bedroom and make sure she's not asleep?"

Mark continued to tap his fingers on the desk as he waited. Beth stared out the window looking out over Boston Harbor and watched a British Airways 747 approach a distant runway.

"No? I see." He covered the receiver with his hand and whispered to Beth: "She was supposed to be working at home on her thesis this morning. Nick was supposed to be joining her there for lunch. He just walked in when the phone was ringing. He doesn't know where she's gone, but he just noticed a note on the kitchen table. He's going to get it and read it now.

"I see. Yes. Well, perhaps she needed a break." Long pause again. Beth picked up the paperweight from the desk. If she hurled it through the plate glass window, would it make anything better? No. Whatever happened, she knew it was time to call a halt to aggression therapy.

"I'm sorry, Nick. I have no idea why she's gone off. I'll call you if I hear from her. Yes. Thank you. Good-bye."

Mark replaced the telephone on its cradle carefully and rubbed his eyebrows with his thumb and forefinger.

"She's gone. Her message said she needed to be on her own for a while. He's distraught. Although he says she mentioned going away last week. What do *you* think? Do you think she's run away because of this?" Mark took off his glasses and pointed them at the article.

"Of course," Beth said with irritation.

"What do we do now?" Mark sat on the edge of his desk.

"Jackie—Nick's wife—informed me that she'd given Leo a letter along with the article, a letter telling Leo that she wouldn't go public with this stuff if Leo left Nick alone."

"Who *is* this woman?"

"Jackie? She's fighting for her husband, I guess. Not having one myself, I can't imagine why she puts such a value on him. She's also devious, treacherous and a pain in the ass."

"She's dangerous."

"Yes, Dad." Beth had a bizarre desire to reach out and touch her father's hand. "She's dangerous. But she's dangerous only because she knows something you never told us."

"I know. I'm—"

"Don't apologize. We'll get into all that later. I think we better fill Nick in on the story. And Meg. And Amy. Even if Leo were to decide to ditch Nick, I don't think Jackie will keep her end of the bargain. Because she'll never get what she wants—she'll never get Nick back. And she'll always blame Leo."

"You're right."

"*I'm* right?"

"Yes," he said slowly. "You're absolutely right, Beth."

"Whoa. You never cease to amaze me. Well, in that case, I'd also suggest that Charlie and Jimmy come in on this family powwow. It was hard enough for me to find out this shit. And I'll bet anything I'm the one of the four of us who can handle it best. In a way, after thinking about it, after the first shock wave passed, I wasn't all that surprised. Meg and Amy will need some help. You know, Amy might know where to find Leo."

"You don't think Leo's done anything—"

"No, Dad, I don't. I did for a while there, but not now. Leo couldn't hurt us like that. And although I hate to admit it, she couldn't do that to Amy, especially. You know how close they are."

"Beth? Is it ridiculous for me to say I love you?"

"Dad—" Beth smiled her angel's smile. "Save it for Oprah."

* * *

Meg picked up the telephone in Mr. Armstrong's office. When she'd been called from class, her first thought was that Eddy was having a panic attack at home and needed her immediately. "It's your father," Mr. Armstrong's secretary Nella explained as she walked a pace ahead of Meg down the corridors. "No one has died. Don't worry. I always think someone has died when I get an unexpected call. So I make sure to check for you. So you wouldn't be worried while we walked to the office."

"Thank you," Meg said, aware that she had stopped listening after "No one has died." Why would her father be calling her? Did he have an inside track on the presidency appointment? Did he know Charlie hadn't gotten it? Meg stopped, cursing herself. Charlie was no longer a part of her life. She had to get used to that fact.

"Come on, Meg." Nella waved her along. "Your father's waiting."

Nella could have entered some speed-walking competition in the Olympics. Despite the fact that she weighed at least 250 pounds.

"Dad? What happened?"

"I need to talk to you, Meg. You and Charlie."

"I'm here. I'm listening."

"No. I don't want to speak over the phone. Could you call Charlie and ask him to meet us at my house in half an hour?"

"Dad," Meg said slowly, stalling for time. She couldn't tell him about packing all her bags that morning and deciding finally to leave Charlie. She hadn't told Charlie yet. "I can't leave work in the middle of the day. And there's no way Charlie—"

"I'm afraid you have to."

"It's that important?"

"It is."

"And Charlie *has* to be there?"

"Yes."

"Then maybe it would be better if *you* called Charlie."

"Fine," Mark sighed. "I'll call him. And I'll see you both at two o'clock."

"Has someone been hurt?"

"No."

"Is this about the presidency?"

"No, Meg. This is a family matter."

"Everyone is going to be there?"

"Yes."

"Can't you just tell me—"

"No. I'll see you then."

"All right." Meg hung up.

This is the last thing I need, Meg thought. A family meeting with a husband who doesn't know he's no longer part of the family.

She'd been staring at the phone on her desk for an hour, waiting for Patrick to call and explain why he hadn't shown up. Every few minutes she'd pick it up to see if it was still working and hear the deadly dial tone. Of course, she should call *him*. She had every right to be furious. After the play, Charlotte had asked where Patrick was. Amy had lied for him, said he had an important appointment he couldn't miss. The look of disappointment on Charlotte's face should have been enough to send Amy into paroxyms of anger. Instead she kept thinking of legitimate reasons for his absence. Maybe he'd gotten lost. Maybe he'd misplaced the sheet of paper with the address on it, maybe he'd been in an accident.

When the phone rang, she jumped, startled. She didn't have to prepare to be forgiving. She already was.

"Amy."

"Dad." She wanted to hang up immediately. Patrick might be trying at this very moment.

"Amy, I need to see you. And James. At two o'clock at my house."

"Why? What's happened?"

"I'll explain when you've arrived. No one is hurt. I need to talk to you both. Meg and Charles are coming as well.

Can you call James, please? Tell him it's important."

"He's at work. So am I, Dad. Is this really so crucial?"

"It's crucial. Yes."

"Okay. If you say so. I'll call him now. Is Leo coming too? Should I call her?"

"No. You don't have to call her. Just call James."

"Fine," Amy replied irritably. "I'll see you at two."

Damn, she thought as she hung up. I don't feel like calling Jimmy. What's the big deal? It took her a few minutes to locate Jimmy at his office and have him summoned out of a meeting.

"Dad just called. He wants to see us. Now. I mean at two. At his house."

"Why?"

"I have no idea. He's probably going to announce his engagement to someone we've never even met."

"I'm working, Amy—"

"I know. So am I. He says it's important, though. Crucial."

"Couldn't he wait to announce it until this evening or something?"

"Jimmy. Don't ask me. All I know is that we're supposed to be there."

"Do you want me there?"

"Dad wants you there."

"I see," he said, the coldness in his voice now matching hers. "I'll be there, then."

Chapter Twenty-One

MARK HAD MOVED from Chestnut Street to a small house on the outskirts of Brookline, a fifteen-minute drive from Cambridge and Boston itself. He had eschewed a bachelor pad in the heart of the city, preferring a place that hid comfortably in leafy, suburban surroundings. Meg guessed that her father's neighbors had at first tried to engage him in evening games of bridge and social dinner parties, but soon gave up, regarding him as a lone wolf—someone they'd wave to occasionally, but never converse with for more than five minutes. After a few years, they probably even gave up making comments on the assorted women who seemed to pass through his door. Mark would be a respected part of the scenery, but never a factor in the community. Because he was unfailingly polite, they respected his privacy.

That is what Meg had done toward the end of her teenage years—respected his privacy, left him alone. She'd turned her attention to her sisters, to boyfriends, and then to Charlie, and placed all her unspecified yearnings in her feelings for them. As she rang the doorbell of his house, she wondered how she was going to react to what he had to tell them all. Whatever it was, she knew she wouldn't get angry with him. That was Beth's role.

How did that old nursery rhyme go? Monday's child is fair of face, Tuesday's child is full of grace, Wednesday's child is full of woe, Thursday's child has far to go—etc. In the case of the Preston family, Meg reflected, various roles seemed to have been assigned to them at birth regardless of which days they'd been delivered to the world. Beth was the outrageous, truth-at-any-price wild child; Amy the solid, dependable, rational child; Leo the beautiful, empathetic one—and Meg? She was the one who had wanted someone else, anyone else, to define her role for her. Because she herself hadn't had a clue.

"Right," Mark said, after Charlie, the last to arrive, had entered. "I know it's difficult for everyone to cram in here, and I'm sorry to have interrupted your working day." He'd brought his kitchen chairs into the living room to accommodate everyone and they were seated in a circle, as if they were about to play a child's party game or conduct a séance. "I have something very difficult to tell you and I'm not sure where to begin. Would anyone like something to drink?"

"Let's leave the drinks till later," Beth remarked. "When we really need them."

Meg, the minute she had seen her father's face, knew that this gathering was desperately serious. She looked over at Amy for some elucidation, but obviously Amy had no idea of what this was all about, either. The only person who knew was Beth. Beth had been there with Mark when Meg arrived. Beth and Mark had seemed to be in cahoots, somehow. As soon as Meg had asked where Leo was, Mark and Beth exchanged a glance. "She's not coming." Beth had replied. So what was Nick doing, sitting there beside Amy? Meg asked herself. *I'm the oldest*, I *should be the one who knows what is going on. Goddamn Beth.*

"Wait a minute, Dad. Where's Leo? I know Beth said she wasn't coming, but where is she?" Amy turned to Nick. "Where is she, Nick?"

"I'll explain that," Mark said.

"Excuse me," Charlie said impatiently. "Can we get on with this? I've got an important meeting—"

"Charles. I'll do my best to make this short. I need some uninterrupted time, however."

"Go ahead, Mark," Jimmy said. Meg noticed that Jimmy and Amy were scrupulously avoiding looking at each other. Well, she had deliberately avoided Charlie's gaze, too.

"As you know, Victoria was devastated by Steven's death."

Why wasn't Beth shouting "screw Steven"? Amy wondered. Where was Leo? Why did Jimmy have to be here to hear a rerun of the family tragedy? Was this some anniversary of Steven they'd all forgotten? Oh, God, she thought, looking over quickly at Steven's photograph, will my dead brother *never* leave us alone?

"And she was unbalanced by it. Mentally unbalanced."

Why isn't Beth shouting "tell us something we don't know"? Meg wondered. Where's Leo?

"I could go into a long explanation as to why I didn't get Victoria the help she needed, but right now it will have to suffice to say how sorry I am and how guilty I feel."

Christ, Beth thought, looking at her father. He might just cry. Too little too late.

"Again," Mark continued, "as you know, Victoria took a trip to England with the Garden Club. I thought it would be beneficial for her. I thought a change of scenery might help. I was very, very stupid."

"It's not *your* fault she had the accident there," Meg quickly put in. Why did that comment come out in the voice of a little girl? she asked herself. Why did it sound like a whine?

"Well, that's what I have to talk to you about. Your mother didn't have a car accident in England. I lied."

"Is she alive?" Amy asked, looking around the room wildly, amazed at the fear she felt. "Is she still alive?"

"No. She's dead." Mark shifted uncomfortably in the small kitchen chair. "She died in England. However, not in the manner I told you."

"Mark," Nick said gently. "Are you sure you wouldn't like a drink yourself?"

"No. Thank you, Nick. I'll wait."

Her father had lied. Meg couldn't believe it. She just managed to stop herself from reaching out and grabbing Charlie's hand to steady her sinking heart.

"What happened was this. Your mother went on the trip, but on the morning they were due to fly back here, she took a walk through Hyde Park. And when she was on this walk, she saw a little boy who had wandered off from his mother. As I understand it, Victoria must have thought that little boy was Steven. He was a toddler. Eighteen months old. Victoria took him, she grabbed him in her arms. Then she walked off with him."

"She kidnapped a child?"

"Yes, Charles. She kidnapped a little boy."

No, Amy thought. I can't stand this. I've got to get out. But there's no place to go. Where's Leo? I need Leo. I need Patrick.

"After a while, Victoria brought this boy back to her hotel. It's hard to know exactly what happened next. Perhaps the little boy started to cry and wouldn't stop. I don't know. Presumably, that's the case. The police assumed that was the case. They believe that Victoria tried to stop him from crying. She lost control."

"Dad," Amy pleaded. "Don't. Don't say anything more."

"He has to," Beth said. She rose from her chair between Mark and Nick, went over and crouched next to Amy, putting her arm around her.

"Beth's right. I have to," Mark said sadly.

Nick pulled out two cigarettes, lit them both and passed one to Meg.

"Thank you," she whispered.

"Victoria lost control and the child died."

"How?" Charlie asked. "How exactly did the child die?"

"It appears that she was shaking him to stop him from crying. He died."

"How can you *shake* someone to death?" Meg cried. "There must be some mistake."

"It appears that she shook him against a wall. It doesn't take much to cause irreparable damage to an eighteen-month-old's head. Perhaps she realized as she was shaking him that he wasn't Steven and flew further into madness. I don't know. But *she* didn't know. Victoria didn't know what she was doing. She didn't know her own strength. She was insane."

"What happened then?" Charlie questioned.

Lawyers, Meg thought. Dispassionate lawyers.

"After seeing his lifeless body, Victoria must have realized what she had done, or had some glimmer of it. Enough to send her across another line." Mark stopped, looked up at the ceiling for a moment, then down at the floor. "She killed herself."

"How?" Beth asked. This was the one fact she hadn't been told yet.

"She hung herself. In the room."

"Where did she get the rope? How did she do it?" Beth persisted. And why did she choose *my* eleven-year-old method? she asked herself.

"She knotted one of her sheets. She found a door in the bathroom that would sustain her weight." Mark sighed. "I didn't do an investigation of my own. I don't know the exact chain of events. That's all I know."

"Where were the other Garden Club ladies while all this was going on?" asked Charlie. He was relentless. Meg wanted him to stop cross-examining Mark and walk out the door. She never wanted to see him again.

"They had to leave for the airport. They tried to find her but couldn't. That must have been while she was in Hyde Park. It seems that she took the boy out for an ice cream before she brought him back to the hotel. I guess she was gone for quite some time. They called me in a panic from the airport to tell me she had disappeared and I insisted that they catch their plane. I didn't want to inconvenience them. I said I'd handle everything and that I was responsible for finding her." Mark shook his head. "I was trying to—"

"You were trying to be accommodating. As always," Beth interjected.

"What kind of ice cream?" Meg asked.

"What?"

Everyone in the room was looking at her.

"I'm sorry," she said, staring at the floor. "I just wanted to know."

"The police there called me a few hours later. A maid had discovered the bodies. I flew out that evening."

"Leo knows all this, doesn't she?" Nick turned to Mark. "She found out somehow. That's why she's gone off." Mark nodded.

"Jackie told her," Beth said.

"Who's Jackie?" Charlie leaned forward.

"Jackie is Nick's wife," Beth replied. "She went to London over the weekend. On Saturday a child was abducted from a hospital outside of London. There was a front-page article on it in the Sunday paper there, complete with a history of other similar incidents. Our mother got a few paragraphs, under the heading of worst-case scenarios. You know: some abducted children are returned home safely, some never make it. Read all about it. Jackie saw the name Victoria Preston, she saw the reference to Victoria Preston's nationality, she probably made a few phone calls. She got the story. Your wife's a real piece of work. Nick."

"Jesus." Nick put his head in his hands. "And she called Leonora?"

"No. She went to see Leo with a copy of the article and gave it to her. Then she came to see me with another copy."

"Why you?" Nick queried. "How does Jackie even know who you are?"

"It's a long story. I'll explain it later. Anyway, Jackie told me she'd written a letter to Leo, informing her that if she left you alone, the Preston family could avoid a public airing of this juicy bit of gossip. Jackie knows Dad cares about the family reputation. And she knows Leo wouldn't want to hurt Dad, or any of us."

"How did you manage to avoid any publicity *then?*" Charlie addressed Mark.

"I pulled every string I had. I called in every favor I was owed. What makes news in England isn't necessarily a big story here."

"But some people must have found out. England isn't Outer Mongolia," Jimmy commented.

"This happened at the time of Charles and Di's wedding. No one there could think of anything else. The story of Victoria's—" Mark paused. "The story didn't get the coverage it would have otherwise. If people here know about it, they've certainly kept quiet on the subject in my presence. Occasionally I'd think that someone from our circle must know, that a child at one of the girls' schools might overhear her parents talking and say something, but that never happened." He lifted his head, looked quickly at his three daughters. "Did it?"

"No," they answered in unison.

"Fortuitous timing," Charlie commented. "Charles and Di were *the* hot topic."

"What happens now, Mark?" Jimmy reached out and put his hand on Amy's. "What can we do to help?"

"Mom murdered a *child?*" Amy stood up, brushing Beth's arm and Jimmy's hand away. "She battered a child against a wall?"

No one spoke.

"Where is Leo? Nick—tell me where Leo is."

"I don't know, Amy. She left a note saying she needed to be on her own for a while. I thought you might know where she's gone."

"*I* don't know." Amy couldn't stop shaking. "I have to go to the bathroom."

"Amy—" Jimmy got up, took a step toward her.

"No. Leave me alone. I'll be all right. I'll be back. And I'm not going to hang myself from the door. We have the same DNA, but I am not *anything* like my mother." Amy rushed out of the living room and up the flight of stairs.

"Jimmy. Why don't you and I get everyone some drinks now. Is that all right, Mark?" Nick asked.

"Yes, of course. There's some white wine in the fridge. And a bottle of scotch and a bottle of vodka in the cabinet by the sink. There is some tonic in the fridge, too. Orange juice is—"

"Jesus, Dad. You're not the bartender at the Ritz. They'll figure it out."

Nick smiled at Beth.

"Yes, we will."

This is like Mom's funeral, Meg thought. Drinks. Civi-

lized behavior. Should I go make some cucumber sand-
wiches? Is that the appropriate response when you find out
your mother has killed an innocent child as well as herself?

Amy huddled in the corner of her father's bedroom, the
phone on her lap. She punched the numbers out, and, when
she got a response, spoke urgently. "Would you mind terribly having Charlotte for the night?" she asked Emma's
mother. "There's been a small domestic crisis. Oh, thank
you. I'll take Emma any night you like. I promise. I owe
you." She pushed the dial tone button, punched another set
of numbers. Jimmy had been astounded, when they first
began to see each other, by how easily she could remember
addresses and phone numbers. It was a talent she hadn't
truly appreciated herself—until now.

"Patrick—"

"Ames. I'm sorry about missing Charlotte's play this
morning. I was having coffee with an old friend who has
just come back from New Orleans and—"

"Patrick. Listen. I need to talk to you. Something horrible has happened. I'm falling apart. I need your help. I
need you to calm me down."

"Is Charlotte all right?"

"She's fine. It's to do with my family. The past. Please.
I need to see you."

"Sure. When?"

"At five? You know that bar we used to go to on Mass
Ave?"

"Fender's? Does it still exist?"

"Yes. I drive by there all the time. It's still going. Can
you meet me at five?"

"Ames—how serious is this? I'm supposed to be—"

"It's pretty serious."

"Okay. See you then."

Meg looked up at Amy as she reentered the living room.
What was going through her sister's mind? Amy was still
shaking, but her face seemed more composed, less lost.
Beth was busy helping Jimmy and Nick hand out drinks.
Meg was looking for a cue from her sisters' behavior, some

hint as to how she should react herself. Had Amy and Beth already processed this information and moved on? They hadn't fainted, they hadn't screamed. Their mother had bashed a child's head against a wall and there they were, acting as if life could continue normally. Were they going to discuss all this as if it had been a movie they'd seen the previous night? Where were the murdered child's parents right now? What were they doing? Meg kept staring at the faces around her, waiting for something to change.

"The question is," she heard Charlie say, as he reached out to take the vodka and tonic Beth handed him, "can we control this situation?"

"Of course we can," Beth answered assuredly.

She can't be getting a kick of this, can she? Meg asked herself. Now that she has been vindicated. Now that we all have to admit what Beth has been saying all along: our mother was a monster. There are no more excuses, there can be no more pity.

"After the original shock subsided, I thought this through rationally," Beth continued, perching on the edge of Jimmy's armchair. "Jackie is trying to blackmail Leo to stay away from Nick. All we have to do is tell our story to an appropriate publication; we have to 'out' ourselves before Jackie outs us. It's simple."

"I don't think that's necessarily a wise move."

"Worried about our career, are we, Charles? My career is dead in the water too, you know. Expressing anger physically is exactly what my mother did. Think of the kind of clients I'd get through my doors when this comes out. But I wouldn't be overly concerned about your reputation in the academic community. After all, you aren't tainted with the brush of the Preston family madness. You only married into the crazies. People will understand."

"I doubt that," Charlie answered, glaring at Beth.

"Why? Because marrying the daughter of a murderess shows bad judgment?" Beth smiled. "I suppose you have a point there. Time to hone your other skills, I suppose. There's always rugby coaching."

"Do we have to do this?" Jimmy asked. "Can't we stop all the banter for a few minutes? I think everyone is in some stage of shock. We should be concentrating on finding Leo. It must be hell for her to be dealing with this on her own."

"She'll call me," Amy said dully. "I'm sure she'll call me tonight. She probably tried to call me this morning when I was at Charlotte's play."

"She might call Nick," Jimmy said softly. "In a situation like this, she might need to talk to Nick before anyone else."

"That's ridiculous," Amy snapped.

"Why? He's the man she loves. Wouldn't you automatically turn to the man you love at a time like this?"

Meg could hear Jimmy's anguish, his pleading voice. She looked at Charlie. Was he anguished? Yes. She could see it in his face. But the anguish was on his own behalf.

"We can't forget that Leonora is dealing with all this information *and* emotional blackmail. For all she knows, Jackie hasn't told anyone else about her discovery. I'm sure she doesn't think Jackie told Beth. Leonora will want to protect her sisters," Mark stated.

"Which means she'd leave me," Nick said. He rubbed his face. "She may feel she has to choose between me and you—her family. If she doesn't want Jackie to spread this information, she'll decide to disappear. I know her. She'll think she's doing the right thing, saving everyone by disappearing forever."

"She wouldn't—" Meg turned quickly to Nick. "You don't think she'd—"

"No," Nick responded immediately. "Leonora believes that life is a gift, that it's sacred. She wouldn't hurt herself. She'd lose herself somewhere."

That's what I was going to say, Amy thought. She stared at Nick, studied his tired face. Could he know Leo as well as I do? Could he possibly love her as much as I do? The first response I have to this bombshell is to call Patrick and arrange to see him. I wasn't thinking of Leo then. I was thinking only of myself. Nick might love Leo with a self-lessness I don't have.

Amy felt tears forming as the self-laceration began in her mind. *My mother murdered an innocent child, Leo's suffering on her own somewhere and all I can do is think of Patrick.* Jimmy's right. Leo needs Nick right now—someone who will think of her needs. I'd probably start talking to her about Patrick within a few minutes. What's wrong with me?

She switched her gaze from Nick to Jimmy.

Why don't I cancel my meeting with Patrick and let Jimmy back into my life right now?

Because I don't want to. Because I'm going to be selfish and willful and let my emotions go berserk.

Like mother, like daughter.

"Amy? Are you all right?" Beth's question snapped her out of her reverie. She palmed the tears from her cheeks and nodded.

"So this is how things stand at the moment. Leo doesn't think Amy and Meg and I know the gruesome story, right?" Beth tossed her hair back from her head in her most imperious gesture. "She's somewhere trying to decide whether to tell us or run away on her own forever. Is that the general consensus?"

"I'd like to discuss how you propose to broadcast this story, Beth." Charlie stood up. "And I'm very worried about Leo. However, I'm sure she'll turn up. Meanwhile, I have to go. Meg, honey—" he leaned over and kissed her on the top of her head. "I'll be back home as early as I can be and we'll talk things over. Mark—can I safely assume that you won't do anything precipitate on the publicity front without consulting me?"

"Jesus, Meg. Where'd you find this guy? In the Reagan White House?" Beth narrowed her eyes. "Nick, give me a cigarette, will you? Kids divorce their parents these days. I wonder if I can divorce my brother-in-law."

"Could I have one as well, Nicholas?" Mark asked, with a shy smile that grew swiftly into a broad grin. "I don't know any precedents for a divorce case like that, Beth, but I'm certainly willing to do the legal legwork for you."

"Yeah, Nick. I'd like a cigarette too," Meg giggled, not understanding where the laughter was coming from, but feeling as if it might never stop.

Amy watched, dumbfounded as Nick handed cigarettes to Meg, Beth and Mark. She listened to Meg's laughter, which spread to Mark and Beth, stopping all conversation. Her father never smoked. He never laughed like that, not with his daughters. An unprecedented alliance had been formed, at Charlie's expense. Seeing the fury on Charlie's face, Amy felt a fleeting pang of pity. It was replaced, un-expectedly, with her own laughter.

The Preston family was in hysterics.

"You're all crazy, you know that?" Charlie barked. "You're victims of post-traumatic stress or some shit like that, so I'll forgive you. And I'll talk to you later, Meg."

"Fine," Meg managed in the midst of another spasm of laughter. "Later."

Chapter Twenty-Two

SHE WAS AWARE of his presence before he spoke. He took off his coat, placed it on the coffee table and sat down in the chair opposite hers. They both stared at the Christmas tree in the corner of the room.

"It's nice," he finally said, pointing at the tree. "Not too garish."

"Thank you for coming." She reached for her earlobe. "I have no idea why I called you. Sometimes I do impulsive things. Now that you're here, I don't know what to say."

"You did a good job of describing yourself. I recognized you immediately. But you shouldn't have said 'thin.' You should have said 'too thin.'" He waited for a moment, but she didn't say anything. "Leonora. You're in trouble, aren't you?"

"Yes." She frowned. "I don't know how to say this." She twisted in her chair. "I don't know how to say it and I don't know why I want to say it to you. But I will. My mother killed a child."

"You mean when she ran over your brother?"

"How do you know about that?"

"I'll explain later. That's the child you mean, though, isn't it?"

"No. Another child. A different child."

"When?"

"Fourteen years ago. She murdered a child in London."

"Why?"

"I don't know. I read a newspaper article about it this morning. I hadn't known until I read it. It didn't say why she'd killed the child. Why do I feel as if I'm reading from a script? It doesn't seem real. I can't believe it."

He was silent, resting his elbow on the side of the chair, his thumb underneath his lower lip.

"Would it help you if you knew why she did it?"

"I don't know."

"Leonora." He eyes seemed to be concentrating on the angel at the top of the tree. "What exactly does this change in your life?"

"Everything," she mumbled.

"Because you feel some responsibility for the act itself, don't you? You feel guilty. Even though you had nothing to do with it, you feel like an accomplice."

She looked at him then face on. For the first time.

"How did you know?"

"I lived in Australia for a long time. When I was there, in Sydney, I had a girlfriend named Janet. We had a very volatile relationship, to say the least. Wild passion, wild fights. It got too much for me and I ended it. A couple of months later, I met a very sweet woman—Nancy. We dated. It wasn't serious. Anyway, Janet arranged—without my knowledge—to meet Nancy. They went for a walk. Janet slashed Nancy's face to bits with a knife. Nancy had reconstructive surgery. Her face was put back together pretty well, but it was never the same. Of course we stayed together then, Nancy and I, because—I don't know—because it seemed the right thing to do. But it didn't work out."

"What happened to Janet?"

"She went to jail for a year. I left the country a month before she was due out. I felt responsible for ruining both their lives."

"That's why you were so freaked out by Beth's strange behavior."

"You got it. That's my story. My deep, dark secret."

"But you weren't responsible."

"And you are?"

His voice was different from the one he'd used on the telephone. It had a magical calming effect Leo felt immediately.

"Stuart—tell me what I'm supposed to do now. Beth and Meg and Amy don't know about my mother—what she did to this child in London. The man I'm living with—Nick—he's separated. His wife is the one who found the article in the paper, an article partly about my mother. Am I going too fast?"

Stuart shook his head.

"Nick's wife said that if I leave Nick alone, she won't tell anyone. I don't want Meg and Beth and Amy to know. It's too painful. It will wreck their lives."

"It will wreck their lives—it will wreck *your* life—only if you let it."

"Why didn't our father tell us what had happened? He must have known. I don't understand."

"Maybe he thought it *would* wreck your lives. That you were all too young to understand, to forgive your mother. I saw her that day. She wasn't sane, Leonora. She really wasn't."

"Is insanity an excuse for killing a child?"

"No. I don't think so. It's not an excuse for slashing someone's face, either. Or for leaving your children alone in a parking lot. I'm not trying to comfort you, tell you that it will all go away in the morning. You can't erase the pain. But you can live with it. And so can your sisters."

"Are you telling me that I can—that I should—forgive my mother?"

"I don't know. I haven't forgiven Janet. All I know is that I want people to forgive *me*. And I'd kind of like it if I could forgive myself."

"What would Nick think of me if he knew?" she murmured.

"Oh, I'd guess he'll think you're the scum of the earth. He won't want to go near you. He'll hold up a cross and a piece of garlic whenever he's in your sight. Otherwise, he'll think the same about you as he did before."

Leo smiled wanly.

"I wish you weren't married, Stuart. I wish you could meet Beth. You two should be together."

"I told you already. I'm not married."

"But Beth said she saw your wife when she dropped off the tape."

"If Beth saw anyone, it was my sister. She and her kid have been staying with me for a couple of weeks. They're going back to Florida tomorrow. They just wanted to see some snow up north around Christmastime. Hey, what is this excited look on your face when I tell you I'm not married? How did that tiny baby I saw grow up to be such a romantic?"

"Beth's going to need help if she finds out." The Leo frown returned. "I know she seems tough, and I'm not saying she's vulnerable, exactly, but I think we're all going to need help with this. I couldn't talk to anyone when I found out. I ran away from Nick. I've been sitting here in this grubby Holiday Inn, planning how I'm going to run away. Run away and dodge all these problems. I spent so much mental energy defending my mother. And now—"

"And now you're wondering whether she's indefensible. Look, when Amy—was it Amy? The brown-haired one with the deep eyes?"

Leo nodded.

"Anyway, when Amy told me in the car that day about your mother running over your brother, I almost swerved off the road. It's a Greek tragedy. Your mother must have suffered beyond endurance. As I said, I'm not sure about forgiveness, but at least understanding goes a long way. She didn't do what she did with a cold-blooded desire to hurt, I'm sure. That must mean something.

"I don't know if this will help you, Leonora, but what I've been trying to do in my own mind lately is to figure out to what extent the past has to influence the present and the future. It plays a role, I know. It has to. But it doesn't have to control your life. The past has to be kept in its place, so to speak. Have you ever run in a relay race?"

"Yes, when I was a kid," Leo answered, bewildered by the question.

"Well, I think of the past these days as a baton you get

handed in a relay race. You have to take it cleanly, run as fast as you can with it and then hand it on. You're not allowed to drop it, you have to hold it as if it were the most natural thing in the world, but all the time you have to run *forward* with it. You can't let it slow you down."

"And then you hand it on to someone else."

"Yes. You hand the past on to your children. That has to be a clean pass of the baton too. They won't be able to handle it if you can't. The past is a part of your life. You can't allow it to stop you from winning the race."

"But you ran away—from Australia. Why can't I run away from here?"

"I ran *forward*. There was nothing left for me in Sydney. I didn't have the equivalent of a Nick. Nancy and I weren't in love. We were thrown together by outrageous circumstances. If she hadn't been hurt, we would have broken up within the month. That's the irony of it. That's what I'd like to shout at Janet until my voice gave up. She picked on the wrong person. But you know, there's no *right* person to pick on—some people who are looking for revenge against fate, against a lousy life or rejection or just plain bad luck strike out at the wrong target. Why didn't Janet slash *my* face? That's what I keep asking myself. I don't know the answer."

"You remind me a little of Nick. You both talk in paragraphs."

"What, you're in love with a windbag? Leonora, I'm disappointed."

Stuart didn't look as she had imagined. He wasn't some heroic figure waiting for battle to commence; he was fairly ordinary, with sandy-colored hair, a largish nose and wide-set, David Hockney swimming-pool-blue eyes. Yet Leo could see what had drawn Beth to him, even all those years ago. He was immediately accessible. You wouldn't find, upon closer inspection, any hidden nasty areas of his soul. He was honorable. And he was, Leo thought with gratitude, a rare person. He was trustworthy.

"You're telling me to go back, aren't you?"

"Well, I *should* say that it's entirely your decision. But, you know, I saw your mother that day and I drove off as fast as I could and I do feel responsible. Yes, I'm telling you to go back. I think in your case going back is going forward. I don't know the situation with Nick's wife. I don't know anything about your relationship with Nick. But you're protecting people who can look after themselves. Beth sounds eminently capable of absorbing blows. As for Meg and Amy, I'd guess they can take the heat, too. They're like you—they're fully grown women. Trying to shield them from pain doesn't give them any credit."

"I thought our savior, our guardian angel, was supposed to protect us from pain."

"Look—you guys got yourselves out of that parking lot. All right, I helped, but I was amazed at how together you all seemed. No one was screaming, no one was having hysterics. Beth, I think I remember, started talking about taking a trip to California. You seemed pretty resilient to me. Even when we're discussing the horror of what your mother did in the past, you can suddenly switch to the present and try to matchmake me with your sister. You've got your own life. You should live it.

"Someone once said to me, when I was in pretty bad shape and feeling damned sorry for myself, 'Everyone maintains that they'd like to be happy. But some people don't really *want* to be happy. And some people want to be happy, but can't be. You have to decide first of all whether you want to be happy. And then whether you can be.' What do you say, Leonora: do you want to be happy?"

"Yes," Leo said fervently.

"All right, do you think you can be?"

"I don't know anymore." She put her head in her hands. "I just don't know."

"How can I help?"

"You already have. I don't know why I called you. But I'm glad I did. I needed to talk to someone outside of all this, but someone who had a connection to it, too."

"Well, you find out your mother killed a kid, you're

involved with a married man—I'd say you need a little help." Stuart stopped talking for a moment and smiled. "Or maybe a little break. I'm meeting my sister and my nephew in a half an hour at F.A.O. Schwarz—why don't you come Christmas shopping with us? My sister is a great believer in retail therapy. Why don't you try it?"

"Shopping?"

"Look, I know you think you should be agonizing about everything right now. I'm sure it will take a long time to come to terms, even partly, with this information. But you need to see some life out there. You need to see a little kid looking at a toy store. You need to be reminded that there *is* joy in this world. Take it from me. I shut myself up for so long, I almost forgot there was an outside world. It's important not to get so wrapped up in yourself that you forget."

"But I feel so guilty."

"It can be indulgent sometimes, guilt."

"What, do you mean I'm feeling sorry for myself?" Leo bit her lip.

"You're feeling guilty for something you didn't do."

"I keep thinking of that child."

"Of course you do. I keep thinking of Nancy. But I am not the person who slashed her face. You didn't kill that child. Do you think it helps that child—your guilt?"

"No."

"Is there anything you could have done to help that child?"

"No."

"Well, you can feel miserable. You can feel devastated. But you can't feel guilty, can you? You *would* be guilty if you hid this from your sisters. They have a right to know. You can't understand why your father didn't tell you. I think he made a mistake not telling you. You would be making an even bigger mistake not telling them and disappearing from their lives."

"You're right," Leo said. "I'm grateful to you, Stuart.

You make sense. I was so confused, I didn't know what to do."

"Well, then, come with me now. You can deal with all this later."

"You don't have to work?"

"I'm a guardian angel, remember? I'm working right now."

"You're being mysterious again."

"Come on. F.A.O. Schwarz is in the Chestnut Hill Mall. We can drive by the Star Market and reminisce. After shopping, we'll go get an ice cream with my nephew and then I'll take you back to this Nick guy. He's the one who should be helping you now. If I didn't remember Beth so well, I'd be less willing to deliver you into the hands of another man. But she definitely has first claim on my heart. Besides, you're too young for me.

"I don't get it." Stuart looked puzzled. "What did I say? What's so funny?"

Each time the door to the bar opened, Amy swiveled on her stool to see who was coming in. It was far less painful than craning her neck as she had that morning during Charlotte's play. As soon as she saw the person entering, she'd swivel back and take another long sip of her mineral water. For the first time in her life, she understood why people smoked. It was something to do to pass the time. She hadn't brought anything to read. The desultory conversation she'd started with the bartender had petered out after a few minutes. All her mental energy was consumed by the need to banish from her mind the image of a tiny child lying on a hotel room floor, a tiny child battered to death. The image would appear, she'd struggle with it and blot it out. While she was waging this war, she sat and stared at her glass and swiveled occasionally and felt miserable when the person coming through the door turned out not to be Patrick.

It was now five-forty-five. Amy had downed six glasses of Perrier. She considered asking the bartender to look out for Patrick while she went to the bathroom, but the humiliation that had begun to engulf her at five-thirty was growing to the point where she didn't want to draw any more attention to herself. Already the bartender kept casting "You've been stood up, you poor pathetic female" glances at her. Other patrons had come, had a couple of beers and left. One old man who seemed to live in a booth by the jukebox also swiveled his head whenever the door opened, and looked at her with an expression of hope until whoever had come in walked past Amy. Then the old guy would sigh and roll his eyes. After a while, Amy refused to look in the old man's direction. She kept praying that he'd leave.

When the bartender said: "It ain't Cheers here for you, is it, honey?" she made the move to the bathroom, conspicuously leaving her coat on the back of the barstool. If Patrick came in and looked for her while she was in the ladies', he'd see the coat. She'd worn it to the bowling alley, so he should be able to recognize it as hers. Anyway, the know-it-all bartender would doubtless tell a newcomer who surveyed the room that a woman was waiting for somebody, Amy reasoned. She wouldn't miss him. If he showed up.

How could Patrick not show up? She looked at herself in the mirror as she washed her hands. She'd told him it was crucial that she see him. He must have heard how upset she was. He couldn't leave her sitting in a bar on her own in an emotional mess. Could he?

At six-fifteen, Amy asked the bartender where the telephone was. He pulled one over from the end of the counter and handed it to her. "You can call on this one for free," he said. He sounded as if he was expecting her to pick it up, dial and order her own hearse.

"Patrick?"

"Hi, Ames."

"Weren't we supposed to meet at five?"

"I was there at five. You weren't. So I left."

"But I got here at five past five exactly."

"We must have just missed each other."

"You didn't wait five minutes?"

"I figured you weren't coming."

"Patrick. I told you it was crucial. You didn't wait?"

"You said it was *pretty* important. I don't classify that as crucial."

"Could you come now? I'm still here."

"Sorry. Can't make it. You should have phoned before."

"I should have . . ." Amy couldn't think what to say. She watched the bartender covertly watching her. She turned in her seat and glared at the old man in the booth. Why didn't my mother murder *him?* she wondered. Why did she have to kill a *baby?* "I've got to go," she finished.

"I'll call you tomorrow, Ames. And I'll see you soon," Patrick said.

I don't think so, Amy said to herself, as she hung up. She took a very long time to finish the last Perrier.

"Do you mind if I make one more call?" she asked after she'd paid her bill.

"Be my guest." The bartender turned his back on her. The show was over.

"How much have you had to drink?"

"Two vodka and tonics. And that was a while ago, at Dad's. I'm sober."

"You're shrill and hysterical."

"Two of my favorite adjectives. Why do I think you only use them when you're talking about women?"

"Meg, calm down. You're not being yourself."

"Which is?"

Charlie looked at her blankly.

"I mean, tell me exactly what *myself* is. Am I being myself when I'm cheerful and compliant and cute? Am I not being myself when I'm pissed off and standing up for what I want?"

"Are you going to a feminist meeting tonight? Is this a dress rehearsal?"

"Great." Meg sucked hard on her cigarette. "I find out my mother is a child murderer, you come home and all you want to do is talk about how to keep this under wraps. You don't ask me how I'm feeling or what my emotions are and because I'm angry about that I'm categorized as a raving feminist. This is about being a human being, Charlie. Not about which sex we happen to be."

"I don't understand what you want from me. I don't see how I can help." Charlie threw up his hands. "Your mother killed a child. What else is there to say? What we have to do now is handle the fallout of that act in the best possible way."

"Is it completely ridiculous of me to want some sympathy? You want to talk about the fallout of all this, how it will affect your career. Well, what about mine? Do you think anyone will want me to teach their little children when they find out about this?"

"Exactly. That's why I'd like to discuss whether we have to go public. I don't think it's necessary."

"So you think Leo should leave Nick alone and that we should all hope Nick's wife then shuts up and leaves us in peace."

"Well, it's an option."

"Isn't that giving in to blackmail?"

"There's no money involved."

"Jesus, Charlie. You'd be willing to sacrifice Leo's happiness, wouldn't you?"

"*You're* the one who said this relationship with Nick was a disaster."

"Well, I've changed my mind."

"A woman's prerogative."

"This has nothing to do with being a woman. How many times do I have to say it? This is about being *human*."

"Why isn't it human to wait a while, at least? That seems to me to be a good compromise. You can go public with this story after—"

"After the appointment of the president."

"Right. I'm being honest. You can yell at me all you want, but at least *I'm* being honest."

"Are you accusing me of lying?"

"You lied to me this morning about being pregnant."

"Well, I've lied to you this afternoon, too. I haven't told you a lot. I haven't told you that I've packed all my bags or that I'm looking for an apartment. I haven't told you I'm moving out."

"That makes a whole lot of sense." Charlie's voice managed to register weariness and scorn in equal parts. "This morning you tell me you want a child. This afternoon you tell me you're leaving."

"I'm a woman. I've changed my mind. I don't want to have a child that you *allow* me to have so that I'll shut up and stop bothering you. You don't want a child, I know. You'll treat it differently from Josh and David, and that will drive me crazy."

"I told you from the beginning, Meg—"

"Don't. I know. I understand that I made a mistake thinking that you would change your mind. I take responsibility for that. But that doesn't change the way I feel."

"That's hardly logical thinking."

"No, I suppose it's not. Very little in my life right now is logical. Because I don't understand things. My father can sit there, as he did after you left, and try to explain why he didn't tell us about our mother when it happened, but I don't understand. I don't understand why my mother killed that child. I don't understand what happened in her life and I don't understand what happened in mine. I have no idea why I married you, if you want to know the truth. And I have no idea why you married me. You said at the beginning that you needed me to keep you out of trouble. What does that mean, Charlie? I don't understand."

"Did I say that?"

"Yes, you did. And now I don't understand why you don't remember. It was the first night we met."

"I'm sure I said a lot of things that night. Why is that particular phrase so important?"

"I don't know." Meg shook her head. "It seemed important at the time. I suppose it's not important now."

"You're wondering why you married me. That's important."

"I'm being honest, Charlie. Just like you."

"And what am I supposed to do now? Throw my arms around you and tell you how much I love you and that I'll do whatever you want, whatever it takes to cater to *your feelings*, whether they be rational or not, so you'll stay?"

"I think you're probably just as relieved as I am that I'm going."

"No. I think it's more likely that amongst the list of all these things you don't understand, *I* am number one. You don't understand me, what I need, or how I'm struggling. You think everything is easy for me, you think I don't have feelings myself, so you wallow in your own and get some real pleasure out of being misunderstood. Heartless man versus caring, sharing woman. That's the scenario, isn't it? Oh, sorry. I should be talking about *human beings*, not the sexes, shouldn't I? Well, let me tell you, you've made that impossible by fitting so perfectly into the female stereotype."

"You don't believe that the natural reaction for anyone— male or female—would be to come home and at least try to comfort me for a few minutes before starting in on how this whole business with my mother might ruin your career? You don't think that's the human response?"

"I thought you were strong enough not to need this so-called comfort. You wanted me to play the male, protective role while you simpered in my arms? I gave you more credit than that."

"Simpered. Right."

"You know what I mean."

"Yes, I do. I think we have very different views on the basics of life, on what people need in relationships. I happen to think that you're full of shit. That if the positions were reversed, you'd want to simper in my arms and I'd be *happy* to comfort you."

"Well, you're full of shit on that one, Meg. I'd be perfectly willing to discuss the situation and its implications without getting the mandatory phony dose of 'comfort.' Besides, it seems more than a little perverse to want me to comfort you when you've already decided to leave me."

"You didn't know I was leaving when we started this conversation."

"Jesus. I give up. You want everything your own way. Why don't you go find some little wimpy new-age man who will cosset you and the two of you can go hysterical together? I don't have time for it, I really don't." Charlie paused. "And your chain-smoking. It's disgusting."

"Okay." Meg stared at her cigarette, inhaled, blew out the smoke and watched it drift toward Charlie's face. "I'm sure you're already worrying about the effect our splitting up will have on the chances of your getting the presidency. So I'll tell you right now, it's fine by me if we don't tell anyone about this before the appointment. I'll move out. I can stay with my father until I move into an apartment. He's already proved today how discreet he can be. After the appointment, I think we should get divorced. I don't want any money so you can't accuse me of doing a Helen on you, all right? I just want out. And I'd like, if it's possible, to keep in contact with Josh."

"Why doesn't that surprise me? Meg running home, back to Daddy, back to the little women. Your family always came first."

"It wasn't a competition."

"No. Of course not. And you didn't feel in competition with Helen, did you? Grow up, Meg."

"Yes, I felt in competition with Helen, and that was childish. Growing up is what I'm trying to do now."

"By leaving me."

"Yes."

"Well, if you think I'm going to put up a fight for you when you're in this kind of mood, you're mistaken. I am so tired of hectoring women who need to be fulfilled twenty-four hours a day, I'll be very happy to be left alone. If you come to your senses, you can call me. Meanwhile, good luck. I'll tell you something. If you walked out of my life forever, a lot of my friends would be very pleased."

"I'm sure they would."

Mike and Mary—Meg thought as she went to call her father—*I'll never have to see Mike and Mary again.*

"You know what would be wonderful? If I never had to see Charlie again." Beth lolled back on Leo's sofa, her hands behind her head. "That may be the only thing I'd have my mother to thank for."

"You think they'll split up because of all this?" Nick asked.

"I wouldn't be at all surprised. The Chuckster showed his true colors today. And they're not particularly attractive hues. My friend Robin says that when she first meets people, she says to herself: well—they're fun or they're funny or they're interesting, but what would he or she be like if we were buried together in the sand from the neck down and rampaging killer ants were marching toward us? Would this be the person I'd want beside me? *I'd* rather have the tax man than Charlie by my side when the killer ants approached. Meg *has* to face reality now. She can't bury her own head in the sand forever."

"I have to say, he seems emotionally obtuse."

"Charlie's fine—as long as he's getting his own way. Wait a minute. I take that back. Charlie's *never* fine. He's endurable when he's getting his own way. Otherwise he's unendurable."

"You can be very harsh in your judgments of people, Beth."

"I know. So everyone tells me. But I'm usually right."

"Are you sure about that?"

"People misunderstand me sometimes, that's all. I told Amy once that she and Patrick were incompatible. She took it as a criticism of her, I know. It wasn't. Patrick is a great guy in many ways, but he's also an irresponsible shit. That's the part of him that's incompatible with Amy."

"Did you ever explain that to Amy?"

"No."

"Maybe you should."

"Amy would take it all wrong. She'd think I was saying that she's boring."

"You do have a low boredom threshold."

"I know." Beth nodded agreement. "But you want to know something? That threshold is changing. At this particular moment in my life, I'd be happy for a little boredom. I'd like it if Leo came through the door, threw her arms around you, and you two lived happily ever after. I'd like to live happily ever after myself. I think I'm getting a little fed up with excitement. I might renounce my title as drama queen."

"You could see yourself settling down?"

"Maybe. I don't know. It's a thought, I suppose."

"Are you still furious with Mark?"

"I'm pissed off, yes. I guess I always will be. But I'm not so furious. I saw a link between my mother and me today. I could see myself going berserk with this crying kid and shaking it against a wall. I really could. That scared the shit out of me. It's changed my attitude toward Dad. Not that anyone should expect a radical change in my personality."

"Of course not," Nick smiled.

"Tell me something—was Leo backing out of the marriage before all the high drama today?"

"What makes you ask that?"

"Before I got completely bombed out of my mind on Thursday night, I sensed a slight unease between you two. I figured that might be the cause."

"You figured right."

"She's nervous."

"Yes, she's nervous. She's worried that she's been too impulsive. She's concerned about Thea, my daughter."

"Leo doesn't want to cause anyone any pain."

"Yes. And she doesn't know if she can handle the complications."

"Well, you know I thought this marriage was a huge mistake. This was one time when I was definitely wrong. You two fit together. Despite the age gap. It astounds me, it really does. I'm sitting here talking to you and I feel as if I'm sitting here talking to Leo. Now that could be cloying and worrying—two people *too* close, but in this case it works somehow. You complement each other. I never thought I'd say this, but I think you could be happy."

"This approval isn't some part of a plot to keep us apart?"

"Listen, sunshine, you've got Jackie working full-time on a plot to keep you apart. You can forget about me."

"Jackie."

"Yes, Jackie. Remember her? The one you swore undying love to? Your psychotic wife? Forget blood tests. You and Meg both should have had taste tests before you walked down those aisles. Sanity tests, too."

"What happens if Leonora doesn't come back tonight? Doesn't call?"

"Then we mount a full-scale search to find her—whatever a full-scale search entails."

"Could she be at your summer house?"

"Dad and I already checked that out. No."

"She could be hiding out with friends from college."

Beth paused, swung her feet off the sofa and sat up straight.

"Unless someone else has a key to this place, she's about to appear right now. Leo—" Beth rushed over to her sister coming through the door. "What the hell? Look at all those bags. You've been *shopping?*"

"Retail therapy," Leo smiled, dumping packages on the ground. "You should try it. It's a lot better than breaking things."

"Leonora," Nick said quietly, moving up beside Beth. "You had some terrible news today, didn't you?"

"You know?" Leo turned from Beth to Nick and back again.

"Yes. You know."

"You went out *shopping?*" Beth squealed. "We've been panicking about you and you're combing the aisles of F.A.O. Schwarz? I don't get it."

"It's a long story." Leo took off her coat, moved to Nick's side, put her arm around his waist. "You'll like it, Beth. I promise. Who else knows? Does Amy know?"

"Everyone knows," Beth replied. "We all had a powwow at Dad's house. You missed some great scenes. Dad, Meg, Amy and I even laughed together."

"You *laughed?*"

"Yeah, we laughed and you went out shopping. What else do you do when you find out your mother's a child murderer?"

"I don't understand. I mean, Jackie wasn't going to tell anyone if I left Nick alone. How can she have known I wouldn't?"

No one had made a move to sit down. They were standing in their spots like still-life models.

"Jackie and I have a history I hadn't told you about," Beth admitted. "She came to my office pretending to be someone else in order to get all the info she could out of me on you and the family. As soon as I'd caught on to her little trick, we became what I'd call major enemies. So when she found out about Victoria, she couldn't stop herself from spilling the beans to me too. She just had to gloat. Huge miscalculation."

"Then you told Amy and Meg?"

"Then Dad told Amy and Meg. And Charlie and Jimmy. And Nick."

"Jesus. I need to sit down." Leo walked into the living room, slumped into the chair Nick had vacated. "I need a cup of coffee or something."

"I'll get it," Nick offered. "Beth, would you like something?"

"I'd like a bottle of gin, but I'll settle for a coffee. Thanks, Nick."

"How is Amy?" Leo asked immediately.

"You know, it was weird. Amy seemed much less upset than I would have expected. She seemed distracted. As if she had more important things to think about. It's hard to imagine exactly what could have been more important."

"And Meg?"

"Charlie was such an asshole about it that his reaction blotted out Meg's in a way. I'm not sure how she is, but she seemed pretty strong by the end of the afternoon."

"And you?"

"It was tough at first. I thought we were all doomed. Then I figured we weren't. Our mother was crazy. Our only responsibility in life, as I see it, is not to be as crazy as she was. We can't change what happened."

"The past has to be put in its place."

"Exactly." Beth's eyebrows raised. "That's exactly what I think."

"What are you doing *here?*"

"We were worried about you. I was keeping Nick company."

"Beth—what happened to Mom after—after she'd killed that child? Was that when she had the car accident?"

"No. There wasn't any accident. She killed herself."

Closing her eyes, Leo hung her head.

"I guessed that," she whispered.

Nick brought the coffee in, handed mugs to Leo and Beth.

"Are you all right?" He stood behind her and rubbed her neck.

"I don't know. Why didn't Dad tell us, Beth?"

"He said that he wanted to protect us. I figure he wanted to protect himself, too. His reputation. On the other hand, he's willing to let the story come out now—no matter what the consequences to his job. So maybe he's evolved a little."

"What do you mean—let the story come out?"

"Well, for once Dad agrees with me. The way I figure it is that it will send Jackie bananas if we make sure her little plot does not go according to plan. So the best thing to do is to get the information out before she does. When we were at Dad's, we started to talk about which publication we should go to. I called Oprah, of course—Leo, please—don't look at me like that—it was a joke. Although

who knows? We *could* become minor celebrities for a while
with this one."

"Beth—that's the sickest thing I've ever heard you say."

"Don't be so dismissive. We might be able to help someone, you know. I'm sure there are other people out there
who have run over their children or somehow caused their
children's death by accident. No one has ever focused on
that problem, to my knowledge. It might be important to
convince people that the whole damn family needs help in
a situation like that. Or other tragedies can occur as a result."

"You really think we could help someone?"

"Absolutely. Think about it. We know what it's like to
be the siblings of a child whose death was caused by a
parent. We're in a unique position to help other siblings
who go through the same experience. And while we're at
it, we might just be able to help ourselves. I mean, I *know*
a lot of my reactions to things are rooted in Steven's death.
Aren't yours?"

"Probably." Leo stared at Beth, wide-eyed. "Yes."

"We could make it our cause. I mean, I'm out of a job.
I don't think Meg will find it easy to continue teaching, at
least for the moment. We could convince Amy to take a
break from her brainwork. Christ, we may even be able to
rope in Dad. The Preston family road show. What do you
think, Nick?"

"I'm sure you could help. I'm not sure how you'd go
about it, though."

"Leave that to me." Beth tossed her head. "And now
I'm going to do something tactful for once in my life. I'm
going to leave you two alone. I know I should hug and kiss
you both good-bye, but I'm feeling fragile at the moment.
I don't feel like getting into a touchy-feely farewell."

"Beth—before you go—"

"Yes?"

"There's a present for you in one of my bags—the one
closest to the door—see it?"

Beth went and picked up one of the F.A.O. Schwarz plastic carrier bags.

"Is this it?"

"Yes. Open it when you get home, okay?"

"But it's not Christmas yet."

"I know. You'll understand when you open it. It's a special surprise."

"Beware of sisters bearing gifts," Beth murmured, reaching for her coat in the hall closet.

Chapter Twenty-Three

"WHERE HAVE YOU been? Where's Charlotte?"

"Charlotte is staying with a friend for the night. I've been sitting in a bar."

"On your own?"

"I was waiting for Patrick."

"Oh. I see."

"Jimmy, come sit down. We need to talk."

"I don't think I want to sit down. I don't think I want to talk. You're going to tell me you're going back to Patrick. I don't know what to say to that."

"Come on, sit down." Amy took Jimmy's hand and led him downstairs to the sofa. "I'm not going to tell you that I'm leaving. I'm going to explain what's been happening in my mind the past couple of days. And you can explain what's been happening in yours. Okay?"

"I don't think I have any choice, do I?"

"You *could* walk out on me right now."

Jimmy brushed his hair back in his Bobby Kennedy gesture, placed himself carefully in the chair opposite his wife.

"I'm too tired to walk out on you," he said. "I'll listen to what you have to say. There are a few things I'd like to say myself."

"All right. I'll start. When Patrick showed up out of the blue, I was shaken. I hadn't expected to see him again, and suddenly, there he was. That stirred up a lot of old feelings."

"So you lied."

"What?" Amy sat back. "What do you mean, I lied?"

"I saw you two together that night, Amy. On the porch. The cozy couple in the cold. Did you tell me he'd shown up? No. You came in afterward as if nothing had happened."

"But you were asleep."

"I pretended to be asleep. I wanted to see what you'd do, whether you'd tell me all about it or keep it a secret. You kept it a secret."

"How did you know it was Patrick?"

"How did I know?" Jimmy snorted. "You keep his picture in your dressing table. His picture and your old wedding ring. A nice little shrine."

"Jimmy—you've never been jealous of Patrick. You've always said you wouldn't mind if he came back into town."

"And I thought I meant it. I thought I wouldn't have minded. He's Charlotte's father. I understand all that. But I hated the emotional hold he still has over you. I felt as if everyone was keeping secrets from me. Rachel didn't bother to tell me the simple fact that she was getting married until that awful dinner. You didn't tell me you'd seen Patrick until that awful dinner. I was humiliated in front of your whole family. You and he were seeing each other behind my back. What was I supposed to do—pretend it wasn't happening? Sorry, Amy. You seem to forget. I've been betrayed before. I know the scene."

"I haven't betrayed you. I haven't slept with him."

"Has he asked you to?"

"That's not fair."

"Well, why don't you tell me what is fair? Because I'm having problems figuring it out myself. I was with you this afternoon. I was there to help. And your response was to run to Patrick. *He's* the one you want to be with. Why don't you just admit that and we can go from there?"

"Patrick stood me up this afternoon."

"Please don't tell me that's supposed to make me feel better. Patrick stood you up, so you come back to faithful, reliable Jimmy."

"It's not like that. Let me try to explain. It's got a lot to do with Steven."

"At the risk of sounding like Beth," Jimmy said, "screw

Steven. I don't see what Steven or Steven's death has to do with any of this."

"Listen. No one likes being second best. All of us were second best to Steven in my mother's head. I mean, we didn't even *rate* compared to Steven. And then, growing up, I felt second best to Beth. She was the beauty, the star, the one who got all the attention from people. When Patrick came into my life, I was stunned. I couldn't believe he'd chosen *me*. When he left, I felt, in a way, that I'd gotten what I'd deserved. I wasn't exciting enough. I wasn't interesting enough for him. And then, with you, I always felt Rachel was the one who really held your heart, and although I resented the hell out of her, I suppose I thought that it was natural for you to prefer someone else to me. Leo was the only one in my life I really trusted."

"How many times have I told you that Rachel and I are just friends?"

"I know, I know, but I didn't believe it. And the way you treated Charlotte made me feel as if she were a runner-up too, second always to Zoey. She and I were paired against you two and we came out on the losing side."

"Well, where do I come out in a one-on-one with Patrick? He's the handsome one, he's the goddamn poet. I mean, he came across, from the way you talked about him, as some Byronic figure. Have you ever considered what it was like for me? Having Patrick portrayed as this romantic intrepid explorer instead of the chronic hippie he is?"

"Jimmy—you're jealous."

"You bet I am."

Amy felt a grin spread on her face. She tried to suppress it, but couldn't.

"God, you look sweet," she said softly.

"I'm jealous and I'm pissed off, too," Jimmy continued. "How can you let Charlotte grow up with this complete fantasy? That's what I wanted to know. But it wasn't my place to interfere. I'm not her father."

"I guess I did have a fantasy vision of Patrick. The way

he left—so suddenly—it meant I had a lot of unfinished business to deal with emotionally."

"Are you telling me that the business is finished now? Because he stood you up?"

"Yes, it's finished. But not because Patrick stood me up. My pride was hurt, sure. But a big part of me was *relieved* that he didn't come to that bar. When I married Patrick, I married someone I couldn't possibly have a long-term relationship with. I realized that when he didn't show up this afternoon. We did some fun things, but when I think about it honestly, I remember wishing all the time that we didn't have to be quite so carefree. It was a struggle for me to keep up with him. I'm a homebody, not some wandering Gypsy soul. But I couldn't admit that to myself. I couldn't face the fact that at heart, I *am* a responsible person. It sounded so mundane.

"You know something? I have no desire to swan around the world with Patrick. I don't want to live with him. He drove me crazy when I did. I'd keep rushing to poetry books to look up what he was talking about. Jesus, the time I wasted trying to fall in love with Shelley and Keats was absurd. I like science. That's what turns me on."

"Why have you been acting like a lovestruck teenager this past week—if you don't want to be with him?"

"I wanted to prove something to myself. I think I wanted to be desirable."

"Sexually desirable?"

"Yes," Amy mumbled.

"Don't I make you feel desirable?"

She looked away from his stare.

"Oh, Amy, I'm sorry. I think you're wildly desirable. If I haven't communicated that to you, it's my fault. I apologize. I'm never sure how affectionate I can be when Charlotte's around."

"Does Charlotte remind you of Patrick?" Amy asked, remembering what Leo had said long ago.

Jimmy rubbed his hands on his knees.

"Yes. I suppose if I'm going to be completely honest,

she does. It's her restlessness. I can't help but think she gets that from him. And that you indulge her in it because it reminds *you* of him. I've never been nasty to her, Amy. I've tried to be the perfect stepfather and obviously I've failed. I don't know what a perfect stepfather is supposed to be, though. I don't know what the boundary lines are. So I probably err on the side of caution. Which turns me into the safe, boring insurance man yet again, doesn't it? Sometimes I think I could be more fun, more spontaneous, and then I think—no—that's *Patrick's* role. He's already bagged that one. It would seem as if I were trying to compete with him."

"That's the way I feel. Whenever I think of doing something a little wild or different, I think I'm trying to compete with Beth. That's sibling rivalry, though. What you're saying—"

"What I'm saying is that there is a rivalry with your spouse's ex that must be a different version of sibling rivalry."

"You're probably right. I know that I lumped Beth and Rachel together. I was rivals with both of them in pretty much the same way. Sometimes it feels as if I've been competing with *everybody*. All these years I've been jealous of Steven—we've all been jealous of Steven, everyone except Leo—we've wasted years being jealous of that poor kid. It struck me today, at that bar, that we have no right to be. Steven's dead, and he never had a chance to live, not really. He can't sit here now and say: oh, I wish I were more spontaneous, or I wish I could be number one in people's affections. He can't wish for anything. He never got to fall in love or have children himself or experience all these human emotions. He's dead. It's obscene, truly obscene to be jealous of Steven.

"I'd rather be alive. Even if it means living with the fact that my mother killed that boy, even if it means having doubts about myself and my own worth."

Amy moved to sit beside Jimmy. When he hugged her

to him, she nestled her head against his chest for a long time before sitting back and speaking again.

"I've been so busy competing with Steven's ghost, competing with Rachel, competing with Beth, and even sometimes with Meg. Part of the reason I was so smitten with Patrick in the first place was because I knew Beth found him attractive—lots of women did. Having him for myself made me feel as if I'd scored points in the game of life. I'd won a competition. Christ, I even felt competitive with Nick today over Leo. That's not right. I don't want to be Steven. I have no desire to be Beth. Or Meg. Or Rachel. And I have to let Leo have a life of her own. I don't need to compete anymore."

"Are you sure?"

"Yes. But I need your help. When I was jealous of Rachel you never seemed to understand. You reacted as if I were completely absurd to have those emotions. You didn't seem to understand what effect the way you treated Charlotte had on me, either. I'm not asking you to be her father, Jimmy. All I want is for you to understand that I'm sad you can't love her like a father. And, maybe, just maybe, treat her like a friend instead of a pain in the ass."

"I think I dismissed your jealousy of Rachel because I didn't want to confront my own jealousy of Patrick," Jimmy said very slowly and deliberately. "And as far as Charlotte is concerned, I think I found it hard to get close to her because Zoey wasn't here. Charlotte being around all the time made me miss Zoey more, made me wish she could be with us all the time, too. I must have taken it out on Charlotte in an unconscious way. I know I didn't mean to. I *am* fond of her, Amy. I'll have to learn to express it better."

"Well, it might make it easier that, as of Christmas, Zoey *is* going to be here, living with us."

"What?"

"Rachel and I had a talk. She wants Zoey to be based here from now on. I called her from the bar before I came here and told her that was fine with me."

"You're kidding."

"No. For a long time I've felt slightly out of kilter, off-center. Now I know exactly what I want. I want to concentrate on you and me and Charlotte and Zoey—us as a family. It's possible, isn't it? Or have I screwed things up irrevocably?"

"Amy—nothing is irrevocable."

"Except death," she said.

"Do you want to talk about that—your mother?"

"Yes, I do. I want to talk all night. But I need to find out where Leo is first."

"She's with Nick. I would have told you before, but I didn't want to interrupt whichever way the discussion on us was leading. She called just before you came in. She sounded all right, I promise."

"Then I'll leave her alone with Nick. Let's get out a bottle of wine and call up a pizza place and pull an all-nighter, okay?"

"Can we take commercial breaks for wild sex?"

"You bet we can," Amy laughed. "After all, we're going to have two children in the house pretty soon. We should take full advantage of any time we have alone."

"So Patrick won't show up on the doorstep tonight?"

"No, he won't. If he does, I'll tell him to kiss the joy as it flies. I'll tell him to kiss off."

Beth looked at the black-and-white decor as she came into her apartment and stifled the urge to throw a bottle of mustard at the walls. The minimalist approach to decorating was as complete a failure at this moment as it had been when she was hungover. She needed some warmth, some color, not this sparse, bleak landscape of rooms.

The same scene kept running in her head: that afternoon, at her father's, when Mark had asked Meg why she hadn't told him about the Star Market parking lot incident. His question had been more curious than accusatory, but Beth wilted nonetheless, waiting for Meg's reply.

"I don't remember," Meg answered Mark. "I remember

feeling so lost in that place. I remember Stuart. I remember Mom telling me she thought she'd seen Steven. But I don't know why we didn't tell you about it."

"I suppose I came home very late that night, as usual," he'd sighed. Once upon a time Beth would have loved the guilt in Mark's voice. Right then, however, she held her breath and even resorted to the childish ploy of crossing her fingers behind her back and wishing hard. Please, she'd asked a God she didn't believe in, please don't let Meg remember.

"I guess by the next morning we'd pretty much forgotten about it. After all, it wasn't completely far out of our experience. Mom used to leave us waiting at school all the time," Meg explained. Beth looked to see if Meg tried to catch her eye. When she didn't, Beth felt free to relieve her superstitious fingers.

"I wish I'd known. I'm not saying it would have changed the course of history. But I wish I'd known." Mark took his glasses off, rubbed his eyes. "I don't think I've ever felt as tired as I do right now."

Beth wondered if she was close to shouting out "It was my fault. I'm the guilty one. I hated the idea of having to go visit Victoria in some loony bin. I convinced Meg to keep her mouth shut. It's me. I'll throw myself at the mercy of the court." She decided that she was a long way off from confessing. She didn't want to find out whether her father thought the quality of mercy should or should not be strained. He'd given her points almost all afternoon. Receiving them was an enjoyable enough feeling to make her realize she didn't want to lose them immediately.

Nick had joined in the conversation then, saying that he imagined Victoria might have thought she'd seen Steven on many occasions. The last one, in London, had probably been the only opportunity she'd had of walking off with the child concerned.

"You might be right," Mark had mused. "She certainly didn't tell me about it. Although that's hardly surprising. I avoided any conversations having to do with Steven. It was too charged a subject for both of us. I buried my head in the sand. I have blood on my hands. I'm as responsible for that child's death as Victoria."

Hearing Nick and Jimmy then try to allay her father's fears and guilt was a revelation to Beth. They were both rational, calm, thoughtful and, at the same time, honest. Jimmy had behaved particularly well. He rose in her estimation almost to the point that would allow her to forget he sold insurance for a living. Little did he know that by helping Mark, he was also helping her. Despite all they said, *something* would have changed if she'd told Mark about the parking lot. Of that Beth was sure. She had blood on her hands, too. She'd never liked the look of other people's blood. She could stomach only her own.

Having cancelled her Monday night tennis match with Robin, Beth felt precariously alone. Robin had been pleased to be let off the match—she was still with the old boyfriend. "Great," she'd said. "I'll call him up and we can go to a foreign film. He loves foreign films." Beth hadn't been able to stop herself from saying "Does he have problems with English?" And Robin had hung up, clearly miffed.

Who could she talk to about all this? No one. Leo was where she belonged—with Nick. Amy and Jimmy. Meg and Charlie. Jesus, she thought. Even Charlie would be better than no one right now. That's how low I've sunk.

She went to her stereo system, and turned on the tape machine. The mystery tape began to play, a song that started with the words: "Riding shotgun down the avalanche." It had been one of her special favorites—when she'd believed the rape was from Stuart. Now, as the third line rang out: "This is the best thing and the very most hard," she turned away from the music in disgust. "The very most hard?" she said out loud. "What school did you go to, sweetheart?"

Everyone else was taken care of. Sure, they had to make compromises with their partners, but at least they *had* partners. She was the only one alone. She and her father. The ones with blood on their hands.

On her way to the kitchen to fix herself a drink, she stumbled over the package Leo had given her. "Open it when you get home," Leo had commanded. Well, why the hell not? F.A.O. Schwarz was a children's toy store. Perhaps Leo had given her a doll. A little boy doll she could try to bring back to life.

I'm sick, Beth realized as soon as that thought occurred to her. Diseased. I have to get a grip on things. Soon. Or I'll end up like my mother. What had Amy said when she'd fled to the bathroom? "I am not anything like my mother." Amy *could* say that with a clear conscience. Beth wasn't so sure she could do the same. After all, she looked like her mother. She practiced a therapy involving aggression and the subconscious desire to kill people. How much closer could she come to being Victoria? She could kill someone. Or herself.

Who would be weeping at her funeral? At twelve, she'd imagined her mother throwing herself on the grave, in mourning for centuries. Everyone would be distraught, destroyed, despairing. Now she was thirty. What legacy would she leave behind? Come on, Ghost of Christmas Future, Beth mentally beckoned. Tell me what will happen if I die. Let me imagine the scene.

My old boyfriends will throw a celebratory champagne party. Robin will have a moment of silence and then find a new tennis partner she can beat. Meg and Amy might shed some tears, but they'll probably be tears of relief. My habit of saying exactly what I think in obeisance to the principle of honesty hasn't won me my sisters' total devotion, I know. Even Leo has hinted that I'm overbearing and controlling. What did she say that Saturday morning? Something like "I should really be protected from you, Beth. Stop trying to run my life." As for Mark, he might regret that they hadn't had a better father-daughter bond, but probably be relieved too. He won't have me to kick him around anymore.

I'm not Jimmy Stewart playing George Bailey in *It's a Wonderful Life*. I haven't saved a sibling from drowning. I haven't made a spouse happy. I have no cute kids. I haven't done anything anyone would point to and say: "Without her, the world would be a poorer place." I'm not in any happy-ever-after movie. I can talk to Nick and say that I wouldn't mind settling down, but could I really settle down with some boring schmuck when it comes to the crunch? It might stop the loneliness, but I'd go berserk in two days and end up driving *him* crazy.

If all I can do from now on is feel sorry for myself, I might as well emulate my mother and finish the job I wanted to start when I was twelve years old, right Ghost? And I have enough pills and enough booze to do it.

Picking up Leo's package, Beth tore the wrapping off in furious grabs. Revealed inside was a silver wand. Taped to the star on top was a message written in blue ink: "Little Heartbreaker: Call me." Underneath, in Leo's writing, were the words: "He's *not* married, you idiot. That was his sister. She's almost as wonderful as he is."

Beth stared at the wand and the message for ten minutes without moving.

"Shit," she finally said to her walls. "I *am* in a fucking movie."

"Meg was the first one of the Little Women to marry, Dad, remember? Now I'm the first one to get divorced. I guess that's ironic."

"Are you absolutely sure it's all over between you?"

"Yes," Meg said ruefully. "It's all over."

"What about Christmas. Will you see Charlie then? What are you going to do?"

"Avoid it. I want to hide out for a while. Do you think that's cowardly?"

"No. It's fine, Meg. I'm sorry about this, really I am. I can't help but feel responsible. The news of your mother. The way I laughed at Charles today. I didn't behave well at all, I know. I simply couldn't stand his attitude, I'm afraid."

"I had decided to leave him this morning, Dad. What

happened this afternoon was just more icing on the cake. It's funny, I always thought you liked Charlie."

"I don't hate him."

"That's not even faint praise you're damning him with."

"Please understand. I was fully prepared to get along with Charles because you loved him. Your choice in men is none of my business. You don't need my approval. Nor should you seek it."

"I know, Dad. I know. I won't drag you into a trash-Charlie session. This isn't all his fault any more than it's all mine. I wanted a happy family so much I jumped on anyone I thought might give me one."

"My fault."

"Nobody's fault. I'm not a victim. The only victim in this story is that little boy."

"Yes."

"Dad. Was Mom unbalanced at all *before* Steven's death? You always told us those wonderful stories about her, but it was a little hard to believe in them. Did she show any signs of instability before?"

"No. None. That's part of the reason why I didn't want her hospitalized. I thought she'd come back to herself—given time. I also thought having you four would help her."

"You must have seen fairly early on that having more children wasn't the answer."

"Victoria wanted children. Desperately. I loved her, Meg. I was weak. The weakness soon turned into a feeling of complete powerlessness. I saw that she wasn't functioning properly at home. Instead of doing something about it, I turned to my work—where I had a sense of control. I ran away from it all. Beth was right about me all along. She threw my faults in my face constantly."

"Beth has some faults of her own. We all do."

"At least Leonora's back with Nick. That makes me feel a little better."

"Leo's going to be all right, Dad. We all are."

"What role do I play in your lives now, I wonder? I

wouldn't be so brazen as to suggest making things up to you."

"You know what I'd like?" Meg looked at her father's exhausted face and felt immense pity. "I'd like one Christmas together—all of us together without the past hanging over us like some sword of Damocles. We could try to have one day when we're a relatively happy family, when we forget—if not forget, at least try to overcome—the past. Victoria, Steven, that little boy—everything. If we could have a moratorium on the past and try to be together in the present, I might understand what being a happy family means."

"Do you think Beth would be willing to try that? Christmas together? On those terms?"

"I don't know. It's worth a try. I did her a favor today. She owes me."

"What favor?"

"It's between me and her, Dad. But I want this so badly I'll call in the favor if I have to."

"That negates the whole purpose of the day, doesn't it? If Beth is there because of some pressure on your part? I wouldn't call that a happy atmosphere."

"I resent the idea that this all hangs on Beth. Why should she be the one who controls our family all the time? It's always been that way. I'm fed up with it."

"Then tell her that. Don't tell me. Tell her."

"I will," Meg said with conviction. "I'm getting a whole lot better at telling people what I think."

"I assume Charles experienced the effects of this new-found talent today."

"You assume correctly." Meg grimaced. "Which is why I'll be single again. That's a huge problem. The idea of going back into the dating scene if I ever decide I'd like to spend time with a man again."

"Meg. One piece of fatherly advice. Avoid married men, if possible. It's like fishing—"

"Dad—" Meg interrupted, laughing. "Enough with the fishing, okay? I was never any good at fishing, if you remember. Christ, I can't even fish for compliments. Save the fishing analogies for someone who understands. And don't worry about me and married men. As Charlie would say—"

"Been there done that got the T-shirt," Mark said wearily.

"How did you know?"

"Charles doesn't have a way with words. He uses tired phrases all the time. That one—his favorite—happens to be particularly abhorrent to me."

"He won't get the presidency, will he?"

"I happen to know that he will."

"You're sure?"

"Yes."

"A divorce won't affect anything? It won't ruin his career?"

"Meg, if a divorce affected people's careers these days, there wouldn't be anyone in politics or industry or finance. Half the people in this country wouldn't have careers."

"I'm glad, I really am. I don't want to ruin Charlie by walking out."

"How about the children?"

"Josh and David have Helen. Charlie loves them, too. He over-indulges them sometimes, but he loves them. I think they can survive without a stepmother."

"You seem remarkably sanguine."

"What? Given the fact that I found out my mother killed a child and decided to divorce my husband on the same day?"

Mark nodded.

"I'm probably having a nervous breakdown subconsciously. Amy should do a scan of my brain right now. It's probably on fire. But I'll tell you what is another remarkable thing about today as far as I'm concerned."

"What?"

"I'm sitting here talking to you and I'm not sounding like some whining little girl looking for Daddy's love. I'm not nervous. I haven't even had a cigarette since I've been here."

"That's a shame."

"Why?" Meg stiffened, startled.

"Because I was just about to ask you for one. I think I want to take up smoking. My nerves are completely shattered."

"Well, in that case—" Meg pulled a pack of Merits out of her bag. "I'll join you. We can sit here smoking and pretend we're fishing. And you can tell me what Steven was like when he was alive. Not Mom's version of Steven. I want yours."

"Are you sure? Do you really want to know?"

"Yes, Dad. I really want to know. I want to know everything."

"We seem to be in the habit of taking midnight rides," Nick remarked. "Do you want me to come with you or stay in the car?"

"I'd like to go on my own," she answered.

"Don't disappear on me again, will you?"

"No." Leo shook her head. "Never again."

She knew the way so well she almost didn't need her flashlight, but she used it anyway, picking out gravestones in the dark. Some were unkempt and crumbling, some were fastidiously tended to, with fresh flowers lying like the offerings of love they were, in front of these stone memorials.

Leo reached the family plot in five minutes, keeping her head down against the winter wind. First she touched Steven's headstone, then her mother's. Stepping back, she shone the flashlight on the inscriptions: name, date of birth, date of death. No "may he rest in peace" or "beloved wife of. . . ." Just the simple facts of existence and oblivion. Someday she'd be lying here beside them, Leo reflected. Until that time, the past had to be put in its place.

"Why did you do it? Tell me why," she whispered, knowing all the while that she would never get an answer. Having conversations with her mother now seemed absurd. She couldn't ramble on, detailing what was happening in her life, not anymore. She couldn't forgive her mother, so how could she talk to her?

She wanted to fly to London, seek out the parents of the boy who had been killed and beg their forgiveness. At the same time she understood what a hopeless idea that was. Her need for forgiveness would not help them. They would have spent their lives trying to forgive themselves for letting the boy wander off for the moment it took Victoria to grab him. And trying to forgive, or at least understand, Victoria. Leo was not a parent who had lost a child. She couldn't do anything to help them.

Did that little boy have siblings? Had those siblings lived a life similar to hers and Meg's and Beth's and Amy's? Maybe Beth was right. Maybe there were people walking around this earth who were in a similar position and needed to talk to one another. Maybe she *could* help someone.

Leo moved forward and touched the top of Steven's headstone again, letting her hand lie on it.

"I thought you were up there somewhere looking after us all," she said softly. "But that's a big burden to put on a little boy, isn't it? You were always smiling in those pictures. Why? Did you know something? All these times I thought I've been talking to you, were you listening? Are you the only one who can really forgive Mom? Why can't I stop talking to you? Why do I believe in you still? Why do I *need* to believe in you?"

She stood motionless for ten minutes, then turned around and walked very slowly back to Nick's car.

"I've just been talking to Steven," she said, a few minutes after she got in. Nick hadn't started the car. They were sitting in the dark cemetery parking lot, Leo staring out the window, Nick concentrating on her profile.

"That's good."

"I talk to him a lot. I used to talk to my mother as well, but I'm not sure I can do that anymore."

"You need some time, Leonora. To take all this in."

"Do you think it's crazy? Talking to a dead person I never even met?"

"No. I don't."

"Beth had Stuart as her guardian angel. I never told anyone, but I had Steven."

"That seems perfectly sane to me."

"I don't think I can forgive her, Nick. And that scares me. I'm sure she didn't mean to kill that boy, but it's not like Steven's death, is it?"

"No. It's not." He took her face in his hand and turned it to him. "Leonora. I can't make the pain disappear, but I can try to help you with it. I loved Jackie once and now I'm sure I can forgive her for the pain she's causing. She can't forgive me for leaving her. Beth has clearly had problems all along forgiving *both* your parents. From what you told me earlier, Stuart, the guardian angel, has his own problems forgiving. I think what he said to you makes a lot of sense. We have to try to understand first of all and then see if we can forgive.

"Everyone has his or her own boundary lines when it comes to forgiveness. Forgiveness can be a very personal concept. You forgave your mother for leaving you in that parking lot, you even put a good spin on it—Beth winds up meeting Stuart—whereas I found the same act unforgivable. Jackie seems to have forgiven me for truly vicious things I've said to her in arguments, but can't forgive me for walking out. She could tell a friend about giving you that article and the friend might say: 'Well done. You had every right to do it.' But I can't forgive her for that. We each have different reasons for being forgiving or unforgiving.

"There are some cases where the lines are clearly drawn. A woman killing an innocent child is unforgivable across the board in society, except to the most Christian among us. Your mother, when she realized what she'd done, found her own act unforgivable. She wouldn't have killed herself unless that were the case. Yet there are serial killers out there who have no remorse whatsoever in taking innocent lives. *They* seem able to forgive themselves. Your mother, unbalanced as she was, still had some sense of moral behavior. She knew she'd crossed the line, so she punished herself for her sin. That's something.

"I think all we can do is to try not to do anything we consider unforgivable ourselves, and at the same time realize that others will doubtless do things we can't forgive. And then we have to live with that, with the messy human condition. We have to try to understand human weakness. We have to help each other out here. Maybe when we die, we'll be told what it was all about, maybe we won't. I don't know. I think we have to live with the mess. The complications."

"Will you tell me something, Nick?" Leo was speaking in a whisper. "How could I get so excited about setting Beth up with Stuart *on the same day* I found out about my mother? Stuart pointed that out to me, you know. I've been feeling terrible about it ever since. How could I be so casual about a dead little boy? Now I don't know how I could have gone shopping, either. I feel so squalid, acting as if nothing had happened."

"The way you related it to me, I think Stuart was trying to tell you that you have a life, despite what's happened in the past. Just as he does. You have a right to get a kick out of your sister's possible romance, you have a right to go Christmas shopping."

"On the *same* day?"

"Yes, Leonora. On the same day. Christ, I was sitting in the hospital when my father was dying, and all I could think about was whether you had a boyfriend. It doesn't mean I didn't love my father. We can't stop ourselves from thinking about ourselves unless we happen to be saints. Saints take on everyone else's problems every second of their lives. And you know what happens to saints? They have to die. You can't live yourself if you deny your own needs and feelings all the time. I'm not saying you have to be selfish continually. But you can't deny that you *have* a self. I happen to believe that Stuart *is* a guardian angel of sorts.

I mean, I think he did exactly the right thing by taking you out shopping. He reminded you that you have a life that is independent of your mother and her despair. You owe it to your mother to try to be happy. You owe it to Steven. And to that little boy. But most of all, you owe it to yourself."

Reaching out, Leo grabbed the back of Nick's neck, pulled him to her and kissed him in exactly the same way he had kissed her the first time.

"Is that the speech you're going to make when Beth books us on *Oprah*?" she asked when she let him go.

"I might refine it a little."

"It's a passionate one, though."

"Do you think it would work on TV? I might run over the commercial break."

"Nick?"

"Yes, Leonora?"

"Let's go get a cup of coffee at Dunkin' Donuts."

"I'm not driving you anywhere until you tell me how desperately, totally in love with me you are. I want every passionate adverb in the book."

"I've just done that, idiot. With my kiss. Beth said once that you were dumb. She was right. God, my mouth is *aching*. I need some coffee."

"All right." Nick started the Honda. "But tell me something. Is this Stuart guy handsome?"

"Definitely."

"How old is he?"

"A year younger than you."

"I take back every nice thing I've said about him."

"Thanks for the wand," she said as soon as she heard his *hello*. "I need it."

"I thought you might."

"That really pretty woman is your sister?"

"Mm hmm."

"She doesn't have the best telephone manner."

"Neither do you."

"Okay," Beth laughed. "You got me. What were you doing with Leo?"

"She called me. She needed someone to talk to."

"Why you?"

"When are *we* going to meet, Beth?"

"After all this time, I can't be bothered to play hard to get. Whenever you want. What's made you change your mind, though?"

"Your sister."

"She's beautiful, isn't she?"

"Yes. She is."

"I don't look like her. I should tell you that right now. Lower your expectations. Immediately, please."

"Beth?"

"Yes, Stuart?"

"Hang up the telephone, get in your car and come over here."

"Wow. Macho man."

"Are you going to give me shit or are you coming over here? Beth? Beth?"

The line was dead.

Chapter Twenty-Four

THIS IS A completely crazy idea, Amy thought as she arranged plates and cutlery on the dining room table. But it might just work.

They'd never had a family Christmas, not in the usual sense of the word. When Victoria had been alive, Christmas had been a trial, ranking only a fraction beneath Steven's birthday and the anniversary of his day of death in the "bad family moments" catalog.

On the Christmas after Victoria's death, the family tried hard to be festive but failed spectacularly. Mark decided to take them all out to a hotel for lunch. Beth flirted outrageously with the waiters. Meg gave Mark his electronic fishing tackle present and watched sadly as he looked at it with ill-disguised disdain. Amy spent her time counting how many forks and knives there were in the entire hotel dining room. Nine-year-old Leo looked at everyone expectantly, waiting for them all to be happy and civil to one another, then frowned and pulled at her earlobe as the meal dragged on and it became clear no one was having any fun.

The next year, Mark gave up completely and announced to his four daughters that they could do whatever they wanted to do to celebrate Christmas on their own from then on. This translated into Beth taking charge and driving them to strange places for no apparent purpose. Once they went to a monastery and sat outside it in the car speculating on what the monks were eating. Another time, they drove to a radio station, trooped into the lobby, sat down on plastic chairs and bombarded the receptionist with special requests. "Tell the DJ to play 'Born to Run,'" Amy remembered Beth insisting. "We're orphans. We're in charge of the Bruce Springsteen Orphans Only Fan Club. We've got a lot of clout."

Patrick had joined in on these Christmas excursions for the two years he was with Amy, delighting in the unknown, wacky element. As soon as Meg married Charlie, however, the sisters stopped the car trips and Beth declared that she wanted to spend Christmas on her own. Amy always invited Leo to join her, Charlotte and Jimmy, but the family had never assembled en masse.

Until today. Charlie wouldn't be there, of course, but Amy had made a bold and possibly dramatic gesture by inviting Rachel, Alex and Zoey. Amy was a little worried about Beth's reaction to Rachel, but she put aside her fear in the interest of Zoey. Why shouldn't Zoey's mother, father, stepmother and stepfather sit down amicably together? Why *couldn't* everyone get along? Besides, Stuart was coming. If he was as wonderful as Leo said he was, perhaps Beth would be a little less difficult.

They made an even dozen. There wasn't enough room to sit them all down at the table, but Amy knew she could arrange a nice buffet lunch that they could eat comfortably in the living room, in front of the fire. All right, the odds were against them happily singing carols, but they could have reasonable conversations. At least it was a start.

Our family is like a damaged brain, Amy thought. We've had the equivalent of a stroke, producing lesions that have affected our behavior. It's possible to work around those lesions, to get the brain functioning properly again. Sometimes it takes bizarre tricks, however. Scientists had recently discovered that a person with lesions affecting his ability to feel on his right side can respond, can regain the feeling, if cold water is poured in his left ear. What our family needs, Amy decided, is the equivalent of a cold shower raining down upon us. This gathering may be turning on the tap.

"Charlotte," she yelled. "Come down and help me fold the napkins."

*   *   *

"Patrick." Beth turned over, onto her stomach, resting her head in her right hand, the telephone in her left. "I'm very pleased to hear that you're the one who arranged to have the tape sent to me. Really. I'm glad when you heard it in that bar you thought of me. That's fantastic. You have good taste. But that's not the bargaining power you think it is. I'm losing patience. You've blown it with Amy, okay? Face facts. She's told you you can see Charlotte every weekend if you want to—what else do you expect?"

Beth made a face of complete exasperation as she listened for a moment.

"You can't get her back because she doesn't want to come back, Patrick. She's happy with Jimmy and he's a decent guy. She's been fair to you and that's that. End of story. I don't want to hear you whine anymore. It's boring. Go surfing in Baja. Smuggle some drugs into Thailand. I don't care. Just get off her case. You're only interested because she's not interested in you at the moment. You like the romance of being the spurned lover. Go brood by yourself."

Hanging up, Beth turned onto her side, saying "Jesus, what a jerk."

"The poet?"

"Yeah. He quotes other people's poetry anyway. I don't think he's ever written any himself. If he has I don't want to read it."

"I thought you liked him."

"Once upon a time, maybe. He was different. Not now, though. His act is getting old."

"How's my act?"

"You're the only man I've ever been able to talk to. I trust you, Stuart. I trust you and normally if I trusted someone, I'd be bored as hell. I can't figure out why I'm not bored. Maybe you are. Are you bored? Am I tedious? I bet I can think of something to do right now that would liven things up."

"Wait a minute. Slow down, Beth. You sounded serious for a second there."

"I was. I am."

"How serious?"

"How serious do you want me to be? I mean, I've been in love with you for almost twenty years. I'd call that serious. Or else very, very funny."

Propping himself on one elbow, Stuart reached out with his other hand and grabbed a piece of Beth's hair.

"Look, five minutes after you arrived at my apartment we were in bed having jungle sex. Since that time we've been in transit between my bed and your bed."

"What's wrong with that?" Beth reached out too and pinched Stuart on the butt.

"It's great, Beth. But I wouldn't call it serious."

"Oh no. Is it time to discuss our relationship?"

"I'm trying to tell you that we don't have a relationship."

"You don't want to make a commitment. You know, I've said that phrase myself so often I know it in five different languages. 'Je ne veux pas—' "

"Beth—" Stuart tugged her hair. "I never said I didn't want to make a commitment. I'm *worried* about making a commitment, especially to someone I don't really know, yes. The fact that you are bringing me to this family Christmas today makes me nervous, yes. I feel like you have designs on me and I wish you'd let me in on what they are, exactly."

"I want to marry you and have your children. How's that for a plan?"

"It's ambitious. Christ, you don't even know what I do for a living."

"I don't care. It's irrelevant. It hasn't interfered with our lives so far. Are you unemployed?"

"Not exactly. I am at the moment. But I do have options if I choose to—"

"Okay. Problem solved."

"Don't you think you might be pushing a little too hard? I've told you about my past. You know I've got good reasons to be anxious about a woman so—so committed to me."

"Look. We have the kind of sex people want to read about, right?"

"Yes. I have to give you that one."

"And we've also managed, between rounds, so to speak, to laugh a lot, right?"

"Right."

"Do I smell okay?"

"You smell great."

"So all you're worried about is my fervor? Is that the right way to put it?"

"I think you're rushing things."

"Stuart. Please. We can do all the usual stuff. We can go to movies together and try not to eat our popcorn in some gross, offensive way. We can watch TV together and hope we like the same programs. We can cook a cute little meal of pasta together and laugh sweetly if the sauce splatters over our silk shirts. We can even have our first fight soon, if you want to. I just know that we're supposed to be together, that's all. It has to do with destiny."

"I don't think I believe in destiny. And I think you're looking at me the way you did when you were twelve years old."

"God—I must have been a real slut then."

"Beth—"

"Stuart. If you don't want to continue this relationship, if it goes wrong for you, I'm not going to slash your next girlfriend's face, okay? I'm not going to do anything crazy. I've got a lot of pride and if you decide I'm not the person for you, I can accept that. I'll just think that you're a loser and destiny sucks."

Stuart laughed, but stopped himself abruptly.

"Do you mean that? What you just said?"

"Of course. Look, I'm sure I can find a guy who I find as attractive as I find you. I'm sure I can find a guy who is as intelligent as I think you are. I'm sure I can find a guy who makes me laugh as much as you do. And I'm sure I can find a guy I can show my vulnerabilities to without being afraid—the way I feel I can with you." Beth paused.

"I'm just not sure how I'm going to juggle these four guys in my busy schedule. So, since I have them all wrapped up in one at the moment, I think I'd like to stick with you. It's easier."

"So I should just lie back and relax and enjoy myself?"

"We *both* should. Neither of us has had a particularly good time recently. There are reasons for both of us to be wary about commitment. I think we can help each other, that's all. Just because I happen to see us meeting each other again as the working of Fate doesn't mean you have to."

"Do you still see me as your guardian angel?"

"No. I see you as a sex machine."

"We've got to be up and dressed for this party in ten minutes."

"I know. But ten minutes can be a long, long time, Stuart. When you know what you're doing—which I have already admitted you do—ten minutes can be forever."

"I don't like to think of Thea being with Jackie today. Not when Jackie's in the kind of mood she must be in. I wish Beth hadn't called her. I hate to think what she said."

"I wish Beth hadn't called, too," Nick agreed. "Jackie needs to be placated right now, not inflamed. Beth has some personal vendetta going with her. Calling her to tell her that her scheme hadn't worked, had actually backfired, was the last thing we needed."

"Beth can't stop herself sometimes. Stuart has a calming influence, though."

"I'm looking forward to meeting him."

"But *you're* worried about Thea too."

"Of course I am."

"I'll talk to Zoey about her again. She might know something we don't. Maybe Thea's spending Christmas Day with friends."

"It wouldn't surprise me. I hope she is. And that's ironic. So many past Christmases, when Thea's done the obligatory present-opening and then announced her plans to go to friends' houses, I've wished she had wanted to stay in with us. Now I'm hoping she goes out."

"What do you think Jackie is going to do next?"

Nick pulled the car to the side of the road in front of Amy's house, killed the engine.

"I pray that she's given up now. What else can she do?"

"I don't know." Leo opened her door. "But I'm beginning to wonder if she will ever give up. I think breaking us up has become her mission in life."

"Mission impossible," Nick grunted, reaching behind to gather presents from the back seat. "I thought of buying you a bulletproof vest for Christmas."

"Nick." Leo stopped, halfway out of the car. "That's not funny."

"I know," he said. "That's the problem."

"Look—there are Nick and Leo at the door. You can park right here, Dad."

"Would you mind terribly if we sat in the car for a moment before going in?"

"Why? Are you nervous?"

"Yes, Meg. I am."

"There's no need to be. If something goes wrong, if there are terrible scenes, everyone can blame it on me. I'm the one who suggested we do this, remember?"

"You never told me how you convinced Beth to come."

"Beth *wanted* to come. I didn't pull in any favors. She was the one who suggested we all have dinner that night at Locke-Ober. Some part of her must want to get the family together, too."

"I hope this isn't a replay of that evening at Locke-Ober."

"It won't be," Meg said assuredly. "For one, Stuart is coming. Also, Amy has sorted out the Patrick problem with Jimmy. And Charlie won't be sitting there glowering about his job, either. We might have fun, Dad. We might actually have fun."

"I don't know." Mark shook his head. "People's circumstances might change, but that doesn't mean the whole picture changes. I remember that Christmas lunch I took you all to eat at the Parker Hotel. It was fraught. And very depressing."

"I remember it too. I gave you a present you hated."

"I didn't hate it, Meg."

"Just the way you didn't hate Charlie."

"Meg—"

"Dad. Listen. That's the past. This whole day is about trying to go beyond all that stuff. It's not going to work if you can't drag yourself out of the past. Make the effort."

"What?"

"You heard me. I'm telling you to make the effort."

"You're becoming very proficient in saying what you think."

"You bet I am. Now let's go party. The Preston family: party animals extraordinaire. It's all over, Dad—all that angst, that misery. It's all over. It's finished."

Stuart was sitting on the floor, cross-legged, in deep conversation with Nick, Jimmy and Alex. Amy watched them, thinking how well they seemed to fit together into a male tableau. Nick with his pensive expressions, puffing away on his ever-present cigarettes; Jimmy with his open face, his evident curiosity, his shy grins; Alex unself-consciously animated, waving his hands in the air to illustrate points. And Stuart, who laughed easily, yet listened easily too. They were having a good time, the four of them. They could have been discussing football or finance or females while the women of the piece were listening to Rachel tell a complicated yet hilariously funny anecdote about her next-door neighbors. Even Beth was laughing, implausibly content to let someone else have the limelight.

Beth's been in bed with Stuart all morning, Amy decided. That's why she's willing to take a backseat to Rachel. She's got that lazy after-sex glow to her, and she's wallowing in it.

"They wanted to find out if we could hear them argu-

ing," Rachel explained. "So they staged a fake argument
last night to test how thick the walls were. We were supposed to knock on the walls, like, when we could hear what
they were shouting about. Well, I could have told them
from the start we can hear *everything* the whole time, but
I thought it would be fun to listen to a *fake* argument for
once. And, you know, they start in on some stupid thing
like 'You don't put the top back on the toothpaste' and I'm
knocking on the wall to signal that I can hear, but by that
time the fake argument has become a real humdinger and
they can't stop. I'm *pounding* on the wall and they're
throwing pots and pans at each other and it ended up so
bad we had to call the police. Can you believe it?"

God was in his heaven and all was right with the
world—for once, Amy thought. Mark was playing Scrabble
with Charlotte, Zoey was busy arranging her room for a
permanent move, the food was cooking nicely. Nothing
could go wrong now.

So why should she be assailed by a creeping fear? Amy
wondered. It had something to do with the look in Leo's
eyes. Leo was behaving normally, she was laughing away
at Rachel's stories, but she wasn't comfortable, Amy knew.
She hadn't been from the moment she walked in. Leo was
nervous. Leo was frightened. Amy caught that fear and ran
with it.

Banish paranoia from your brain, Amy told herself as
she quietly left her sisters and Rachel and moved toward
the kitchen. It doesn't help to expect disasters. Expecting
them doesn't make them easier to deal with if they occur.

When the doorbell rang, she didn't jump. She walked
calmly to the front hallway, telling herself that it must be
Patrick. She could handle Patrick now. He wasn't a threat
anymore. She could look at his handsome face, acknowledge that she would always find him attractive and still tell
him to leave. He could see Charlotte tomorrow if he wanted
to. He had no place at this party.

She could sense a stirring behind her, as talk stopped.
She could feel all eyes on her back. As long as Beth didn't

rush up to Patrick, grab him by the hand and usher him inside, everything would be fine.

"Hello," she said to the unfamiliar face. "Can I help you?"

"Is my father here?" the girl asked.

"Thea." Nick rushed up to the door. Amy stepped to the side and watched as he gave her a paternal hug. "What are you doing here? I'm so glad you've come."

"Thea—hey—come in." Zoey had appeared from up-stairs as well now, and Thea stood still in the doorway, looking from her father to Zoey and back again.

"Come in," Amy echoed, noticing the similarity in looks between father and daughter. Thea was tall, rangy, pale. She had Nick's preoccupied face, a face that made her seem older than Zoey or any fourteen-year-old girl.

"What's happening?" Zoey asked with a smile. "I thought you weren't coming." She turned to Amy. "I forgot to tell you. I invited Thea here today, but she said she couldn't make it."

"I'm glad you could." Amy decided to take action. She put her hand on Thea's shoulder and directed her into the living room. "It will take a while for me to introduce every-one and you'll probably be confused, but after a bit you'll figure out who's who."

"I have to talk to you," Thea said, wresting her shoulder from Amy's hand and looking back at Nick, who was a step behind her. "There's a problem with Mom."

"What problem?"

Everyone in the living room was on their feet. Leo took a step forward, then back.

"She's got a gun."

"Oh, Jesus." Amy heard Jimmy's voice.

"Who's got a gun?" Charlotte asked excitedly.

So that was it, Beth thought, looking around the room. An-other rampaging loony wrecks everything yet again. It was laughable, really. The idea that they could all gather to-gether without some devastation ensuing. She should never

have allowed herself to trust the strange feeling of peace
she'd had lately. Or the pretty picture of Stuart, her father,
Jimmy and Alex all getting along as if they'd been old
friends while Rachel told her ridiculous stories and the
smell of food wafted from the cozy kitchen. Christmas bon-
homie. Dream on.

They were all frozen now, in various poses of terror and
disbelief. Jackie had a gun. Of course she did. Stuart's ex-
girlfriend had had a knife. Victoria had used her bare hands
to kill a child. They couldn't sit around happily, pretending
that life could go on with any degree of normality when
the unbearable weight of the past tugged at their heels. Stuart's idea of putting the past in its place was all well and
good, but some pasts refused to lie down. Some pasts were
like those Dennis Hopper villains in Hollywood movies
who keep springing back to life just when you thought they
were dead.

This blissful relationship with Stuart was doomed, Beth
knew. So was any reconciliation with her father. Life was
not about resolutions. Life was about struggle. The emotional sea change she had felt during the last couple of days
was fast disappearing. Now she felt seasick.

Beth emptied her wineglass with one bold movement.
Life is a bitch, she reminded herself. The only reasonable
response was to laugh at the inanity of it all.

"Charlotte—you can watch that new video up in our room,"
Amy said, trying not to make it sound like a command.
"I'll call you when it's time for lunch."

Charlotte hesitated for a second, then grabbed the video
from her pile of presents on the floor and ran upstairs.

"Will you tell me about the gun later?" she shouted from
the landing.

"Yes," Jimmy answered. "Later."

"Come over to the fireplace," Mark addressed Thea
gently. "You're not wearing a coat. You must be freezing."

"Who are you?" Thea asked, not budging.

"He's my father, Thea," Leo said, walking toward her.

"He's right. You should get warm before you tell us about—about the gun."

"Am I supposed to tell everyone? Like I'm giving a talk to my class in school?"

"We're all involved in this." Beth now stepped forward. "I'm Leo's sister. And I know your mother too. In fact she may have bought the gun to use on me. So I think you better tell everyone."

"You don't have to, sweetheart. You and I can go into a separate room and talk this over," Nick said.

"Or the rest of us could go upstairs with Charlotte and watch her video while you talk to your dad. What's the video, Amy? *Pulp Fiction*? *Reservoir Dogs* with a new Bing Crosby soundtrack? No, Nick—" Beth's voice was fierce. "Your daughter better stay right here."

Nothing had changed. Absolutely nothing. Meg watched as Thea gave a sharp look to Nick and then moved toward the fireplace. However outrageous Beth was, people listened and did what she said. All the patterns set during their childhood were still firmly in place. What was the point of trying to grow up, trying to be an adult? Everyone remained a child all their lives, they just had different ways of hiding their childishness. For the first time since she'd walked out on Charlie, Meg felt a wave of misery and remorse. Life would be a lot easier if she had stayed with him. If he'd been here now, he would have rolled his eyes at Beth and Meg could have spent all her energy worrying about his reactions instead of worrying about her own. No way was this family going to get together peacefully. It was a lost cause.

"You're both so screwed up." Thea spat the words out at Nick from her position in front of the fire. "You and Mom. She's running around like some maniac in a Stephen King movie and you're running around with—" she pointed dismissively at Leo. "Some college kid."

"Thea—" Rachel, perched on the end of the sofa, waved

her hand. "Hi. Remember me? I didn't bake cookies for you when you and Zoey were hanging out together. But I remember driving you guys around a lot and I remember you weren't a rude little brat in those days. You were a nice person. Why don't you cut the crap about how fucked up your parents are and tell us what exactly is going on?"

Amy saw Beth make a thumbs-up gesture in Rachel's direction.

"Look. I don't know exactly what's going on, okay? All I know is that Mom has a gun. I don't know where she got it. I don't know what she's planning to do with it, but I walked into her room and I saw it lying on her bed. And she's in such a weird mood I know something's seriously wrong. She's been talking to herself all morning with a really strange expression on her face."

"Did you ask her about the gun?" Stuart questioned, in a gentle tone.

"Yes, I asked her about the gun. She said it was a Christmas present."

"Did it come with a matching machete?"

"Beth—" Mark cut in sharply. "Let's leave the jokes for later."

"Why, Dad? Give me one good reason."

"It's unbecoming."

"Oh, good. Here we go again. All my behavior is unbecoming, isn't it?"

"Dad's just trying—"

"Meg. Why do you always have to come to his defense in such an ass-licking way? He's never done you any favors."

"Since when have *you* done anyone any favors?" Amy heard herself shrieking. "All you do is criticize people and try to get them to do what you want—"

"Such as?"

"Such as getting me to do all the cleaning in the house—"

"You volunteered, Amy, remember? You *liked* all that shit."

"Please," Leo pleaded. "This isn't helping anything."

"You can't smooth things over anymore, kiddo. There's nothing to smooth over. We've pretended all these years, the four of us together, we've pretended—"

"Right, Beth. We've pretended you don't bother the hell out of everyone," Meg snapped.

"You can have this family argument later," Stuart cut in. "Right now we're trying to deal with the fact that an angry woman has a gun."

"No." Meg walked over to Beth, stood directly in front of her. "I want to know something *now*. Who's Ringo? That's what I want to know. Which one of us is supposed to be Ringo? It's me, isn't it?"

"Ringo?" Alex turned a puzzled face to Rachel.

"This must be some Beatles deal," Rachel replied.

"No one is Ringo," Beth laughed. "I never marked anyone down as Ringo. You shouldn't take things so literally, Meg. You're as bad as Amy."

"This isn't funny," Leo said softly. "We'll all go crazy if this keeps going on."

"Meg's as bad as me? That's great, Beth. Is her haircut as bad as mine? Are her curtains as awful as mine? You know, I always thought *I* was Ringo. And I want to know something, too. *I* want to know why you took us to that goddamn monastery and made us sit outside in the car and talk about what food the fucking monks were eating for five hours. That's what *I* want to know. What did you think you were doing, Beth? Did you think that was *fun?*"

"Jesus, Amy. Lighten up. What else were we supposed to do? I mean it wasn't as if our beneficent father had planned a great Christmas for us. I was improvising, that's all."

"So why did you always get to be the one who improvised?" Meg hadn't retreated from her position. "Amy's right. Why did you get to decide where we were going? I was older. I should have been driving. *I* should have been improvising."

"Whoa, doggies." Rachel rose from her seat on the sofa.

"Settle down. Hold on a minute. I'm going to show you something." She grabbed Beth and Meg by their elbows. Amazed by this turn of events, both sisters followed Rachel uncomplaining as she led them to the far end of the living room. "Stay right here for a second, okay? Now Leo and Amy and Mark—you get over here, too, okay. Right. You're all together. I want you all to shut up for a while and just stand here."

"What is this shit?" Beth sneered.

"I think Rachel is demonstrating that you're a family," Stuart commented.

"Oh, please," Beth sighed. "Is this supposed to be news?"

"Hey, it's a technique I learned once," Rachel shrugged. "You're all arguing and you're not seeing the point. You're not seeing what you have in common."

"Our DNA?" Amy asked.

"Yeah, right. Your DNA. Whatever. The rest of us here are all connected to you guys in some way and *we* can see you're a family. It's obvious to us what you have in common. Now Thea is standing here listening to you all fight and she must be thinking you're all nuts because she's just told you her mother has a gun. None of us give a shit about Ringo or monasteries or who drove what fucking car. We want to figure out what to do about this person with a gun. I mean, I don't even know you, Leo, and I'm scared shitless on your behalf. And this cute guy Stuart here has obviously flipped over you, Beth. If I were you I'd want to live to enjoy his attentions. Basically, what I'm saying is like— get serious. Am I right or what?"

"You're right," Mark said. "We have to decide what to do."

"I suggest we call the police," Jimmy volunteered.

"*Now* we're getting somewhere. Good idea, Fishbone."

"Are we allowed to move now, Rachel?" Beth asked.

"Sure. I was just making a point."

"It was a good point," Meg smiled at her. "At least it stopped us momentarily."

"Shit—" Thea suddenly broke silence as everyone moved back to their original positions. "You're all so—" she paused, glancing around the room with a withering glare. "Stupid. You're all caught up in your stupid little lives and your stupid little jokes. I shouldn't have come here in the first place."

"Thea—chill out, will you?" Zoey exclaimed. "This is my family too. They may be stupid, but I can remember times you've been stupid, so don't pull any superior stuff on me."

"I'm sorry, Zoey—" Thea stared at the ground, her voice faltering. "I'm just so confused. I don't know who all these people are. They're all as crazy as Mom. I'm tired and confused. I don't even know if we're friends or not."

"Of course we're friends," Zoey assured her. "Why don't you come up with me to my room now and we can talk about everything. These guys need to decide what to do. We can leave them alone. We've got a lot to talk about."

"Go on, Thea," Rachel urged. "Zoey's missed you, you know. So have I. I remember listening to you two laughing together in the old days. I miss that."

Thea turned to Nick. "Are you going to tell Mom that I told you about the gun?"

"Not if you don't want me to," Nick answered.

"I don't know. I'm not sure I care. I just wish you two would leave me out of things. I don't want anything to do with what's going on. It's your problem."

"I know it is," Nick said sadly. "And I'm sorry."

"Yeah. Sure. Let's go." Thea turned to Zoey and accompanied her up the staircase.

"Calling the police may be a good idea," Mark commented as soon as the girls had closed the door to Zoey's room upstairs. "But I don't see how they can do anything. Jackie hasn't threatened anyone."

"The gun may be unlicensed," Stuart said. "It's against the law to have an unlicensed gun here, isn't it?"

"Yes. But the gun may be licensed. You know it's within her right to bear arms."

"Before you and Stuart get off onto constitutional issues, Dad, I'd say we should call the police and tell them the situation. They'll tell us whether they can do anything or not," Beth remarked. "The last thing we want is Jackie coming in wielding an Uzi. I have to admit Rachel was right. I forgot for a while there how much I have to look forward to. I mean, I haven't even opened my Christmas presents yet."

"Wait a minute." Leo stepped forward. "I don't think we should call the police. I think I should go over to Jackie's house and talk to her."

"That's foolish, Leonora," Mark said. "If anyone goes to talk to her, it should be me."

"No," Nick protested firmly. "It should be me."

"Why don't we all fucking go?" Beth said, "Maybe Jackie's got guns waiting for all of us, little presents wrapped up under the tree. We can have a shoot-out at the Cambridge Corral."

"We can't stop Jackie," Leo continued, oblivious to Beth's interjections. "Dad's right. She hasn't threatened anyone. If we call the police, we're the ones who'll be the aggressors. I don't want to do that."

"Do you want to sit and wait?" Meg asked. "Helen told me the other day that she seriously considered running me over in her car. I believe her. I think she probably came damned close. I think Jackie's a lot more unhinged than Helen was. I think she sounds very dangerous."

"I want to go talk to her."

"Leo—listen to me for a minute. I've been through the wars. You're the last person on earth Jackie would be able to be rational with. The sight of you will drive her crazy." Meg sighed. "You've got to understand. You've got what she wants. This is like territorial imperative. Nick's hers. You're trespassing. Trespassers get shot. I hate to say this at this particular moment, but I saw an Oprah Winfrey program once that scared the hell out of me. A woman who had been left by her husband went out and shot him and his new wife. Killed them while they were sleeping in bed.

She was interviewed in jail and she didn't have the slightest remorse about it. And you know, the audience was cheering her, if you can believe it. Everyone was on her side."

"But it wasn't that way with you and Helen. You two managed to be friendly."

"You're not listening, Leo. I just told you—it *was* that way. We *weren't* friends. Far from it. You have to understand. You're Jackie's enemy. You can't sit down and negotiate a peace. She doesn't want one."

"Meg's right," Stuart said. "I'm in a position to know. We have to take this seriously. I'd say that the best plan would be for you and Nick to clear out of town for a while, Leo. Give Jackie a chance to calm down."

"I can't leave Thea," Nick stated.

"I can't leave you," Leo shot back.

"We've reached a dead end, then, haven't we?" Rachel turned to Alex. "You're the doctor. Any ideas for a remedy?"

"As a matter of fact, yes," Alex said, rubbing the back of his neck as he spoke. "I do have an idea. Why don't *I* go to this Jackie person's house? She doesn't know me. She has nothing against me. I have a certain amount of training. I should be able to recognize what kind of state she is in."

"Alex, that's very kind of you. But what makes you think she'd let you in?" Nick asked.

"She's a woman, isn't she?" Rachel put her hand up to Alex's cheek. "Just look at this face, will you? No woman would turn this face away. Stop blushing, baby, you know it's the truth."

"She's got a point," Beth chimed in. "Alex is a god in human form."

"I'm sorry," Mark shook his head. "This doesn't make any sense. Even if Jackie let Alex into her house, what pretext would he have for delving into her emotional state, much less asking her what weapons she happened to have lying around?"

"Alex can get silver out of a stone," Rachel said with evident pride.

"Isn't that supposed to be blood?" Amy asked.

"Whatever. You know what I mean. Once he's got his foot in the door, he can do anything." Rachel stopped, put her hand to her head. "Shit, sorry, Fishbone. I don't mean to say that you couldn't, you know—"

"It's okay." Jimmy winked at his ex-wife. "Really. I'm comfortable with my limitations."

"So that's the plan? Alex is the Trojan horse?" Mark queried.

"What do you think, Nick?"

"I don't know, Stuart. I probably have less idea than anyone these days what will work with Jackie."

"I think it sounds worth trying." Meg moved closer to Leo on the sofa and put her arm around her.

"It's so off the wall, I do too," Beth echoed.

"And so do I," Amy assented.

"I've got my mobile. I'll call you from there when I know what's going on."

Alex was using his doctor's voice, Meg reflected. It was amazing how effectively authoritative it sounded.

"Thank you Alex," Nick said with a somber expression. "Let me give you directions on how to get there."

As Nick went into the hallway with Alex, Amy turned to her sisters. "Somehow I don't think we'll be eating much for a while. I'm going to go turn off the stove."

"So what do we do while we wait for the doctor's report?" Beth asked. "Play Charades?"

"Later, Beth. Nick—why don't you let me get you a drink?" Stuart asked.

"Thanks," Nick replied, coming back down into the living room. "I could use one right now. I'm not so sure this is such a good idea."

"Believe me, it is," Rachel countered.

"How did you and Alex meet?" Mark asked, in his most polite voice. "Why don't you tell us the story, Rachel? We could use some diversion."

"Okay." Rachel beamed. "It's so cute. You'll love it—"

"Don't leave out any sex parts, Rach," Beth interrupted. "That's what we all really want to hear."

Stuart handed Nick a glass of whiskey, walked over to Beth and put his hand over her mouth.

"It's time you were muzzled, sweetheart. Let Rachel tell her story."

For the next twenty minutes, Rachel proceeded to narrate the history of her first encounter with Alex, starting with the clothes she had chosen to wear on the afternoon of the party, progressing through a detailed description of Alex's moves on the dance floor and, finally, ending with a breathless summary of all Alex's heroics in the realm of asthma research.

"It's like when he started telling me about his work, I thought: wow, maybe *I* should get asthma and be his guinea pig. You know, let him experiment on me."

"Don't even think about saying anything," Meg heard Stuart whisper to Beth.

"That's a lovely story, Rachel. Really romantic— Jimmy, will you get the phone?" Amy asked her husband. "It might be Alex. He may be lost."

"Jackie may not have let him in," Leo said, the corners of her mouth twitching as she watched Jimmy disappear in the direction of the hall telephone.

"Alex doesn't get lost," Rachel commented, turning to Meg. "He's real centered. He always knows where he is."

"Alex is a prince." Beth nudged Leo with her elbow and winked at Stuart. "Alex will save the day. He and Jackie will probably be out shooting skeet this afternoon. I'm sure he's a dead shot."

"That's not funny," Rachel turned on Beth. "He's doing you a favor. Don't make fun of him."

"Well, excuse me for trying to bring some levity to the room."

"Levity?" Rachel looked at Meg, then Leo. "Levity? What's she talking about?"

Jimmy appeared from the hallway, brushed his hair away from his forehead, and said in a strained voice: "That was Alex. She's not there. He said the door was open, though, and he took it upon himself to walk in. No trace of Jackie. No trace of a gun, either. He had a little prowl around the place."

"Wait a minute. We're all panicked over nothing," Amy said. "I just realized something obvious. How would Jackie know my address? How would she know Leo and Nick are here?"

"Right," Rachel smiled. "I guess we don't have anything to worry about anymore. She's gone somewhere else."

"Where's else, I wonder?" Mark began to pace the floor.

"I told her." Beth reached out for Stuart's hand. "I told her when I called her to say her little blackmail scheme hadn't worked. I said we were all going to have a celebratory Christmas lunch."

"But you wouldn't have said *where* we were having lunch?" Meg's tone was incredulous. "Beth? You didn't tell her Nick and Leo would be *here*, did you? Beth?"

"I left the message on her answering machine."

"I know you did, Beth. But what did you say?" Nick kept his voice neutral.

"I said she should come join us. I gave her the address. I—it was a joke," she finished lamely.

"Boy, you sure know how to get in people's faces, don't you?" Rachel commented with an awed voice.

"God, Beth." Stuart shook his head. "You're an unguided missile."

"I know. I'm sorry." She leaned against Stuart and hid her face in his chest.

"I think we should clear the house," Mark said quickly. "I think we should leave immediately. We can all go to my house and call the police from there."

"I think," said Rachel, "we forgot something crucial. We forgot to lock the door."

They all turned to see a woman standing on the threshold of the door, a gun in her hand.

"I'd guess that's Jackie," Rachel added. But no one was listening.

Chapter Twenty-Five

BETH HAD NEVER been in an accident. She'd listened half-heartedly once when Robin described a car crash she'd been involved in. "Yeah, right," she had wanted to interrupt. "Everything was in slow motion, it was if it were happening to someone else—blah, blah, blah." Since one of Robin's legs and three of her ribs had been fractured in the smash-up, Beth decided to take pity on her and let her tell her story unhindered.

Now she understood how strange it was to feel time wind down. Jackie was walking toward the room, not exactly waving a gun around, but moving it from side to side in a sweeping motion. An absurd amount of time elapsed between steps. Beth found herself noticing Jackie's clothes—blue wool pants, a white silk shirt, no sweater or coat—and thinking: she must be freezing. The next thought was: how can she wear wool pants and carry a gun? Leather, sure, jeans, sure—but wool? This can't be happening.

"Am I interrupting the party?" Jackie asked, staring at Nick. "You should have invited me. I wouldn't have had to gate-crash."

"Jackie—put the gun down. There are children upstairs. *Thea's* upstairs, for God's sake."

"I don't care who's here. Why should I? You don't care about anyone. Why should I?"

She's crazy, Beth thought. *But this is happening. That's a real gun. And for the first time in my life, I'm scared.*

Beth had unconsciously moved toward Leo. Amy and Meg had as well, effectively blocking her from Jackie's range. Mark, Jimmy and Stuart were making the same moves in Nick's direction.

"Stay away from him," Jackie ordered the men. "And

you—" she pointed her gun at Beth. "Get away from your sister. She can't hide from me."

This is some fucking melodrama, Beth wanted to say. They're not supposed to run soap operas on Christmas Day. She wanted to say a lot more too, but she knew that for once her mouth was not an appropriate weapon in this battle.

"Do you know how to use that gun?" Stuart asked in a calm, controlled voice.

That's a voice that can talk people off ledges, Beth thought. *Jesus, that's a voice I love.*

"Yes, I know how to use this gun," Jackie answered. "I aim it at someone I hate and I pull the trigger."

"What about the—" Stuart took a step forward as he spoke.

"Shut up. And stand back. You think you can talk me out of this. Whoever you are. I don't care who you are. You all thought I'd just disappear, didn't you? You thought you could have your parties and laugh at my expense—"

"Nobody was laughing at you," Stuart said quietly. He had followed Jackie's order and stepped back a pace, but he was the focus of Jackie's speech and her stare. Beth realized that this was how it was supposed to be, that Stuart was the only person in the room who had any chance of coping with Jackie.

"I have my rights."

"I know. I'd like to know what you're going to do now." His voice was as soothing as her gun was terrifying.

"I'm going to shoot the thief. The person who stole what belongs to me. The person who stole my life. I thought I could get it back. I tried to get it back. Without the gun. But I need the gun to get it back."

"You won't get Nick back if you shoot Leonora," Stuart said.

"I don't want her to have him," Jackie turned her stare from Stuart to Nick. "I don't want her to have you," she repeated.

"You've been hurt," Stuart said simply.

"I've been robbed," Jackie replied.

"You've been hurt enough. You shouldn't hurt yourself by using that gun."

Beth saw Jackie's eyes narrow as the words Stuart spoke entered her consciousness. She was thinking. At least she was capable of thought.

"Jackie—" Nick broke in. "Thea's upstairs. Put the gun away. You don't have to do this."

"Yes, I do. You want to talk me out of this, don't you—" her eyes had traveled back again to Stuart. "You've got a nice voice. It would be nice to talk to you. You'd probably understand. It *sounds* as if you would. You might understand pain and humiliation and loss. You might understand why I need to do this." She paused. "Which one of these women belongs to you?" Her gun followed her eyes as she looked at each woman in the room.

Beth felt Jackie's gaze move away from Rachel and lock in on her. She tried to rid herself of any emotion, she tried to look at Jackie as she had looked at her those times in her office, with contempt. She knew if she betrayed the slightest feeling of fear, Jackie would turn on Stuart. And Stuart was their only hope.

"I don't believe it," Jackie laughed, breaking eye contact with Beth. She turned back to Stuart. "You're crazy, you know. I'm not. You are. You're involved with *her?* That pathetic excuse for a shrink? You're certifiable. Now, Leonora, I'd suggest you step out of that circle that's protecting you. Unless you want to cause a lot of people a lot of harm—unless you want me to start by shooting someone else. I'd be more than happy to start with Beth."

"Jackie. I'm the one you're angry with." Nick pushed Jimmy and Mark to the side and took a step forward. "If you have to shoot anyone—"

"Shoot you? You want to sacrifice yourself for your beloved. Oh, God, Nick, you're funny. You've seen too many movies in that job of yours. This isn't about you. I just said that. This is about *her*. I don't hate you. I hate her. Oh, I know I'm not supposed to kill people just because I hate them." Jackie heaved an exaggerated sigh. "But you know something? I don't care anymore what I'm supposed to do. She didn't care when she had her affair with you, did she? She wasn't *supposed* to do that. She wasn't *supposed* to screw a married man, was she? There aren't any rules anymore. No one plays by the rules. So I don't either. Come on, Leonora. I'm tired of talking. It's time."

Beth felt Leo trying to break through the circle she and Amy and Meg had formed. She felt Leo's tiny hands trying to push her to the side. She felt herself stiffen against them, her body taking on a solidity she didn't think she possessed. She and her sisters were rocks. They wouldn't let Leo pass.

Beth saw him then. He was suddenly standing behind and above Jackie, at the top of the steps leading down to the living room. Jackie had left the door open when she'd come in and he'd managed to enter and approach unnoticed while she'd been talking.

I know him, Beth thought.

Time, which had been so slow, suddenly picked up its pace.

"Put the gun down," he said.

I know him.

Jackie turned her head to the side. She didn't move her gun.

"Put the gun down."

He was in uniform. He had his own gun. It was pointed at Jackie.

"Come on, lady. It's Christmas. I'm sure you've got your reasons. But we've all got better things to do."

Oh, shit. That's something I would say, Beth thought.

Jackie swung the gun then and fired. Beth couldn't believe how loud the sound was. She couldn't believe what she was seeing. Nick threw himself on top of Jackie. For a moment it looked as though they were having a crazy form of sex, writhing on the floor. Stuart was beside him within a second, grabbing the gun, which Jackie had dropped when she'd been tackled. Charlotte was screaming something upstairs. Zoey and Thea came running down. Beth saw blood pouring out of the policeman. She saw another policeman come through the door with what looked like a doughnut in his hand. She felt Leo finally push past her. And then she felt her own blood drain away from her body. She saw strange yellow colors circling in front of her. She felt her legs collapse.

Chapter Twenty-Six

LEO COULDN'T STOP trembling. She could have been swathed in layers of heavy fur and still she would have been possessed by constant tremors.

They'd been taken to a small lounge on the fourth floor of the hospital. In one corner stood a large TV, its screen a blank, waiting to entertain. Two young men sat in another corner, connected to IV poles. They were both wearing baseball caps that they'd occasionally remove as they talked, revealing their bald heads. Both of them had glanced up when Leo, Meg, Beth and Amy had been ushered in, but had gone back to their conversation without any other acknowledgment.

"Do you want me to try to find you a Valium or something?" Beth asked.

Leo shook her head. The only words she had spoken since the shooting had been to ask to go to the hospital where the policeman was and to tell Nick she didn't want him with her.

"Leo—please tell us what you're thinking. It's killing us seeing you like this," Meg begged.

Leo didn't respond. She couldn't. How could she put her thoughts into words? It was impossible. A man might die because of her. She was responsible. How could she have started a relationship with a married man? How could she have driven someone to the point of murder? It wasn't worth it—love wasn't worth that kind of price. She should have run away from Nick, from everyone, that day she'd read about her mother.

"You can't blame yourself for this," Amy said softly. She was crying, Leo realized dimly. How lucky Amy was to be able to cry.

"It's strange, isn't it, that his name is Steven. It's like some strange twist of Fate," Beth said to no one in particular. "You know he stopped me for speeding just a while ago. He let me go without a ticket. I couldn't believe that was him again."

No, no. It's not strange, Leo thought. It's not strange at all that he's named Steven. Go away, she wanted to say to her sisters. This is between me and God—no one else is involved.

"You can't blame yourself," Amy repeated. "You're not responsible for the act of a crazy person."

And who made her crazy? Leo looked down at the floor. It seemed to be miles away.

"Leo—I really think you should see a doctor. You've been through so much lately. You need medical attention." Meg turned to Amy for support, but Amy was too focused on Leo's face to respond.

"Where is the fucking person who'll tell us what's happening? Jesus, I hate hospitals." Beth began to tap her foot impatiently. "I can't believe I fainted. I always thought I could stand anything. But everything seemed to be happening so fast. I couldn't understand why she shot *him*. It must have been what he said about having better things to do. That must have flicked some switch."

"It was something you might have said," Meg commented.

"I know. I thought so too. My kind of dismissive comment. Christ, I'm glad I kept my mouth shut for once in my life."

"Are you sure you don't want Nick here?" Amy asked Leo.

Leo shrank back in her chair.

"Okay," Amy soothed her. "But what about Dad?"

She shook her head.

"He's going to be all right, Leo. I can feel it. He won't die," Meg said, trying, but failing, to sound assured.

I tracked Nick down, Leo thought. I could have left him

alone and I didn't. I kept going after him. What kind of person am I?

"Kiddo—please. You're scaring us. I've never seen anyone tremble like that. Talk to us, please." Beth reached out for Leo's hand. "You've got to calm down. Really. You have to."

When there was no response, Beth looked at Amy and Meg with a desperation she couldn't remember ever feeling before, not even that night she'd thought briefly about ending her own life. Jesus, I love her, she thought. What can we do? "Amy," she said. "Say something. You might be able to get through to her."

Amy didn't bother to wipe the tears from her cheeks. She looked at Leo disintegrating before her, falling into tiny pieces. Nothing anyone had ever said about the workings of the brain could help Leo now, Amy knew. Nor would funny references to TV shows they'd watched as kids.

Why won't they go away? Leo wondered. Why do they keep looking at me like that? It's my fault he was shot. They don't need to be here. If the policeman hadn't been shot, what would have happened? Jackie would have shot me. That's what *should* have happened. But that wouldn't have been as painful as this so of course it didn't happen. I have to be punished in the most painful way possible. What had Stuart said? The past is like a baton in a relay race? That's right. He said you have to keep running forward with it. Until? I should have asked Stuart that question. Until when? Until you die? Or until you hit a solid wall of shame, misery and guilt and wish you were dead?

"Leo." Amy knelt down at her sister's feet, put her hands on Leo's shaking knees. "Don't do this. You're turning into Mom."

"What?"

"You're behaving like Mom."

"No." Leo shook her head.

Meg and Beth exchanged glances, amazed to hear Leo finally speak. Meg nodded in Amy's direction, a silent signal to Beth to let Amy continue uninterrupted.

"You're taking responsibility for an accident, just like she did. That's not fair. Not to you or to anyone who loves you. You'll destroy the people who love you if you do that."

"It's different," Leo mumbled.

"How is it different?" Amy pressed.

"Mom running over Steven *was* an accident. I chased Nick. I did something wrong, something I knew was wrong. It wasn't an accident."

"You never planned to fall in love with a married man, Leo. I know this is a tired argument, but it is also a true one. If Nick had been happily married, none of this would have happened. He didn't get involved with you for a lark. He *adores* you. It is not a criminal act to want to get out of a lousy marriage. Do you blame Nick for what's happening now?"

"No. Jackie was right. It's not Nick. It's me. It's my fault."

"It is *not*." Amy had tightened her grip on Leo's knees and raised her voice. "Falling in love *is* like an accident. You had no intention of hurting anyone. You didn't set out to hurt this woman. We're all sorry Jackie is in such a state, but I'm afraid she has a responsibility for that, not you. Her life is a mess and that's very sad. It doesn't help anyone if your life is ruined too. Don't you care about Nick? About us? You can't be like Mom, Leo. You can't let guilt destroy the rest of your life. You just can't. Whether you like it or not, there are people who love you in this world and you have to be the best person you can be for them."

"But what if he dies, Amy?" Leo bent forward and grabbed Amy in a fierce embrace. "What if he dies?"

"He won't," Amy whispered to her sobbing sister. "He can't."

Meg saw that Beth was crying now as well. They were all crying and Meg understood that they were crying not only for the Steven of their present but for their mother and their dead brother and the child in London and everything terrible that they had never been able to cry about together before.

"Jesus," Beth said finally, wiping her face with the sleeve of her sweater. "I don't think I can take this kind of emotion. I really don't. I mean, isn't it time for me to say something sharp?"

"You don't have to," Meg replied.

"I don't? Shit, that's a relief."

"You know something, Beth?" Meg smiled at her. "I think you can relax now."

"But not too much." Beth returned her sister's smile.

"Of course not. We might need your brand of light relief again sometime."

Leo let go of Amy and sat up in her chair.

"I don't know what I'd do without you," she said simply, looking at her three sisters in turn. The trembling had subsided slightly.

"Yeah," Beth said. "The Little Women. We're good with tragedy, aren't we? You know I never admitted this to you before, but I went to see the movie. They weren't bad, those broads. I still can't figure out why Mom didn't name one of us Jo, though."

"The eternal mystery," Meg commented. "We're not supposed to know."

The nurse entered the room then, a young blonde who looked tired and cross.

"Excuse me," she said, "You're waiting for news on the policeman who was shot, am I right?"

"You're right," Meg said immediately.

"He's going to be okay. He lost a lot of blood and he was critical for a while, but he'll be okay."

"Steven." Leo drew in her breath. "He's going to be all right."

"Yes. You're not immediate family are you?"

"It depends on how you look at it," Beth replied, smiling her angel's smile.

*   *   *

They all thought they were so superior, they all thought they could throw me away. They didn't understand about love and they didn't understand me. Now they do. Now when it's too late.

He promised to stay with me, to love and to cherish me till death did us part. What made him think he could break that promise and walk away? That's what I'd like to know. What gave him a right to lie to God? What gave her the right to step into my place as if I were dead?

I deserved to be loved. Nick loved me once. I had the letters to prove it.

Then he stopped loving me.

He kept saying we'd been heading for a divorce for a long time. He kept saying how much we fought. As if any marriage doesn't have fights. As if it could possibly be perfect.

That's all people do these days. Break up if it's not one hundred percent perfect. There's no sense of decency. There's no integrity. There's no shame.

Other wives rip up their cheating husbands' clothes or ruin their cars or spend all their money. Other wives go to divorce courts and accuse their cheating husbands of abusing the children. I wouldn't do that. I didn't want to hurt Nick. I wanted to get rid of her, the person who had robbed me. I wasn't crazy. I was looking for justice.

And now I'm the one in jail.

That policeman shouldn't have talked to me like that.

I made a mistake. I shot the wrong person.

I don't remember actually pulling the trigger. All I remember is his blood. And Nick's body on top of mine.

And Nick's body on top of mine.

Epilogue

"THIS IS FANTASTIC," Meg said, raising her head from the paper and looking at Leo. "You've written it beautifully. It works perfectly with what Beth and Amy and I have written. If I can edit them all together, I think we have a great magazine piece here."

Leo smiled tentatively.

"I thought it might be too emotional."

"No, not at all, it's an emotional subject. We've *all* been emotional. But we haven't overdone it either—none of us has been sloppy."

"Of course we haven't been sloppy," Beth said crossly. "We're not sloppy types."

"I hope it helps someone," Leo said.

"I think it will," Amy joined in. "There aren't a lot of people in our situation, not a lot of children with our kind of family history, but there must be a few with similar backgrounds anyway."

"God. Poor bastards," Beth remarked, taking her boots off the table and sitting up straight. "You know, Meg, I like the way you've done this place. It's much nicer than your house was."

"I rented it furnished, Beth."

"Oh, shit. I've done one of my famous insults. I didn't mean to, really. I'm trying to reform."

"For our benefit?" Amy asked.

"For my own benefit."

"Why do I think Stuart is involved in this transformation?" Meg queried.

"Because he is, of course. Listen, I'm in love. I admit it. It might just make me a nicer person. I might even start complimenting people."

"Boy, you're not turning over a new leaf, Beth. You're turning over a whole tree," Amy laughed.

"Stuart's worth turning over a forest for." Beth reached out and picked up her glass of wine.

"Has he told you yet what he does for a living?" Leo asked.

"Yes."

"So what does he do?" Leo pressed.

"Well, I know we've been avoiding the danger topic here, so I better not say."

"I don't understand. What are you talking about?" Meg leaned forward.

"Okay. I'll tell you. He does what he did on Christmas."

"Beth," Amy sighed. "What does *that* mean?"

"He talks people out of things. I knew it when I heard his voice that day. I thought—this is a voice that talks people down from ledges. And that's exactly what he does. He worked for the police in Australia. He was the person they'd call if someone were threatening to jump off the Sydney Bridge or holding someone hostage in the Opera House or whatever. That's how he met Janet—the face-slasher. He had talked her out of jumping off the roof of a building and then the sap started dating her. No wonder she went wild. She was crazy to begin with."

"That's incredible," Leo exclaimed.

"I know. He almost pulled it off with Jackie. I really think he might have if she hadn't figured out he was connected to me."

"Then *he* should have been the one to go to Jackie's house, not Alex," Amy said.

"He hadn't worked for a while. He wasn't sure he could function well anymore. That's why he let Alex go. It's lucky it happened that way. He told me he wasn't sure if he would have called the police the way Alex did when he found Jackie's house empty."

"Is he going to try to work for the Boston police now?" Meg asked.

"Not yet. He's taking a break from all that. He's not

sure he wants to go back. It's not exactly a stress-free job and he wasn't making much money, either. Which is why he lives in such a dump. But you know something? I think he should do it. I think he's right for that kind of work."

"Wow, I'm impressed," Amy said. "Jimmy said something to me that Christmas night, though, when we got back from the hospital. He said Stuart was the kind of guy you'd want at your bedside if you were dying. I thought that was a strange thing to say, but I know what he means. There's something about his voice."

Beth nodded.

"Nick adores Stuart, too," Leo added.

"I suppose I should be worried about a guy all these men find so wonderful."

"Very funny." Amy shook her head. "I have to say, it's odd hearing all these romantic things coming out of your mouth after all your lectures to us about the unimportance of the male species. Aren't you worried about dwindling?"

"Nope."

"So you didn't mean all those things you said about men and women and people in relationships wanting to kill each other?"

"I did then, Amy. Not now."

"Well, I'm the odd one out now." Meg refilled her glass of wine from the bottle on the table in front of her. "I'm the only one without a man. And I'm feeling as if I'd been let out of jail. I can't imagine myself ever getting married again."

"I didn't think I'd get married again after Patrick left," Amy commented. "Things can happen, though. Things can change."

"And things can go wrong," Meg said sadly. She glanced at Leo and saw her frown. "Still. Things can go right. What's happening now between you and Nick?"

"He's concentrating on Thea at the moment. What she went through that—that day. It wasn't good. She has to deal with the fact that her mother's in—you know, in jail. He's back at their house, looking after her. Where he should be. And that's good for me. It's giving me space and time to think."

"Are you coming to any conclusions?" Amy asked.

"I love him. I don't know if that means we can be to-gether after all that's happened. It's such a wreck. But we see each other a lot. He loves me in a way no one has ever loved me. I know that. I can't imagine my life without him. I think we just have to wait and see what is possible and what's not." Leo tilted her head to the side and rubbed her face with her hands. "It sounds as if I'm being rational, doesn't it? But I'm not really. I've been a hopeless romantic from the first moment I saw him. He keeps saying we'll find a way to be together, and I'm beginning to believe him."

"Well, I'm a big fan of Nick's. And as part of my ref-ormation, I should tell you that I like Jimmy too, Amy. I think he has a depth to him I was too superficial to see. But, having said all that positive and uplifting and self-deprecating junk; I want to say something else. I think that the four of us better be a seriously tight unit from now on."

"What do you mean, Beth?" Leo's eyes widened.

"I mean—what do we have here? We have Nick and Stuart and Jimmy who all get along like a house on fire— probably because they were together in a house *under* fire. And we have Dad, who seems to have taken those three guys to his heart with a passion and keeps planning all-male fishing trips. So there's a whole lot of family feeling among the men in our lives—sorry, Meg, but I'm sure who-ever your next choice is will probably fit in too. I mean after Charlie anyone has got to be a welcome—sorry. I'll stop right there. Anyway, I think we shouldn't give up our position, our power. The four of us always had a power. I've got a new take on men now, but that doesn't mean I've forgotten what assholes they can be. Not entirely. So we better be a powerful force ourselves. We better be as together as the Beatles were before Yoko and Linda. Even if that means I have to be Ringo."

"Oh, God." Amy put her head in her hands and began

to laugh. "Not them again. Not the fucking Beatles."

When the doorbell rang a few minutes later, Meg answered it with tears of laughter in her eyes.

"Happy New Year," Jimmy said, kissing his sister-in-law on the cheek. "We come bearing gifts. Champagne."

He was followed through the entrance by Stuart, Nick, Mark, and finally a redheaded woman.

"Uh-oh," Amy whispered to Leo, pointing at the woman.

"Your father has an announcement to make." Stuart took off his coat, walked over to Beth, and put his arm around her. "He wanted our support when he made it."

Mark took the redhead by the hand and led her into the center of Meg's new living room.

"I want you to meet Susan," Mark said. "Susan and I are planning to get married next month. I know this may seem sudden to you, but we've been seeing each other on and off for a few years now."

Jimmy uncorked a bottle of champagne with a loud bang.

Susan had an uncomfortably shy look as she shook hands with Meg, Beth, Amy, and Leo.

"Are there any glasses?" Jimmy asked.

"I'll get some," Meg answered quickly. "Come on, come help me, will you?" She turned to her sisters.

In the kitchen, Meg made no move to find new glasses. The four sisters looked at one another. Eight eyebrows raised. Beth was the first one to speak.

"She looks about thirty years old."

"She might look younger than she is," Amy said weakly. "But it's hard to imagine having her as stepmother."

"This is a disaster," Meg stated.

Leo burst out laughing.

TURN THE PAGE FOR AN EXCERPT FROM

FOREIGN CORRESPONDENTS

THE NEW NOVEL FROM CINDY BLAKE
NOW AVAILABLE IN HARDCOVER
FROM ST. MARTIN'S PRESS

"YOU'RE SETTING THEM up on a television show?" Bernice asked, wondering, as she always did when she saw Anna, what Mr. Anna had been like and where he was now. Everyone seemed to know that Anna had been married, but no one could say what had happened to the man. Anna didn't have any pictures of him, never mentioned his name and immediately cut Bernice off the one time she'd asked her about him.

"What's wrong with that?" Anna stared at Bernice across the table.

"Isn't that a little over the top? Meeting on a television show?"

"Funny—that's the phrase everyone used when I explained Simon's potential in the marketplace. Over the top, they kept repeating. Have you forgotten how I succeeded with Simon?"

"I wish I could forget." Bernice felt her shoulders sag in despair. Simon the Skunk. Her nemesis. The very mention of his name brought back memories of a whole childhood spent listening to her father's bedtime tales of Simon the Skunk and his Robin Hood–like exploits in the Forest of Dean. She hated that shitty skunk almost as much as she supposed Fergie's kids hated Budgie the bloody Helicopter.

Every night when her father came to tell her another episode in Simon the Skunk's life, Bernice would recoil from the smell of his Paco Rabanne aftershave, as if it were an odour let off by Simon himself. She had no interest in Simon's cute antics and was horrified when her father announced he was trying to sell the tales of Simon to a publisher.

Anna was his agent. Anna and Simon together made her

father famous. The fact that Bernice's father was named
Simon and he had called the skunk after himself was somehow so embarrassing that Bernice cringed with shame every
time she saw *any* kind of animal. Upon hearing that Simon
the Skunk was to become a national figure, a new version
of Paddington Bear, she punched her bedroom wall and
wept with despair.

"I can do for Clare what I did for Simon," Anna said
proudly.

"What, you're going to turn her into a skunk and send
her into a forest?"

"Very funny. No, I'm going to bring her to life. I'm
going to force her into a situation she'd never have the
nerve to bring about herself by setting up this meeting with
Carl on American TV."

"But—"

"Do you have any idea how intense this correspondence
has become?"

Anna interrupted, her eyebrows moving up and down
with a rapidity Bernice found disconcerting. How old was
Anna? Hard to tell, and Bernice had never asked. Somewhere in her late thirties, possibly early forties. Closing fast
on past it, anyway. Is it hard to pull after forty? she thought
of asking Anna but, noticing the silver penknife on Anna's
desk, decided to stick to the subject at hand.

"It doesn't sound too intense to me. Clare talks about
Carl fairly often, but always as if he's a good friend, a pen-
pal type of bloke."

"It's more than that. I've seen the letters—she gave them
to me. She's terribly close to him, you know. She confides
in him."

"You think she's fallen in love with Carl?"

"Do you?" Anna cocked her head to the side and smiled.

"Anna—God!—you really think they'll get together if
they meet?"

"Maybe." Anna's smile transformed her momentarily
into a young girl.

"What is all this? Are you giving up being a literary agent and starting a dating agency?"

"Don't *you* think they should meet?"

"I don't know. I suppose so. But on TV?"

"It's as good a place as any. Plus, then we all get to watch it. What's the point of arranging a meeting if we don't get to see it ourselves? Cupid likes to watch his arrow hit, you know."

"It's certainly dramatic."

"Romantic *and* dramatic. Exactly." Anna clapped her hands. They were ringless, Bernice noted, and fairly plump. Yet Anna's frame was thin. She could wear miniskirts or tight jeans with ease and grace, but she had never deviated from just-above-the-knee-length power suits. Today she had an ice blue number on with a white silk blouse. Bernice found herself looking at her own deep purple fingernails, black baggy jeans and black sweatshirt. The contrast was faintly alarming.

"Look, Bernice—let me put it this way—if you knew the Prince was out there with the slipper trying to find Cinderella, and you also knew exactly where Cinderella lived, wouldn't you do something to get them together?"

"I'm not sure. Aren't you supposed to let the Prince find his own way?"

"Come on—everyone needs a little help these days, even Princes. *Especially* Princes."

"Excuse me, but where exactly does Jeremy Letts fit in to this scheme?"

"I'm not sure. He may end up winning, as usual, I just don't know. Listen, Bernice, it's simple. I read all the letters and I got caught up in them—in the possible romance of them—those two together. And once I'd decided that they should meet, I went for it one hundred per cent. Which happens to mean, in my case, television. It *is* over the top, I agree. But that's the way I work, that's the way I think. It's the American in me I've been denying for too long, all right? If they met in a bar or at the top of the Empire State

Building or whatever it would be the typical, usual story. This way, it's different. It's glorious."

"So Jeremy be damned?"

"I figure Jeremy can take care of himself. Besides, even though my gut instinct tells me Carl Lioce is a good-looking, presentable man, I can't be sure, can I? Clare could be sick at the sight of him. He could be a real dog."

"Anna."

"You know what I mean."

"So you've already talked to the producer of the show?"

"Mmm," Anna nodded. "Actually, he's an old flame of mine. He's just the type to be running a show like *Magic Moments*."

"And it's like *Surprise, Surprise!*?"

"Right. It's the American equivalent. People meet people they haven't seen for years, couples get reunited, all that heartrending stuff. Clare and Carl meeting for the first time will be right up their street."

"I don't understand. Why don't *you* go with her? Why me?"

"Because I am pulling the wool over her eyes, Bernice. I'm telling her that she's going to appear on this show to plug *Breathing in the Dusk*. How many times do I have to explain this to you? She *thinks* she's got a new, trendy American publishing company which has bought the rights to *Breathing in the Dusk* and is now going to publicize it. She doesn't know it is all a setup to get her on the air, on a live television show in New York where she will meet Carl. I know she'll be angry with me at first for tricking her, no matter how well it goes with Carl. She'll need a cooling-off period. That's what you're there for."

"I think this could all turn out very badly," Bernice frowned. "And I still don't understand. How are you going to get Carl to be on this show too? Are you going to tell him he's there to meet Clare? He doesn't sound like the type of man who would like to have a first date on nation-wide TV."

"Leave that to me. I guarantee it will be a surprise for

him too. For both of them. And don't worry if it does go badly, if they dislike each other on sight, for example. It's a cable show based in New York. It's not broadcast nationwide."

"Oh. Well, that's a *huge* relief."

Bernice stopped silently comparing clothes with Anna and started silently comparing hairstyles. Anna often changed the way she wore her hair. Today it was in a bun on top of her head, fashioned into a mound like Patsy's in *Ab Fab*—a beehive.

The last time she'd seen Anna, a month ago, her hair had been à la Jennifer Aniston in *Friends*. Was Anna conscious of modelling herself on female television stars, Bernice wondered, or was this reflecting a deep, hidden, unconscious desire for screen fame? Was that why Anna was so keen to get Clare on television? Was she living vicariously?

Bernice forced her eyes from the top of Anna's head, then forced her mind back on track.

"Do you think Clare will really believe a television show wants to plug *Breathing In the Dusk*? You need a plumber to *un*plug that book. It's so stiff, the pages have arthritis. Oh, Jesus—" Bernice sighed. "I didn't mean that. But this plan is totally absurd, Anna. Clare is not a good candidate to be surprised on live television, even a non-national cable programme. She's not going to gush and enthuse, you know. She's not like that. It's as if you wanted to turn Maggie Thatcher into Paula Yates or something."

"Bernice," Anna leant back in her chair, "I'm paying for this trip."

"Does that include," Bernice leant forward, "an upmarket hotel?"

"Absolutely."

"And restaurant meals?"

"As long as they're not excessive."

"And what's my part in all this?"

"You calm her down afterwards. Explain to her that I

set this up for her own good. Also, make sure she doesn't
catch on to anything beforehand."

"What's in it for you, Anna? You're paying for our trips,
putting us up, what do *you* get out of it?"

"You know something?" Anna swivelled her chair and
looked out of the window, her eyes travelling across Hamp-
stead Heath. "I have no idea. Maybe I'd like it if someone
did something like this for me. Or maybe it's the story. I
want to find out what happens next in the story. The letter-
writing part is finished, as far as I'm concerned. Now it's
time for some action."

*Cricket was in a bad shape in this country before Jeremy
came onto the scene. We'd been humiliated in the World
Cup, which is, I suspect, like the World Series over
there, or the Super Bowl—in other words, the really big
match. But you don't play other nations in baseball or
American football, do you? The difference here, you see,
is that we do. When other countries consistently beat us,
we feel ashamed. There's a national malaise. My husband changed all that . . .*

Clare stopped, staring at the words "my husband." Why
was she carrying on this absurd charade? Why lie to Carl
of all people? And what would Anna think, if she *did* ever
manage to read the entire manuscript? How humiliating.
She could try to explain by telling the truth, of course.
She'd made a comment in a letter, saying that, if she were
ever to find her husband in bed with her best friend etc.,
etc., and Carl had misunderstood, had taken her literally,
instead of realizing that she was positing the worst-case
scenario of discovering someone you love with someone
else. Carl had written back and said that unlike her, he'd
never married. Well, she *could* have set him straight in the
next letter, but she hadn't.

Why not?

Partly because she liked the idea of stopping any romantic thoughts which could spring from this correspon-

dence dead in their dangerous tracks. It made life simpler and the letters easier to write. If she had protested, if she had said, "Carl, I'm *not* married. Jeremy and I are a couple but we're not married," wouldn't that have sounded as if she were opening some kind of door, particularly as Carl had just told her *he* wasn't married? With this one deception, she'd managed to squelch any potential embarrassment.

Now, after almost a year and a half's worth of letter-writing, she knew Carl well enough to believe he wouldn't have forced any romantic issue between them even if he had known she was single, but back then, back at the beginning of it all, she wasn't as confident. After all, he was a man, and men were always *thinking* of sex, weren't they?

Wasn't that what Billy Crystal had said in *When Harry Met Sally . . .* that it was impossible for men and women to be simply friends? Well, it wasn't impossible in letters, especially if one of the letter-writers was married.

But it was more complicated than that, Clare knew. She was practising in her letters, getting used to the idea of being Jeremy's wife. He hadn't asked her to marry him yet, but he might, and if he did, she wanted to be prepared.

"Clare, you ginormous bitch!" Bernice had exclaimed after Clare had announced that she and Jeremy were going to live together. "Why does everything in your life seem to work out so perfectly?"

Bernice had asked this in a tone of undisguised, though supposedly lighthearted jealousy. Bernice believed Clare led a golden, trouble-free life. To protest, to say, "Hang on, it's not always the way it seems, *I* have problems too" would appear to be begging for undeserved sympathy.

Clare knew that Bernice had been adopted as a child and that for very good reasons Bernice felt misunderstood and unloved. Clare also knew that Bernice saw the good-looking, attentive, famous Jeremy and assumed all was idyllic in Clare's life, just as she had assumed, when they were little girls together, that Clare's asthma was nothing more than a minor medical inconvenience.

How could Clare explain her unhappiness to Bernice? The task was similar to explaining cricket to Carl. The subtleties, the nuances seemed ineffable and, at the core, faintly ridiculous.

What would happen if she said, "Jeremy's too good. He's too nice. Everyone tells me how lucky I am to have him and it drives me wild. His constant good behaviour makes me want to do something wicked. He is robbing me of my self, bit by bit. When we have people round for dinner, he insists on cooking. When we've finished eating, he leaps up and clears the dishes while I sit there listening to other women marvel at his helpful nature. He doesn't lose his temper. He pats me on the head like a dog when he leaves the house.

"If he is so clearly the 'nice' one in the couple, who am I? If he is so clearly the successful one in the couple, who am I? I could sit back and decompose slowly and he would carry the weight of this relationship in his handsome arms with consummate ease. Sometimes I think he could point to an ashtray on a table and say 'This is Clare' and everyone would nod and smile.

"I am living with a perfectly nice, caring man and I yearn for a tough, difficult character whom I could scream bloody murder at—someone whom my friends would occasionally come round and console me about. 'I don't know how you do it, Clare,' they'd murmur. 'You're amazing.' A man who was dangerous and tricky and not entirely safe."

But what would Bernice do if I said all this? Wouldn't she say, "Spare me the sob story. You don't know what it's like *not* to have anybody—you've had it all too easy—all your life. How can you possibly whine about a man being *too* nice and *too* supportive when I am aching for any man who will offer me any kind of love on a permanent basis? *I* would take Jeremy's love and run on it happily for the rest of my life."

She would be right, of course.

So I don't say anything to Bernice. I just nod and smile

like some lucky dumb animal when she tells me how perfect my life is. And only once in a while, at times like this, do I admit to myself that my life isn't perfect. And I wonder what it would be like to be Mrs. Jeremy Letts.

Pushing her unfinished letter to Carl away, Clare picked up the postcard she'd received from Angela Rae that morning. It showed a white beach with a grass hut in the background. Turning it over, she re-read the one-line greeting.

"What are you doing with your life?"

"I'm taking care of your house." Clare answered the question out loud. "I'm trying to keep it clean and tidy and I'm answering your mail occasionally and I'm waiting for Jeremy to come back from South Africa. If I knew how the hell I could find you, Angela, I'd write to you and tell you how grateful I am for this house, how pleased I am to live amongst your few possessions.

"I won't tell you I've bought a television; I suspect it might drive you mad. I won't ask you when you're coming back because I know you won't answer. I won't mention that I'm afraid you might die at some point during this seemingly endless sailing trip. I certainly wouldn't dare to say how much I've missed you. Or how lost and alone and strangely *thirsty* I often feel. Carl's the only one I can talk to about you. Carl's the only one who understands."

It was getting to be a bad habit, Clare realized. The way she kept re-reading letters from her correspondence with Carl. She'd go to her study desk in the same way Bernice went to the refrigerator. Guiltily, yet savouring the prospect of a treat. No one would understand this particular addiction, or what craving it satisfied, but more and more often she'd go and pull out the letters, devour the words and then place them back in their drawer.

This time she tried to excuse herself by pretending she had to file Angela's postcard in its proper place, in the drawer below the Carl–Clare letters. As soon as she'd put away the postcard, she gave up any pretence and indulged herself.

Letter Eight

March 30

Dear Carl,

*You're right. It's time we were on a first-name basis.
You know, this is a fairly tiny island nation on the large
scale of the world, and living here can be claustrophobic. That's why, I suspect, people tend to keep their distance, be more reserved than in an open, ranging
country like America. An American friend of mine here
who now says she hates the States, still admits to missing
the idea of getting in her car and driving across country
for days on end. "Hitting the end of the road in Scotland
is a lot different than hitting the end of the road in
California," she sighs. "And the M1 doesn't really live
up to Route 66."*

*So we're physically and psychologically bound.
Country lanes are beautiful but very, very narrow. There
are hedges everywhere. People need their space, obviously, so they keep it inside themselves. Americanisms
have crept in on us—people in shops often say "Have
a nice day" too, but it's very rare to enter into a conversation with a stranger.*

*The English are known to be eccentric, particularly
members of the upper classes, but we're not idiosyncratic. I think eccentrics are often quite similar in their
eccentricity—they share many of the same peculiarities—
so they're easily recognized and satirized. People who
are truly idiosyncratic—well, let me put it this way—I
don't know one English person who would write letters
to unknown names in foreign telephone directories.*

*That's why it was strange to come downstairs and
discover Angela Rae in my mother's house that evening.
I found it hard to believe that she would have remembered my name, much less looked me up again after six
years. I thought she had been pleased to get rid of me
in the airport. Pleased to be shot of me for ever.*

*After we'd shaken hands, she ordered me to change
my clothes.*

"*Dress for roulette,*" she said. "*That means no jeans.*"

My mother, who, I suspect, was relieved whenever I left the house, nodded to me, motioning for me to go back upstairs and get ready. I did just that, throwing on a skirt and blouse, wondering what the hell was going on.

Angela had a black cab waiting outside. And Angela, being Angela, didn't speak on the ride to the Ritz. I'm wrong. She said one sentence. "*Your mother should never have married your father, but she should have had you even though she doesn't seem to know that, so I suppose there's some sense in it all.*"

We strode through the lobby of the Ritz. Angela never walks, she strides. I was having trouble keeping up with her. She was dressed impeccably, in a tailored dark blue suit. But she still looked like a witch.

"*Stand beside me at the roulette table,*" she commanded. When we entered the casino she told me to keep my mouth shut and watch.

She then proceeded to win four hundred pounds. I think it took her about half an hour.

We left the table and she strode to the Palm Court, where we sat down. She ordered two glasses of champagne.

"*You're old enough to drink now, thank God,*" she said. "*I'm not in the mood for Coca-Colas.*"

"How did you find out where I live?" I asked.

"*Clare, there are a few important points to understand in life. The first is that you shouldn't ask questions which aren't relevant to the occasion. The second is that you deserve to be surprised.*"

"Why did you bring me here?"

"*So that someday, any day in the future, when you want to, you can tell this story to someone. Who will be just as interested in the answer as you are right now.*"

"*Will* you *tell this story to anyone?*"

That was the first time I heard Angela Rae laugh.

She has a girlish laugh, Carl. A tantalizing laugh. Flirty and fun and enticing.

"Yes," she answered, "I'm sure I will. But I'll probably change some of the details."

"Which ones?"

"None of your business."

That reminds me, you see, of your mother, that day with Danny, the boy who tried too hard. Your mother knew what was best left unsaid, just like Angela.

Angela Rae gave my life meaning. She wasn't a fairy godmother. Oh, she gave me a glass of champagne that evening, she gave me many glasses of champagne on many subsequent evenings. But she wasn't a warm person, or a visibly affectionate one. We've never hugged or even kissed each other on the cheek. I've always been frightened of her. But she's the only person who believes in me.